D1797553

UNTIL DAYLIGHT BREAKS

UNTIL DAYLIGHT BREAKS

ROGER CONWAY-HYDE

SilverWood

Published in 2013 by the author
using SilverWood Books Empowered Publishing®

SilverWood Books
30 Queen Charlotte Street, Bristol, BS1 4HJ
www.silverwoodbooks.co.uk

Copyright © Roger Conway-Hyde 2013

The right of Roger Conway-Hyde to be identified as the author of this work
has been asserted by him in accordance with the
Copyright, Designs and Patents Act 1988.

All rights reserved. No part of this publication may be reproduced,
stored in a retrieval system, or transmitted in any form or by any means,
electronic, mechanical, photocopying, recording or otherwise,
without prior permission of the copyright holder.

This is a work of fiction. Names, characters, places and incidents either are products of
the author's imagination or are used fictitiously. Any resemblance to actual events or
locales or persons, living or dead, is entirely coincidental.

Because of the dynamic nature of the Internet, any web addresses or links contained in
this book may have changed since publication and may no longer be valid. The views
expressed in this work are solely those of the author and do not necessarily reflect the
views of the publisher, and the publisher hereby disclaims any responsibility for them.

This book is to be sold subject to the condition that it shall not by way of trade or
otherwise, including the electronic media or cinema, be lent, re-sold, hired out or
otherwise circulated without the author's prior consent in any form of binding or cover
other than in which it is currently printed and without a similar condition including this
condition having been imposed on any entity.

ISBN 978-1-78132-141-6 (paperback)
ISBN 978-1-78132-142-3 (ebook)

British Library Cataloguing in Publication Data
A CIP catalogue record for this book is available from the British Library

Set in Bembo by SilverWood Books
Printed on responsibly sourced paper

Acknowledgements

I thank my wife Rosemary, Abdul Osman, the late Douglas Sutherland, together with Paul and all friends associated with "H1" and "H2" for their generous aid, support and encouragement during the writing of this book without whom it would never have found its dawning, or would ever have been written. In addition, I give my thanks to Michael Walsham who untiringly has given his support since the story's conception, also my neighbour Neil, my brother Richard and my nephew Andrew for all they have contributed in the planning.

Foreword

Roger Conway-Hyde is a man shrouded in one thousand and one mysteries. A member of a family that has had an inside track into the way international relations have developed over the last 50 years. His knowledge and experiences have been poured into his works, distorting the lines of plausible fantasy and a frightening reality. Conway-Hyde's fictions are sometimes a danger close to truth, causing us to question the fragility of the status quo in which we inhabit.

After a receiving a priority call from Whitehall, Commander Derek Thompson travels to London, on what seems a disturbingly pressing matter. The Russian Navy had implied the maiden voyage of their state of the art nuclear submarine was inevitable. Thompson travels to Northwood HQ and sets up surveillance teams to monitor the movement of the enigmatic *SSBN Gorbachev*. Suspicions of Russian manoeuvres have been elevated since the launch of their innovative new space platform *Vostok*. Soon, Commander Thompson and the world will see the importance of the Russian modern warfare advances.

Across the pond in Cape Canaveral, General John Kemp is assisted with his floored yet bright young protégé Lieutenant Logan 'Smartie' Smart. The two task themselves with proving their conjectures about the Russian movements. Pooling resources with the UK and NASA they try and link the inexplicable catastrophe's in the Atlantic Ocean, with seemingly un-accusable Eastern Bloc. General Kemp contacts his British counterpart Admiral Marchant who relays Whitehall's findings. This alone isn't enough to put Russia in the frame, but can they prove their gut feelings before World War III erupts? Are the actions of the ex-communist states bitter and maniacal or justified after years of ridicule and insult?

Providing a peek behind the TOP SECRET curtain that countries use as safety blanket, something for the public to look toward and feel comfortable knowing that there is someone who has it all under control. *Until Daylight Breaks* condenses the Superpowers of the world down to a handful of men who have their fingers on the big red buttons. This portrays a scary reality, that a person just like you or me could become an envoy of the end.

Jordan J. Key

Chapter One

Nearly sixteen years had passed since that fateful day of 11 September 2001 when an international terrorist organisation destroyed the World Trade Centre in New York killing over three thousand people; since then, America and Great Britain together have sought to rid the world of terrorism.

Both countries now war weary, having been pounded daily by those seeking to exploit whatever morsel of news or event, which would heighten the very delicate state of any lull in the constant fighting, whereby such press reporting would only enhance the inevitable reign of fear and terror on innocent people.

Severomorsk Naval Base, Russia

On board the Russian Navy's strategic nuclear ballistic submarine, *SSBN Gorbachev*, Ivargo Ivanov had heard news of the earthquake.

For the past four days Ivanov had tried to get any information concerning the whereabouts of Mika Belinka. He looked at the photograph standing on the shelf in his temporary cabin: it was a picture taken in 2009 on the date of Mika's twenty-first birthday. His emotions were aroused; Mika was a most beautiful creature. The picture showed her long blonde hair wistfully blowing in the wind as she received her citation honours. Ivargo hoped and prayed that she had survived. His thoughts were troubled by the news which recently had come through regarding the second earthquake. It told of the immense proportion of damage and size of the disaster. Ivargo could only trust that some guiding light was watching over Mika.

As the rank of Lt. Commander, Ivargo Ivanov had been assigned a new job and position. He was now the top man in charge of environmental and state planning under Nuclear Marine Operations of the *SSBN Gorbachev*. The position held full control of any issues that would indicate areas of programming and planning in the field of nuclear activities during any peacetime operation. Other than direct intervention from the Kremlin, no one else, only Ivanov, was authorised to handle any affairs that would engage matters under this strategic operational planning department. When occurring under the umbrella of nuclear operations, the submarine would be directly involved under the mighty naval power of Russia and the Commonwealth of Independent States of Russian countries [CIS].

Lt. Commander Ivanov alone would report on all adverse issues which happened under his department's control. He was responsible for ensuring no strategic information was released or exposed inadvertently, implied or hinted, having been involved with any national or international incidents. Nothing was to be brought about by the department to embarrass the Kremlin or be breached through such intervention of any public sector by ill-contrived rhetoric. If this position was ever to exist Ivargo was to scramble a full alert, and thereafter screen all operations.

The Lt. Commander had been made fully aware concerning all strategic programmes; he was also to monitor activities in space undertaken by the Russian space programme and monitored by the FSB [Russian Federal Security Bureau]. His orders were that at no time was any information to be found in the hands of any unauthorised party.

In recent years America had engaged full production of the Trident and the Tomahawk [SLCM] sea launch missile programmes together with a further advancement of the AGM-129 ACM advanced cruise missile. The Kremlin considered that the American State Department in Washington, contrary to any world opinion, had always wished to display that the Americans still had the largest submarine afloat and, more importantly for that matter, America had the biggest fleet size. Russia and the FSB assumed the American State Department had always insisted this be confirmed but Russia considered it was done in order to play down growing international views of the West's increasing concern, and a common belief in America carrying out the destruction of its nuclear arsenal regarding all medium range nuclear rockets.

There were no longer any serious nuclear deterrents available to counter-attack aggression if made by any unforeseen enemy.

Early in April 2017, the United States Military Space Division launched the last of their ageing space shuttles named *Columbia* on what was classified as a highly secret mission. There were no press or media releases concerning the launch but the Russians had given great emphasis and concern to all its departments regarding America's actions.

Recently in May, Russia had restarted work on the development of their failing independent Russian space platform, *Mir*. Secretly, the Russians had begun building a new space station named *Vostok*. On the surface,

Russia wanted the world to see they were doing the right thing and were not involved in anything untoward to upset international planning.

Finally, it was agreed with America an inspection would be made. World opinion openly suggested that in building a new space station Russia had installed, up in the exosphere, an arsenal of nuclear laser guns, missiles and other alien objects. Russia welcomed the suggestion of the proposed inspection and, with glasnost, assisted in inviting the investigation to be organised.

The Kremlin published new pictures taken in space from its space records of previous missions carried out with the Americans. They showed the world a past space programme regarding the re-commissioned Russian reusable space plane *Cosmos 1374*. Details were released showing the newest update of the Russian Space Launch Vehicle. Pictures televised all over the world showed the latest launch from Kapustin Yar of recent coverage screened by Russia of the Russian shuttle orbiter with its SL–X–17 launcher converted to carry the SL–W shuttle modification, and showed the shuttle landing in readiness for the next Russian and CIS space station programme.

The world's international space agencies were notified, and Russia acknowledged full details of the mission to anyone who wished to know. They confirmed they had extended the size and programme coverage of its building operations in space, all of which had now advanced considerably since the platform's launching in the year 2000, and suggested all countries of the world would be amazed by their advancement in this field of technology. The space platform was lending itself to take on the appearance of a mini city in space. Moscow claimed this was to be the new travel era of the future for which Russia was exceedingly proud; it was to be even better than the success made by America of their Saturn Titan Moon programming which had been completed during 2004.

From countries that had been fully involved with the exploration of outer space, it was suggested past eligible space mariners could be chosen in order to make a journey of inspection. It was arranged that three fully laden spacecraft would be launched. Everything concerning coverage of each epic take-off and landing held the world in suspense. All went exceptionally well. The spectacle was applauded. Congratulations were in order. Russia had achieved a triumphant international success. An accolade was extended to all involved.

America offered availability of the NASA space operation and any emergency service to be actioned at any time. This ensured, in case of a full emergency, a backup programme was available in case the Russian space platform met with any unforeseen difficulty. America's space agency, NASA, was placed on full operational alert. Two, now ageing, space shuttles, *Discovery* and *Endeavour*, were made ready for take-off in case any mishap occurred.

Within three weeks of the space inspection success a Russian military space shuttle, totally undetected, docked at the space platform. There was no report of any launchings by the Russian news agencies; only a small press release announced that Russia was to undertake refurbishment of certain areas of their space platform as a precautionary annual routine operation. Any launchings concerned with the situation had been successfully carried out.

NASA Ground Control and Tracking, Cape Canaveral
US Military and Naval Intelligence Department

The officer in command of operations for NASA, in conjunction with both military and naval intelligence was General John B. Kemp. A well-encrusted veteran of the American space programme, he had been involved since the early 1970s and had been primarily involved with the Apollo and Saturn moon rocket operations.

Sitting in his office, the General was carefully studying a file he had received marked urgent — TOP SECRET/HIGHLY CONFIDENTIAL. In reading the file of red striped pages, Kemp realised only a few senior staff members of both the military and naval sections of the State Department in Washington knew of the file's details. He knew that if what he had seen ever fell into unauthorised hands or the contents of the file became known to any person not clearly instructed, the whole position of Western security could well be exposed and escalate with sufficient aggression to provoke and bring about World War Three.

General Kemp's working day had long ended. He was somewhat irritated by the file's implications but in turn he did respect its top secret intentions. Sitting back in his chair, he removed his reading glasses. Rubbing his eyes, now strained through immense concentration, he picked up the receiver of an internal telephone and called the night security guard.

The guard soon arrived. The General, with great caution, systematically checked the file was fully intact and complete. The locking catch was then sealed. He got up and placed the box file in to the wall safe. Gathering up his personal brief, he checked that all security switches on the laser alarm and mechanical systems were set at green.

Kemp passed his briefcase to the security guard then pulled the office door shut. Two keys were set into their respective keyholes. He first turned each key clockwise to engage the computerised programme then turned them anticlockwise twice to engage the locking of the doors on to a time lock. The locks would be released at 08.00 hours the following morning.

A faint whirring sound was heard, then several clicks. Finally a mechanical grinding noise sounded as the locks and alarms engaged. At that moment all the lights dimmed and moments later the security guard closed and locked the front door of the building.

Seconds passed as the rear lights of the General's black limousine disappeared in to the darkness of the night.

A village in Hertfordshire, UK

Just before 06.30 hours on 28 July, Commander Derek A. Thompson RN left his house in the Chiltern Hills, north of Berkhamsted. A beautiful summer morning greeted him as he closed the front door of his house.

On walking down the hill, the Commander noticed – high up in the troposphere – vapour trails discharging from two intercontinental jet aircraft which gradually had distanced themselves, having changed course. As the sun began to rise into the upper heavens, each vapour trail hung in the sky and glowed. Soon the white wispy colour slowly began to change, now becoming tinged with an orange pink glint.

At about 04.00 hours Commander Thompson had received a priority call from Whitehall. It requested he be in London by 10.00 hours to await collection by car for an emergency visit to the Royal Naval Intelligence Centre at Northwood. All he knew at this stage was that the matter concerned the possibility of an imminent departure of Russia's newest nuclear submarine.

To date, no knowledge was forthcoming from anyone. No department really seemed to know what the vessel was, its battle power or what speed the submarine was capable of doing. All information from reliable sources was that the submarine had been named after the past Russian President, Mikhail Gorbachev.

Commander Thompson caught Marshall's, the local express commuter coach service in to London. The journey was fairly quick: about one hour twenty minutes. In consideration of all the unresolved problems continually experienced by the rail service, the Commander thought the coach service always seemed capable of beating the total rail and underground journey time in getting to Victoria. He considered the coach bettered this time by at least fifteen minutes, and the scenery and comfort were felt to be appreciably more interesting, and caring.

London, W1

Just before 08.00 hours the coach stopped at its final destination a little way from Victoria Coach Station.

After stepping off and crossing Buckingham Palace Road, then Eccelstone Bridge Road, Commander Thompson thought he might take in a little breakfast before walking to the office in Whitehall. He often stopped at a little Italian bistro café in Eccelston Road if time allowed.

"*Buon giorno, signor* Derek. What canna we interest you in today?" Antonio greeted him. "Maybe a cappuccino and a Parma ham roll?"

"Thank you," replied the Commander.

Luigi appeared from down behind the counter. "*Mamma mia, signo*r. It is a little early for you today, yes?"

Commander Thompson smiled as he collected his coffee and ham roll then made his way to a table near the green door. He sat down and began to read his *The Times* newspaper. As always the Commander's instincts alerted him. He glanced around the café to check who else was sitting down. There were always a few people chatting while having an early morning coffee. His eyes caught sight of a man at a table at the back of the café. Normally, Thompson would not have considered studying him carefully but for the fact that the man was wearing a dark navy raincoat. Thompson thought this seemed very strange seeing the temperature outside was already twenty-three degrees and warming to a lovely day. *Mind you*, he thought, *London was always full of surprises regarding people's habits of dressing*. He gave a quick glance at his watch then looked up at the two brothers. In nodding at Antonio and Luigi he said, "I must be going."

Thompson got up and hurriedly paid the bill then departed. On leaving the bistro he walked towards Buckingham Palace Road.

The traffic lights changed for pedestrians to cross. Immediately taking the opportunity, Thompson made his way across the road and set a course for Whitehall by way of the Victoria Plaza. He walked down through Victoria Station, out across Victoria Street then onwards to Parliament Square after which he would cross into Whitehall.

Stopping for a moment on the other side of the road in order to check his bearings, Thompson noticed the man he had seen in the café was facing his way but couldn't cross the road due to the change of the traffic lights.

On the Commander went. He soon crossed the concourse and entered Victoria Street. About halfway along the street, he developed a firm belief somebody was following him. Immediately the Commander swung round, but there was no one to be seen. At least, nobody at close quarters. Certainly no one that would give him cause for further concern. Thompson composed himself. He bent down and picked up his newspaper from the ground where it had fallen when he'd turned sharply. As he started to rise, he recognised a shape under the shopping arches on the opposite side of the street. It was the same man that had been sitting in the café wearing the raincoat. Thompson saw he was just standing there looking over towards him. The nature of the man's position certainly confirmed to the Commander his instincts were spot on. He paused and thought for a moment, not wishing to give any undue cause for alarm or sense of danger.

Yes, Thompson thought to himself, *I should change my course.* Immediately, he took a left turn through some small passages and headed towards Seaforth Place knowing this would lead him past Petty France then to St James's Park. It would not be too long before he would enter his office via a back entrance in Horse Guards Parade.

Picking up his pace, the Commander crossed Buckingham Gate then entered Vandon Street to take a right turn into Vandon Passage. *Good,* he thought to himself. *No sign of anyone following.*

He turned into the passage. As he did so he stopped and froze. At the other end of the passage was the dark outline of the shape of a man wearing a raincoat. *Well,* thought Thompson, *I'd better take steps in case of any trouble.* The man was smaller than he was and appeared to be younger.

Being fully trained in combat tactics, Thompson prepared himself for any eventualities. He momentarily waited while pausing to light a cigarette but already the man had begun making his approach – stalking his prey. Still Commander Thompson waited. Inhaling his cigarette he was trying not, in any way, to seem nervous or ruffled as to the suddenness of the situation. By now the man was within twenty feet of him.

"Excuse me, are you Commander Thompson?" the man called.

Derek Thompson was nearly taken off his feet by the sheer surprise of the person speaking his name. "Yes," he said.

"I am sorry to surprise you, sir. I was instructed to contact you and to do so at the café in Victoria. I was about to introduce myself but before I had a chance to speak, you were up and away. My name is Bluntly, Staff Sergeant James Bluntly."

Commander Thompson was still not sure of the man, disconcerted by his unorthodox approach. "Do you have any form of identification, Staff Sergeant Bluntly?" He noticed the man went to make a move to put his hand inside his coat pocket. "No! Just stay there as you stand, and don't try to move."

Bluntly made no attempt to move.

Reacting cautiously, Commander Thompson began to search him. "Thank you, but I'll check myself."

"It's in my left pocket, sir," Bluntly said. "I was ordered to meet you as soon as possible. A message was telephoned to your home to give you an update regarding the change of plan, but unfortunately you had already left."

Commander Thompson found Staff Sergeant Bluntly's full security clearance card in his pocket as he had stated. Relaxing his stance and now being somewhat amused by the complete turn of events, Thompson smiled. "I don't mind telling you, Bluntly, I was getting ready to knock your bloody block off. I would have done so if you had turned out to be one of them."

Staff Sergeant Bluntly looked a little warily at the Commander. "That's quite all right, sir. It's all in the line of duty. By the way, sir, the car is just over here."

Derek Thompson was pleased his driver showed he had a sense of humour. Maybe, he thought, the journey from Whitehall wasn't going to be a dull one after all.

On seeing the parked vehicle, he commented, "Mmm! I wondered how on earth you got here so quickly from the other side of Victoria Street. When I first noticed you, you were on the other side of the road near the Army and Navy Store."

On hearing the Commander's comment, Bluntly's face was a picture. They both laughed.

It was now 08.50 hours. *It could still be possible,* thought Commander Thompson, *for us to be in Operations HQ at Northwood before 10.00 hours.*

Soon, the car disappeared into an ever-increasing volume of London traffic that would eventually clog and jam up until at least mid-morning.

Severomorsk Naval Base, Russia

Slowly, almost silently, the dark shape of the *Gorbachev* moved along the water. Only a small wake could be seen reflecting on the sea as the nuclear submarine stealthily moved forward quickly disappearing into the dark water under a moonless night sky.

It was 01.00 hours on the morning of 30 July.

The submarine's captain did not know the destination of his mission nor was he yet at all sure of what his mission was to involve. Captain Nakita Narodny was given strict instructions: he was not to open the sealed envelope containing top secret orders until after sailing a preset course westward for one hour. He was then to complete his task from the time of leaving the safe haven of Russian territorial waters.

The sea was slight and the temperature outside in the night air was cold. A hint of night frost could be felt. Most of the vessel's one hundred and fifty crew were resting.

Before turning in for the night the concern that was felt by most of the submariners on board was that departure now seemed imminent; so suddenly, all crew members were disallowed any shore leave for twenty-four hours. Each member was instructed to go about his or her routine business on board in the normal way. Some of the crew, sleeping different watches, would not, upon waking, be aware the submarine was now at sea.

The strategic nuclear ballistic submarine, *Gorbachev* was built as a credit and fine example to the shipmasters of the Russian Navy. Its keel was laid down in 2009. Delivery to Severomorsk in the Motovsky Gulf for fitting out was completed by the end of December 2013.

Finally, at a displacement of thirty thousand tons, the *Gorbachev*, an advanced formula of a Borei Buluva class VI nuclear ballistic submarine, was ceremoniously commissioned for operations under the newly reformed Russian Navy's Northern Command.

The submarine took on its operational crew and captain during March 2017.

Equipped with the latest specialised sonar, radar and detection instruments of a hunter-killer nuclear ballistic submarine class, *Gorbachev* had been installed with a new highly sophisticated and sensitive tracking operations room. It was especially built to handle top confidential and high priority communications. In the ship's manual, the record showed the special operations room reference was logged as: ONLY TO BE USED IN MATTERS OF GREAT IMPORTANCE.

Prior to the submarine's sailing the FSB had been very nervous of any information being released regarding this room's existence. The Department for Environmental and Strategic Planning of Nuclear Marine Operations had rigorously been instructed to ensure that no information was given. Any such enquiry made, other than by an authorised party, was to be reported immediately to FSB Headquarters.

The Department of Nuclear Marine Operations was notified about what might happen to any of its officers if any unauthorised information was found to have been leaked. Lt. Commander Ivargo Ivanov was congratulated by his superiors for his good work in ensuring that the vessel's confidential files were never put at risk or in any danger from unauthorised parties. This confirmation had been received shortly after the *Gorbachev* had slipped its moorings.

The submarine having set sail, Ivargo Ivanov's position returned to monitoring control operations on shore. Although this position was still very involved with the rusted hulks of rotting radioactive submarines, now with the *Gorbachev* underway, this allowed the position on shore to become more relaxed.

Ivargo Ivanov desperately wanted some form of relief from months of stress and the acute pressure of the operations around him. His thoughts were constantly of Mika Belinka: there had still been no news of her whereabouts. However, small consolation was to be considered by Ivargo that at least no report had been received stating that Mika had been found listed as one of the thousands missing or dead. He prayed it was not so. Ivargo's mind drove him to believe the whole situation regarding Mika was his fault. He kept thinking that if it weren't for him she would never have gone away. He began to believe only his selfishness and utter stubbornness had forced the issue.

Ivargo remembered the time, just two weeks before her departure, when Mika had come to his flat on Friday evening. They had gone out for a meal then joined a party and sang and danced with friends until the early hours. He drove back to his flat and Mika had told him how much she had enjoyed herself.

A nightcap of coffee and vodka were considered a good idea. Ivargo poured out the drinks in the sitting room. Mika rose from where she was sitting and kissed him. He lifted her into his arms and carried her in to the bedroom. Mika nibbled his ear lovingly and again kissed him. He carefully eased her down on to the bed. She helped him remove his jacket, tie, shirt and trousers.

Mika eagerly wanted Ivargo, his love and everything he could offer. But she wasn't so sure about one thing: she did not want all the official strings attached to Ivargo's job.

Ivargo slid off Mika's dress and bra and gently caressed her breasts and nipples. Mika began to show her emotions giving soft moans of desire in her eagerness for more pleasure. Eventually, Ivargo could not control himself any longer. He lifted her body slightly and carefully entered her. Beads of perspiration formed on their bodies as temperatures rose.

The bedroom soon filled with the sound and heat of their passion. Mika quietly wept at the sheer ecstasy and joy of being loved and wanted. After a minute, Ivargo leant over and kissed her. She responded then moved back and sipped her glass of vodka. Ivargo lit a cigarette, then took Mika's glass and topped it up with the remains of his drink and sipped from it as if it were a loving cup.

Ivargo remembered it was wet and cold on that Saturday morning. He had discussed with Mika what he thought they should do over the weekend that followed. In passing, he had asked Mika if she would reconsider getting married. Mika had not replied.

Later that morning, Ivargo had to go on duty at the department. He remembered Mika was annoyed over the same thing happening time and time again. Ivargo could still hear her screaming words at him as he was closing the door while leaving. He thought of the time when his duty had turned from a simple function into a major control operation. When he had returned to the flat, very early that Sunday morning, he had talked several times on the telephone with Mika. He thought and hoped she would understand. In order not to wake her, he eased open the door of the bedroom and pushed through an enormous bunch of flowers in case she was awake.

There was no response.

He paused, thinking she must still be asleep. Finally, pushing the door open wide enough for him to ease through, he saw that the bed was made up. An envelope was on the pillow.

> *Dear Ivargo,*
> *I have patiently waited hoping you might come. I am fond of you, but I cannot agree to marry you right now. I need to think about our relationship. I am going away to visit the Caspian Sea and Armenia for around three weeks. I will give you a definite answer upon returning.*
> *Now and then, maybe once a month, you wish me to come and see you for a weekend. Then I find that you're called away to your work. You keep on leaving me all alone. Work always comes first.*
> *Ivargo, please do not use me. If we're to marry, I would commit to you totally...*
> *Can you do the same?*
> *Love Mika*

Ivargo remembered that after reading her letter his heart sank. He sat on the bed feeling so empty. He didn't really grasp or understand what Mika had written nor did he really fathom what she was trying to tell him. All he now thought about was for Mika's return. He prayed that he would see her again in three or four weeks. Even worse, he had begun to believe he had driven her away and that was why she had not been in contact.

When news came of the two terrible earthquakes, the stress of not knowing if Mika had survived or maybe was injured, even dead, was intolerable. Such strain was beginning to take its toll. On top of all this the pressures of the strategic confidential operation regarding the sailing of the *Gorbachev*. Ivanov was driven near to his wits end.

Lying back on his bed just looking up at the ceiling of his room, his eyes were like two dark hollows. His face was grey, near ashen, through the recent long hours of strain. Added to this, now he had the worry he might never see Mika again. Totally exhausted, sleep finally came to his rescue.

Royal Naval Intelligence HQ, Northwood

It was two days, four hours and fifty minutes since Commander Derek A. Thompson had settled into a constant pattern of surveillance regarding the file on the *Gorbachev*. He looked up at the clock. On checking the time and wishing to take a well-earned break, he thought a strong coffee was in order.

Thompson had been on duty since 23.00 hours. It was the turn of his group's operation in action of their first sequence of being night watchman. His eyes watched closely the large screen map marking latitude and longitude of the vast intelligence radar plotting system of Royal Naval Command. The screen map had initially been set to cover areas of the Northern Hemisphere and Arctic. Currently, the map showed the last known positions of American, British and Russian nuclear-powered strategic ballistic hunter-killer submarines.

Since Wednesday, Thompson had been brought in to command and control a team of very efficient men. Six eight-hour watches had been set covered by three groups. Each group contained nine operators with a co-ordinating officer of the watch. Keenness and concentration was the Commander's ally, and his highly trained staff were offering him these facilities. All these attributes were a necessity in order to keep up a constant vigilance towards seeking out an unknown enemy. The long arduous hours of watching, everyone waiting for the unexpected at any time. Thompson appreciated the immense determination of his men. As for the bare facts available on record for notifying where and what each submarine was doing or where they might be, especially the Russian submarine *Gorbachev*, all of the allied listening stations throughout the Northern Hemisphere were primed and actioned to report.

Shortly after 01.00 hours, a small bright red light began to show on the screen, flashing the position of some unidentified craft that had been located in the vicinity of Latitude 72.0 N – Longitude 33.0 ENE. Confirmation of the exact location was being received and transmitted by undercover references FZ3253–P935. These references indicated that contact had been established and acknowledged by loyal Finnish agents. The Northwood operations room suddenly became a beehive of intense activity; was this possibly the moment everyone had been waiting for? Computer bells were ringing as printing machines began to spew out paper. The message read:

01.07 AM★★★FZ2353–P935/300792–53: OUT★★★★MSSGE – URGENT – REPEAT URGENT
SSBN G O R B A C H E V ★★ LOCATED ★★ PROCEEDING TO AREA WEST-SOUTH-WEST 90KMS EAST MURMANSK – STOP – DO WE CONTINUE WATCH – STOP – DO NOT CONSIDER KREMLIN WILL ALLOW US AROUND FOR TOO LONG – STOP – EXPECT RESUMING OF PERSISTENT 24 HOUR JAMMING – STOP – HAVE A GOOD TIME HUNTING – STOP – TTFNFN2353–P935 ★★★ IN: 01.08 AM – STOP – END MESSAGE

Commander Thompson beamed a smile of delight to his operators. "Well, we might now find out what Moscow has kept us all guessing about," he said as he paused and read the message again. "Please notify both US Military and Naval Intelligence at the Pentagon State Department, and the CIA of this news. Record only basic message details; we do not wish to have the Americans try to spoof our scoop and good fortune, do we now?"

All of the operators grinned at each other in response to the Commander's remark. Everyone in Commander Thompson's group congratulated themselves. It was at least six hours before 'A' Group would be stood down. Plenty of time, thought Thompson, for his men to show their skills.

Privately, a message was immediately dispatched to No. 10 Downing Street informing the British Prime Minister of time and movements of the *Gorbachev*. The *communiqué* further acknowledged that the US State Department had been informed.

NASA Military and Naval Intelligence, Cape Canaveral
It was 20.45 hours EST on 29 July 2017 and senior officers of the State Department had just informed General Kemp of the departure of the Russian submarine. He was requested from that moment to be on full alert

regarding matters of national security. If at all possible his personal lines of communication were to be made free and open on a twenty-four-hour basis for receiving 'hotline' telephone calls.

The General set in motion all instructions necessary for special communication clearances then sat down at his desk and dialled his wife. The telephone rang a few times: "Deirdre, something important has come up. I'll either be very late, dear, or will call you in the morning."

The General's wife wished her husband a pleasant evening. "Don't forget to eat something and, John, do try to get a break and some rest if you're held back there all night."

"I will, darling," he replied.

Royal Naval Intelligence HQ, Northwood

It was 02.00 hours BST 30 July 2017.

Commander Thompson noticed the small flashing red light had moved steadily on a course west-north-west; its routing currently placed the position of the *Gorbachev* approximately forty-five nautical miles north of the most northerly point of the Norwegian coast.

At Sea

On board *Gorbachev*, Captain Nikita Narodny, as instructed, was breaking the seal of his Top Confidential Mission Orders. It was well over an hour after sailing. The instructions read:

> ALTER COURSE DIRECTION TO 73.0 NNW – 13.0 WSW – STOP – AFTER FOUR HOURS THIRTY-FIVE MINUTES ARRANGE IN READINESS ALL MANPOWER TO MEET IN THE SPECIAL OPERATIONS THEATRE – STOP – AT 06.00 HOURS MOSCOW TIME AWAIT YOUR NEW MISSION INSTRUCTIONS – STOP – END MESSAGE

Captain Narodny immediately obeyed instructions and gave the order to alter course and he soon felt the submarine begin to move to starboard. Captain Narodny was not unduly concerned at this time as he was more intent in ensuring the submarine was working well. Currently, it appeared to him that the *Gorbachev* was capable of performing every function it was designed for. Certainly, he thought, the Buluva class submarine a lot smoother than the earlier Typhoon and Delta IV and V class submarines, and was by far way ahead of its much older Victor III class predecessors.

The *Gorbachev* was a larger vessel than Captain Narodny had first imagined. Conditions of both working areas and crew quarters had shown the submarine had a wider area of space. However, nothing seemed to show any unnecessary wastage in respect of the *Gorbachev's* broader design.

Captain Narodny had spent many long hours at the shipyard during the fitting out, emphasising the importance of human comfort. He had past realised it was near impossible to have any design modification and alterations made, but his bitter experience of long voyages in older submarines made him continually aware of the problems of bad air, lack of space and, above all, personal comfort. The Captain had constantly brushed heavily with Moscow on these particular matters. He had previously been severely reprimanded in condoning these new conditions that appeared to embark upon the luxury of an international five-star hotel. Finally, before the completion of fitting out, plans for the *Gorbachev* were rethought regarding its interior design. At the time of sailing, and all the changes having been finally accepted, Captain Narodny felt satisfied he had achieved a standard that would enable his crew to work in the submarine on long sea voyages. Conditions below certainly had been improved compared with past standards. Everything in regard to the *Gorbachev's* crew quarters was considered now as being assets of reasonable comfort. The Captain had pointed out to the crew this was due, in all probability, to the submarine having to be away from its home port for at least six months at a time, and possibly longer, depending on the type of mission.

Appreciating the submarine's new-found qualities, Captain Narodny was pleased with the results training his crew had shown.

He wrote in the ship's log:

To date, no problems have been experienced in the nuclear reactor room. The submarine has acted very well during its preliminary sea trials. The vessel has handled with perfection and has maintained all functions.

He thought that the submarine appeared now to purr as it sped along at thirty knots below the surface at a depth of one hundred and twenty feet. It was slightly faster than he had considered, seeing that the *Gorbachev* was so large, but all seemed to be sound and in good working order.

The day had been a long one. Captain Narodny felt it was time to get some rest. He notified the bridge and officer of the watch he was turning in. "If by chance any adverse conditions are experienced, it is essential you call me immediately and tell me about the problem. I'll be in my cabin and do not wish to be disturbed unnecessarily until my alarm call scheduled for 05.40 hours."

As he lay on his bed, Nikita Narodny kept thinking hard as to what this particular mission might be about; everything was instructed to be handled once the submarine was underway. It just seemed a little odd but he wasn't too bothered about it. He just liked to have some idea what his task was going to be. He began to wonder what type of sea conditions the submarine was going to sail through so he could ready his crew. His mind not really coming up with any ideas, he placed the book he was reading back on the shelf above his bed then switched off the light. Eventually, he fell asleep.

The time was 02.15 hours.

The officer of the watch had previously acknowledged the Captain's orders and went about his duties.

Chapter Two

The White House, Washington DC

Late in the evening of 29 July, news received in the Military and Naval Departments of the White House dealt with the presumed sailing of Russia's newest nuclear ballistic missile submarine. The details available gave little cause for concern. All the information was forwarded to the President who after consultation with his military and naval advisors considered, as a precautionary measure, the same details be delivered to Naval High Command at Charleston, South Carolina. Instructions were also given to dispatch a copy to SMSB at Farslane, Scotland, and thereafter the matter would be handled under the joint co-ordination of operations by USAF and NASA through their respective military and naval intelligence sections and other specified departments.

Naval High Command, Charleston, South Carolina

The US Naval High Command received and acknowledged the message. As requested, it was ensured utmost caution was given due consideration in case of any pending embarrassment.

A message was immediately coded then dispatched to one of America's fastest hunter-killer submarines, the *SSN Bowevil*, currently on operations somewhere in the Arctic. The message read:

ALTER COURSE EAST-SOUTH-EAST – STOP – PROCEED TO MONITOR POSSIBLE INTRUSION TO YOUR AFFAIRS – STOP – DO NOT REPEAT DO NOT ENGAGE YOUR PRESENCE – STOP – ONLY MAINTAIN ADVISING US OF THE INTRUDERS CURRENT POSITION – STOP – DO THIS EVERY TEN MINUTES IN ORDER FAIRLY CLOSE CONTACT CAN BE OBSERVED – STOP – END MESSAGE

SSN Bowevil acknowledged receipt of the message and confirmed it had altered course as instructed. The *Bowevil*, one of the revered 37+11+18 Virginia class nuclear missile submarines had been fitted out to carry eight twenty-one inch torpedoes and handle the Harpoon and UGM-109 tactical Tomahawk SLCM Programme. The submarine had been modified from earlier Los Angeles class predecessors. It could master a speed of thirty knots and carried four additional firing tubes to accommodate the M48 lightweight torpedo.

From Charleston, South Carolina, the US Navy's largest operational nuclear submarine, *SSBN [X] Intrepid*, set sail. Its destination was recorded as unspecified; its mission was logged as Top Secret and Classified. This submarine displayed all the attributes of being the *crème de la crème* of *SSNB [X]* type submarines; it was swift, silent and sophisticated in all its trappings. The American Navy built the submarine to excel the previous 7+6+11 Ohio class. However, *Intrepid* had never really been seen other than by US Military top brass; its evasiveness gave rise to a rumour it was the biggest thing the US Navy had ever built. Records suggested the submarine had a displacement of twenty-five thousand tons when dived. The truth about this had never really been substantiated. Russia did not try to disclaim it, nor did they consider it being of any great interest.

The *Intrepid* supported a crew of one hundred and forty-one enlisted men including twelve officers. The ability of the *Intrepid* to outrun the *Bowevil* was never tested. Both top operational speeds were logged in records as the same. One exception: the *Intrepid's* true displacement tonnage when dived was twenty-five thousand tons, the *Bowevil's* was only seven thousand eight hundred tons dived.

Royal Naval Intelligence HQ, Northwood

Commander Thompson, while sipping his cup of coffee, took a look at his watch. It had been a long night of intensive activity. A hum of excitement kept the pressures and tensions of surveillance on a high which created good morale all round. The clock on the wall of the operations room registered the time as 05.32 hours. The flashing red light had slowly advanced its way further westward. It had changed direction shortly after 02.00 hours and was now on a more northerly course. The whole night had been very active once it was established the Russian submarine had sailed. Many questions were put forward and many interpretations were being sought as to why the Russians had sent *Gorbachev*, their new submarine, out on undisclosed operations. For what purpose was it proceeding in a north-westerly direction?

Outside, the dawn of the July day was breaking. Commander Thompson knew his group's watch had just over one and half hours longer to maintain their vigilance. He took a break from the operations room and asked if Staff Sergeant James Bluntly was about. An orderly soon found Bluntly and directed him to the Commander's room. On arrival, Thompson enquired if he was able to handle a special assignment of a personal nature. He gave Bluntly a fifty pound note and requested him to go and complete an errand. Commander Thompson instructed him to ensure he was back by 07.30 hours at the very latest. The Staff Sergeant understood all he had been asked, saluted then went on his way.

It was 06.06 hours.

The Commander had returned to the operations room and he saw that everything appeared to be functioning on an even keel. He then entered his office. On doing so, by habit, Thompson looked up at the huge operational surveillance screen showing the world. He noticed the flashing red light had moved further westward and was now a little further north of the position he had previously seen. This showed the Russian submarine's position to be not very far from Jan Mayen Island.

Thompson settled down at his desk with a fresh cup of coffee and continued to survey the screen through his office window. As he took another sip, the area where the red light was flashing suddenly went dark and blank.

"Good God!" Thompson said. "The bloody red flashing light has just gone and disappeared!" Slightly embarrassed, still completely astonished and at a loss as to what so unexpectedly had happened, he called to fully check that all systems were functioning correctly. The time of the Russian submarine's disappearance was recorded at 06.09 hours.

It was now 06.17 hours. Commander Thompson was in the process of confirming to Royal Naval Headquarters and Operational Control a full account of what had transpired. "Admiral, there was no suggestion made at the time of the recorded change of surveillance that there were any signs of a problem. At 06.09 hours the red signal light just simply vanished."

"All right, all right, Thompson," Admiral Raymond J. Marchant replied. "Well, we shall just have to find it again, won't we, Commander?"

For a moment Thompson was not quite sure how this was going to be achieved. He was thankful there wasn't going to be any area of recrimination. "Do you think there may have been a horrible disaster, sir?"

"Well, Thompson, if that is the case, then at least there would be one less for us to worry about for a while. However, sadly, if it were true what a tragic loss of human life. We'll just have to wait and see. At present, Thompson, I do not know. But I must say, I do have a really sneaky feeling about this one." The Admiral paused for a moment rubbing his chin while deep in thought. "Mind you, it could possibly be a red herring. Anyhow, the Yanks have a fast hunter-killer submarine up around there, one which we have just been informed about. Have its details put on the operations screen. Place it up with the usual US Navy references. Note it under its name *SSN Bowevil*."

"Yes, sir. Right away." Thompson gave a sigh of relief. He was pleased somebody else had now motivated some direct assistance even though it was declared to be the Americans.

Admiral Marchant continued, "Be sure you mark the screen with an odd colour. Do it so we can distinguish it from the normal run of Yank vessels. The reason I request this, lad? It's simple. The American Navy believes we think their ship is operating somewhere north of Greenland, but the true fact of the matter is we have it placed, although unknown to them, just east-south-east of Kong Oscar Fj. This is the American sub's real position, thanks to our good friends in Scoresbysund. I am pretty sure this cannot be too far from where we recorded the Russkies last position, eh?"

Thompson passed no comment.

"Well, dear boy, you had better get to it. Oh, by the way. I am sorry, Derek, you won't be going off duty at 07.30 hours but your boys will. I'll need you to spend at least another hour or two briefing the new watch, Group C. Then I think you can stand down for a bit."

"Why, thank you, sir." Thompson felt he needed two more hours work like a hole in the head.

Marchant continued, "Mind you, don't go disappearing off anywhere as I'll need you to re-brief me before you leave operations."

"Yes, sir," Thompson replied.

Commander Thompson instructed his group's watch operations regarding the placement of the US Navy's submarine *Bowevil*. He asked if any communication had been made possible in order to establish contact with both the Norwegian and Finnish listening posts.

"No, sir. Nothing as yet. We are still experiencing constant jamming. Presumably, this is being done by the Russians."

"All right, men, don't worry. Just keep trying." Thompson gave the matter some thought. Maybe the jamming and the sudden disappearance of the *Gorbachev* could well have had some connection. Could it be possible that what Marchant had said had some sort of bearing on the matter? Perhaps this wasn't altogether to be passed over as a myth.

It was 07.30 hours. Commander Thompson stood down Group

A operations. He congratulated them on their night's work and further confirmed they could all depart from their watch knowing they had scooped a first. The Commander continued speaking, "Also, it may not just turn out to be simply a routine operation, pending on the element of a potential total disaster. I stress this to you all, as Group A watch, in order to keep your spirits high. That little red dot you found might be the start of something which eventually could turn out to be pretty big."

At Sea

At 06.00 hours local time, the *Gorbachev* was north-west of Jan Mayen Island and was set in readiness for receiving completion of its new instructions.

Just before 05.45 hours, Captain Narodny had summoned all of the special operations room staff and entered the highly top secret and sophisticated surveillance room.

At 05.58 hours, the computer and its monitoring systems were poised, waiting receipt of the coded instructions being transmitted from Russia. All crew operators were sat in place ready to decode the incoming message.

Exactly on the bell of 06.00 hours the monitoring equipment came into life. It was as if someone had created an electronic fireworks display. Coloured lights, which eventually instigated the illumination of the observation screens, began pulsating in lines. Flickering lights on the receiving system confirmed reception, and that decoding of the transmission had begun. Within seconds the deciphering computer started to print out a message. It read:

GORBACHEV IS NOW OPERATIONAL WITH DIRECT LINKS TO MOSCOW AND THE SPACE PLATFORM VOSTOK – STOP – TEN MINUTES FROM THIS TIME – STOP – YOUR VESSEL WILL BECOME INVISIBLE FROM ANY ENEMY – STOP – YOU WILL BE ABLE TO HUNT, TRACK, AND KILL AT LEISURE – STOP – INTERNATIONALLY EVERYONE WILL BE ADVISED AND BELIEVE YOUR SUBMARINE WAS LOST ON ITS MAIDEN VOYAGE – STOP – DUE TO THE INVENTION AND CREATIVE GENIUS OF OUR SPACE PLATFORM OPERATIONS – STOP – YOU WILL BE VEILED AND COCOONED FROM ANY FORM OF CONTACT OR TRACKING BY AN ENEMY – STOP – YOU WILL SOON FIND WITHOUT ANY DETECTION – STOP – YOUR SUBMARINE WILL BE ABLE TO MONITOR, TRACK, ENGAGE AND DESTROY ANY ENEMY – STOP – THEN CONTINUE TOTALLY UNNOTICED – STOP – GOOD LUCK AND GOOD HUNTING – STOP – END MESSAGE

Captain Narodny read out the message to the whole ship's company. He personally was slightly astonished in regard to its content and implications. However, in being singled out by Moscow, and on having had a brilliant and unblemished record, was Moscow now confirming his promotion? Moreover, he was sure Moscow would not be in the least surprised regarding the *Gorbachev*'s reply:

GORB/MSCW 06.05 A.M. REF: 300717 MSSGE STARTS
WE WELCOME THE HONOUR BESTOWED UPON US – STOP – ARE WE
TO UNDERSTAND THAT PRIOR CLEARANCE IS TO BE MADE – STOP
– OR MAY WE HUNT AT WILL – STOP – END MESSAGE

An immediate response was given. It read:

MSCW – GORB 06.07 A.M. REF: 300717 START
CLEAR ANY TARGET PRIOR ENGAGING – STOP – AS PREVIOUSLY
STATED GOOD HUNTING – STOP – END MESSAGE

At 06.08 hours, Moscow linked operations with the space platform *Vostok* and put in to service 'Operation Invisible'. The *SSBN Gorbachev* was now undetectable by any enemy, any intelligence agency or listening post. All had deemed it to have put its light out. It was believed the submarine had simply vanished.

NASA Military and Naval Intelligence, Cape Canaveral

It was 01.17 hours on 30 July. Kemp was working his way through the mass of operation intelligence reports which had accumulated in the short space of time since news was released about the *Gorbachev*.

After a long evening of co-ordinating operations with the military and naval departments everyone swiftly set about his or her tasks. All had played down the sailing of *Intrepid*. Moreover, the engaging of the *Bowevil* being moved on to red alert operations in order to maintain any form of contact with the Russian submarine was viewed with some scepticism.

A red light began flashing above the telephone on the General's desk; the line was only used in cases of extreme emergency. Kemp picked up the receiver. He listened in near disbelief. "Yes, yes. Oh my God! No trace, nothing? What the hell could have happened? Has anybody made contact with the President? Oh! Okay. Jesus, those poor bastards! I know they are supposed to be the opposition but nobody wants to die that way.

This is dreadful. Whereabouts did this happen?"

There was a slight pause. "Near Jan Mayen Island, General."

"Good grief!" retorted Kemp. "They would never have had a chance of survival in those waters. Do we definitely have confirmation the Russian sub was lost?"

A sullen voice in reply came over the telephone. "Yes, General. We have received a full message from the Politburo in Moscow."

"This is dreadful," the General quickly responded. He enquired, "Do operations in London know about this?"

"I am advised, General, all major powers have been notified formally of the loss of the *SSBN Gorbachev,*" came the reply.

The General answered, "All right. Thank you very much for the message, sir. I'll finish up here then close the file."

"Do finish up, General. However, I wish you confidentially hold your file open at least until a full report has been mustered for release."

"Okay, sir, I'll do just that." The line went dead.

Kemp was staggered by the news. He was mentally drained and physically tired due to the recent unbelievable stress, and now this. Still he kept thinking about the terrible loss of life and what an awful way to die. "Jesus Christ!" he said to himself. "The Russkies really have lost their newest and biggest piece of nuclear submarine equipment." Finally having cleared his desk he telephoned security to set the alarms then closed his office door and departed.

Royal Naval Intelligence HQ, Northwood

It was 07.36 hours. Commander Thompson sat down to face the new Group C watch. As expected, a full complement of operators had mustered, instructed in readiness, to be prompt for 07.30 hours.

With the standing down and exchange of duties having been formally completed, he addressed his new operational staff and logged the time as 07.37 hours on 30 July 2017. "Well, gentlemen, I won't beat about the bush in trying to teach you any simple elementary stuff. The fact of the matter is, during the night, Russia set sail on its maiden voyage their newest and biggest nuclear submarine the *SSBN Gorbachev*. This department had managed to track it down. It had followed the sub's course and change of movements all through the night. We successfully monitored its speed and even managed to plot its position at all times. Everything had been going along quite perfectly until just after 06.00 hours. It was then, gentlemen, the bloody thing just vanished. As you can imagine, for a while, all hell let loose." Commander Thompson paused. "Now, as of one hour ago, Moscow released a full report. It stated that the *Gorbachev* was lost with all hands on her maiden voyage. The position and location where the submarine foundered were given as being in an area just south-east of Jan Mayen Island. Every surface vessel in the area has been requested to keep a sharp look out for any sign of wreckage. Currently, there has been no trace reported."

Again, Thompson paused for a moment and looked around the operations room to see if everybody was fully attentive. "Well, gentlemen. Our job has been instructed. We are not under any circumstances to stop keeping a constant watch and look out for the submarine. Our groups, by this I mean all watches, have been officially ordered not to abandon at any time nor stand down from any existing responsibility from the current task. Anything, I repeat, anything that could locate it, or may give any of you the minutest opportunity or clue, is to be reported to me, immediately. I trust I make myself very clear to all of you. Remember, nothing is to be left unquestioned. The true fact of the matter is headquarters do not believe the story that Russia has paraded to the international press, and have further advised the military establishments of every major power in the world of its opinion.

"We are asked not to even think nor consider that the damned submarine has sunk. It is in this respect we shall therefore put into operation the programming of a new file. Please integrate this into all existing programming. The name of the file is to be called 'Operation Blindfold'.

"The previous watch has spent last night gleaning the vessel's information from our records. You are instructed to fast copy all this information after which please place your computer logs into a simulation mode. From this moment on, you will keep the main screen operating as it stands. It is still to involve all other records, data and tracking. However, you will show the marker of the *Gorbachev* as still being fully operational but it will now be coded under the new file reference, Operation Blindfold.

"Gentlemen, I trust all of this means something to you. Please now reset your computers to run in an auto channel modular."

Instantly, all operators pushed the select buttons on their programmers. Commander Thompson continued. "When we wish to check the computer's data record findings automatically, for purpose of analysis, the programme will change on to the main screen revealing only the computer's brain functions under a programmed simulation. This will enable it to confirm, at that time, what it believes the submarine might possibly be doing. Hopefully, it may give us an accurate assessment of where it could be positioned. With this taking place, see to it that you all are ready and fully informed. I trust all is clearly understood?"

"Yes, sir," came the reply.

The Commander continued. "Please carry on, Group C watch. Kindly ensure, at a minimum, that each computer check is made at intervals of thirty minutes. Pass the report back to the duty officer of the watch when it is completed. By the way, who is that?"

A reply came from the back of the room. "Lieutenant Henderson, sir."

"Fine. Henderson, I'll need to brief you personally on one or two matters before we break up."

"Right you are, sir," replied the Lieutenant.

"Has everyone understood the situation?" asked the Commander.

"Yes, sir," came the response.

"Then please proceed."

The Commander entered his office and beckoned Henderson to follow. "Sit down please, Lieutenant."

"Thank you, sir."

Commander Thompson looked him straight in the eye in order to gather what reactions would be given to his next request. "In a moment I am going to give Admiral Marchant a telephone call. I'll confirm to him everything I have put into motion this morning. Is that clear, Henderson?"

"Yes, sir."

"I'll also request you be left in control. I mean, while I am hopefully able now to get some shut-eye."

Henderson gave a quick nod of his head.

Commander Thompson continued, "Therefore, I trust you will not let me down, eh?"

"No, sir. I mean yes, sir."

"By the way," the Commander said, "Admiral Marchant might just unexpectedly call in to see what is happening although I am sure he would contact me first prior to doing so. However, he may have considered I have been on the go for nearly fifty hours non-stop so he might just allow me to have a little longer respite." Commander Thompson sipped his coffee. "Cover yourself well, Henderson. I'll be depending on you now. That is all."

"Thank you, sir." The Lieutenant then stepped out of the office.

Commander Thompson lifted the telephone receiver and dialled the Admiral's number.

"Yes?" Marchant answered. "Oh, Thompson it's you. Is everything running smoothly?"

"Yes, Admiral." Thompson then gave his report. It was received with full approval.

"Okay, me lad. You had better go off and get a bit of shut-eye otherwise shortly you won't be fit for anything."

"Right you are, sir." Commander Thompson thanked the Admiral for his clearance, and then said, "By the way, sir, I have already advised the senior officer of the watch, Lieutenant Henderson, to contact you — that's if anything comes up."

"Jolly good show. However, I am sure he will first get you up if any problem arises. Off you go now." Marchant thanked Thompson for a fine effort and a good night's work. He asked him to contact him after he had got some well-earned rest.

Chapter Three

It was nearly ten hours since news regarding the loss of the *Gorbachev* had been broadcast across the world. Every naval institution sent messages of condolences expressing their sympathy for the extreme loss of life. In addition to messages regarding the tragic loss there were offers giving full assistance to help trace the wreckage, even to possibly assisting a recovery of the submarine's nuclear reactors.

At Sea

In Moscow, the Presidium, as instructed, ensured it had covered every eventuality in respect of any exposure concerning engagement of all activities between the Russian submarine and space platform *Vostok*. Finally, when the shut down occurred, it was immediately requested that an Elbrus class research and recovery ship, plus one Kara- class light cruiser the *Nikolayev*, be dispatched to the area of Jan Mayen Island. Also, an older ship, the *Kirov*, already out on patrol, was moved into the area.

As a show of strength, the Russians ordered a full aerial surveillance and reconnaissance operation be put into action. A Tupolev TU142MR Bear MR J aircraft equipped with MOD3 operated by the Russian Naval Air Force, in order to maintain and sustain an all oceans link between Nautical Command activities and any nuclear missile armed submarine operation, was directed to fly over the area. As a long-range aircraft, this particular type had already received its nickname from NATO Operations. The 'Big Bear' was able to fly under almost any weather conditions.

Without any news or knowledge of what the world was grieving about, Captain Narodny was checking the plotting of the submarine's next course and position.

Currently, the *Gorbachev* was just south of the Arctic Circle, positioned 68 0. N.–25 0. W. The submarine was at a depth of fifty feet, and had been following the course of a large ore carrier. Captain Narodny had been carefully constructing the possibility of making a full practice attack. A ship was showing on the submarine radar and Captain Narodny thought it was an opportunity not to be missed. However, the weather up top was foul. A storm of nearly force twelve was raging.

The *SS Andros*, a Liberian–registered ship under time charter to the Dresser Corporation of America, was slowly proceeding on its voyage. Its destination was Bergen, Norway. On the bridge, Captain Ronald Rossway was looking through the window into a constant deluge of lashing torrential rain. Visibility was very poor, about two hundred metres, and the sea very rough. Each time a huge wave crested over its bows, the ship reached.

"Range, eight thousand five hundred metres and closing," the *Gorbachev*'s operations room sounded its advice of co-ordinates to the bridge.

"Please contact Moscow for clearance," Captain Narodny instructed. "Request if we can proceed to engage. Advise we wish to create the possibility of our first practice attack. Thereafter, it may become the real thing." The minutes ticked past.

"Moscow have acknowledged, Captain Narodny, sir," came a response.

As soon as the confirmation was cleared Captain Narodny immediately motivated his submarine crew into action. "Surface! Surface! Surface!" he ordered. "We have been given full clearance from Moscow to conduct our submarine's first battle trials. An ore ship is our target. If we are successful it will be recorded that the ship simply foundered in heavy seas with no survivors."

Captain Narodny continued the process of broadcasting details of his message to the whole submarine's company. "By now, you all are aware our submarine has been recorded as having presumably been sunk, supposedly lost on its maiden voyage. Also, I am sure you are all aware we are now undetectable. Therefore, before we can handle more important targets, we must first ensure we can successfully handle all of the new equipment. In this respect, and in regard to what we are about to embark upon, please do not fail our illustrious and gallant vessel. That is all."

Captain Narodny and his officers mustered in readiness to go up on the deck of the conning tower. The submarine heaved heavily in the huge sea. Captain Narodny knew very well if he was to achieve any form of success, he was at all times to maintain the position of his submarine being undetected.

Again he spoke to the submarine's company. "As yet nobody has successfully fired an atomic-powered laser gun from a vessel at sea. Therefore, it must be tried and tested in order to achieve progression in its field. So, in order that it may be improved and operations be maintained we must carry out these tests." In finishing his address the Captain spoke quietly to his confidant, Lieutenant Bishkoff. "In this case the weather will be our only ally, Number One."

As the hatch to the upper deck was raised, water poured in drenching an able seaman whose task it was to raise the hatch at the same time a howling wind came down the aperture of the enclosed conning tower.

Standing unsteadily on the bridge of the *SS Andros*, Captain Rossway engaged in checking the ship's radar in order to ensure that its course and heading were clear; he saw that the nearest ship on the screen showed a ten thousand metric ton Japanese cargo ship called *SS Kuji Maru*. However, its route took the ship on a course well astern of the *SS Andros* about six miles due south, and making headway on a south-westerly course. There was another ship twenty miles north of the *SS Andros* plus two more were about sixty-five miles ahead of its current position.

"Cup of coffee, sir?" enquired Midshipman Evans.

"Thanks. A coffee would certainly warm the cockles of my heart. The weather's ghastly."

Evans replied, "It must be one of the worst storms this year, sir."

Soon the water came to the boil; it was bubbling out of the kettle as Evans poured its steaming stream into two large mugs. "Here's your coffee, sir," said Evans, handing the piping hot mug to his Captain.

"Thank you very much. I believe you're right about the sea, Mr. Evans."

At that moment a monster wave lifted high over the ship's forecastle. It came crashing down on to the forward hatches. A wall of seawater raced foaming, along the deck momentarily submerging everything below its water line. The huge wave continued forward smashing against the hatches amidships then it cascaded onward towards the main superstructure aft. On its journey, the water swallowed up anything that was loose or partly secured on deck where such items were savagely ripped off and dragged back into the sea. Suddenly an inflatable craft, which had partially broken free from its mooring, seemed to raise itself up in defiance of the advancing aggressor. The force of the raging sea snapped it away from its deck position, tossing it high up in the air; it then keeled upside down then overturned disappearing over the ship's port side as the vessel's deck slowly reappeared in levelling it out from the foaming seas below.

Captain Rossway looked back from the bridge window and shouted. "My God, that was a bloody big wave! Mr. Evans, you had better ensure that Sparks sends a message out to all shipping confirming how bad the local weather condition is. Please ensure you mark the storm's east-north-easterly progress. Also, have a message sent to our agents in Iceland telling them to expect an unscheduled visit from us for storm repairs. Notify them we should be docking in Reykjavik hopefully late morning on 31 July."

"Right you are, sir," responded Evans.

Captain Rossway continued to shout above the noise. "Mr. Evans, you are also to alert the Dresser Corporation. Ask them to make all necessary arrangements with our agents. Do this just in case we suddenly lose radio contact. Express in the message that next time it would be our wish to take the more southerly route to Bergen. They are well aware it may take slightly longer, but in seas like these we may well at anytime have our cargo shifted."

On board the *Gorbachev*, Captain Narodny was advised the ore carrier was at a range of five thousand metres. "We do not want any problems now do we? My God, Bishkoff, this damned weather certainly is rough. Do you know, I am almost certain the world will believe the *SS Andros* most definitely will have foundered in this heavy sea. Prepare to lock on to target."

Captain Narodny's order rang out from the bridge throughout the submarine. The sound of slowly turning ball bearings was heard marshalling the immense machinery placed on the forward deck of the submarine. It was a sinister looking object of black tungsten steel, torch-like in shape. A sealed turret enclosed the extended barrel piece which housed the automatically controlled computer link to the space platform *Vostok*.

Captain Narodny continued issuing his instructions. "Alert Moscow again. Advise them we are now very close to our target. Have them confirm we still remain fully undetected. State everything has gone to plan and in accordance with the manual's instructions. Re-confirm the target ship is an ore carrier, the *SS Andros*. Ask if we may now engage on to the target and kill!" The *Gorbachev* waited. Then a response came:

MSCW/GORB 12.48 HOURS 30/07/17 TS: CON/0356400-2
YOU MAY ENGAGE AT 10.15 HOURS YOUR TIME – STOP – YOU ARE
SYNCHRONISED AT THIS TIME WITH THE SPACE PLATFORM VOSTOK
– STOP – GOOD HUNTING – STOP – END MESSAGE

Captain Narodny acknowledged receipt of the message from Moscow. He checked his watch. It was 09.51 hours. He requested the crew of the special operations room to co-ordinate operations with the space platform *Vostok*. "Order that suspension of the Space Cocoon programme now be made safe." The time for this was to be synchronised and set at 10.15 hours.

"We have exactly twenty-three minutes and thirty seconds to firing, Captain," came a voice over the internal speaker being relayed from the special operations room.

Captain Narodny picked up the bridge microphone. "This is your Captain speaking. Comrades, we are about to embark on a new dimension of discovery in regard our country's defences on earth and in space. We have been allowed to exercise the first firing at an enemy of our newest weapon – the atomic-powered laser gun. We are now in communications with our comrades in space and are cleared and co-ordinated for firing at the time of 10.15 hours. It is vital we do not expose ourselves to any detection. Please be advised, Moscow has acknowledged to the *Gorbachev*, good hunting. That is all."

On the bridge of the *SS Andros,* Captain Rossway and his number one were in the process of receiving news from the wireless room. It was confirmation and acknowledgement of messages sent to *SS Kuji Maru,* Iceland, the ship's charterers and owners.

Visibility appeared to be slightly improving and the submarine was now at a distance of about three thousand five hundred metres. The torrential rain had eased a little, but the *SS Andros* was still rolling very heavily in the high seas. The ship's radar showed nothing had really changed or had altered in regard to previous readings.

The time now was 10.11 hours.

In checking and seeing everything was in order, Captain Rossway thought he could go below to his cabin for some rest.

Evans, at that moment with his binoculars raised, was scanning the waves through to the horizon. He was trying to establish from where the next huge wave was coming from. "Slightly to the port beam, sir," he called. "Yes. There's another very big sea coming."

"Steer into it, Number One," Captain Rossway replied.

The *Gorbachev* rolled then dipped slightly each time a huge wave came from its stern. The submarine glistened, like the wet fur of a black panther stealthily stalking its prey.

"Range, three thousand two hundred and forty metres and closing," came a voice from below reporting to Captain Narodny who by now was standing watching from the enclosed conning tower bridge. He commented, "Thirty-nine seconds to go, Lieutenant. Start counting when we reach twenty seconds."

"Yes, sir," Lieutenant Bishkoff replied.

On board the *SS Andros*, Midshipman Evans had moved his position and was now watching the sea directly over the ship's forecastle. A huge wave passed; the ship was now in its trough. Slowly the ship's bow again began to rise in meeting a smaller wave. Evans had his binoculars trained slightly to port. Again he began to do a sweep. "There's another huge sea coming, sir," remarked Evans to Captain Rossway who had decided to remain on the bridge a little while longer.

"All right, Evans, I'll take her through this one," said the Captain as he raised his glasses to follow the sea's pattern. Slowly he panned across the waves towards the horizon. Visibility was about three thousand four hundred and fifty metres. "Great Scott!" he yelled. "In heavens name, there's a damned submarine out there! It's right slap-bang in front of us. It appears to be on a collision course! Quick, Evans, check the radar."

Evans did as he was commanded. "Nothing is showing, sir," he said quickly responding. At the same time he grabbed his binoculars to look in the same direction as Captain Rossway.

Visibility at that distance was still not good. Evans began sweeping his glasses up across the waves. Suddenly, he saw what Captain Rossway had presumably seen. It seemed and appeared to be the huge black shape of a submarine lying dead ahead of the bow of the *Andros*. "It's a submarine all right, sir! Good grief! What a submarine!" shouted the midshipman.

Momentarily, a small blip appeared on the radar screen. Captain Rossway blurted out an order, "Get Sparks to immediately send this message out to all comers on the open frequency!" Evans quickly took down the details:

HAVE FOUND SUBMARINE ON SURFACE AT 09.0 N – 66.0 W – STOP –
TIME 10:14:55 HOURS – STOP – END MESSAGE

At that moment a flash of light engulfed the bridge of the *Andros*. Then, there was nothing.

On the conning tower bridge of the *Gorbachev*, at precisely 10.15 hours, everyone saw the atomic-powered laser gun spit forth a beam of red light. The gun emitted an unprecedented force that struck *SS Andros* directly on the bow. Instantly it glowed through the main section of the ship's forecastle and hull. The beam then shot up through the deck to the aft section of the vessel's superstructure. The *SS Andros's* bridge was struck right in the middle of the main aft stack. The glowing red beam bore an immense gaping hole right through the ship. In a matter of fifteen seconds there was nothing to be seen. Only a few bits of flotsam and jetsam were left floating on the sea.

The *Gorbachev* had made its first kill. Immediately, Captain Narodny acknowledged confirmation of the successful hunt to Moscow and to the space platform *Vostok*.

Soon reports were coming in from the international media. They advised confirmation of the tragic loss with all hands of the ship, *SS Andros*. The news statement confirmed that the ship, an ore carrier of twenty-five thousand tons, had sunk very suddenly in severe weather and heavy sea conditions somewhere off the south-east coast of Iceland.

On board the United States Navy's hunter-killer nuclear submarine, *Bowevil*, news of the sinking and loss of the *SS Andros* had been received. Although understanding the disaster had happened in extremely severe weather conditions everyone was quite amazed how it could be that a ship only five years old should have somehow foundered in such a swift manner.

Immediately the news was received, Captain Jack Maxman ordered a special clearance be authorised from the top which he hoped would enable the *Bowevil* be ordered to carry out an underwater search to try and locate the wreck of the *Andros*. Captain Maxman had very quickly reacted to the sinking; he was puzzled as to why the disaster had occurred. *Maybe*, he thought, *if the Bowevil was lucky enough to locate the sunken ship some clue could be given as to why the ship sank so quickly.*

NASA Military and Naval Intelligence, Cape Canaveral

Kemp had spent only a couple of hours back at his house. He was just settling himself down when the security officer called him and urgently requested that the General should come back to the office as soon as possible. The officer informed Kemp it certainly appeared that a flap was on. An instruction clearance, marked 'TOP PRIORITY', had just been received from the *SSN Bowevil*.

Events of the past two days were still sending vibrations back and forth to the White House. Kemp thought the loss of the Russian submarine *SSBN Gorbachev* was to be treated as a serious concern and great worry. London secretly had advised him he was now to be extra cautious and vigilant regarding this delicate situation.

In the meantime, Kemp had been notified that the *Bowevil* had been immediately dispatched to the disaster area. However, it was also believed the Liberian-registered ore carrier *SS Andros* had tragically foundered.

Personally, Kemp thought the whole thing stank.

Having returned to his office, Kemp was still feeling a little weary having had very little sleep. He sat at his desk caressing a large black coffee. Finally, in settling down, the first task he knew he had to deal with was the urgent matter concerning the message and request made by the *SSN Bowevil*.

While sipping his coffee, Kemp began to consider certain implications in regard to certain irregularities found in the *Gorbachev* file. At that moment the red telephone on his desk, the hotline, began to ring.

It was a little after 06.30 hours EST, the morning dawn had already echoed its chorus of song and now a carpet of rich, serenely golden clouds began to spread across the sky.

"Good morning, General," said the voice. "I wonder if you could please find time this morning to come down to NASA Tracking to see me? I wish to show you something in respect of what, since midnight, our Space Monitoring Operations have delivered to me."

"Okay, Mac," replied Kemp. "I'll be there in about an hour. Is that goin' to be all right with you?"

"Great stuff, John."

"Anyhow, what's the problem, Mac?" beckoned the General.

Professor Macdonald Burston was a long-time friend of Kemp, a veteran of the NASA Apollo Space Programme, the same as the General. Many times in the past they both shared each other's problems regarding what they jointly deemed as 'phenomenon', or 'unexplainables'.

Macdonald Burston, 'Old Buster', to his close friends, lowered his voice in reply to the General's last comment. "I cannot really discuss it on the telephone, John. Come on now, just get your feet into gear and get on over here then I can talk to you."

"Okay, Mac, I'll do just that. Bye for now."

Kemp replaced the receiver. As he did, he thought it highly odd for Old Buster to blow in like that on the General's operational hotline. However, in responding to the intrigue of his friend, he thought he had better pack up the files on his desk and make a move as the Professor had suggested.

Just as the General was leaving, the hotline rang. By now he had already closed his office door. After a few rings the telephone automatically switched itself through to the security desk so that a message could be taken or recorded.

"Good morning. This is Admiral Raymond Marchant. I had hoped to catch General John Kemp in his office. Could you ask him to urgently return my call? He has my private number."

"Certainly, Admiral," replied the security guard.

"Thank you very much." The Admiral rang off.

Next, he picked up the telephone receiver and tried Commander Thompson at the Royal Naval Operations Room at Northwood, but he wasn't in either.

Marchant picked up his gin and tonic and carried on studying the many intelligence reports received over the past twenty-four hours. "Damn it. I just know those bloody Russians are up to no good. Why the devil is it when you always want to get something started, or quickly sorted, the whole ruddy world seems to disappear into the woodwork?"

He carried on thinking aloud, "People today no longer seem to have either the willpower or the stamina to stay at their post until the damned job is finished. Huh! It would never have happened in my day. Goodness me, if we all had suddenly disappeared, we would have been flogged... No. On reflection that was a little bit strong, and well overboard. But for Christ's sake, why is it, there never seems to be anybody about when you really want to talk to them?"

After further deliberation, Marchant raised his glass and approvingly took a deep draw. He then continued, quietly grumbling to himself about the fact of now having to wait for nearly two hours for the arrival of Commander Thompson. "It just wasn't on! On the other hand I suppose the man has to rest. Damn it! I'll just have to wait regarding this delay, too."

Looking for something else to occupy his mind the Admiral picked up his notebook and began to doodle.

It was just after 13.00 hours. Commander Thompson had rested well. He was an hour earlier than his duty demanded when entering the operations room. He had considered it was far more useful for him to be on hand, just in case any further news had been reported other than to remain laying in bed fretting about it.

"Hello, sir," Lieutenant Henderson announced greeting the Commander as he entered.

"Good afternoon, Henderson. What's been going on? Anything urgent or of a drastic nature to report?"

"Sir, the *Bowevil* altered its course a couple of times. As it is now, it appears to be heading towards the south-east coast of Iceland."

"Thank you, Henderson. Has there been any intelligence information as to why the *Bowevil* has moved its position?"

"None reported as yet, sir." Henderson continued. "By the way, Commander, Admiral Marchant telephoned for you about an hour ago. He wanted to know if you had arrived back in operations."

"Okay, Ian. Thank you for the message. I'll contact him directly." The Commander ordered coffee then entered his office and began dialling the Admiral on his private line.

"Hello? Who's that?" was the opening retort.

"Good afternoon, Admiral."

"Ah, Thompson. Good, you're back sooner than I had expected. Now, dear boy, about the US Navy's hunter-killer submarine, *Bowevil*."

"Yes, sir," Thompson replied.

"Watch it very closely for a while, will you? We don't want the Yanks to start queering the scene, now, do we, eh?"

"No, sir."

Marchant continued. "Personally, I think the US sub has gone looking for that freighter that foundered."

Thompson didn't reply but,he felt that the Admiral might be mistaken.

"Now then, Thompson, be sure what I am going to say to you is kept very tight under your hat. Do you hear me?"

Thompson still didn't move or pass any comment. He just sat there at his office desk with the telephone poised at his ear and carried on listening.

"Right. Total assumption, Thompson, total assumption!" Marchant coughed, wishing to clear his throat." Now then, I still think that Russian submarine is somewhere around. As much as I have said it before, I can't yet prove it. I want you now to become all ears and eyes. Is that understood?"

Thompson continued listening.

Marchant kept talking. "No discussion out of bounds with anyone. Do you hear, Thompson? I don't want anyone alerted whatsoever concerning matters regarding this subject. I duly trust I have made this abundantly clear to you?"

Thompson still said nothing and continued to take stock of the situation.

Marchant carried on with his address. "I seem to have a very funny feeling about the whole thing." He paused to take a sip from his third gin and tonic.

It was then Thompson spoke. "I fully understand, sir. But could you give me any reason why you should wish your mind to rest upon this assumption?"

The Admiral exploded, echoing down the telephone. "Assumption, damn it! Now listen here! You just darn well accept that what I am telling you is fact. Don't you dare try and put back your reply to me in such a manner, certainly not one that would seem to imply you doubting my thoughts. I openly resent anyone who cares to interrupt me, even more so, answering in the absurd manner of some young upstart. Is that quite clear?"

The Commander didn't move he did not wish to be drawn by the Admiral's comments nor did he wish to give Admiral Marchant any cause to accuse him of anything untoward.

"Heavens above, Thompson, I should have thought that by now you would have known better. Now then, please mark well what I have said and at all times do try to remember it. Is everything now quite clear with you?"

Thompson quickly tried to correct the situation. "No, sir. I mean..."

Admiral Marchant interrupted. "Now then, lad, come on please just go and do what I have asked. You will soon find out what I have been telling you is the truth. Mind you, if it does very quickly become a reality I again shall be talking to you about the same subject in the near future. Is everything now very clear in your mind?"

Thompson hesitated, still unsure of what Marchant had been saying to him. However, he knew if he were to argue he would jeopardise matters. "Yes, Admiral."

"Good. I am now going to partake in a late lunch. I trust everything regarding this current circumstance is now fully understood. "There was a long pause. "Well, Thompson?"

"Yes, sir. Err, quite clear. Quite clear thank you, sir." Thompson was left thinking, *What on earth have I done to deserve this lot?*

Marchant interjected. "If you can put this one to bed, we shall have to see what we can do in keeping your name in line for something special in the future."

When the Admiral rang off, Thompson put down the receiver. His ears were still ringing to the sound of Marchant's voice. Carefully, he reflected on what Marchant had said, not forgetting the implied possibility of a promotion. That was, of course, if this operation just happened to work out to his advantage. Smiling to himself, reflecting on the Admiral's comments, Thompson left his office for the rest room.

General Kemp arrived at the NASA Tracking Control Centre. He was a little later than he would have wished; his limousine had suffered a slight mishap on the freeway which had delayed him for over thirty minutes. As the vehicle entered the security gate the driver's electric window slid down whereby he announced, "General Kemp is here by the personal request of Professor Burston."

The sentry guard lifted the telephone and called through to the Central Control Building. "Priority One clearance given," came the reply.

The black limousine sped forward along the driveway. Soon it rolled into the V.I.P. parking lot.

As Kemp stepped out he asked his driver to wait.

Professor Macdonald Burston had received the message informing him that his long-time friend John Kemp had just arrived. On hearing the news, he came to the reception to meet him.

Walking through the main lobby entrance the General saw the Professor. "Hi there, Mac," Kemp called, striding forward, his hand outstretched to greet him.

"Hello, John. It's good to see you again."

"How's business in your neck of the woods?" Kemp responded warmly.

Macdonald Burston was very pleased to see his friend. He had known Kemp since the early days of the Apollo moon missions, and valued his friendship. In the past, he had found the General's perceptiveness and sometimes unorthodox ability to approach and unravel problems normally left sitting in the pending file a hidden asset. However, the Professor also realised and knew such files were left due to nobody else wishing or having neither nerve nor any courage to stick their necks out. Macdonald Burston respected John Kemp as nearly always being the one man who'd seek to turn those pending files upside down. He also knew the General would never let any of them stand too long on any shelf in order they might be seen left to gather dust.

The General spoke. "Well, Mac. It's not like you to bell me on the hotline. Something must be bugging you mighty strongly which must be really hottin' up in order for you to do that."

Professor Burston stopped General Kemp short and requested he follow him. Leading the way he said, "Please come into my private office, John." His office faced eastwards towards the distant huge launching pad of the Saturn/Shuttle space complex.

The General had looked at the site earlier when getting out of his limousine. "My word, Mac, the view you have from up here sure is somethin'. In fact, it's positively stunning."

"I suppose it's not that bad."

"Buddy, modesty will never become you. In the whole time you have had this room I'll bet you haven't missed a launch yet." Kemp walked over to look out of the wide expanse of glass.

"You're right, John. I have always been pleased with this office; it sure brings back many memories of bygone days. Anyway, a couple of old veterans like us could spend weeks reminiscing and I didn't bring you all the way over here just to do that." Professor Burston was pleased to see his friend; he smiled at the General in response to his remarks.

"Well, Mac, what's all this intrigue about? What in heaven's name is near to boiling point? Why did you bring me over here?"

The Professor took a file from the centre drawer of his desk and handed it over to the General. "Hey, John, have a look at these high altitude pictures. I've just received them overnight from US Airforce Strategic Command. The pictures have been taken during the past six weeks. I am advised they were taken at a height of between sixty-two miles down to ninety-six thousand feet."

Kemp studied the content of some of the photographs. He saw an American Air force spy satellite had taken the first of them. Some of them he didn't recognise at all. Others he couldn't really make a lot of certain shots. What he did see in several of the pictures could only be described as a cone or a funnel shape formed of fluorescent lighting. As Kemp continued to peruse over the photographs, he spoke. "Yes, Mac, finally I think you have got one on me. Mind you, I must say that I have never seen anything quite like that before." Kemp paused placing his hand to his chin. Momentarily, he showed an expression of deep thought. "Hey, Mac, hold on now. Maybe, for just a moment there, I was a little bit too hasty."

"Yes, John? Do you really think then we may have stumbled across something?" asked the Professor.

"Woah back a bit, Old Buster. Now just hold on a moment. Maybe. Mind you, except for one thing. Well, I don't know. But, look at this one here. It reminds me of a photograph I saw some years back taken on a return journey by one of the Apollo moon missions. Heck! I'm almost sure it was something similar, looking at that sort of thing."

"Really, John?" the Professor remarked.

"Certainly. I do remember at the time everyone was carping about it.

They thought finally that they had found the solution to what might have been the ultimate cause in leading to resolving the saga of the Bermuda Triangle. Mind you, nothin' further was ever really investigated into the subject. If it was, it never became public knowledge."

For a moment the General pondered. "Yes, I do seem to remember, come to think of it. I believe the file was presumed lost, or was recorded as havin' been shredded."

Kemp set about laying all the photographs spread out on a huge glass table. He laid them out in sequence, first starting with a row of the pictures taken about six months earlier. He then laid down underneath them the latest photographs that were barely twenty-four hours old. When he finished he commented, "Hey, Mac, if we both didn't know anything different I'd say we could well have been the first pioneers into finding out what a space weather system looks like. Mind you, I must say these darned objects certainly seem to be somethin' like a spate of highly charged space tornados."

"You may well be right, John, and could possibly have struck on something there. Maybe, finally out of all of this, we could be the first to discover what these things really are. However, I must say currently the whole thing really beats me." Professor Burston thought something more positive might have come from it all what with his close friend being always with his nose to the ground and in the know.

Meanwhile, Kemp was left somewhat puzzled; he was not really sure as what he should do or say. He looked up at Macdonald Burston, "What would you like me to do with these pictures, Mac?"

The Professor was still thinking. "I'm not exactly sure. What do you think should be done with them?"

"Well, I suppose I could take them back with me; have our boys run the data through our intelligence computer in order to see what G.O.D. can make of any of it."

The General's computer was originally given a title of the *Computer Graphics Operational Defence System*. Over the years it had become affectionately nicknamed G.O.D. The reason given for this extraordinary title was mainly due to the fact it always seemed to have an answer for everything that was programmed into it.

"Mac, did Strategic Air Command and the US Airforce send anything else with these pictures?"

Professor Burston thought for moment. "As a matter of fact, John, yes they did. It all came sealed in a black box."

The General turned and pointed to where a box was standing. "It's that one over there, the one standing on top of the filing cabinet."

On seeing the familiar shape Kemp beamed a great big smile. He felt as if something, a new beginning, was going to unfold. "Well, if you don't mind, Mac, I'd like to have these pictures and all these details released into my operations, and on an official basis. That is, of course, depending on whether you can get full clearance. If you can I'll get the show on the road for you. Then hopefully, Mac, possibly you can get something off to me? Let's hope I can come back and really give you some answers to this very strange puzzle."

Professor Burston smiled. In showing an air of excitement, he said, "Why, thank you, John. Somehow, I just knew you would come up with a bright idea. Are you able to arrange to take all this stuff away with you?"

"Sure I am," Kemp replied.

Macdonald Burston continued, "Okay, then I'll arrange for a fax message be sent to your office advising an official confirmation of release and that clearance has been given. I'll do it while you are travelling back. It has been grand meeting you again, John," said the Professor smiling. "Mind you, let's not make it such a long gap next time."

Macdonald Burston helped Kemp collect up all the photographs, plus information necessary for assisting the computer programming.

Kemp acknowledged his assistance. "Thanks a bundle, Mac."

As Professor Burston lifted the black box down from the filing cabinet, he replied. "Glad to be of service, old buddy."

Out of instinct, Kemp took a last careful look about him to see if there was any vital information left behind. "Well, Mac, don't worry. I'll be back again to take another look at this incredible view you have."

"Sure, John. Be my guest, anytime."

Both men left the office.

Kemp pushed the button on his pocket bleeper to warn his driver he was soon going to be at the front door.

"That's neat," remarked the Professor.

Kemp replaced the little machine back into his side pocket. "It sure saves you a heck of a lot of time. You'll see the limo will be outside the door even before we reach the reception area."

Soon they turned left from the corridor into the reception area. Through the huge glass window at the front door Professor Burston could see a large black automobile. "My word, John, that sure is some limo the department gives you these days."

Kemp smiled. "Next time you get the chance to visit me, you will have to come over to my place. We will do it when we have checked all of your info out. Hopefully by then we could well have cracked the problem. If needs be, I'll send the limo over to collect you."

Macdonald Burston looked at the highly polished vehicle. "Yes, I should like that a lot." The Professor offered the General a courtesy handshake. "I'll say bye for now, dear friend."

Kemp nodded. "Don't work yourself too hard, you old devil! Oh, by the way, Mac, I nearly forgot. Thank you for the opportunity to renew our friendship, and also for the files."

As Kemp walked down the steps the driver stepped out. He placed the file container and documents briefcase into the limousine's boot. It was not very long afterwards the black limousine turned out of the parking lot, and soon it sped away down the drive then on to the open freeway.

Chapter Four

At Sea

Moscow sent a message of congratulations to the *Gorbachev* in confirmation of receiving the submarine's message acknowledging the successful firing of the atomic-powered laser gun. Captain Nikita Narodny beamed a smile of delight as he read out details of the message to the submarine's company. There were rapturous cheers and congratulations all round. The crew spontaneously burst into a chorus of the Russian national anthem. The time was 15.30 hours.

Since the sinking of the *Andros*, the *Gorbachev* had remained submerged. A course had been authorised set for the open Atlantic. The crew hopefully thought it might now be the time to sail into less troubled waters. However, a second sea trial had to be arranged. It was planned that an attempt be made to fire the atomic-powered laser gun, underwater, at a surface target. As an alternative, a night trial was to be considered that was to take place on the surface, at a flying target. It was to be logged as the trial for covering sea-to-air combat.

Captain Narodny was fairly cautious regarding the proposal of any underwater trial. In past testing of the atomic-powered laser gun certain fatal mishaps had occurred. One time in testing, records stated the space platform's radio wave screen protection had not disengaged at the synchronised time. This had resulted in the total destruction of a prototype atomic-powered laser gun. There were many fatalities. Records confirmed the injured were left maimed, all suffering for a very long time from the disastrous circumstance and wrongful testing. The matter of *Gorbachev's* atomic-powered laser gun trials had been advised by Russia's naval superiors to be considered a captain's decision.

NASA Military and Naval Intelligence, Cape Canaveral

It was 11.40 hours, 30 July. General Kemp spent an uneasy night. He had been woken several times during the early hours. His department required clearances regarding details concerning new operations of the *SSN Bowevil*.

The General also learnt the sad news regarding the *SS Andros*. *Dreadful bad luck* he thought to himself. *The loss of such an experienced skipper, who came from a well renowned seafaring family in New England.* Still in deep thought, he was now concerned with the photographs that Professor Macdonald Burston had officially handed over to him. Already he had organised the Graphical Operations and Defence Departments to set programming the data into the computer. Kemp had given full clearance for *G.O.D.* to be engaged to receive the complicated input of all classified data gleaned from the pictures, plus full records of surveillance and all air reconnaissance details that had been collected by the United States Air Force under the authority of Strategic Air Command.

US Air Force Lieutenant Smart, 'Smartie' Logan had been seconded concerning the highly technical schedule to act as Kemp's aide.

"Seems a very bright young lad," the General said when thanking the Military and Naval Staff Department for sending him over.

Lieutenant Logan knocked on the General's office door and waited.

"Come in!" Logan entered. General Kemp continued, "Hello, Logan. Are you settling in okay? How is *G.O.D.* treatin' you today?"

Logan smiled at the General's comments. Somehow he had the feeling he had just been raised on to the celestial platform of heaven, seemingly for a personal visit. "Well, sir…"

"Yes," Kemp replied.

Logan continued, "The computer will take at least three or four hours to digest all of that input, sir. I also believe the machine is well capable of handling it." Logan confidently passed his remark not knowing quite what he had just said.

The General retorted and belted back at Logan. "Capable, Mr. Logan? Capable? Now, just let me tell you, you young whippersnapper. *G.O.D.* is the best computer going. Over these past years it has been involved with analysing the full space strategy programme. It followed that through and completed it right to the second." The General paused. "May I also state it was done both swiftly and with total accuracy." Again he paused. "It covered all of NASA's space launchings, even probably those that took place before you were wet behind the ears! These were all handled in the same way." General Kemp coughed. "Capable, you say, Logan! You know nothin'!"

The Lieutenant was stunned. He tried to say something. "Well, sir… I mean, err…" He was still catching his breath, gulping from the broadside and onslaught Kemp had just blasted at him.

However, as quick as the situation had flared up General Kemp soon stopped his huffing and puffing. He replied. "I'm sorry, youngster, but you kinda get very attached to toys, big ones, or even small ones," the General chuckled.

Logan gradually eased his tense facial expression. He produced a slight smile then motioned to speak, but Kemp interrupted him and continued, "I have always held, with tremendous pride, a soft spot for G.O.D. Nobody of this department, past or present, has ever, nor will they at any time in the future, specify that G.O.D. is merely *capable* of doing its job."

Kemp took a sip of his coffee. "Logan, it's the best. The best that America, *IBM*, and the whole darned shooting match can put together! I now trust that's okay and fully understood by you, son?"

Hesitating, Logan replied, "Yes, sir."

Replacing his coffee mug on his desk, Kemp looked up. "Now, young man, what was it you wanted to see me about?"

Logan leaned back in the chair and began easing himself into the conversation. "Well, sir, the first feedback from the computer we received," Logan paused, "Err, G.O.D. General, reveals the circular shapes are in fact radio wave graphs of a very high intensity. Each programme was separately fed in according to the record of its date, time and place, exactly as the data information that had previously been confirmed, sir." The Lieutenant placed on the General's table a copy of all the graph reports. He placed them against each dated block and photographs that the General had previously laid out.

Kemp got up from his desk and moved over to the table to have a look. He stared at all the computer's output. He said nothing for at least five minutes and then spoke. "Okay, young'un. What do you make of that?"

"I don't really know as yet, sir," Logan replied. He didn't want another avalanche of fire and brimstone from the General to burst forth and come breathing down his neck. The situation Logan now secretly had named to himself was to become none other than the 'devil's mouth', reflecting the wrath of the General's tongue.

Kemp spoke. "I tell you what, Logan."

"Yes, sir," replied the young man.

"Can you set up an extra, but separate, programme? See to it, it holds in addition to the first input the exact timings of all past events. Select to show these when processing. I've requested you do this in order to have G.O.D. give a coded printout of the radio wave cones as we see them in the pictures. Do please remember to operate this programme to be synchronised and locked on to the same dates and times of the current information we have received. I believe these will then simulate the setting of each area, both longitude and latitude. Do it to cover timings and dates recorded at sea, plus any area of land mass that shows a recording of the space tornados being beamed towards the earth at any specific recorded time. Cover every individual piece of information we have received on this subject. I wish it to be done when the final printout comes through. By then, hopefully, we should have covered every angle G.O.D. feasibly could have foreseen or deemed to have conjured up." Kemp stopped for a moment to take a sip of his coffee then continued. "Lad, let me say I have a wild hunch as to where all this might lead us, but I am not saying anything about it just yet."

"Right, sir," Logan replied.

Kemp turned round. As he did, he looked straight at Logan and spoke enquiringly, "Well now, Smartie, when do you think you will have all this lot ready for me?"

Logan paused, lowering his head for a moment in deep thought. "I should hope to have it ready at around 15.00 or maybe 16.00 hours, General." The Lieutenant looked up, smiling.

"Okay, I guess that'll be all right. Mind you, if at all possible can it be quicker?" The General wanted to get on and began to show his impatience.

Logan gave a salute. "I'll do my very best, sir." He then departed from Kemp's office.

Again, Kemp began to peruse the new data Logan had delivered to him from G.O.D. He placed all the printouts with the original pictures on a table. Taking off his glasses, he scratched his head. Deep in thought he then muttered to himself, "For godsakes! Somewhere in amongst all this lot there must be an answer or at least a simple clue to the supposed phenomenon."

Kemp entered his office and on his desk he saw a white envelope marked with a red stripe and the words 'TOP PRIORITY-URGENT'. Quickly he opened it, read the first page then immediately set about contacting Admiral Marchant. The General knew it was very late at night in London, so he called the Admiral's private line. The number rang. There was a click. The General then spoke, "Good evening, Raymond. I got your message advising you had called. What can I do for you?"

Admiral Marchant was sitting in his comfortable chair sipping his aperitif before having supper. "Ah, John Kemp. Thank you for calling back. I tried to get you earlier, but unfortunately I had just missed you."

"That's quite all right. Anyhow, I needed to speak with you on one or two matters."

"Please go ahead," Marchant invited.

"Well, Admiral, can I trade one?" requested the General.

Raymond Marchant was not really one to ever trade anything. He would merely enquire as to the status quo of a particular subject then take matters from there. He acknowledged Kemp's request, but considered he should make the first move.

"John, we have received firm evidence your submarine, correction, the US Navy's sub *Bowevil,* has gone looking for a lost freighter called *SS Andros.* Can you corroborate this information to be correct, General?"

Kemp was a little surprised by the forwardness of Marchant's line of remarks. "Pure speculation, sir. Pure speculation, but I won't deny it."

Kemp laughed at the mere suggestion of the idea after which he considered the matter was at an end. "Admiral Marchant, may I ask you a very direct and open question in friendship?"

Marchant answered, "Certainly, by all means."

The General was hoping that maybe he could clear any further skeletons from the cupboard. "Do you believe the *Gorbachev* was truly lost, Raymond?" There was a very silent pause.

"Hello? Hello, Admiral? Are you still on?" Kemp muttered, "Damn it. I've gone and lost him."

"I am still here, John," said Marchant, and then enquired, "Is this off the record between us?"

"Sure," responded Kemp.

Marchant replied, "Well, what do you think?" still not wanting to make any first move.

Kemp knew what the Admiral's last comment meant.

The Admiral quietly stated, "Good, that makes two old timers' instincts both seem sound in body and mind."

They both enjoyed a good chuckle.

Kemp spoke. "You know, I cannot put my finger on it yet, Admiral, but, as sure as hell is hell I'll get to the bottom of what it is those damned Russkies are up to. What d'yer say to that?"

By now Marchant was relaxing his stance a little towards the situation. "I believe, John, I will join you on that one if you need me. Or, if I can be of any help or assistance please do not hesitate to call me."

Kemp smiled. "Why thank you, sir. Oh, one moment, Admiral. I have got one for you to fathom out."

"What one is that?" Marchant quickly responded, but was immediately taken aback by Kemp's reversal.

The General answered, "I said I have a puzzle for you to confidentially consider."

"Okay, let's hear it, John," the Admiral replied.

Kemp asked, "What would you consider a group of bright fluorescent spiral-type lights descending towards our planet from outer space were to be?" There was a slight pause. Kemp continued, "If you could solve that one for me today, Admiral, you would certainly relieve me of what I consider and believe to be my next mystery headache of the moment. Or maybe, for that matter, the biggest one for this year. Got any ideas?"

Marchant had just stopped to take a sip of his drink. "Well, John, I might be able to assist you, but it would need you giving me greater insight. Why don't you forward to me any relevant material available on the subject and I will see if we have anything here to compare your details with."

Kemp was pleased with that suggestion. Furthermore, he knew if British Naval Intelligence had picked up information which happened to be anything like both the USAF and SAC had discovered, then maybe there could be envisaged a final outcome, or at least a positive idea as to what the darn thing was. "I will do just that, sir. Thank you for the suggestion," came his reply.

The Admiral answered, "Not at all. Thank you for the offer, John."

Marchant had already begun to think back over the past two months. He was not sure whether the Royal Navy had received from their resources any information that was remotely like Kemp was requesting. A thought then crossed his mind that he could call up an old school chum he had kept in touch with, Professor Albert Ponsonby. He was the Senior Professor of Physics and Scientific Radiology at Jodrell Bank in charge of the second largest fully steerable radio telescope in the world, the Jodrell Bank Mark 1A 76-metre dish. Marchant thought if anyone knew what these things were, Albert Ponsonby would. The Admiral's train of thought was broken by the continued conversation from General Kemp.

"Well, Admiral, where do you think the *Gorbachev* is at this moment?" Kemp thought he would send in a final broadside for a closing reaction. He was still hoping for some lead as to what Marchant might have up his sleeve.

"I have not the foggiest idea, John. However, taking all details into account of what we have now imparted concerning Russia's two missing FSB agents, you would do well first to check these matters in your own back yard. At least in your doing a surprise pounce on certain top people. Let us say, for example, those persons you would normally believe are safe, such persons sitting quite close to the top of the tree, someone who is in a respected position and very able in keeping a watch on every move.

Someone, a special person, other than your number one man. One who is capable of discreetly controlling everything like a great big queen wasp." The Admiral's voice deepened in beginning to exert an air of premeditation. "John, someone who you would normally have assumed to have been totally sound. It is that sort of person who probably knows even more information than the President of the United States of America does himself. One thing I am fairly certain of, I believe you really do have such an enemy."

Kemp felt a wet cold shiver going down his spine; he was very surprised to hear what Marchant was eagerly hunting for and equally aiming to get at. Even more so, the General was suspiciously sure Marchant must have received some very positive information, which had allowed him now to be so profound.

"Well, General, I expect I'll be hearing from you shortly. If not, I will be in touch by next Monday. Then I will give you a full report and update regarding your 'demons from outer space'," Marchant chuckled.

Kemp wasn't quite sure what Marchant was implying by the word 'demons'. "Thank you very much, Admiral, for the advice. I hope you don't consider naming your file, 'Space Ghostbusters'!"

Marchant silently laughed to himself; he did not want to completely ruin the platonic relationship which had formed mutually over past months through their telephone acquaintance. However, he couldn't resist the golden opportunity of considering naming the service file as 'Operation Ghostbusters'. Nothing more on the subject was said.

The Admiral kept a broad, beaming smile as he replaced the receiver after wishing Kemp goodbye.

It was now very late into the evening of 31 July. Admiral Marchant no longer felt hungry, he was feeling tired from a long eventful day. As he finished his nightcap, he decided he would telephone Commander Thompson before turning in.

Royal Naval Intelligence HQ, Northwood

The operations screen showed clearly the latest movements of the US Navy submarines the *SSBN Intrepid* and *SSN Bowevil*.

At Sea

The British strategic nuclear missile submarine *HMS Excalibur*, known affectionately as the 'Sword of the Sea', was still three hundred miles south-south-west of the position fixed where it was thought the *SS Andros* had foundered.

HMS Excalibur had been on operations in the southern Atlantic Ocean overseeing patrols around Fortress Falklands. The Ministry of Defence had not considered replacing its tour of duty earlier than expected but the nuclear submarine, having been drawn into Operation Blindfold, now left a gap in Britain's Southern Defence Patrol. Due to the circumstances regarding *SSBN Gorbachev* this essential priority had now taken precedent.

HMS Excalibur, although smaller than both its Russian and American counterparts, had one thing superior by far – its speed. *HMS Excalibur's* keel was laid down in 2009, the completion of its building was finalised in the autumn of 2011 and on 12 May 2013 the submarine was commissioned and taken over by its one hundred and thirty-five crew and twelve officers as an official 0+1+(3) Astute class strategic nuclear missile submarine. It was listed as sixteen thousand tons dived. The submarine had four torpedo tubes that would fire in anger a new lightweight Tigerfish Mark MU92, wire/guided/acoustic homing torpedo. Additionally, the *Excalibur* also carried 'Super Spearfish' torpedoes. These advanced weapons were equipped with a new type of on-board digital computer, which permitted a sophisticated adaptive operation of the weapons guidance system, which enhanced the torpedo's homing sonar sub-system. Its warhead consists of a newly developed EHE device capable of penetrating modern advanced separated outer skin and pressure hulls now used in the latest submarines.

As the submarine thrust along at nearly thirty knots through the turbulent seas of the mid-Atlantic Ocean, *HMS Excalibur* forged a massive sea surge ahead of its bow. Commodore Christopher Brianston-Green RN had received classified operational orders delivered from Northwood Royal Navy HQ *HMS Excalibur* was to arrive soonest in the area and vicinity where the *SSBN Intrepid* was sailing.

Commodore Brianston-Green's instructions read:

…YOU ARE THEN TO SHADOW AND COVER THE TASK OPERATIONS OF SSN BOWEVIL – STOP – STILL CONTINUE TO MONITOR THE MOVEMENTS OF SSBN INTREPID – STOP – KEEP A CONSTANT WATCH ON BOTH SUBMARINES WHILE GOING ABOUT THEIR DAILY MISSIONS – STOP – END MESSAGE

It was advised in the Commodore's *communiqué SSBN Intrepid* was to be found positioned about sixty miles north-east off the coast of Iceland at 13.0 W – 63.0 N. *SSN Bowevil* was covering a zigzag search course. Its last known position was recorded being south-west of Iceland at 23.0 W – 62. 0

N. Information received alleged the submarine was carrying out a bottom survey of the ocean bed but was believed to be trying to locate the wreck of the *SS Andros*.

Out in mid–Atlantic the *SSBN Gorbachev* had settled down to completing its revised monitoring operations under the cover of 'Operation Invisible'. In co-ordinating instructions with the Russian space platform Vostok this was to handle and maintain control of its cocoonment. The submarine had soon to be ready for stage two of the sea trial testing programme.

NASA Military and Naval Intelligence, Cape Canaveral

It was Friday, 31 July. Time 13.30 Hours.

As instructed, Lieutenant Logan began to set and program the operation records into G.O.D. He fed the computer a full revised list of data regarding the mysterious fluorescent cylindrical funnels of light which the department now considered was to be some kind of space tornado. The new data program he had constructed was to form a simulated scan pattern of radio waves. Logan knew the immense pressure he was under. Six, maybe seven hours could be foreseen in order to allow the input schedule to enter and be digested by G.O.D.

For nearly two hours Kemp had been sitting in his long-backed easy chair carefully dissecting the program data 'Smartie' Logan had delivered to him from G.O.D.'s pre-analysis printout. He got up and walked over to the large glass table and laid each section out across its clear expanse. The first section dealt with a lot of information collected from past military shuttle landings. The second section had been compiled from data gathered by a United States Navy's Satellite, which was very successful in its field. A new version of the satellite had been launched just over a month ago; its job was to deal with upper hemisphere atmospherics registered under the name of Scientific Naval Oceanic Weather Module Intelligence in Space as a testing unit. This very sophisticated piece of sensory equipment had now been adopted under NASA's wing, and its file log reference name for classified operations was *S.N.O.W.M.I.S.T.* '*U*' or, 'Flaky' which NASA's operations room had affectionately decided to call it.

Kemp often used the invisible space sphere, this being way beyond its purported limits. In past years, he had synchronised *S.N.O.W.M.I.S.T.* '*U*' for gleaning data from some of NASA's pre-flight information of military launchings. The *S.N.O.W.M.I.S.T.* '*U*' had been a classified hidden asset to his department covering every launch since making its debut in June 2011.

Now Kemp needed to find a similar inspiration; he knew he had to try to seek a solution regarding the problem of the 'space demons'. At present, the mystery wasn't giving itself up easily. The *S.N.O.W.M.I.S.T.* 'U' Data Information System had shown that, since starting its upper hemisphere atmospherics monitoring from the beginning of May, many of the weather intelligence pictures had begun to pick up signs of the fluorescent-lighted spirals. Since then, these were increasingly beginning to form a path earthwards. Predominantly their first activity had centred on obscure areas near the Black Sea. At around that time a United States Military 'Spy' satellite had detected that a Russian Civilian Space Associated marine ship, the fifty-three thousand five hundred ton Gargarin class *Kosmonaut Yury Gagarin,* was being used for investigating upper atmospheric conditions, and had been checking on operable space vehicles. Currently the ship was positioned in the Black Sea and the US Military Department concerned in vetting the matter discounted any connection the department had dismissing any theory that such a ship, a civilian operation at that, could in any way be involved in something military-wise. Later that month the same US 'Spy' Satellite picked up similar sightings in the Indian Ocean; these observations together with the previous sightings reopened the file. In all, there had now been over thirty sightings recorded during the past six weeks, these fixings being prior to those recorded over the past week. It was noted that earlier occurrences bore no real resemblance, size or comparison to those recently seen against the latest recordings taken on 29 and 30 July.

Kemp began to set little red markers out on a large transparent map which he had laid across the glass table. Most of the sightings were centred on a vast area of the Independent Federal States of Russia.

MARKER ONE: 4 MAY 2017. TIME: 17.00 HOURS
AREA AND SECTION: BLACK SEA.
MARKER TWO: 19 MAY 2017. TIME: 08.23 HOURS
AREA AND SECTION: DJIBOUTI, GULF OF ADEN AND INDIAN OCEAN.

Markers numbered three to twelve were centred over areas of the Ural Mountains.

Looking more closely at the world map the General saw two of the spirals had shown themselves to occur above Kapustin Yar, Russia's Central Asian Space Launching Centre. The remaining markers displayed a series of strange sightings over very odd areas. The space spirals were seen over various unusual places in both the Pacific and Atlantic Oceans. *Even more curious,* thought the General. He noticed most of the remaining markers were scattered about over the inner Arctic Circle; others appeared to be centred fairly close to Greenland and Iceland.

Deep in concentration, Kemp paused for a moment and sighed, then muttered to himself, "Maybe when Logan comes forward with completion of a full synchronisation of all the input data, hopefully this will allow us a greater understanding of these strange phenomenon."

The red telephone rang on Kemp's desk breaking the late afternoon silence of his office. In checking the time on his watch he lifted the telephone receiver. The time was nearing 17.30 hours EST.

Royal Naval Intelligence HQ, Northwood

"Is that you, General Kemp?" a voice asked.

"Yes, who is this?" came the General's reply.

"Admiral Marchant here. What is happening at present with you, John? I am just about to turn in so I thought I'd better give you a call to see if you had managed to accumulate any more information about your space demons," the Admiral chuckled.

Listening, Kemp sat at his desk and frowned.

"I have alerted Professor Ponsonby, John. He has agreed to play ball. I wish to assure you, General, I can now offer my fullest assistance regarding this matter." Marchant paused and took a sip of his nightcap.

Kemp, a little taken aback and somewhat surprised by Marchant's forcefulness hesitated for a moment then replied, "I am not at all sure what I can do for you at present, Admiral. I have had no further input; therefore I have nothing further to say on the matter. Mind you, I will look forward to receiving any suggestions you may wish to make, but without any commitment on my part, I would prefer the matter remains solely on your side of the pond. I trust you will understand."

Upon hearing Kemp's blocking remark Marchant felt he might possibly have overdone things. He was very tired; his day had been a long and arduous one. "All right, John, I accept. I think there's a reasonable degree of purpose and understanding behind the meaning of your request."

Kemp held back his reply. He wondered if he had upset Marchant in any way. Normally at this hour they would both have had a polite late afternoon discussion. Sometimes it would border on sensitive issues but now, in beginning to feel very weary having continually worked through his day of rest and on top of a very busy week, the General felt he didn't want any more harassment. Looking at his watch the General knew it was now late evening in Britain. Again he began to wonder whether or not he had actually upset Admiral Marchant. It appeared to Kemp that Marchant had suddenly cut short what normally was their joint social weekend call.

Marchant, however, was almost sure Kemp was holding back his answer.

"I quite understand, General, in you not replying to my comments. However, please kindly remember I have already begun investigating matters on this side of the pond. Therefore, I will ignore your implied spell of silence. Please remember that if I am able to uncover any further information which might well assist you, I do trust we shall be able to intelligently talk about it between us. Or, am I to understand from your lengthy period of silence that you have nothing further to say on the matter?"

Marchant by now was back on form and he continued to push his point. "General, may I mention something about this discussion as you have suggested? If so, I hope it will be held sometime early next week. For that, I am sure you would agree the whole matter might well have been something connected with our joint instincts. Therefore, and in this regard, I request your not holding back now!"

Suddenly, as if that last remark finally had activated and triggered a prime signal, Kemp erupted, "Damn it, Admiral Marchant! Will you kindly shut up! Stop meddling in matters that may not really concern you!" Kemp was reeling at the pace the Admiral was setting. It had been a long stretch of working – nearly seventy-two hours had past. Now, quite unexpectedly, he had flipped.

However, Marchant was fuelled up so much so by Kemp's retort that he did not consider any form of retreat. He weighed into Kemp's sudden outburst.

"Do I imagine, General, this subject of 'Ghostbusting' in space is now giving you cause of some major concern? Surely to God, Kemp, you certainly must realise, and now quite understand, your bunch and department is totally incapable of really knowing what the hell is going on. Huh, you don't even seem to know A, who, your enemy is and B, nor do you appear to have the foggiest idea of how many aliens might be sitting amongst you, and for that matter even in your own camp. I'll now leave you with that horrible sinister thought. I bid you good afternoon."

Finally, incensed to boiling point the General retaliated, "What in heavens did you say? Jesus Christ, Marchant! Who in bloody hell's name and damnation do you think you are?"

Kemp was too late. His ranting and ravings were to fall on deaf ears. Marchant had already put down the receiver.

For a moment, Marchant stood still grinning like a Cheshire cat. He then turned, picked up his drink and drained the glass in complete satisfaction. He continued to chuckle muttering to himself, "That should keep Kemp on his toes. It might finally crack the nut."

His watch showed it was nearly 21.00 hours.

He picked up the telephone and placed a call to Professor Ponsonby. "Albert, sorry to interrupt your evening. Just telephoning to confirm our arrangements. I'll be there as planned on Tuesday morning at 11.30 hours."

"Right you are, old boy," replied the Professor.

"Sorry to have troubled you. Go back and enjoy your supper," responded the Admiral.

NASA Military and Naval Intelligence, Cape Canaveral

Lieutenant Logan had begun extracting the computer printout from *G.O.D.* It was a little after 18.30 hours EST. Hour after hour of feeding information into the computer had not dulled his tenacity, nor had it tarnished the zest of his task in continuing to compile and collate *G.O.D.*'s answers.

A telephone rang in the computer room. Lieutenant Logan leant over his desk and picked up the receiver. "Logan speaking. Oh, good evening, General. Yes, yes, *G.O.D.* has begun producing an answer, sir."

General Kemp was pleased with Logan's efforts. "How long do you think the whole operation might take, Lieutenant?"

Logan was not quite sure what to say; he didn't think the processing would be finished for at least another three hours. "Well, General, I think we should be having a result hopefully sometime late this evening, sir."

"Good," came the General's reply. "Logan," General Kemp continued.

"Yes, General?" replied Logan. He waited for any possible onslaught.

No, lad," replied the General, "I am not going to chew your butt off for the delay and time it is taking you. That will not help towards any kind of end result."

A little surprised by Kemp's comment, Logan answered, "Thank you, sir."

Kemp said. "I think you can leave *G.O.D.* to enjoy its just desserts. I am sure it will still be there at 08.00 hours EST tomorrow morning. Say, why don't you pack up at about 19.00 hours. I'll be able to give you a lift back to your digs if nothing else crops up."

"Why, thank you very much, sir. That would be very useful. I might just have time to get out and see what this Friday night has to offer. Maybe go dancing."

"That's the ticket. Find yourself a chick, and live it up."

At Sea

The *Gorbachev* was sailing in calm waters two hundred miles north of the islands of the Azores. Captain Narodny had allowed the crew to relax for twenty-four hours. He also needed time to consider which condition of testing was finally going to be chosen, this being one that would ensure total success, and cover the full safety of his submarine and crew. He carefully approached the problem from two angles. The first was to consider possibilities of there being any catastrophic problem. If the test of the underwater firing failed he had to weigh up what the total consequence would be. Complete destruction? Moreover, he was very concerned regarding exposure and the possibility of the submarine being found. The second angle was to wait until nightfall then surface. There were nearly seven hours to consider the outcome of that position. In any event, Captain Narodny knew he would have to alter course to a more northerly position if he was going to achieve either of the submarine's objectives.

"Captain to bridge. Increase our speed to twenty-five knots for the next four hours. Alter course to 52.0 N − 42.5 WNW. Please advise when the new course setting is fixed."

Friday, 31 July 2017, the time was 13.00 hours. Slowly the huge submarine turned to starboard, cutting a wake of white foam across a calm sea under a clear blue sky.

Chapter Five

At Sea

The afternoon had allowed the *Gorbachev* to proceed on the surface undetected by any visual or radar contact for nearly three hours. The huge black steel shape left its wide white wake disappearing into the calm waters of the deep blue Atlantic Ocean. Captain Narodny had pushed the submarine to its maximum speed of nearly thirty knots.

It was a little after 17.00 hours. Nikita Narodny continued his progress report in making plans to ensure both the space platform *Vostok* and Moscow were fully advised regarding the expectant second sea trial.

The atomic-powered laser gun was ready.

Decisions as to whether the sea trial was to be an underwater operation or a sea-to-air demonstration had not yet been finally established. Only Captain Narodny knew how or what the outcome would be. Official instructions received from the Russian Naval Command, ordered by the *FSB*, the Dumo and Federal State Presidium jointly co-ordinated with the space platform *Vostok*. It demanded a further acknowledgement and clearance of the final decision. This was to be revealed only by them.

At Longitude 09.0 N. Latitude 66.0 W.

Hurricane force winds and past weather conditions had moderated a little now becoming gale force 7 to 8 backing south to south-west. For the past six hours the *Bowevil* had been monitoring the progress of its robot deep-sea submersible bathysphere, named *Itromps*. The sphere had received its nickname from the US Navy's Institution of Technological Scientific Research of Ocean and Marine Plant Study.

At a depth of about eleven thousand feet the ocean bed was peaceful and still. There was very little movement or life to be picked out by the submersible's searchlights. Only the occasional brilliantly-coloured sea worm or the fluorescent lights of a deep-sea angler predator could be seen through a small vision porthole.

Captain Jack Maxman laid out his sea chart; it had a diagrammed criss-cross pattern of a navigational zigzag course marked out on it. Slowly the pattern size had diminished until *Itromps* either located a target, or it had moved on to another section of new ground.

Over the past hours of searching, twice the crew's spirits were raised. In each case it turned out to be the grave of a merchant ship sunk during the 1939-45 war. In studying a video recording the first sunken ship's fate seemed to show it had been devastated by a terrifying bombardment from a surface raider. It bore all the hallmarks of having had its main superstructure blown away. The ship's forecastle was heavily corroded but still it held the four-inch naval gun which had been hurriedly welded on to its deck to avenge such an attack. It gave the stricken ship an air of proud defiance.

The other ship appeared to have been a medium-sized oil tanker that had broken in two at the time of its death plunge. The camera on *Itromps* clearly showed a gaping hole in its port side, also a massive gap across the top deck of its forward section which could well have been the result of a torpedo attack. *Such a dreadful death* thought Captain Maxman. He had seen many pictures of the Second World War depicting and portraying heroic actions of the world's Merchant Navy. Maxman always shuddered at the sight of critically injured seamen being rescued from stricken oil tankers, their faces showing utter total distress. Scenes of the crew choking slowly to death having swallowed a seawater cocktail laced with burning oil and black burnt tar while trying to escape. Lungs stripped of their use, the black mass finally sealing a dying man's fate and finally clogging the vital passageways of life.

Captain Maxman ordered the wrecks to be marked and registered as war graves. He asked the information be forwarded for checking details against all existing records kept in international world archives. This was done for possible identification.

Instructions were given to the ship's chaplain to offer a prayer of remembrance, and he was instructed to record the same procedure for his weekend sermon in respecting of the dead, and giving a presence for the future. The chaplain was requested to speak to the *Bowevil*'s crew to remind them of the vital need and purpose of the US Navy to have submarines like *SSN Bowevil* at sea in order to maintain vigilance and act as a deterrent.

At 16.15 hours, 1 August, *Itromps'* sensors picked up a distant silhouette and shape of another sunken vessel. The crew in *Bowevil*'s monitoring surveillance operations room had been carefully finalising new plotting markers on the chart in section forty-six. These markers were co-ordinated with the latest sonar readings made by the submarine in trying to assist detection of any bottom seabed readings.

Section forty-three had begun at 16.07 hours and was logged and positioned as 90.06 N – 66.05 W. The *Itromps* television camera computers had been fed information that when deciphered was reprogrammed from data received by the *Bowevils*'s tracking of the submersible's laser beam search probe sensors.

As the *Itromps* searched the area, it was clear that the seabed had been disturbed as there were millions of particles of sediment that had been stirred up by a recent major upheaval.

The *Itromps* was between twenty up to fifty feet above the surface of the seabed and at a depth of nine thousand two hundred and sixty-eight feet. Visibility was murky, however the beam of the searchlight was so intense it was able to penetrate such darkness up to a distance of about eighty feet.

It took some time for signals to be received by the *Bowevil*.

Likewise, the slow-moving *Itromps* was in no desperate hurry to receive its programmed responses.

Within two minutes of *Itromps* sending a message, *Bowevil*'s reply was being transmitted back.

The submersible's speed increased to five knots.

Enclosed television cameras moved their positions to face forward. There was still some distance to be covered. The *Bowevils*'s operations room estimated that the unknown target was less than twelve hundred metres away.

Only its navigation lights glowed on *Itromps* outer panels to assist its direction thus saving any unnecessary loss of power.

On hearing that the *Itromps* had possibly detected another large sunken object, Captain Maxman entered the OPs Room of Intelligence and Surveillance. "Good afternoon, gentlemen."

The room's occupants immediately moved to salute.

Captain Maxman halted them requesting they continue with their surveillance duties without engaging in such formalities. The television monitor showed nothing but the darkness of the oceans murky depths. This increased the room's tension.

Itromps was still too far away to achieve any real clarity of picture.

About five minutes had passed and the submersible bathysphere was now closer and at a distance of eight hundred metres. The *Bowevil* sent forward a signal to *Itromps* that would automatically turn on the small high-density searchlights. As the lights lit up, the screen of the television monitor changed from very dark grey to a deep bluish blackness which glistened with spotted fluorescent colours of gold, red and green. The tempting baits of deep-sea anglerfish made these lights as they swam to and fro in front of the camera lens.

The situation of good visibility was still obscured by clouds of very thick sediment still gradually settling down from whatever had disturbed the seabed. From the bathysphere the small searchlights shone straight ahead. Slowly its cameras raised their angle from the seabed in order to allow an early sighting of the big shape which the sensors had now fully locked on to. Soon, with the seabed disappearing, the lenses lengthened their focus of camera vision, but still nothing clearly registered on the video screen.

The seconds ticked by.

Gradually, in the murky distance, an unclear outline of a large sunken ship began to appear. Its shape became visible at just over four hundred metres.

The *Bowevil* programmed another signal to *Itromps*.

Moments later the submersible's small lights went out. Now in total darkness the bathysphere still slowly progressed forward.

Captain Maxman and the *Bowevil*'s intelligence surveillance operators all sat expectantly watching the television monitors.

The computer VDU printout showed *Itromps* was two hundred and twenty metres from the wreck and closing in on the unidentified object.

Captain Maxman ordered the main searchlights to remain switched off until the sphere had reached a distance of one hundred and twenty-five metres from the registering wreck.

Further signals were given; these directed *Itromps* to make its approach from either the bow or the stern section of the sunken ship.

Gradually the deep-ocean craft moved to starboard and made slow but steady progress at a level of about twelve to fifteen metres from the seabed.

While passing forward small pieces of wreckage became visible. These appeared as the *Itromps* neared the front end of the wreck.

One hundred and thirty metres showed on the VDU monitor.

Suddenly all the television screens lit up; the *Itromps* four main searchlights turned on again.

There now was a stony silence in the operations room.

At the first sighting of the wrecked ship it could not really be clearly recognised. Its bow had taken on a very strange appearance looking something like the huge jaws of an attacking great white shark. *Itromps* was now about seventy metres away from the bow section of the wreck. The picture showed the top edge of the forecastle disappearing away to the distant stern and there was little change in the ship's line or contour until, at its bow, a huge jagged aperture made the ship take on the appearance of rows of pointed shark's teeth.

Captain Maxman and some of the crew members stood staring in total disbelief. Their faces had the look of shock and absolute amazement. The size of the gaping hole was over twelve metres across.

Itromps was now directly ahead of the sunken ship's bows.

No comment or whisper could be heard from any of the *Bowevil*'s crew; all were stunned by what they were seeing.

In the dim reflection of light showing on the starboard bow, just beneath the forward deck, a camera showed the partly remaining letters of the ship's name. The letters read *SS And....* There was a small gap where the next letters should have been.

The camera was carefully programmed and was focused to zoom in to take a closer look in order to see if the missing letters were 'ros'.

Captain Maxman was satisfied his crew had located and found the sunken wreck of the *SS Andros*. He also now knew the ship had not just foundered on that fatal morning of 31 July. Something, an unknown thing of great force, had ripped through the ship taking with it the lives of a gallant sea captain and its crew of thirty-three men.

By now the *Itromps* had begun to enter the ship's hull and darkened aperture. The searchlights shone a beam showing a path that seemed to pass right through the hull of the ship as far as was visible.

There was no sign of there having been any sort of fire.

Each bulkhead had somehow been cleanly severed; the force of an unexpected explosion inadvertently had blown nothing away.

In moving forward the searchlight beam now reflected an eerie blue-green glare as *Itromps* carefully ventured along an unbelievable passage of destruction. Soon the beam shone into the black depths of the Atlantic Ocean.

The submersible had steered its way clear of the gaping shaft that had been bored right up through the hull of the ship, and had now found clear water.

The top deck of the sunken ship appeared suddenly as *Itromps* dipped and was thrust forward with the current having been released from the depths of the ships skeleton now left empty as an eerie cavern.

The cameras refocused revealing a sight equally as awesome; the main white superstructure aft took on the appearance of a giant Polo mint. A massive hole had been cut right through the bridge area and crew's quarters. It was as if a chef had cut through a soft oblong butter pat leaving a neatly grooved incision.

Itromps continued to move forward.

The submersible had soon carefully navigated the ships deck surface then entered the wide aperture of the main stack superstructure, and slowly the cameras panned around the bridge area.

Suddenly, the lenses caught in their sight a swollen deformed body; it had become trapped and entangled by loose wiring and cables. Eventually, pinned down, the suspended captured torso had been finally trussed against the ship's instrument panel. A set of binoculars still hung around the dead man's neck. It was Mr. Evans, the ship's number one. His eyes were still fixed ahead gazing in terror, and their pupils had disappeared where all that remained were two transparent eyeballs. His face was almost unrecognisable.

Itromps stealthily moved onwards passing up through the ceiling of the bridge into the crew's rest rooms. Other wreckage was strewn about together with several bodies of crew members that had been fatally pinned down by the sudden swiftness of everything, and the force of the final death plunge of the stricken vessel.

Captain Maxman told the crew of the *Bowevil* the missing crew of the *SS Andros* had been located. He advised there was nothing unusual to be seen other than the ship had obviously foundered in very heavy seas and met its cruel fate after shifting its cargo.

In the submarine's operations room the observation, surveillance and intelligence officers were all sworn to total official secrecy. All were to be granted the privilege of one months extended shore leave on medical grounds. Since seeing those awful sights all the *Bowevil's* crew were experiencing a constant torment; these being a recurrence of nightmares and an acute feeling of depression and fatigue.

Captain Maxman had received new instructions from Naval Headquarters, Charleston, South Carolina. He was to completely suspend all further operations and was ordered to code scramble everything recorded back to home base. Instructions were given to lock away the evidence in the ship's strongroom, and this meant all video film, computer data and anything else concerning the affair.

The *Bowevil* was ordered to immediately return to its home base after collecting and securing the *Itromps*.

It was nearing 18.30 hours by the time the submersible was engineered in to the *Bowevil*'s aft flooded sea storage hold. As soon as the water level had subsided a special crew picked from the surveillance department entered the submersible; they removed both underwater camera films placing them into a sealed container marked 'TOP SECRET DATA'. It was immediately dispatched to the submarine's strongroom.

Captain Maxman had soon cleared all instructions regarding the top priority coded messages. These were sent as ordered, everything being finally completed in just over four hours.

Chapter Six

NASA Military and Naval Intelligence, Cape Canaveral

At 18.40 hours, Kemp had been alerted and was advised that it was very urgent his staff remain in the department as an urgent scramble of coded messages were currently being received in Washington and at Naval Headquarters. He was advised it was regarding data the *Bowevil* had retrieved from the ocean bed concerning the wreck of the SS *Andros*.

Kemp put down the hotline telephone and then rang through to speak to Lieutenant Logan. "I am sorry, Smartie. As of now, lad, we are both destined for late operations. You had better go and get yourself a bite to eat then meet me back here at about 19.30 hours. By that time I should have more news and hopefully a good idea of what the flap is about!"

Serveromorsk, Motovsky Gulf, Russia

The clock had just struck midnight as Lt. Commander Ivargo Ivanov returned to his flat. He had come from a late duty at the Russian naval base and Department of Environmental and Strategic Planning of Nuclear Marine Operations where he had been hearing hourly newsflashes about the extraordinary exploits of a young lady.

Headline news confirmed, against immense odds, the lady had survived both earthquakes and then had set herself up as a staging post for incoming rescue teams. The media had begun releasing these stories since early morning when they confirmed she had somehow engineered the finding of five live survivors who were still entombed.

Apparently, and by complete chance, an aerial rescue team found the lady during one of their helicopter search patterns. Until now, the media had been unable to establish the name of the person who had won the hearts of everyone, so they went by the name of 'Blondie'.

Ivargo Ivanov didn't need to hear or read any more. He knew that Mika Belinka was alive.

Before leaving, he arranged that his department send a discreet message to the Caspian Sea Office of the Department of Environmental and

Strategic Planning of Nuclear Marine Operations in Armenia to the town of Baku. This office was under the control and co-ordination of the Federal State Department for the Caspian Sea. As yet, no telex communication had been possible due to the complete breakdown of communication lines caused by long overdue maintenance. Therefore, Ivargo had to rely on the express courier service. He was advised delivery would take up to five days; his message was sent late on Saturday afternoon and, *Hopefully*, he thought, *it might just reach Baku by Friday, 4 August.*

Ivanov realised there was nothing else he could do other than to wait and pray for a response. The Lt. Commander's Saturday duty was fraught by many worries and excitement. Ivanov had received instructions from Moscow advising he was to go to England in order to visit the British Admiralty and meet his official counterpart; as he read his orders, he saw the officer was named as Commander Derek A. Thompson RN.

His mission was advised as top secret. At all cost the Lieutenant had to ensure there was no leakage of information concerning any environmental or strategic state planning of nuclear marine operations. Ivanov was especially asked to look out for any warning signs that might advise where western superpowers were trying to obtain classified information as to the mysterious disappearance of *SSBN Gorbachev*. Ivanov was requested to ensure the safe custody and security back to Moscow of a steel box plus its valuable contents. He was instructed the box was to be delivered incognito to London's Heathrow Airport under the designation and order of the Chief of Staff, Headquarters FSB Moscow. Under no circumstance whatsoever was the box to be opened. Full diplomatic clearance had been arranged.

The Lt. Commander was ordered to stay in London for a few days. He was to ensure no leakage of information concerning the operation fell into the hands of the Central Intelligence Agency of the United States of America. His departure date to London had been set for Friday, 4 August. Ivargo was first to travel by train from Severomorsk to Moscow. There his papers would be given to him upon his arrival after which he would be collected from Moscow's new railway terminal and delivered to Sheremetyevo Airport. This would enable him to catch a direct Aeroflot flight to London. Arrangements were cleared for him to stay at the Russian Embassy where he would be advised British Naval Intelligence had full knowledge of his pending visit, and also that his name was logged with records at the British Navy's Headquarters at Northwood.

J. F. Kennedy International Airport, New York

The warm late afternoon sun of the first day in August accompanied the hustle and bustle of passengers queuing for last minute reservations at New York's J. F. Kennedy International Airport.

There was a lot of excitement centred on the departure desk of Air India. This day was a special one for the Air India staff. It was the inaugural flight of the airline's new McDonnell Douglas MD-12 jet aircraft, the first to fly under their airline's national flag. Air India was especially concerned to ensure full security procedures were carried out prior to departure. The Air India New York representative office had received an anonymous message; it confirmed there was likely to be a terrorist attack against the Indian Government by a group of Sikh extremists. It further stated, a bomb would be planted on one of Air India's airliners routed to Bombay. As yet, no time or date had been given. Now a second written message had been received. It read: *Beware. You are at great risk if flying Air India on Saturday, 1 August.*

It was now 18.00 hours. Air India's Flight AI 102 was destined to depart at 20.15 hours with its first scheduled stop being London Heathrow for a fuel stop. The landing at London Heathrow was scheduled for 08.05 hours. The aircraft's new departure and take-off would then be scheduled at 09.30 hours BST destination Bombay, India, departing as a direct flight.

At Sea

The *Gorbachev* had reached a position that was approximately one hundred and sixty miles due south-west of Greenland. The submarine's course was set to continue north-north-west. There had been a number of reports of large icebergs being seen further south of the normal ice flow limit, and these being near to the vicinity of where the submarine was currently sailing. Captain Narodny requested a full up-to-date computer printout of the latest surface to horizon radar sonar scan.

The time was 17.00 hours.

It was not long before the radar screen operators reported there were a number of fairly large icebergs in the area. With the Arctic's major ice flow appearing to melt a lot quicker every year – supposedly caused by the greenhouse effect – a greater volume of ice flow was now being found much further south than in previous years.

A very large iceberg showed on the radar screen about five nautical miles due north-east from where the *SSBN Gorbachev* was sailing.

Captain Narodny requested a message be sent to Moscow in order clearance be granted with the space platform *Vostok* to release the space cocoon at exactly 17.30 hours. This was so an underwater sea trial could be carried out. The target was to be a very sizeable iceberg.

Captain Narodny considered that he was enhancing his crew's practise and also, hopefully, assisting the safety of international shipping lanes by demolishing a dangerous obstacle to all merchant shipping.

A voice came on open speaker from the operations room to the bridge. "Moscow confirms acceptance of the synchronised time for joint release with the space platform *Vostok*, sir."

Captain Narodny calmly replied, "Thank you, operations. What range are we at present?"

"Range, eight thousand two hundred and twenty-three metres. Target depth, one hundred and twenty-nine metres. Submarine depth, seventy-five metres. Speed, thirty knots, sir."

"Action Stations! Action Stations!" Narodny's voice rang out loud and clear over the submarine's tannoy. The crew swiftly mustered themselves to battle stations awaiting further command.

"This is your Captain speaking. As you are all aware I am ordered to carry out further sea trials for this submarine regarding our new type of armament. An opportunity has conveniently been supplied by Mother Nature in order *Gorbachev*'s second sea trial can take place. There is a very large iceberg weighing heavily in the sea ahead of us at a distance of about seven thousand five hundred metres. We have received full clearance to engage and destroy it. This action is timed for 17.30 hours. You are all further to be made aware that precision in regard to this engagement has to be absolute. If successful the *Gorbachev* will have performed something that, until now, has never before been mastered.

"I place my total trust and belief in you all. You in return will ensure this submarine carries out both its duty and task successfully. We have seven minutes to effect target synchronisation. Remember, all of you, if in any way you are wrong regarding the premeditation of your actions, I may not have an opportunity again of wishing you all 'Good hunting'." The tannoy went silent.

An eerie peace was felt throughout all quarters of the submarine. A movement was heard forward; the large frame of the atomic-powered laser gun, its co-ordination controlled by computer.

"What range do we have now? What is our target depth?" Narodny requested.

"Range seven thousand metres. Target depth one hundred and sixty-five metres, sir," came a response.

"Ten, nine, eight, seven, six, five, four, three, two, one..."

It was exactly 17.30 hours. For a moment the dark blue sea turned into a radiant orange; the *Gorbachev* became engulfed in a deep glow of light as the atomic-powered laser gun spat forward a beam of brilliant gold and reddish fire directed at the massive frozen object.

Watched by Captain Narodny through the main periscope, the impact showed a majestic blue-white pillar erupting. It exploded with the force of a giant steam pressure cooker coming to the boil. It seemed as if a massive ice cube maker had been suddenly turned on. For miles around the sea was showered by millions of ice cubes which had shot upwards above the area where the iceberg had been.

Then, by an extraordinary circumstance of nature, the evening sunlight created a most amazing sight. An iridescent spectrum; a circular rainbow constantly turning and changing colour formed as the tiny ice flakes began melting into rain thereafter falling seawards.

The second sea trial was heralded a complete success.

Narodny enquired whether the periscope camera had filmed the incredible spectacle. He was advised a film video would be ready for replay in a few minutes. The Captain then beckoned one of his officers on the bridge to send a message to Moscow. It acknowledged the *SSBN Gorbachev* had successfully carried out its underwater sea trial. It was hoped its third sea trial, a sea-to-air operation, would commence at the earliest opportunity.

"You have done well, my crew," said Narodny. "Let us hope our third sea trial can also meet with as little trouble."

J. F. Kennedy International Airport, New York

Air India Flight AI 102, New York to London, was now showing on the departure board. The schedule roster advised the flight would be departing on time.

In the British Airways Terminal Departure Lounge various people were milling around. Some were shopping, and others were enjoying some light refreshment due to news of the extended delay of the departure of Flight BA 182 bound for the north of England to land at Manchester Ringway Airport.

The Boeing 777-300ER aircraft was fully booked with a mixture of business and first class passengers. A number of British servicemen travelling back on leave were diverted from Belize due to severe weather conditions. These had been rescheduled to join the flight. A lot of these were infantry soldiers leaving for their final operations in Afghanistan after enjoying an extended summer furlough.

The aircraft had a total of three hundred and eighteen passengers including flight crew booked for the flight plus fourteen cabin crew. Everything had been provided for comfort and convenience. A revised departure time was now scheduled for 20.30 hours.

The time was 20.00 hours. Airport tannoy speakers began announcing the final call for Flight BA 182 in order baggage checking and security clearances could be made. However, a third luggage screening which British Airways baggage controllers and airport security had called for had caused a further delay.

Both authorities had made independent checks with acoustic laser sensors, the newest and latest form of safety function. The new machinery, which had recently been installed, had only become operational over the past few days. The laser unit system, world renowned for its ability of accuracy in detection with near one hundred percent reliability, had been adapted over many years derived from the previous cosmic core and sonar methods.

Previously in testing, the machine had been put into service by US Military Land Forces together with the Navy. These units now replaced the old sonar and earlier crude screening programs which were well overdue for replacement and now classed obsolete.

In the International Departure Terminal, Air India's Flight AI 102 had closed and the brand new aircraft, photographed by press and aviation magazine coverage, had now left its podium for departure.

Soon, clearance for its take-off was given. The noise of the engines increased as they thrusted to full power. The aircraft gathered speed along Kennedy International Airport's easterly runway. Gradually, the MD-12 aircraft began to lift up its nose as its huge shape ascended into the late evening sky.

On the flight deck the crew were busily checking post take-off procedure.

The co-pilot logged the take-off time as 20.19 hours.

By now the next aircraft had positioned itself for take-off.

British Airways Flight BA 182, after all its minor problems and baggage delays, eventually became airborne at 20.25 hours.

At Sea

The success of the second sea trial had elated the morale of Captain Narodny's crew. Everyone off duty was celebrating the great achievement over the late evening dinner table when the klaxon alarm sounded 'ACTION STATIONS'.

The time was 22.25 hours.

"This is your Captain speaking. Comrades, opportunity comes our way again to test our gallant submarine with its third sea trial. Our radar surveillance operators have made contact with three flying objects. These could soon come within range of our armament. If time will allow, and complete caution shown, it could result in a positive outcome. As yet, we have no form of aircraft identification at this stage. In my placing you all into a state of readiness, I am sure either one of the targets will prove suitable."

In the Air

The east-bound Air India Flight AI 102 progressed at a speed of five hundred and twenty miles per hour flying at a height of thirty-three thousand feet. Its position was about two hundred and twenty-five miles due west of the *Gorbachev.*

The British Airways 777-300ER Flight BA 182, flying at a height of thirty-seven thousand feet, had found a jet stream tail wind and was powering forward at four hundred and ninety miles per hour. Captain Adamson was pleased with his aircraft's progress in trying to make up some of the delayed time; his aircraft was approximately one hundred and eighty-five miles south-west of the *Gorbachev.*

West-bound, a Boeing 747-400 cargo freighter of the German airline Lufthansa, Flight LH0873C, was steadily battling its way against a two hundred and twenty mile an hour headwind in the Atlantic jet stream. The aircraft flying at thirty-one thousand feet; its speed of five hundred and thirty miles per hour still left no impression in trying to make up lost time. The jet was already fifty minutes behind schedule and the German aircraft's position was about one hundred and forty-five miles due east of the *Gorbachev.*

At Sea

Captain Nikita Narodny felt elated after his actions of the past few days. Adrenaline was again pumping through his body like a two hundred mile an hour express train. With the excitement and fulfilment of this wonderful achievement he had an immense feeling of pride serving his country. Soon, he thought, his submarine would be able to challenge anything or anybody in respect of its new unbeatable supremacy.

With nerves as cold as the arctic winds, and a calmness which never disturbed any of his crew, Narodny ordered a time be set for synchronising with Moscow and the space platform *Vostok* the next exercise. The requested timing was 00.35 hours, and he awaited clarification. "Please have Moscow acknowledge clearance for a sea-to-air trial and arrange that the space platform *Vostok* confirms clearance in order the cocoon screen of Operation Invisible at 00.34 hours will be cleared to allow completion of *SSBN Gorbachev*'s third sea trial."

It was very early in the morning in Russia.

During the night Moscow and the space platform *Vostok* had shortened their manpower to a skeleton staff force; nearly everyone had finally turned in to get some sleep. The sound of soft snoring could be heard from the sleeping quarters of the cosmonauts on the space platform.

Just two operators were left on watch.

It was 04.45 hours Moscow time when clearance was finally received.

By now, Air India's Flight AI 102 was approximately ninety-five miles west of the Russian submarine's position. The Lufthansa cargo plane, call sign Delta, Boxer, Alpha, Uncle, Alpha, Flight LH0873C, was eighty miles east of the *Gorbachev*. The Flight BA 182 had steadily been progressing eastwards cruising in the fast jet stream, and was also about ninety-five miles from where the black steel shape of death and destruction laid waiting.

Narodny requested new details regarding the approaching aircraft. Finally, when hearing there were three targets sighted, his spirits quickly rose with the excitement. It was decision time. He had to choose whether to lock the armaments sights on to the target approaching from the east or consider aiming the laser gun at the two targets flying close to one another swiftly approaching from the west.

The bow of the *Gorbachev* was facing northwards.

"Bischoff, please acknowledge to Moscow we will be concentrating on the targets approaching and closing from our port beam. Confirm we stand ready for action."

In the Air

The time was nearing 00.30 hours on 2 August. Air India's Flight Captain Naresh Patel, a well-seasoned flyer, had just acknowledged a radio message from Captain Walter Schmidt of the approaching Lufthansa cargo flight. He confirmed he could see the flicker of the oncoming aircraft's main wing and fuselage lights. He estimated the distance between each plane was about forty miles.

The German airline captain verified he had seen the main lights of the approaching AI 102, and of the British aircraft Flight BA 182. Captain Schmidt confirmed the British Airways 777 aircraft appeared to be a good seven thousand feet above his own flight path, and also that of Air India.

At 00.34 hours and 38 seconds, Lufthansa Captain Schmidt had observed a series of strange flashing lights. On the flight deck of the Air India aircraft, Captain Patel had also logged the same strange sighting.

Within ten seconds of his logged sighting there was a blinding flash whereby the shockwave violently rocked both aircraft as they were nearing to pass by each other.

Within a sixtieth of a second of 00.35 hours, an almighty explosion ripped through the night air just as the British Airways Flight BA 182 should have passed directly over the position of the waiting submarine.

At Sea

Captain Narodny looked up and, in near disbelief, he saw wreckage from the stricken aircraft begin tumbling seawards in two huge fireballs.

In the Air

Captain Schmidt frantically grappled with his aircraft's controls; everything had happened so suddenly. He thought that his outer port engine and wing tip had completely disappeared. His radio navigator was already sending out a full 'Mayday' rescue alert. Schmidt's co-pilot, Hans Jurgens, went aft to check out the structural damage. The huge Boeing cargo aircraft was beginning to make horrendous noises and sounded as if it was descending on its final death plunge.

Co-pilot Jurgens, secured by a wire lifeline cord, held on to the side strapping attached to the cargo bay wall. He could see a gaping hole had appeared in the roof of the jet. A piece of wreckage painted in familiar colours of red, white and gold of Air India's livery was now an addition to the cargo hold. This wreckage had fallen through the jet's roof and lodged itself into the top of one of the cargo containers fastened to the main deck of the German aircraft's cargo bay. It looked to him to be like the shape of a main passenger door with the escape chute still attached. The noise it was making sounded like a constant roll of thunder; the exploded escape chute was flapping wildly having been drawn back out of the gaping hole in his aircraft, and was flying around in the German aircraft's slipstream.

Jurgens felt the huge cargo plane, after flying steadily at thirty-seven thousand feet, had suddenly begun to plummet earthwards. Schmidt was frantically trying to pull the great beast out of its ever-steepening dive. His whole body was shaking from the immense vibration caused by an increased yawning movement of the stricken aircraft. He felt that he was not going to be able to regain control. At the time of impact Schmidt knew his co-pilot had been checking the cargo hold. "Hans! Hans! Get back here! I need you to try to manually lower the aircraft's main wing flaps. Maybe we can slow the big bird's speed down. You will have to do it very slowly or we may end up forcing the aircraft to breaking point."

In the total mayhem around him Hans Jurgens, still very calm and cool, went about his business and obeyed his captain's orders. Very slowly the flaps soon began to extend.

Luckily the aircraft never received the full force from the blast of the explosion which had disintegrated Air India's massive MD-12 jumbo jet. However, the falling wreckage had inflicted serious damage to the Lufthansa aircraft. As for the British Airways 777-300ER aircraft, it had completely vanished.

Millions of pieces of wreckage had scattered hitting the ocean surface about ten to fifteen miles east of where the *Gorbachev* was sailing. Wreckage from Air India's Flight AI 102 had fallen entering the sea nearly twenty miles east of the Russian submarine.

The crippled German Boeing 747 cargo plane was still descending fast. However, its speed had reduced which now enabled the wing flaps to gradually be eased back allowing Schmidt to control the aircraft's descent.

Schmidt called to his flight officer and navigator, Franz Oltman. "Do you have any response from the Mayday call yet?"

Franz Oltman calmly acknowledged that the control tower at Gander, Newfoundland, had responded. "They want to know if we are going to make it, Herr Captain."

Schmidt was amazed and looked back at Franz Oltman. "Great! Tell them, no problem. Advise them we are in the middle of having a ball up here. Our present state has somewhat improved and somehow all our systems are still running, but we have suffered severe external damage.

"Jesus Christ, Franz! Tell them we have advanced from our previous advised position a further sixty miles. We are operating only on three engines. The weather outside is a little cold for this time of the year. As yet, however, we have had no snow flurries. Hell dammit! Don't they realise at all what we have just come through? Tell them we have had suffered one hell of a massive systems problem. Surely they're not expecting us to perform the greatest of miracles, or are they? What in bloody hell's name do these jerks think we are doing up here?"

Oltman gave a slight smile.

Schmidt spoke again. "Sorry, Franz. Advise Gander that both our wings are still intact and we are in the hands of guardian angels – God and our manufacturers the Boeing Aircraft Corporation of Seattle." He paused not really believing Gander did not seem to understand how bad the situation was. "Tell them until all systems become a little more stable we shall let them know of our progress every sixty seconds."

Schmidt was still slowly bringing his badly damaged aircraft back from its near-death fall when co-pilot Jurgens entered the cockpit. Jurgens had received a nasty gash on his arm when having lost his balance at the time the aircraft had begun plummeting.

Jurgens spoke, "Herr Captain, the top deck is in a shambles. We have a large aperture in the aircraft's upper outer skin. We appear to have lost some of our cargo through it. However, at the same time, it seems we have acquired a new emergency exit. It would appear this exit has been made possible by the courtesy of an Air India Flight AI 102."

"Why's that? What do you mean?" Schmidt said somewhat alarmed. "How on earth do you think that could have happened?" he asked.

Jurgens replied, "I cannot really say but I would guess it was probably due to an extremist's bomb. Unfortunately, in our continued run of bad luck, we just happened to be in the wrong place at the time of the bomb's detonation."

Jurgens was not really feeling himself. He was desperately trying to steady his big frame.

In the noise and din Schmidt shouted back, "Yes, Hans, but, what were all those flashing lights? And where the devil did the British Airways jet vanish to? Franz said there seems to be no sign of it on our radar anywhere."

Jurgens' face began to slightly discolour; he was losing a lot of blood from his injury.

Franz Oltman had also noticed his colleague was looking frail. "Hey, Hans, sit down will you. Let me do something with that wound."

Jurgens looked at the navigator. He felt his mind was beginning to muddle. "Okay. But the loss of two aircraft within five or six miles of each other?"

Oltman gave Jurgens a painkilling injection."There. That should ease things a little. Right, now let me dress that open wound and bandage it."

At that moment the cargo aircraft suddenly gave a tremendous jolt. Luckily, Oltman was holding on to Jurgens by the left sleeve of his blazer. Jurgens gave a loud shout but his feet gave way. Losing his balance he fell against the aircraft's bulkhead; there was a sickening crack as his arm struck the aircraft's framework. At the same time his head crashed against the cabin wall. This blow immediately knocked him unconscious and he fell helpless on to the flight deck floor.

Franz Oltman stood smiling at the ridiculous situation. "Well, Walter, now we have become an air ambulance as well as a crippled cargo plane."

Schmidt spoke. "I think we are all going to be lucky, Franz. I think I might be able to put our big beauty back on to its autopilot. We are flying steady and at a ceiling of fourteen thousand feet. All fuel lines appear secure for the one starboard outer, and two inner port engines. I think our remaining port side engine and its wing is currently holding its own. Franz, I hope this should now allow me to go aft and investigate all for myself. I need to find out what had caused that major jolt. Please keep an eye on Hans. Make him as comfortable as you can. Don't forget to watch the altimeter and, Franz, do ensure we remain steadily climbing a little instead of dropping back and downwards on our height, okay."

As Schmidt entered through the flight deck door and into the top cargo bay, Oltman accepted with pride he was all but in control of flying the stricken aircraft. "No problem, Herr Captain. As you previously stated, we have at this altitude a secret band of angels flying with us on each wing."

In total dedication and calmness of the situation both officers grinned at one another. Each one knew how desperate the situation really was and that everything was very much a matter of touch and go.

Schmidt entered the top cargo hold and he could see the extensive damage caused by Air India's cabin door. It had settled into a fixed position between two LD3 flight cargo containers already fastened by clamp and chain runners to the main floor area of the upper cargo deck. The massive jolt appeared to have been caused by the final departure of the large emergency inflatable escape ramp when it had ripped itself away from the cabin door vanishing out through the hole made in the aircraft's roof.

Seeing there was no sign of his co-pilot coming round in order to quickly establish what damage had been caused, Schmidt considered he had to fully investigate everything for himself. He had to be sure the aircraft would be capable of making its flight to Gander and, more importantly, safely land. In taking the cargo lift to the lower deck, it bumped as it came to a halt. When the door opened Captain Schmidt was immediately sucked forward; his body sped along the top of the cargo freight canisters to the brink of a large hole that had been ripped out of the bottom side of the aircraft's underbelly. The statutory fastening of a retractable lifeline saved him. Luckily, once fully extended, the retractable lifeline began to automatically rewind itself.

Under the ever-watchful eye of the flight navigator, the huge aircraft continued to make steady progress still maintaining its flight course under control of the autopilot.

It was then that Schmidt's voice sharply broke the cabin's silence. Oltman heard it over the internal intercom. The Captain yelled, "Franz! Franz! Is everything okay?"

"Is there anything wrong, Herr Captain?" Oltman yelled nervously.

The Captain's voice then calmly replied, "No, nothing really to panic about, Franz. However, I think I have just received my first natural unassisted flying lesson. You know as you get older you are told to exercise more. Well finally, I appear to have taken my doctor's advice and jumped."

As he listened, not really understanding the Captain's predicament, Oltman said, "I hope God has also allowed your feathers to sprout, and your wings to quickly grow."

Amidst the horror and fear of the ridiculous situation, they both laughed loudly.

By now, Schmidt had been automatically winched back along the top of the sealed cargo containers. Catching his breath he radioed through to the flight deck. "Franz, do not consider coming through to the cargo bay on the lower deck. We are in pretty bad shape down here. I confirm the main factor that is keeping us secure is the design of the interlocked containers. It is these that are acting as the aircraft's main underframe. I am afraid we have lost most of the outer aircraft underbelly. Anyway, not to worry, thankfully our electrics still appear to be complete. The main hydraulics plus wire tracking for elevation, also our flap controls, are all sound."

Oltman listened carefully to all his Captain had said. Suddenly the aircraft hit a violent wall of air turbulence. "Herr Captain! Jesus Christ!" He had not expected anything quite like that to happen.

"Where in bloody hell's name are you, Captain?" Oltman yelled, in his sudden panic, and the aircraft's shaking having now past, it was then that Franz Oltman realised what Captain Schmidt had said to him. He immediately called him back. "Where in heavens name have you been in order to make that kind of stupid statement?"

The seconds passed away but there was now complete silence.

"Herr Captain? Herr Captain? Where in God's name are you?" Forty very long seconds passed.

"Do not worry, Franz," came back the quiet sound of Schmidt's voice. "Currently I am dangling between the lower port deck and aft starboard cargo containers. I am looking out into a clear night sky and at the ocean far below us. It is very cold here but my thermal suit is keeping me warm."

"Holy jelly beans!" Oltman sat nearly frozen to his seat.

"Do not worry yourself, Franz. If the winch continues to hold and pulls me in I should be with you in a few minutes. Remember what I said. On no account are you to venture down here otherwise you might find that you will not be as fortunate as I was. Just keep on watching that our aircraft's nose is pointing in the right direction. You are doing a grand job, Franz, a grand job. By the way, what are our present altitude and instrument readings?"

"Fourteen thousand two hundred and twenty feet. Speed, four hundred and ninety miles per hour. Fuel, One Hundred and ninety-two thousand pounds," Oltman reported as if he was the talking computer voice of the automatic pilot.

"Fine," Schmidt responded, "as long as I can get back then everything should be considered as being reasonably satisfactory. In the meantime try and keep yourself warm."

Within himself, Oltman began to feel a little uneasy. He had been trying to work out how to be in three places at the same time. Recognising he was officially the navigator, but also the only person on the flight deck, he uttered to himself, "Yes, Franz you're doing a grand job. You're now the acting pilot and the co-pilot, and also working in your own capacity as the navigator. My oh my, what a fine time to receive such a fast promotion!"

Franz looked around the cockpit and then over to where Hans Jurgens was lying. "Oh, my heavens! I almost forgot one. The doctor. Yes, I am also the in-flight doctor. That will do nicely for my log report!" His mutterings were suddenly cut short. A loud voice came in over the radio.

"Lufthansa LH0873C, are you receiving us? Over. LH0873C, come in please. This is the voice of the chief traffic co-ordinator at the Gander Control Tower, Newfoundland. We now have you on our main radar screen, Captain Schmidt. How do you and things stand at the moment?"

In a state of near panic Oltman froze. "Jesus heck! What the devil should I do now?"

Just at that moment the lower cargo lift motor signalled its ascent, and within seconds Schmidt stepped out of the door and entered the flight deck. He looked a little pale.

Oltman gave a sigh of relief then enquired, "Are you all right, Herr Captain?"

The Captain paused to take stock of their present status. "I'll be all right in a moment. However, I must first answer and reply back to Gander

Control. It has to be done immediately in response to their request."

Schmidt was glad to be back; he was pleased to be sitting back in the pilot's seat where he felt most at home. In settling down he began checking the autopilot and instruments, and as he did this he spoke into the headset microphone. "This is Lufthansa Flight LH0873C. I repeat, LH0873C. We read you clearly Gander Control. Over."

There was a slight crackle and a voice spoke, "Still with us then, Walter?"

It was Werner Lotz, a long-time friend and veteran air traffic controller. He had aspired to become Chief of Operations at Gander, Newfoundland. "I understand, Walter, you are having one or two problems. We'll keep this channel band open. It will be completely clear just in case any new emergency crops up."

Walter Schmidt knew his old friend's dry sense of humour and replied, "Why, thank you, Werner. By the way, what do you consider to be an emergency? This plane is very lucky to still be in the sky. If we are able to make it back you will see for yourself what a state it is in. No, Werner, better still, do not worry about us too much. We are sure as hell having a wonderful time up here." Schmidt wasn't going to let on quite how serious the situation was.

Werner Lotz knew his friend would never reveal how bad his problems really were, well, not until he had officially lost his aircraft. He tried enquiring, "Walter, can you, or somebody, please tell me what on earth went on up there about an hour ago? How badly damaged are you? We have not received much data from anyone. No one knows what happened."

Schmidt knew he couldn't really reply to Werner Lotz over the air about how bad his situation was. "Werner, what more can I say other than we have been lucky so far."

Lotz replied, "I am sure about one thing, Walter. We have checked. Sadly two other jets, an Air India MD-12 super jumbo, Flight AI 102, and a British Airways 777-300, Flight BA 182, have both been lost. However, the odd thing is that there was only one explosion."

"My God!" said Schmidt. "I wonder did they actually hit each other! Was it a mid-air collision?"

There was no reply.

Schmidt carried on speaking. "What a terrible mess. By the way, Werner, I think you had better let somebody know that somehow we have acquired one of the Air India flight's main cabin doors, and it's sitting embedded in our roof. I think it was from the starboard side."

Lotz cut in and roared, "You say you have WHAT on board?"

Calmly, Schmidt continued, "I said we have one of Air India's cabin doors currently sticking out of our roof."

Stunned, Lotz replied, "How do you know that it is an Air India cabin door, Walter?"

Schmidt could not believe his ears, "For heavens sakes, Lotz! I have been back there to check the upper cargo deck myself. What's more, you can tell them we shall be billing their airline for a new outer starboard engine, a wing tip, plus, I think, a whole new underbelly refit while they are at it."

Lotz could sense his friend's wrath was building.

Again Schmidt spoke, "Now will you please leave me in peace to try and fly this plane on to *terra firma*? By the way, I am dreadfully sorry to hear the news of the loss of the two planes."

After a long silence, Lotz spoke. "Walter."

"Yes," came the reply.

Lotz continued, "It has just been reported to us both aircraft losses are understood to have been suspected terrorist bombings. Keep in touch with me. Call me every few minutes will you?"

Schmidt's voice came back sounding very down. "Okay."

Lotz signed off, "Good luck, my dear friend."

The radio contact went silent.

Hans Jurgens stirred and said, "What in hell's name has happened to us?"

Franz Oltman got up from his navigator's seat and went over to assist Jurgens. "Hans, you must try to get back to your co-pilot's seat. Somehow, over an hour ago, for a few minutes we got caught up in another world. By the way, how are you feeling?"

Jurgens was still not too sure of his condition. "Numbed, otherwise not too bad. I broke my arm, didn't I?" He could feel the splints under the bandages Oltman had supplied.

Oltman knew that if he didn't move his patient soon the aircraft might suddenly lurch and then matters would become far more serious than they were at present. "Now then, Hans, with my help are you able to get yourself up and make it back to your seat?"

Jurgens looked about him for some extra support. "I think so, Franz."

Oltman eased his arms around Jurgens' chest and then began to lift him. "Okay, let's go."

Schmidt settled the shaking aircraft as best he could while Franz

Oltman assisted Hans Jurgens back into his co-pilot's seat. Gently and carefully, Oltman eased his colleague down around the controls and then steadily engineered him back into the seat Jurgens always referred to as his international home. Oltman moved across and returned back to his navigator's desk.

Schmidt looked over at his co-pilot then turned and looked over his shoulder at Oltman. The navigator was preparing everything and clearing his desk board ready for action.

The Captain broke the silence of the cockpit. "Well, my dear friends, if we can stay with it, I estimate we have about two hundred and sixty miles to go until we reach land. Our big bird does not like being nursed one little bit. I think she has already given up the ghost but I am confident I will be able to coax her back, and I hope that will ensure a long holiday coming up for us all, assuming I can get us down on to Gander's runway in one piece. Anyway, good luck to both of you."

In the clear night sky the Lufthansa cargo plane groaned its way westward. Landing time, if everything held itself together, was anticipated being just over fifty minutes away.

The time was 01.45 hours.

At Sea

The *Gorbachev* was barely moving having just fired its atomic-powered laser gun on what appeared to be a faultless sea-to-air third trial.

Captain Narodny acknowledged to Moscow he believed he had made a successful strike. Observers on the bridge saw the gun successfully fire, and within moments they registered the explosion after which it was recorded bits of aircraft began to rain down on them from all directions. The crew confirmed a large piece of fuselage fell into the ocean about ten miles off the Russian submarine's port beam. When all this had started to happen, Captain Narodny immediately ordered for the submarine to dive. He gave orders for the *Gorbachev* to maintain a slow speed and head off on a south-south-westerly course.

A few minutes of silence had passed when the Captain's voice came over the ship's tannoy. "Comrades, I congratulate you all in respect of our success of the third sea trial. Moscow has confirmed it had been reported that two large aircraft are now missing somewhere in mid-Atlantic. Thank you again. Please enjoy your rest."

It was now, 01.55 hours.

★

Forging ahead at a speed of thirty knots, *HMS Excalibur* was about sixty miles from the disaster area. The Royal Navy's intelligence operations at Northwood had given clearance for the submarine to continue at best possible speed. Commodore Brianston-Green was instructed to try and make contact with the US Navy's nuclear hunter-killer submarine *SSN Bowevil*.

News about the tragic loss of the two civil aircraft and information relating to the cause of the destruction were just beginning to filter through. The information stated terrorist bombs were the likely cause of the disaster. This theory had been based upon all collected data which was in the process of being received by the radio room.

An urgent message had just come through; it was being cleared marked: for the attention of Commodore Brianston-Green. The message was headed and marked: 'TOP PRIORITY AND STRICTLY CONFIDENTIAL'.

Gander Airport, Newfoundland

In Newfoundland, the Gander Control Tower had been watching on its main radar the slow but steady progress of the approaching Lufthansa jet.

It was now 02.10 hours.

Crippled, yawning violently, the aircraft was now less than sixty miles from the airport's main runway. Emergency fire crews and ambulance services had all been put on full alert; they were on standby, instructed to roll immediately the huge jet came in sight of the runway.

Fatigued, aching through the stress and strain of his ordeal, Captain Schmidt looked as if he had aged about ten years. His co-pilot Hans Jurgens sat uncomfortably in his seat. The pain of his injured arm was finally giving him spasms of nausea and blackouts.

Franz Oltman stuck grimly to his task. He was constantly poring over his maps and charts ensuring that no mishap or error of calculation would lead the aircraft off its plotted course.

Oltman called out to his Captain. "Walter, what is our wind direction and current air speed right now?"

"Headwind one hundred and thirty knots. Gander weather reports conditions at the moment are fairly clear. However, they do state there's a bit of a blow locally whereby the wind strength is expected to increase during the next hour."

Schmidt looked across at his navigator. "I think, Franz, we should be okay, but as you are readily aware our fuel capacity is likely to be the big problem. I would say we have only about sixteen thousand pounds of the liquid gold left. Our height is now rapidly dropping; we are constantly slowing down due to the increasing headwind. If I try and conserve anything more by coming down nearer to our normal landing speed, and with this being done too early, we might suddenly and quite unexpectedly all become amphibians. It sure is going to be touch and go. Hey, fellows, I will keep you both posted if that time ever gets to be close and critical. Okay?"

Both officers had listened in total silence and jointly gave a nod in ensuring they understood the meaning of their Captain's very sombre words.

Schmidt continued. "But, one way or another, I reckon we will be landing in about ten or fifteen minutes."

By now, in the distance, Schmidt could see the lights of the town of St. John's on the Avalon Peninsula.

As the aircraft grew closer to is destination, it began its final descent.

With the Boeing jumbo's speed decreasing, the altimeter quickened. As its arrow rounded the dial it showed the aircraft had dropped from twelve thousand five hundred feet down to six thousand five hundred feet.

The jet's speedometer read one hundred and eighty miles per hour.

Gradually the wing flaps extended and this started to cause a strange vibration which now began to rock the aircraft's port side.

Schmidt quickly glanced at his instruments and was trying to find what the fault might be. He could not see anything that seemed unusual but he knew something was not quite right.

In altering its course, the aircraft now banked away to starboard.

Schmidt could clearly feel the very unusual sensation.

Franz Oltman also felt it. It seemed like a strange form of lurching.

Franz broke the electrifying tension in suddenly shouting out, "Jesus, God, you cannot go and do this to us now! Dammit, surely not! Not after all we have bloody well just gone through! Where are those goddamned guardian angels now?"

The quiet voice of Hans Jurgens responded to the fear in Oltman's voice. "Don't worry or panic about it now, Franz. It's a ruddy miracle that Werner has been able to get us back this far. Remember, the aircraft is having some minor problems. It has a new observatory in the roof, a gaping hole in its underbelly, no outer starboard engine and no wing tip," replied Jurgens with a grin on his face. But inwardly he was fearing his own words.

At that moment a violent juddering suddenly shook the whole aircraft. One of the outer starboard main wing flaps snapped off spiralling away into the darkness.

Schimdt could not exactly know what had just happened but he knew his aircraft and announced, "It's cracking up, boys. I really don't think it wants to stay alive up here with us much longer."

Oltman felt the sweat of fear soaking into his shirt collar. He nervously began calling, "MAYDAY! MAYDAY! MAYDAY! Gander, this is LH0873C. We are going down. We are about twenty miles out. Serious malfunctions have now occurred; our main outer flap on our starboard side has just disintegrated. We have veered off our course and are rapidly losing height. We have very little fuel left in order to sustain our flight path." Oltman tried to speak calmly trying not to show his acute fear, while carrying on giving Gander Control and Werner Lotz what could be the last words heard from Flight LH0873C.

Desperately fighting with the aircraft's controls Schmidt knew he still had to try something in order to pull the great bird back from imminent destruction. He was aware anything was possible by the book, but considered he might have to create a new chapter regarding rules and instructions for pending crash procedure. Above all, he had to try everything that would ensure his survival and that of his crew. However, he was beginning to feel that maybe this time even his luck was running out. Lifting his arm upwards, Schmidt turned on all the aircraft's main landing lights. He then motivated the release of the plane's undercarriage.

Everyone felt the motion of the jet's hydraulics and heard the wheels lock in.

Captain Schmidt gave a sigh of relief. "Thank heaven for small mercies."

The stricken aircraft was now shaking and frantically swaying. The Captain's eyes watched the clock recording the seconds slipping by. The fuel gauge registered the aircraft's tank level was down to less than five thousand five hundred pounds.

The plane's air speed was holding at one hundred and fifty miles per hour.

A constant Mayday call echoed and Franz calmly continued to carry out his duty to whatever end. Hans Jurgens had passed out.

The runway with its lights full ablaze came into view. The aircraft rapidly made its last seconds of flying in a desperate effort to maintain sufficient height and course. Frantically, rocking from side to side, the engines wailing a horrendous groaning sound with the aircraft's speed now falling below one hundred and forty miles per hour, the huge Boeing 747's nose suddenly dipped sharply. Walter Schmidt finally knew this was the end. He calmly leant forward and turned off all ancillary electrics and then extinguished the cabin lights. Schmidt knew he had done all that was humanly possible. Slowly he leaned back in his pilot's seat and then pulled back the stick with all his remaining strength.

He held his breath.

The starboard undercarriage hit the raised grass verge and the outer beacon landing lights at the beginning of the main runway approach at Gander International Airport. There was a huge impact as the port side wheels hit the tarmac. Two tyres immediately burst. The aircraft's massive airframe again groaned and creaked under the strain and then started to disintegrate. Moments later the nose wheel made violent contact with the ground as the aircraft reeled onward from its initial touchdown. Unbelievably, amidst a huge cloud of dust and engine exhaust, Lufthansa Flight LH8073C rocked heavily as it bounced its way along the runway. There was a sudden tremendous roar as the three remaining engines were thrown into reverse thrust. Pieces of the aircraft continued to fall off. With the aircraft speed showing ninety miles per hour, Captain Schmidt engaged the brakes. He pumped at them frantically hoping his stricken metal friend would not finally attempt give up now. Willing it, coaxing it, and trusting it would hang on long enough to ensure both he and his crew hopefully could still survive, Captain Schmidt threw all the electrical switches back to 'ON'. He knew this would certainly be his final act if any sparks were to ignite a ruptured fuel line.

Fire attendants, their red lights flashing and sirens wailing, screamed along racing at a safe distance behind the crippled aircraft. The sparks and flashes began to disappear as finally the jet began to slow.

There was a tranquil stillness in the flight deck cockpit. Franz Oltman looked across to his Captain. Tears of joy were streaming down his cheeks as he spoke, "Bloody hell, Walter. You're a flippin genius! An amazing bloody genius!"

Gradually the huge cargo plane slowed and taxied to a halt.

Captain Schmidt looked down from the cockpit window and quickly estimated the plane could be less than twenty metres from the end of the runway.

From the control tower at Gander International Airport, and through many windows of the airport buildings, everyone from flight traffic controllers to general administration staff had seen the flight come in. Now there were shouts and cheers of jubilation. Some of the secretarial staff were overcome with tears of relief and happiness.

The peaceful scene in the aircraft's cockpit was interrupted as Werner Lotz spoke to Captain Schmidt. In the background noise of his headphones Walter Schmidt could hear the sound of hands clapping and cheers of jubilation echoing. In a state of near exhaustion he struggled to take a handkerchief from his trouser pocket to mop his dripping brow.

Again the voice of Werner Lotz came through his earphones. Captain Schmidt rested his head in his hands as he heard the control tower speaking a message relayed by a recorded computer voice calmly advising:

"This is Gander Control calling Lufthansa Flight LH8073C. Welcome to Gander International Airport. Welcome to Newfoundland. Please ensure all aircraft personnel clear Customs and Excise authorities before leaving the airport. Thank you, have a nice day."

Chapter Seven

NASA Military and Naval Intelligence, Cape Canaveral

A package was placed on the desk of the Head of Security it was marked: 'URGENT' For the of attention: GENERAL JOHN B. KEMP. It was a large red striped parcel, which had just been delivered by a speed courier service from the United States Naval Headquarters at Charleston, South Carolina.

Just after 21.45 hours, on 1 August, General Kemp had been out for an evening bite to eat having earlier met Lieutenant Logan back at his office.

One hour had passed.

Kemp had busily been reconstructing past events regarding the matter now generally referred to as the 'Space Demons file'.

The General's security phone rang. "Yes?" He said in answering.

"Sir, I have just cleared the delivery of a very important package received from Naval HQ Charleston. Shall I bring it through?" enquired a night duty security guard.

Kemp replied, "Call Lieutenant Logan have him collect the package and deliver it to my office, right away."

"Right you are, sir. It will be done at once."

The security guard cancelled the line and immediately connected a call through to Lieutenant Logan's extension. The telephone rang in the computer room and was soon picked up.

"Yes? This is Lieutenant Logan speaking." The guard delivered the General's message.

Logan responded and promptly left his office to collect the delivered mail. In proceeding onward to the door of General Kemp's office, Logan knocked then entered. "Good evening again, General. The night security guard called requesting I deliver this package to you, sir. Will that be all?" Kemp looked up. He hadn't noticed Logan enter.

Lieutenant Logan had automatically entered just in case the General may have been engaged on an important telephone conversation.

The General spoke, "Ah, Logan! Good, thank you for bringing the dispatch programmes over. Now then, young man, I want you to be in on this operation right from the very start. I think you might find it most interesting. I'm sure you will certainly benefit from the experience. Here now, place that box on the table and open it. Please bring over whatever is inside it. Okay?"

Kemp turned back to face the large glass table and complete what he was doing; as he did so he said, "I won't keep you a moment. I just want to finish something which I have been analysing. "He carried on plotting a piece of red cord around a series of flag pins he had marked and dated and had set out on a big chart of the world spread across the table.

Logan opened the box.

There were seven digital recordings tightly packed in side it. Each was security coded and sealed. Logan was not aware what the recordings were about and patiently waited for the General's further instructions.

A couple of minutes passed.

Kemp turned to see what Logan was up to and said, "Well, Logan, I wonder what in hell's name Naval HQ has sent us that is so important at this late hour."

Immediately Logan responded, "They look like seven sealed videos, sir."

Kemp gave him a very blank look. "Well, Smartie, you had better set up the screen so we can see what it's all about. How many recordings did you say had been sent?"

Logan repeated the number as he manoeuvred the mobile projector unit into focus in line with the white screen on the wall.

Kemp rose from his desk and crossed over to sit in an easy chair. As he did so Logan set in motion the recording marked, NUMBER ONE.

The General beckoned him to sit down in another easy chair and said, "Well, young man, it looks like it's goin' to be a very long night. Seven tapes you said? Mmmmmm! The time now is just after 22.15 hours. I think we should be all finished up here by about dawn."

Logan looked across at the General disbelieving, not really knowing if the General meant what he had said.

The screen lit up.

Numbers began decreasing from ten to zero flashing in black and white until the edited film heading came up on the screen: 'CHARLESTON NAVAL HEADQUARTERS – CLASSIFIED REPORT'

SSN Bowevil – Itromps – SS Andros

General Kemp spoke, "Well, me lad, I hope you remember your official secret code. Not a word about this lot to anyone, do you hear?"

"Yes, sir," replied Logan. His pulse had already begun to race and the adrenaline flow. He felt very privileged but also wondered why Kemp was letting him view this confidential information.

The first thirty seconds of film showed the release of *Itromps* from the *Bowevil's* outer storage tank. The huge steel door slid slowly back. Shortly afterwards the main headlights of the submersible came into view as the tiny vessel eased its way out into the ocean's depths. The film continued showing the dive and covered the set search patterns. It also monitored the finding of two Second World War wrecks.

After an hour had passed, the second recording was started up.

Kemp considered it was time for a bit of refreshment but he wanted to see what Logan was thinking of the film so far. "What do you think of that little swimming machine, Smartie?"

Logan smiled. "It sure was fascinating, General. By the way does the Navy have many of these gadgets, sir?"

Kemp at first hesitated then replied, "No, Logan, this one is brand new and very special. Please do not refer to *Itromps* as being a mere gadget. It certainly is not that. If you call it a gadget again you might lose a future opportunity of being involved with a highly specialised team. I mean one that looks after the submersible's well being. Now then, let's have that drink I mentioned. What poison would you like? Tea, coffee or a glass of bourbon?"

Logan stood in silence pondering his thoughts on what Kemp had said. He then remembered a drink had been offered. "Coffee please, sir."

For a moment the General looked at him curiously then acknowledged his request. "Okay, Smartie, you can pour the coffee. The percolator is ready. Would you be so kind as to pour one for me? I'll then add the strengthener of a little sour mash; that should put a little pep into it." Kemp ambled over to the drinks cabinet and took out a bottle of *Jack Daniels,* and poured into one of the 'Tutbury' heavy Edinburgh crystal tumblers. He took a quick gulp then said, "Now then, Logan, let's get back to work."

Lieutenant Logan dimmed the office lights as the large video screen again lit up. Soon the digital recording started rolling and showed NUMBER TWO.

Itromps came partially into the picture taken by one of the outer wing cameras. It showed the submersible cruising along the seabed. The next focused on distance pictures, and then the image of a large wreck began to appear. Kemp spoke out in surprise. "Great Scott, Logan! Just look at that! It's that big ore carrier, all right, but what on earth has happened to it? Christ, look at that bow section! Holy cow! Apart from it looking not unlike a bloody great white shark, what in heck's name could have done something like that?"

Both Kemp and Logan stared in awe at the screen; both were speechless as the amazing pictures showed something totally out of the extraordinary had happened to the SS *Andros*.

It was 00.40 hours, 2 August.

By now, the General and Logan were nearly exhausted by the sheer horror of what they had seen. Again, the recording needed changing. Kemp thought it was time for another pause.

"Well, Smartie, it must be time for a short break. I think you had better pour me another drink. I suggest you also get yourself one too. Heaven knows I am sure you could do with one. While you are getting on with that, I am going to make a private call"

Logan nodded and then smiled. "No problem, General. I'll take care of them. You're right about me having a drink, sir. I could do with a stiff vodka."

The General responded, "Help yourself, lad, and don't you worry. I'll make sure you get back home in one piece."

Logan laughed at the comment as Kemp got up from his easy chair and moved to his desk. On sitting down Kemp picked up the hotline receiver and began to dial.

"Yes! Who the bloody hell is this calling me at this time? Doesn't anybody in the world sleep anymore?" Admiral Marchant had been sound asleep when the telephone rang.

"Good morning, Admiral. It is General John Kemp speaking."

Admiral Marchant was still a bit sleepy. "Who did you say? No, don't know him! You have telephoned the wrong number!"

Kemp shouted back hoping Marchant would hear him and not put the receiver down. "No, no, it's General John Kemp speaking." There was a slight pause.

The Admiral retorted, "Who did you say?"

By now Kemp was beginning to get a little irritated. He decided it was his turn to sound off. "Admiral Marchant! Will you please just back off for a second and let me speak!"

There was a sudden pause.

The Admiral answered. "Oh, General Kemp is that you? In heaven's name man, what on earth is it you want from me at such an ungodly hour? Do you not realise it's only five o'clock in the morning over here?"

Kemp decided to let Admiral Marchant calmly settle back into his stride; he thought it was best to wait until the Admiral had finally blown his lid or had run out of things to say.

Suddenly, there was what appeared to be another long pause of silence.

Admiral Marchant spoke. "General Kemp, are you still there?"

"Yes, Admiral, I was just waiting until you had settled down. I presume by now you are fully awake?"

"Awake, did you say? Awake? Dammit of course I'm awake. Why on earth did you telephone me if you thought that I wasn't going to be awake? Heavens above, man. If you haven't got anything important to tell me, other than your wishing to see if I was awake, then you can bloody well buzz off! If, however, you do wish us to speak just reply by saying yes."

On the other side of the pond in Kemp's office, Kemp had called Smartie Logan over to the telephone and instructed that as soon as the British Admiral had stopped his blabberin', Logan was to join the General in shouting back the word YES! When the retort came Marchant halted, his ear ringing from the onslaught. He replied stating, "So, we are now in joint agreement. Right then, if you do have something to say, then say it."

At first both Logan and Kemp were grinning like two Cheshire cats, each near laughing hysterically.

The General placed his hand over the phone. "Come on, Smartie. We must not let this situation get out of hand."

Logan was trying not to laugh. "No, sir. I mean, certainly, sir. Please excuse me, General. I must go to the men's room." Smartie swiftly left the General's office.

As soon as the door shut, Logan fell about laughing.

A curious security guard rose and stood at his desk not quite sure what he was witnessing.

Logan saw him standing there and staring at him. He quickly recovered his composure and headed towards the men's room.

In the meantime Kemp had taken a large sip of his glass of sour mash; he then began to tell the Admiral all he had seen concerning the pictures taken by the *Itromps*. He acknowledged the *Bowevil* had scrambled the evidence through the system by microcoding. The films on being processed were then released to all confidential departments.

The General then took the Admiral through what had been discovered and Marchant was fascinated. "Well, thank you very much, John, for the information. I am very sorry for the opening charges reeled at you for waking me up. You were right to call me when you did. However, I do stress it is not really very wise to telephone me between 02.00 hours and 06.00 hours. By this time even my brain has generally had enough. Anyhow, thank you very much for all the highly confidential input. I trust we shall speak again a little later in the day. Goodbye for now." Admiral Marchant was just about to put the receiver down when he remembered something. "Oh, by the way, it was a shocking situation for that Captain. What did you say his name was?"

Kemp reminded him.

"Oh yes, Captain Rossway, the poor fellow. We will have to discuss the matter further after you have seen all the digital recordings. Thank you again for calling, John. Bye for now."

"Goodbye, Admiral."

The line went dead.

Logan entered the General's office just as the receiver was being replaced. Kemp spoke, "Well, Logan, have you recovered, lad? I must say that was quite a barnstormer with Admiral Marchant. Anyway, we had better get ourselves back to work otherwise we'll still be here when the janitors come in to clear up."

Kemp looked at his watch. The time was 01.15 hours.

The video screen lit up and began to show *Itromps* proceeding through the massive aperture at the bow of the sunken ship. It then moved upwards through to the deck top, thereafter aft to the gaping hole where the bridge used to be.

Suddenly, Kemp beckoned. "Logan, please stop the machine. I need to pay a visit in order to check the plumbing. While I am gone see if you can fathom out what made such a horrendous mess of that ship. I would gladly accept any form of suggestion, even a wild guess. I must say it sure has got me flummoxed."

As Kemp was leaving, Logan passed a comment. "Maybe, sir, the space demons got at it."

The mere thought of that sent a cold shiver down Kemp's spine.

Logan used the break as an opportunity to replenish his drink; he also topped up the General's glass. *Only two more tapes to go*, Logan thought to himself.

It was not long before the office door opened and Kemp stepped back in.

He spoke, "Are we ready, young man? Before you proceed to set the machine in motion, have you had any more thoughts?"

For a moment, Logan did not know what to answer. It was as if he had just dried up. He coughed then said, "Well, sir, do the US Navy have anything like a rocket or missile that's big enough to bore a hole or cut a path through an object like a ship without it exploding?"

Kemp smiled. "That's not completely unimaginative, Smartie. However, I have yet to see the latest Saturn six rocket take-off to a target at zero height without demolishing whatever it impacted against. No. No, I think we will switch on the video and take in more of this near fictional disaster."

Kemp eased himself into his lazy chair and lit a cigar.

"Okay, sir?" Logan replied.

The General gave a nod.

Logan turned down the lights as the screen began to show images of the *SS Andros's* aft main stack.

As the General sipped his glass of sour mash and puffed at his cigar, the *Itromps* now entered the broken structure. Logan made one or two notes and a quick sketch of the angles he was trying to estimate the width of the gaping hole. The submersible moved up into the area where windows of the bridge had been. Logan was in the process of taking a large gulp of his drink when the ghostly face and shape of a drowned torso came in full view of the camera. His glass slipped from his hands; it fell to the floor shattering into many pieces.

Kemp straightened sharply. "Jesus Christ! I see they didn't bother to edit anything. How awful! What a terrible way to have died."

Logan ran out of the office, just making the men's room before throwing up.

Kemp felt sorry for the lad. Neither he nor Logan had any knowledge or pre-warning that such a horrific sight was going to be kept on record. The General had a lot of sympathy for Logan who on just returning looked as if he had just sailed through a hurricane.

"I'm sorry, Smartie. I must say that dreadful sight completely took me by surprise. My, My, you're looking a bit green about the gills. Here, young man, force this one down your gullet. It'll make a new man of you."

"Thank you, sir." Sheepishly, Logan took the glass and downed its contents in one.

Kemp poured himself another stiffener. "Have another one, Logan, but might I suggest you sip it this time. I haven't too much stock of fifty-year-old brandy, on board."

Logan nodded as he sipped. A feeling, something like an explosion of fire, then hit his stomach. A sensation of rapid warmth soon felt its way through his body. Eventually it made his cheeks and face glow.

Kemp watched as his young officer seemed to be back in control.

"Okay, lad, now let's get on with the finale. By the way, I would like to look at your notes when we have finished screening."

Logan nodded. At that moment his head began to swim into the happiness of intoxication. He smiled a wide Cheshire cat grin back at the General then turned on the video. The pictures showed the submersible moving painstakingly slowly as it edged its way forward.

Soon, Lieutenant Logan sank peacefully back in his chair and fell asleep.

Kemp continued his vigil; he was trying to find any possible solution as to what might have been the cause of the dreadful catastrophe. As the last videotape ended the time was nearing 03.00 hours.

The General nudged Smartie Logan and helped him to his feet. He called the security guard to assist helping the Lieutenant to the limousine. Kemp then went about his usual routine of locking up. As he did so, he came across Logan's notes. There were a lot of scribbled near illegible writings the Lieutenant had written. What fascinated the General was the weird science fiction sketch Logan had drawn. He folded it and placed it into his case. He then turned out the light and closed the door.

The Admiralty — Whitehall, London

Commander Thompson's telephone rang while he was in the bathroom shaving. He quickly made his way into the lounge to pick up the receiver.

"Good morning, Thompson. Did I wake you?" Admiral Marchant enquired.

"Not at all, sir. I was in the process of shaving."

"Well, Thompson, I am calling you in regard to important information I have received overnight. I wish you please to make note. I now have very firm knowledge from reliable sources the *SS Bowevil* has located the wreck of the *SS Andros* although I do believe I am still to receive confirmation. Anyway, be advised the vessel did not as previously stated founder in that very bad storm last week. It was sunk."

"Sunk!" Thompson blurted out.

The Admiral heard the alarm in Thompson's voice to which he replied, "Yes, sunk. She was bored apart from end to end by some unknown force."

Thompson listened in near disbelief to what Marchant had to say. "Will we be receiving any ratification in regard to the horrible circumstance that happened, sir?"

"I cannot really say, Thompson, but rest assured I do somehow smell that a huge rat is going to rise up from the depths of the ocean sewers regarding this matter. It's going to be an ugly one. I also think those Russkies are going to be behind it." The Admiral snorted and coughed at his own suggestions.

There was a slight pause as Thompson composed himself. "Yes, Admiral, and were there any further details?"

"Yes! Certainly!" Admiral Marchant snapped. "You will double all operational surveillance in regard to watching both the *Intrepid* and *Bowevil*. I want an hourly report forwarded to me at the Admiralty. Is that clear?"

"Yes, sir. It will be done, Admiral."

Marchant continued, "If there is a change of course, any adversity or strange happening, I want it all reported. Do you hear? At all times keep me well informed and give me an up-to-the-minute report."

Thompson sensed there was a big flap on." I will see to it immediately, sir."

"Fine. I'll await your progress report on my desk by mid-morning. Goodbye for now."

"Thank you for the instruction and message, Admiral."

Marchant blew his nose. "That's quite all right. Now go for it." He coughed then closed the call.

Royal Naval Headquarters, Northwood

Commander Thompson hurriedly dressed himself. In no time at all he headed for the operations room and then the sanctuary of his office. As far as sleep was concerned it had been a very late Monday night.

Tuesday, 2 August was a bright morning. It appeared to be the beginning of a warm sunny day.

As Thompson entered the office he saw that Lieutenant Henderson had already arrived.

It had just past 07.00 hours BST.

The smell of percolating ground coffee reached the Commander's nostrils. He looked into the operations room but there was no sign of the Lieutenant. A lot of messages were on his desk with a pile of internal clearances which had to be quickly made. Commander Thompson thought it wise to tackle the backlog; he sat down and began to busy himself with the mass of paperwork.

After five minutes had elapsed, a large mug of hot black coffee appeared on the Commander's desk. He looked up quickly.

"Good morning, sir."

"Why, thank you, Henderson."

The Lieutenant commented. "I see, sir, you are another one that has set about hunting the early worm?"

Both of them looked at each other and smiled.

Thompson said, "That is good coffee, Ian. Please sit down. I want you to personally take care of something for me. Very early this morning Admiral Marchant called me. I am sure something huge is coming up and it's about to cause a big flap."

"Right you are." Henderson answered.

The Commander continued, "It's essential you immediately double up on all operations regarding the surveillance of the two American nuke submarines. I will require a full update and confirmation to be made within the next hour. Thereafter, you must report to me every hour until further notice. I want the first report on my desk by 09.00 hours. I expect to hear from you shortly regarding the new position of *HMS Excalibur.* Please inform me immediately when any signals come through."

"I understand, sir. It will be done."

"By the way, Ian, have you heard the early morning news?"

"No, sir, not yet. I only got to the office shortly before you arrived."

Commander Thompson spoke, "I heard the five o'clock bulletin on the radio giving details of a terrible tragedy. A shocking business, Henderson. It appears that sometime during the night two jumbo jets have been blown up somewhere over the mid-Atlantic. One of them is believed to have been a British Airways plane. I understand from HQ Special Ops, *HMS Excalibur* has been ordered to rendezvous in the area and its commander has been instructed to surface to confirm the sighting of any wreckage. We should be receiving an updated report shortly. Please keep me posted. Let me have any news regarding the disaster plus any details as soon as you have it on those Yankee subs. That will be all."

"Yes, sir," replied the Lieutenant who then turned on his heel and promptly left the Commander's office.

The time was 07.25 hours BST.

Chapter Eight

At Sea

The mid-Atlantic sky twinkled a beautiful starlit arena from horizon to horizon. A first glimpse of dawn's pale light could be seen across a fairly calm sea.

By now, *HMS Excalibur* was nearing a position previously recorded, and still marked on its radar screen where a blip had momentarily appeared, and was now logged as an unidentified sighting.

Only when notification came through from Naval HQ Northwood about the disaster did Commodore Brianston-Green indicate to his fellow officers the radar mark recorded at 64.0 N − 28.7 WSW timed at 00.36.28 hours, 1 August, was to be considered the possible wreckage of the aircraft.

The Commodore was conscious that the blip had remained visual on the screen for nearly two and half minutes. Then it had just disappeared. At the time of 00.34.16 hours, *HMS Excalibur* also recorded, almost at the same latitude and longitude reference, another radar blip. This one stayed on screen and then also disappeared after about two and half minutes.

"It doesn't really quite tally does it, Bergman?"

"No, sir," replied Lieutenant Archibald Bergman, senior officer of the watch.

Commodore Brianston-Green checked his watch and said, "Mind you, it won't be long now before we can surface to see for ourselves what all the commotion and kerfuffle is about. I would estimate allowing for our present speed and the current, plus any drifting, we should surface at about 04.00 hours."

HMS Excalibur surged through the ocean at nearly thirty knots. All speed possible was called for after receiving notice from Royal Naval HQ regarding the disaster. The smooth design and classic shape of the British built *SSBN* class submarine gave it an appearance like that of a fearful giant killer whale racing through the sea after its prey.

Nearly three and a half hours had passed since Brianston-Green issued his instructions. After everything had settled down he finally took the chance to grab a little rest.

The noise of the telephone ringing in his cabin broke the Commodore's sleep. Quickly turning over in his bunk he picked up the receiver.

"Good morning, sir. The time is 03.25 hours. We'll be nearing the area of the mystery radar contacts in about twenty minutes." It was the voice of Lieutenant Bergman.

"Are there any orders, sir?"

Brianston-Green acknowledged Bergman thanking him for his wake up call. "No orders at present, Lieutenant. I'll be up on the bridge in a few minutes. Thank you, and out."

Lieutenant Bergman logged his message in the duty watch manual then notified the surveillance and operations room of an imminent visit by the Commodore.

Wreckage of Air India's Flight AI 102 and fragments of the British Airways Flight BA 182 had drifted only slightly from the scene of impact. A lot of bodies were evident bobbing about over the wide area of the disaster zone. Flotsam and jetsam, life jackets and pieces of aircraft, all were scattered within the immediate disaster area and eventually spread over a distance of about six miles.

Commodore Brianston-Green arrived on the bridge having paid a visit to the operations room to determine and check on the present position of *HMS Excalibur*.

The order rang out.

"Reduce our speed to ten knots. Prepare to surface."

Immediately the submarine began to slow then gradually climb to periscope depth.

"Surface! Surface!" Came the sharp cry.

It was a clear early dawn sky. The moon, still up, was beaming down eerily reflecting on the gently rolling waves.

Brianston-Green requested the main periscope be made ready for an infra-red night scan to see if anything might be picked up between the submarine and the horizon.

"Bergman, have we made contact with anything on the surface that is showing on the radar screen?"

"Nothing as yet, sir," Bergman replied.

Slowly, majestically, the shape of the submarine began to break the surface. No detection or any sightings were made prior to *HMS Excalibur* emerging from its hiding place beneath the waves of the darkened Atlantic

Ocean. Outside, the temperature was in the low forties Fahrenheit.

The Commodore gave an order. "Bergman, you had better go up top to see what might be about. Take six able-bodied men with you, plus the night vision cameras. Do it in case anything unsuspected or any wreckage, large or small, might be floating around enabling identification."

"Yes, sir," Bergman replied.

Six seamen were instructed to go up top. Each lookout was given clear instructions what to look for. Once any positive sighting had been made they were to report back immediately.

It was 03.50 hours.

HMS Excalibur slowed to a leisurely five knots.

Lieutenant Bergman had placed his men in a prominent sighting pattern. Each of them had begun a first scan; this was made covering a distance within the confines of a two-mile radius from the submarine's position. They tried desperately to quickly pinpoint what the radar had picked up nearly three and half hours before.

"I have a sighting, sir," came a shout.

"Six degrees to port, distance being about two thousand metres." One of the observers had located a large object floating on the surface. "Sir, it looks like a large piece of an aircraft tail section, and rear wings of a jumbo jet aircraft."

Luckily, the concealment of an air pocket behind the aft toilet section had enabled the tail section of the aeroplane to stay afloat.

Lieutenant Bergman trained his binoculars towards the advised direction. "Okay, I have it now. Thank you, men." Bergman picked up the calling phone. "Sighting confirmed. Commodore, I think you had better come and see this for yourself, sir."

"All right, I'll be up right away," came the reply.

"Engine room, reduce speed to three knots. Slow ahead," came the command.

As Brianston-Green made his way up to the flying bridge, a salute greeted him as he stepped out on to the deck top.

"Stand easy. Please carry on, everyone. We haven't got very long before it will be daylight." The Commodore felt a tinge of emotion as he saw floating bodies of children near the wrecked tail wing tip. "We'll collect any little pieces of wreckage, and pick up as many bodies as we are able, so our submarine can do the honourable service of giving them a decent and honest burial at sea. Lieutenant Bergman, you had better organise a deck crew to stand ready."

"Aye, aye, sir. It looks as if there are a lot of dead bodies down there."

"Stop engines," the Commodore ordered. "Dispatch the deck crew forward. Secure all lifelines."

On board the submarine's main deck, a dozen sailors began to muster. Each was given boat hooks for assisting with the collection of wreckage and allowing any drowned torsos to be heaved to.

HMS Excalibur gently rocked in the slight swell.

Within twenty minutes of starting the search and rescue operation a total of nineteen bodies and dismembered torsos were solemnly lifted from the sea.

Sailors were openly crying at the sight of such horrific scenes all around them. Soon, only two hundred metres away from the submarine's hull, the main tail and rear wing section of the British Airways Boeing 777-300ER aircraft appeared. Its markings, registration G-BHBP and the name *Osprey* were clearly seen in the beam of the submarine's rescue searchlights.

"Commodore, sir," Lieutenant Bergman called. "There appears to be more than one aircraft's wreckage around here. Look there." Bergman pointed to his left. "Yes, that's it, near that tail section over there. Those seats floating past it are clearly marked Air India, sir. Do we have any sort of confirmation that there were two aircraft in the disaster?"

Brianston-Green took note and studied the terrible sight. "I must say for one aircraft there IS definitely an awful lot of flotsam and jetsam about. Send a message to HQ advising the following: 'TIME: 03.55 HOURS 2 AUGUST 2017. FROM: EXCALIBUR. SURFACED 03.50 – STOP – FOUND BA WRECKAGE – STOP – ALSO UNEXPLAINABLE – STOP – APPEARS POSSIBLY TWO AIRCRAFT ARE DOWN – STOP – SEATS LOCATED IN WATER ARE AIR INDIA – STOP – TWENTY-SIX BODIES ACCOUNTED FOR – STOP – PLEASE ADVISE STATUS AND INSTRUCTION – STOP – SIGNED CMDRE BG RN – END MESSAGE'."

By 04.45 hours, at least sixty bodies had been found.

HQ at Northwood had acknowledged two aircraft were reported missing. A third aircraft although damaged had made a safe landing in Gander, Newfoundland.

The operations room began sending out messages requesting assistance from any ship within the immediate vicinity. *HMS Excalibur* requested they immediately alter course and proceed to the disaster area to help in the rescue. Three ships responded; all were over two hundred miles away and would not be able to reach the area for at least eight to ten hours. *HMS Excalibur* had been requested by Royal Naval HQ to consider using part of the submarine as a temporary mortuary.

Brianston-Green acknowledged he had facilities for carrying a limited number of corpses, but he considered a humane burial at sea should be agreed for the bodies the submarine had already accounted for.

By 05.05 hours the tally of corpses had risen to ninety-seven. The main torpedo room, the forward four torpedo tube areas, plus the free outer utility seas chamber areas, were now filled to capacity.

"Commodore, it is impossible to house any further dead in the makeshift mortuary. Do I have your permission to detail the crew to bury any more bodies collected at sea at an agreed time?" Lieutenant Bergman knew however compassionate the circumstance was, the situation now warranted and demanded alternative measures to be taken.

Brianston-Green thought for a moment. "Yes, Lieutenant, you do that. By the way, Bergman, I am going to consider mentioning in dispatches to HQ that your handling of the whole ghastly business has been exemplary. I must say you have conducted everything with the utmost consideration and reverence. It is with my most humble esteem and thanks that I will send this message. In it I'll also mention those members of the crew who openly volunteered to assist you. *HMS Excalibur* honours this deed of compassion together with its show of extreme kindness given towards the dead. I will forward your request to Northwood so condolences can be notified to the bereaved. You may authorise a burial party for 05.35 hours. By that time I should have received full confirmation and acknowledgement from HQ."

It was just after 05.15 hours when *HMS Excalibur* received a response from HQ in reply to its signal. The message read:

TIME: 05.15:28 HOURS 2 AUGUST 2017
FROM: NORTHWOOD RN HQ REF: 0023/097E
HOLD TO CAPACITY THE DEAD – STOP – BURY HUMANELY AND COMPASSIONATELY AT SEA AS MANY AS IS POSSIBLE – STOP – COLLECT ANY PERSONAL EFFECTS – STOP – DEPART EN ROUTE TO RENDEZVOUS AREA RE: SSN BOWEVIL BY 06.00 HOURS LATEST – STOP – THANK YOUR CREW FOR OPERATING SUCH A MAGNIFICENT FEAT IN THE TRUE TRADITION OF THE ROYAL NAVY – STOP – END MESSAGE

Commodore Brianston-Green thought the message should be read out to the whole ship's company. After completing this task he checked with Lieutenant Bergman what time the burial detail would be ready on the main deck, and when the service should be held. Bergman acknowledged everything had been made ready. The Commodore called the ship's chaplain and confirmed the service burial time was to be 05.30 hours. The delay was due to the signal response from HQ arriving later than expected.

The officers and all hands were to be present on deck at the prescribed time. At 05.28 hours, operations temporarily ceased and all movement or motion came to a halt.

At 05.30 hours the ship's chaplain began the order of burial service and the task of committal of the dead to the deep.

As the pale light of dawn begun to break on the ocean's far horizon. Only the moaning of the breeze could be heard and felt while whistling around the conning tower mingling with lapping sounds of ocean waves washing against the submarine's hull. The echoing of the last post from the ship's bugler disappeared into the distance as the burial service reached its completion. Suddenly, in the twilight of the dawn's sky, strange flashing lights could be seen no more than five or six miles from where *HMS Excalibur* was lying stationary.

Lieutenant Bergman and the Commodore both looked up to watch the atmospheric spectacle. It lasted no more than twenty or thirty seconds. About a minute later, the same thing occurred again.

Below, the submarine radar momentarily showed a small blip on the screen during the time of the vivid flashes of light.

"I wonder what all that was about?" Brianston-Green commented to Bergman.

"It's all very strange, sir. Never seen anything quite like it."

By 05.53 hours the crew had dispersed below deck. Preparations were being made for *HMS Excalibur* to get underway as quickly as possible.

About six miles away, to the west of where the British submarine was lying, the *Gorbachev* had been slowly circling just below the ocean's surface. Captain Narodny was watching the surprise appearance of the British strategic ballistic missile submarine. It was the first time he had actually seen one. He was intrigued. The lines and shape of the British submarine were much smaller than he had imagined. He thought it most unfortunate the British submarine was on the ocean surface at the time the space platform *Vostok* wished to change and increase *Gorbachev's* strength of radio beam to enhance the invisible cocoon.

Captain Narodny knew the change would reveal a sky of flashing lights, but he recognised his submarine's position was far enough north for any chance sighting being mistaken for the *Aurora Borealis*. He hoped the flashing lights would be mistaken for them.

However, Captain Narodny was not too sure if it was a seasonal occurrence. He now would just have to wait and see if the British submarine delayed its departure, if having become suspicious.

Through the periscope, Captain Narodny watched the submarine get underway, slowly moving eastwards. He saw it gradually sink deeper in to the water. Then the conning tower of *HMS Excalibur* finally disappeared beneath the waves.

As the distance between the disaster area and the unknown watching eyes of the undetected Russian submarine continued to extend, Captain Narodny lowered the periscope. He was relieved he had not been detected. Moreover, his operations room reported the British submarine was pursuing a course east-north-eastwards and was neither turning back nor engaging any form of battle tactic.

Chapter Nine

NASA Military and Naval Intelligence, Cape Canaveral

It was late morning on Wednesday, 2 August. General Kemp had been busy compiling all data received from the United States Air Force Strategic Air Command, and the Scientific Naval Oceanic Weather Intelligence Space Testing Unit.

Both he and Lieutenant Logan had arrived just after 09.00 hours.

Kemp felt in fairly good shape considering the late hour they had both finished.

Logan was feeling pretty grim and had a fiery headache. Not only did this hamper his good intentions, but also having watched the horrific pictures of the wreck of *SS Andros*, his mind was all sixes and sevens.

Kemp lifted the intercom telephone, pressed Logan's extension and waited. The bell seemed to ring for at least two minutes before Smartie Logan lifted the receiver.

"How are you feeling now, Logan? Are you up to it yet?" said the General.

"Struggling a bit, sir," came back a meek response.

Kemp chuckled. "Well, fuel yourself up with a few mugs of hot strong black coffee then see if you can have *G.O.D.*'s completed programme on my desk within one hour.

The telephone went dead. Logan sank to his knees. He still felt in a state of drunkenness. "Oh Jesus Christ! I am never goin' to touch another drink," he muttered to himself while slowly trying to lift his body up off the floor. *Yes, black coffee. The General could well be right. That's it, a hot pot of strong black coffee.*

After five minutes, the percolator was ready. Shaking with the DTs, Logan tried to pour himself a caffeine fix. In seconds the desk surface was covered with spilt coffee.

Logan looked at the mess. Gradually the lake began to spread. Soon a river of coffee started to flow along the desk towards *G.O.D.* Logan began to panic. The surging wave now gathered speed. At that moment there was

111

a knock on the door. Logan didn't wait to see who it was. He picked up the first pile of paper he could lay his hands on to stem the tide.

In the doorway stood General Kemp and the security officer Sergeant Lance. They burst into laughter at the sight of Logan trying desperately to rescue G.O.D. from its peril.

"I think we'd better sit you down for a while and see if we can tackle the rescue job of G.O.D. ourselves. Just you concentrate on doing one thing: start drinking that black coffee, and gallons of it. That's an order! Do you hear me, Logan, an order!"

Sergeant Lance helped Logan to his chair and placed a mug of steaming hot coffee beside him. "Now be a good chap and do as the General has told you to, sir."

"Okay," mumbled, Logan.

"Sergeant!"

"Yes, sir." Lance quickly responded to Kemp's call.

"Hey Lance, Lieutenant Logan was not in this state when I picked him up this morning. Just look at him now. I wonder what could have done this?"

"I really don't know, sir," Sergeant Lance replied.

"You'd better call for house maintenance to come and clear this mess up. When Lieutenant Logan has decided to come to, we might find time to get some work done around here."

"Yes, General. I'll deal with it right away, sir."

"When you have that organised, Lance, would you come and see what we can achieve in getting G.O.D. to deliver this report. We might as well leave Logan to carry on dreaming for a while."

They both laughed at the sight of the Lieutenant slouched in the chair sleeping like a baby.

"At least the mug is empty, General," said Sergeant Lance trying to soften his commanding officer's wrath.

"Okay, Okay. First, I'll go back to my office for an hour. Then I'll have a spot of lunch. Let me know when everything is back on an even keel. Thank you for assisting, Sergeant."

Both men departed.

Lieutenant Logan lay back peacefully. He was sound asleep. What he did not realise was that he had just topped up his alcohol intake. At the time of still feeling very fragile he had filled the percolator with water. In doing so he had brought about his own downfall. In his haste to set it up he had grabbed the two full glasses of clear liquid that stood on the desk beside *G.O.D.* During the previous evening he had filled the two glasses with Kemp's vodka to give himself a good supply for the late night thrash. When Sergeant Lance poured out the mug of coffee he unknowingly had administered to Logan the perfect leg collapser: hot black coffee laced with neat vodka.

It was nearly 14.00 hours. Lance was out and about checking on his security round. He had returned to see how Lieutenant Logan was fairing. Logan had curled himself up into a ball and was snoring quietly as Lance entered.

"Lieutenant Logan, sir," He called.

There was no movement.

Again Lance tried to rouse him. "Sir! Lieutenant Logan, sir!" He shook him, *Hells bells! I believe the sonofabitch is still legless!*

Sergeant Lance knew that if General Kemp saw Logan still in this state, there would be hell to pay.

The smell of freshly made coffee soon filled the air. Sergeant Lance knew the General would be back around 15.00 hours.

Before leaving, Kemp had asked Lance to try and perform a near miracle. He requested him to ensure Logan was alive and kicking by the time he got back. In addition to this, the General had demanded the completed programme was to be on his desk by the time he returned.

Lance stood at the main entrance checking to see if any emergency instructions or urgent messages were to be handled. Nothing seemed to be unduly pressing. *Good*, he thought. He picked up the first aid box and returned to the computer room. Lance carefully placed the box on one of the tables and opened it. Everything from morphine to pep pills was in it; layers of bandages, boxes of plasters, major surgical apparatuses.

The Sergeant muttered to himself, "Where in hell's name is it?" He carefully kept turning over all the medical equipment. "Ah! There it is. Great! Hopefully that will do."

As Lance walked over to the Lieutenant's desk he began humming a tune to himself. He poured out two mugs of fresh strong black coffee.

On picking up a mug plus a small glass bottle he had taken from the first aid box, Lance went over to where Logan was still laid out, deep in the land of nod.

The Sergeant gently eased off the top of the bottle. He lifted Lieutenant Logan's head and waived the bottle under the Lieutenant's nose.

At first there was no reaction.

Suddenly, Logan began to grunt and snort as the heavy odour of strong smelling salts took effect. "What! Where! Who the hell? Great onions, Sergeant! What is that stuff?" cursed Logan.

"An old-fashioned remedy, sir."

"By heck, it sure packs one hell of a punch. What the hell happened anyway? One minute I thought I was coming to then wham! After that, I don't remember anything."

"Here, sir, drink this. I am sure it will make you feel a lot better." Lance handed him a mug of coffee. "By the way, Lieutenant, sir, I don't think you will find this to be as powerful as your last mug. You somehow unknowingly poured two glasses of vodka into the percolator mistaking it to be water. Mind you, from what I have already heard I can quite understand, sir. You were probably not very stable on your feet. Well, not enough to go to the rest room to fill the coffee flask with some fresh water." Sergeant Lance began to laugh.

Logan also saw the funny side of the story. "Gee! I must say that sounds like I have goofed. This is mighty good coffee, Sergeant. I can already feel my senses beginning to revitalise. I hope there's more brewing up from where this has come from?"

Sergeant Lance was relieved to see Lieutenant Logan getting back to his normal self. "You bet, sir. I suppose I had better now tell you the worst."

"Why, what's up Lance?"

"Sir, it's now 13.45 hours. General Kemp ordered me to get you back into shape and ensure you are fit and in good workin' order before he returned. He also stressed he wished to see the full revised printout and have all the information on his desk by the time he got back. Only you know about that, sir."

"That's correct, Sergeant."

"Well, sir, I must tell you the General is expected back at three."

"Hell! That means there is only forty-five minutes to get *G.O.D.* to give up all. Jesus! I hope that in God's name I can get it to function in double quick time. Oh hell! I swear I'll not touch another drop. Hey, Sergeant, can you get all that printout paper levelled and placed at *G.O.D.*'s disposal? I'll get on the keyboard and VDU to start processing the output programme. It shouldn't take too long seeing I have it already co-ordinated and channelled. Sergeant, if we can keep our heads, we have a good chance the General won't get wind of my three-hour *siesta*. How about it, Lance?"

Logan knew his back was against the wall. "I promise I'll owe you one, Sergeant."

Lance was a likeable, easy-going giant of a Negro from Savannah. He could quite easily crush the bones of any opponent. To his close friends he was called 'Hester'. On hearing the Lieutenant's offer, Lance smiled at Logan. "One day I may well hold you to that one, sir. Now, what is it you want me to do?"

Soon, the noise of G.O.D. functioning could be heard, and a printout began of the full analysis sequence confirming a timetable and program of events which had happened over the past six weeks. "How are you feeling now, sir?" Lance enquired.

"I could still perk up a little more but I'm sure I'll survive. Thanks a million for all your assistance. I couldn't have achieved this without it. Is there another mug of coffee goin'?" asked Logan.

Sergeant Lance willingly refilled the Lieutenant's mug. "Well, I had better warn you, sir, the General will be back in about twenty minutes. I do hope you're a goin' to be ready for him otherwise we are both in for one hell of an afternoon."

"Okay, Sergeant, I've got the message loud and clear." Logan checked the printout schedule then noted how long the laser printer would take. "It looks like it'll be a close run thing, but if G.O.D. is willing we should just about make it on time."

Both Logan and Lance laughed.

Gradually the pile of printed paper thickened.

It was just turning 15.00 hours when Kemp's black limousine entered the driveway and moved towards the building's front entrance. By now G.O.D. was in overdrive. Paper had practically been tumbling out of the printer under the strain of its high-speed production. Logan had begun compiling the sheet schedules in readiness for delivery to the General's office when the telephone rang.

Sergeant Lance picked up the receiver, "Computer room, Lance speaking."

The sound of General Kemp's voice boomed and echoed down the telephone.

"Yes, sir. One moment please. I'll put Lieutenant Logan on the line."

Lance handed the receiver over to Logan.

"Good afternoon, General," responded Logan. The General's voice could be heard firing many questions at Logan.

"Yes, sir, I'll be delivering the printouts to your office within the next fifteen minutes."

Further instructions were retorted at Logan.

"Right you are, sir. Much better now, thank you."

The call finished.

Logan looked at Lance." Well, I don't know how I have managed to get off with this one. Or do you think the General was standing on the sidelines waiting to attack? Anyhow Sergeant, as I previously said, truly I owe you one."

"Why, thank you, Lieutenant. I'll book it down and hold it in lieu. Is there any more that I can do for you, sir?"

"I think that's it for now, Sergeant. Unless you can wait a minute or two to give me a hand carrying this lot through to the General's office."

"That'll be no problem at all, sir."

At 15.12 hours there was a knock on General Kemp's office door.

"Enter!" boomed the General's voice.

Both Lieutenant Logan and Sergeant Lance stepped in carrying a stack of paper printouts. Each pile was ceremoniously laid out on the large glass table. Kemp looked warily at Lieutenant Logan then at Sergeant Lance.

"Is everything one hundred percent, Sergeant Lance?"

"It sure is, sir", said Lance.

"Fine, fine. Have you got your marbles back yet, Lieutenant?"

Logan looked up. "I am sorry for the delay, sir, but I understand I nearly somehow almost blew my head off again this morning."

"We all have to learn, young man. This time it was your turn. I trust by now you will have learnt to be a little more responsible. That is, of course, if there is to be a next time, Logan. Okay, let's see if all the hard work has paid off."

At 15.25 hours Sergeant Lance returned to his security desk. He left General Kemp and Lieutenant Logan busily studying the completed programme.

Two hours later a fresh pot of coffee was ordered.

"Well, Smartie, I must say that was very well done. Fascinatin' ain't it?" He patted him on the shoulder for having programmed and achieved a nearly one hundred percent accurate graph. G.O.D.'s findings revealed some of the times and dates corresponded with information received over the past six-month period. Over that time the Russians had caused immense jamming of the international radio airwaves. Furthermore, and far more serious, G.O.D. had calculated one of the so-called space demons was proven to have been directly over the vicinity of the chart reading 09.0 N – 66.0 W at the time of 10.15 hours on Sunday 30 July. It was exactly in the area where the SS Andros was assumed to have foundered and sunk.

Both Kemp and Logan stared blankly at each other. What was it that had caused the destruction they had seen on the video recording the previous evening?

"Logan," the General said quietly, "not a word about this to anyone. Do yer hear me, lad! Not a damn word. When all these pieces finally fit together it will be anybody's guess as to what confounded mess it could all lead to. You had better now pack up and get yourself off home. Have a good night's rest, lad. You've earned it."

"Okay, General. And thank you regarding the other matter, sir. I mean, for being easy on me."

"You have done a mighty fine job here. Did you think, lad, I was going to break you for that? Ah! Full of…" Kemp refrained from going any further. "Logan."

"Yes, sir," Smartie replied with an air of caution.

"Be a good lad and pour me a large glass of sour mash. Do have one for yerself, boy."

"Right you are. Thank you, sir. But, General, if you don't mind, I will refrain from any temptation for myself tonight."

Kemp smiled as Logan brought him his drink. "I quite understand, Logan. Off you go now. I'll see you back here tomorrow. Make it 08.00 hours sharp."

Logan closed the door as the General picked up the phone.

The time was 19.25 hours.

"Hello? Is that you Admiral Marchant?"

"Can I enquire as to why you are calling me, General?" His voice wasn't ice-cold but he didn't want any slip-ups this time too. What he did want was to get as much information as he could without disclosing what the British Navy had so far been able to probe.

Kemp ignored the Admiral's first comment. "Good evening, Raymond. I know it's late with you. I trust your past weekend wasn't so busy that you were unable to find time to visit your friend at that place you mentioned? Where did you say it was?"

There was a slight pause.

Admiral Marchant knew the damned Yankee was out fishing for news. The Admiral coughed attempting to clear his throat. "Well, General, before we get on to anything else, and in particular the subject you mentioned, I believe first, by rights, you should have some answers for me concerning the SS Andros."

Kemp was drawn in by Marchant's surprise remark. He thought for a moment before speaking. Surely to God the British Navy hadn't already received knowledge of what the *Itromps* had discovered. He knew Northwood HQ was good, but surely not that good.

"Well, Admiral, currently we are still checking things out. We really haven't too much to go on just yet. I am hoping our boys will make contact quite soon."

Marchant could feel the General was on his old kick of cat and mouse so he decided it was now time for him to become the cat.

"General, indeed you surprise me. I had hoped you would already have realised we are also observing the *SSN Bowevil*. In this regard, we noticed it had moved from its fixed position and now is sailing in a west-south-westerly direction. Seeing this to be so, I was going to request from your department some assistance hoping you would allow for another change of course. Let me further advise, our Navy will officially be calling on the naval resources of the United States Navy to request a rendezvous with one of our submarines at the disaster area where the tragic loss of those two aircraft appear to have happened. Quite obviously, and now after what your have hinted, this will not be possible." Marchant paused for a moment to take a sip of his nightcap then continued, "General, it seems very odd to me both aircraft were reported to have exploded within seconds of each other. What do you think, John?" Marchant carefully eased back the tempo of conversation.

He considered it was time for the General to slowly begin to bleed.

"Well, Admiral, the General paused, "you're right. *SSN Bowevil* has finished her task. Mind you, as yet, there have been no unusual reports of anything to the contrary."

Admiral Marchant didn't hesitate to strike. "John, do you really expect me to believe you haven't found that ore ship yet! Come on now, *SSN Bowevil* did find the *SS Andros* didn't it?"

General Kemp's wind quickly vented from his lungs; he found himself bruised and cornered. "You are right, Raymond. However, as yet, we have not been able to ascertain exactly how it sank." Kemp thought his opening remark would halt the current trend of combat tactics.

Marchant began to silently chuckle to himself.

Now for the real bait, he thought, and considered it was time to place a large piece of well-matured farmhouse cheddar in front of the General's nose. "Well, John, at least we agree on one thing. It wasn't the weather that sank that ship, was it?"

"Damn it, Raymond, what do you want me to tell you? That an alien, possibly made the bloody great hole we found right through the ship, or maybe you think we might know something further? Let's say, a new type of weapon? Something that some nation or superpower has made, a superpower which by now has probably taken leave of its senses and begun firing the damned thing in all directions? How bloody absurd."

Marchant thought Kemp had fallen in love with his piece of cheese from the moment he unwrapped it and placed it before him. But he was a little surprised as it had exceeded his expectations.

Catching his breath he spoke, "Anyway, John, one thing for sure, I am by now certain we all would have located the thing on radar, and more than likely our assailant would have disposed of the aggressor. However, General, you seem to be fairly sure in your own reasoning therefore I'll withdraw my thoughts from this conversation. Oh, by the way, thank you. Yes I did have a very successful visit to Jodrell Bank. I am able to confirm Professor Ponsonby acknowledged there was nothing more to be said regarding the space demon theory, and any problem that meets the disillusioned eye. He has willingly joined the Operation Ghostbusters team. The following data is what I have already received. Please allow me to read you part of his report."

There was a rustle of paper as Marchant turned over the pages. He then began to read:

"30 July 2017. 06.08 hours.

"With reference to the immense radio interference experienced your information concerning any issues about operations in the area near Jan Mayen Island. This has given us sufficient data to enable that we may advise the following:

"The radio beam as detected and analysed is deemed to have extended from the Earth to approximately six hundred and fifty miles above the planet's surface at its peak. Thereafter, and somehow, it has returned as an even greater force making contact with the Earth's surface somewhere near the Arctic Circle, this being three hundred and fifty-nine miles at its fall. Jodrell Bank Tracking has located near the vicinity of its peak the Russian space platform *Vostok*. As yet, it is not clear if this radio beam has any link with this space platform."

The report continued:

"30 July 2017. 10.15 hours.

"Again, very strong radio beams were detected coming from outer space towards Earth. Its detection point was isolated near Iceland. Jodrell Bank Tracking, in again seeking the source, recorded the position of the Russian space platform to be in the direct line of the beam. It is our firm opinion that the radio beam could possibly emanate from the space platform itself, but we do stress this position has yet to be ratified. A twenty-four hour round-the-clock surveillance is being maintained covering both the movement and orbit of the Russian space platform. We are boldly stating that there is very real evidence that the Russian space platform *Vostok* certainly did have some serious part to play regarding these mysterious radio beams all of which are logged and recorded."

Admiral Marchant finished reading and waited for any reaction or comment from General Kemp.

There was a long pause of total silence.

"Are you still there, General Kemp?"

There was no answer.

Slightly irritated the Admiral thought, *Well, what do you think of that? All that reading and no reply.*

"Come, come, General, what have you got to say about that lot?"

While listening, Kemp had been checking over G.O.D.'s printed graphs to ensure the Jodrell Bank data definitely checked out with the combined sightings and timings of those advised by the United States Air Force Strategic Air Command. Together, it matched!

"Hell's fire and rattlesnakes!" exclaimed Kemp. "Raymond, I knew it! I darned well knew it! Those conniving Russkies are definitely conjuring up something very nasty. Admiral, I am sure you will now agree about that. Furthermore, you know that we shall have to combine our evidence, but I like you, as yet, cannot detect any motive or purpose behind what the hell it is those damned Russkies are up to."

Marchant interrupted, "Hey, hey, John! Now simmer down. I hope you've got those reports of yours totally under wraps. It goes without saying if this lot gets out there would be a total panic."

"I also do trust, Admiral, that your files cannot be got at. I'd hate it if we both went off half-cocked at this moment in time." The General, now very agitated, realised if the bubble was now going to burst he had no reason to fear anything seeing he had his closest of allies there to back him up. If the position really did become too hot for his own comfort he hoped he could rely on Raymond Marchant.

Admiral Marchant was completely satisfied he now had General Kemp totally engulfed in his sphere of operations. In regard to Northwood HQ sustaining any information about US Naval affairs, the Admiral estimated Kemp would keep him abreast of all issues that in any way were too difficult to investigate. To quell any undue concern, Marchant thought he had better lay foundations to achieve his aim.

"Well, John, we shall have to wait and see what our submarines can trace, but maybe we already have something unwittingly recorded on video which could have got by us unnoticed. I'll do my best to see that our boys put a fix on anything unusual. Of course, I trust you are in full agreement with everything I have said?" There was no reply. "Well, I think that about wraps things up for now, don't you?"

Kemp pondered for a moment then replied, "I guess so. There's not a lot we can do about it now. Well, not until all the evidence surfaces supporting our current findings and joint suspicions. Raymond, we shall just have to keep plugging at it. I'll say goodbye to you for now."

"No problem, John. Thank you for the call."

"You bet. Thank you very much for all the info regarding Jodrell Bank Tracking. Bye for now."

As Kemp put down the telephone he began muttering to himself, "I darned well know those Reds are up to something. I just wish to heck I could put my finger on it."

The time was 20.30 hours EST.

General Kemp called Sergeant Lance. He requested his car be brought around.

Time for home he thought to himself as he walked along the corridor.

"Night, Sergeant. See you at eight sharp, unless something else comes out of the woodwork to upset the night."

Sergeant Lance smiled back then acknowledged. "Good night, sir."

As the glass door closed behind him, the General's silhouette disappeared into the back of a black limousine. A roar of the vehicle's engine was heard and then it was gone.

Sergeant Lance walked slowly over to the main door. He placed the key into the internal lock which then activated and set all the external night alarms. He then made his way back to his desk and turned on the television. He settled down to watch a replay of the weekend's baseball league games.

Chapter Ten

Royal Naval Headquarters, Northwood

The heavy aroma of Lieutenant Henderson's percolating coffee filled the operations room. Henderson had been on duty since 06.30 hours awaiting the arrival of Commander Thompson.

The night operations log showed there had been navigational changes regarding the position of *HMS Excalibur*. Northwood was waiting for Commodore Brianston-Green's full report concerning his submarines rescue mission plus any details of identification of the aircraft involved in the fatal catastrophe.

"Good morning, Henderson," Commander Thompson announced as he entered the operations room heading in the direction of his office.

"Good morning, sir, and what may I ask is the first day of the month of August looking like outside?" Henderson was hoping the weather report was going to be a favourable one.

"It feels a little humid this morning. Do we have any report or news from *HMS Excalibur*?"

"Nothing as yet, sir."

A telephone rang. Commander Thompson answered it. "Yes. Good morning, Admiral Marchant. Just one moment please, sir." He put his hand over the receiver and in a loud whisper called to Lieutenant Henderson and said, "Ian! Do we have any change of course regarding the *Bowevil*?"

"Yes, sir, the Yank sub is heading in a west-south-westerly direction. Speed is estimated at thirty-two knots."

"Good show," responded the Commander. Still whispering, he continued, "Henderson, make sure the information that's given to us is consistent with that given out to the public sector and media."

Henderson gave a sign gesturing he had received the message. He made a note of the Commander's instructions then began telephoning the airlines.

Prior to having a late breakfast, Commodore Brianston-Green had been completing entries into the ship's log.

The time was 08.05 hours, 3 August.

The Commodore lifted the telephone on his cabin desk and called the bridge. "Could you please ask Lieutenant Bergman to come to my cabin?"

"Right you are, sir," came a reply from the officer of the watch. Soon there was a knock on the door of the Commodore's cabin.

"Come in."

"You called me, Commodore?"

"Yes, Bergman, I did. Please sit down. As you are already aware, earlier this morning during the burial service we all saw some form of very unusual lights flashing in the sky. I am sure there's some simple explanation for this, but I must say I have never experienced anything quite like it all the time I have been at sea. Therefore, I wish to confirm to you I have written details of the brief episode into the ship's log. But, significantly and more important, I wish you to take charge regarding any replay and re-tracking of the radio video recorder. This is to be done immediately so we can verify nothing unusual was recorded.

"I request this to be actioned right away owing to the fact at the time of the burial ceremony everyone was on deck for the service. Consequently, our operations were totally unmanned. Lieutenant, any untoward oddity that might turn up out of the blue on the video recorder, please book it in the log. I'll then require a full report. Is that quite clear?"

Bergman nodded his head.

The Commodore continued, "Please kindly observe the strictest security. I request this because I don't want any scandalous rumours being passed about the submarine. I trust that is clearly understood?"

Again, Bergman nodded.

"I also suggest you choose one able-bodied seaman to help and assist you. That is, of course, if you think you are in need of one."

"I fully understand. Thank you, sir. I'll begin operations at once." Bergman saluted then left the cabin, closing the door behind him.

"Bridge to Commodore Brianston-Green. Please kindly contact the bridge," sounded the ship's tannoy.

Commodore Brianston-Green, with the ship's chaplain, had gone forward to survey the state of the humble makeshift chapel of rest which had hurriedly been prepared. They were both passing through some watertight doors when a message bellowed forth. Commodore Brianston-Green unhooked a voice link speaker which was just inside the door's entrance.

"This is the Commodore speaking. Yes, Officer of the Watch. What is it?"

"Sir, we have picked up a very strong radar contact east-north-east of our current position."

"Do we have any idea what it is?" asked the Commodore.

"Not as yet, sir, but it appears to be travelling at a very good rate in our direction, sir."

Brianston-Green paused for a moment. "I'm sorry, Chaplain. I'll have to go back to the bridge. Something unexpected has just come up. I will try and get back to you as soon as possible."

"I quite understand, sir. I'll carry on checking the inventory. Maybe, you can get back to me later on." The chaplain gave the Commodore a salute.

Commodore Brianston-Green then turned and made his way to the bridge.

On board the *Bowevil,* Captain Jack Maxman had acknowledged SMSB at Holy Loch in Scotland and to US Naval Headquarters at Charleston, South Carolina. He had confirmed his submarine would try and meet up with the British Navy's *HMS Excalibur.* It was considered this would be done in case any assistance was needed which could jointly be co-ordinated.

"We have made contact with a large object, Captain. It's coming in our direction from west-south-west and at a distance of about two hundred miles. I would consider at the rate it is travelling, and with our making a maximum speed of thirty-two knots, it can only be that British sub."

Captain Maxman looked at the monitor. "It must be doing at least thirty-five knots plus by the look of things.

"Okay, Number One, send out a friendly coded message. Let it read as follows: OUR WISH TO MEET YOU FOR THE FIRST TIME IS NEAR TO HAPPENING – STOP – LET US HAVE YOUR ETA – STOP – WE CAN THEN CALCULATE YOUR POSITION FROM THIS – STOP – OVER – END MESSAGE. I think that should do it." Captain Maxman gave his officer a wink.

The message went out at 08.25 hours. At 08.33 hours the *Bowevil* received a reply that read:

TIME: 08.32 HOURS 3 AUGUST 2017

FROM: EXCALIBUR REF: CDE: 057/001

TO: BOWEVIL THANK YOU YOUR MESSAGE – STOP – WE ESTIMATE SURFACING IN APPROX FOUR HOURS IF YOUR READING IS

Captain Maxman was pleased the same closed coding had been observed. He didn't want any strange unexpected visit from an unknown predator. He somehow felt the *Bowevil* had already had a narrow miss with an unknown adversary.

"We'll surface at 13.35 hours, Number One. Will you take over for now? I'll be in my cabin." Captain Maxman advised he wanted everything shipshape. This was in case they were to receive any visitors.

Ten miles west of *HMS Excalibur*, the *Gorbachev* was gradually distancing itself. The Russian submarine had followed the British submarine since it had dived at 04.50 hours.

Captain Narodny observed a new blip had appeared on the radar screen. He immediately gave instructions for the engine room to ease back the submarine's speed to twenty knots. "Thereafter, await my further instructions."

Royal Naval Headquarters, Northwood

Commander Thompson observed the time on his diving watch. It was 11.40 hours. Lieutenant Henderson had just delivered an up-to-date report compiled by the airlines so an accurate message could be forwarded to *HMS Excalibur*.

The Commander was in the middle of drafting the final text when the telephone rang.

"Is that you, Thompson?" It was Admiral Marchant. "Have the airlines released any official statement yet regarding the tragedy?"

Commander Thompson hesitated He had a feeling Admiral Marchant might treat the situation as a hot potato. He was pleased that everything up to now had gone according to plan. "Yes, sir, we have just received them. I am in the process of completing a final draft for your approval. I will then dispatch it for the attention of Commodore Brianston-Green on board *HMS Excalibur*."

Admiral Marchant was pleasantly surprised to hear Thompson's remarks. "Good," he said, "read it to me."

The Commander was not sure how to answer the Admiral. He was just in the throes of writing the text and didn't wish to expose any unforeseen technical errors which might have been made.

"Come on, Thompson. What's your problem? I thought you said

it was already done. Now let's hear it." Admiral Marchant was pressing Thompson because he was due to depart for an early luncheon. He had hoped all major obstacles of the day would have been cleared prior to his departure.

"Well, sir, in essence the report covers both airline statements." Thompson was not quite sure what to say next.

"I see. Call me back within fifteen minutes, and by then I hope you might have found time to get the text ready for my approval. Do you hear me, Thompson? Get it done!"

The line then went dead.

Commander Thompson carefully pieced together the final draft. It read:

TIME: 12.15 HOURS 3 AUGUST 2017

FROM: NORTHWOOD HQ

TO: HMS EXCALIBUR

YOUR MESSAGE OF 10.25 HOURS IS WELL RECEIVED – STOP – HAVE ARRANGED EXCHANGE OF THE DEAD WITH THE FLEET AUXILIARY HMS GERIANT – STOP – WE WILL FORWARD TIME AND RENDEZVOUS WITH YOU WITHIN NEXT TWO HOURS – STOP –YOUR ADVICE RE: AIRCRAFT IS AFFIRMATIVE – STOP – BA CONFIRM IN REPORT RELEASED 10.00 HOURS STRONG BELIEF A BOMB ATTACK – STOP – REASON GIVEN FOR THIS IS AIRCRAFT WAS CARRYING BRITISH MILITARY – STOP – PRESS AGENCY IS WAITING FOR ANY CONFIRMATION FROM ANY TERRORIST ORGANISATION TO SEE IF THEY CARRIED OUT THIS COWARDLY ACT – STOP – AIR INDIA HAVE ISSUED A SIMILAR STATEMENT – STOP –THEY AWAIT CONFIRMATION REGARDING BELIEF THAT SIKH EXTREMISTS HAD PLANTED A BOMB – STOP – BOTH AIRLINES THANK THE VIGILANCE AND ASSISTANCE OF THE ROYAL NAVY PLUS THEIR IMMENSE CONSIDERATION AND HUMANE ACTION IN BURYING SOME OF THE DEAD – STOP – DEEPEST GRATITUDE IS EXTENDED REGARDING YOUR ACCOMODATION OF AS MANY BODIES AS POSSIBLE FOR INDENTIFICATION FOR THE CHANCE OF A LAND BURIAL – STOP – END MESSAGE

It was 11.56 hours when Commander Thompson dialled Admiral Marchant's telephone number. It rang a few times before the Admiral answered. "Is that you, Thompson? About time! Well, did you finish it?"

"Yes, sir. After reading it to you, and you giving consent, I'll dispatch it immediately. Oh, by the way, in haste I almost overlooked something. British Airways advised that it had repeatedly received threats; these threats stated that a terrible tragedy would occur if BA continued to allow use of their service by British soldiers. It was the soldiers using the BA flights while returning home from their bases overseas that could have given cause for the flight to be bombed. Personally, Admiral, I do not think this information is particularly relevant for forwarding on to Commodore Brianston-Green." Thompson paused for a moment. He wasn't sure if he had exceeded his authority by making that last remark. "Would you still like me to read the message, sir?"

"Yes, Thompson, please proceed."

The Commander read the text. "Is it all right to send now, sir?"

"Good show, Derek. Right, send that text right away to *HMS Excalibur.*"

Admiral Marchant spoke again. "Yes, the first text you read will do fine. Send it off in its current form, but do hold back that BA reminder. You were right, Thompson, not to include any of that stuff in this *communiqué*. Well, now that's all done I must be off to lunch. Let me know the precise time the message is sent out. I'll speak to you later on when I get back."

"Thank you, Admiral. Have a good lunch, sir," Thompson responded feeling relieved he hadn't had his head taken off for being in any way above his station.

Royal Naval Headquarters, Northwood transmitted the message to *HMS Excalibur* at 12.15 hours. Within half an hour back came a reply. It read:

TIME: 12.40 HOURS 3 AUGUST 2017
FROM: HMS EXCALIBUR
TO: RN HQ NORTHWOOD
WE ARE PROCEEDING NORTH-NORTH-EASTWARDS – STOP – WILL MEET SSN BOWEVIL IN NEXT TWO HOURS – STOP – REQUEST ASSISTANCE IN ORDER TO CLARIFY OUR RECORDS – STOP – AT 04.30 HOURS OUR TIME – STOP – WE HAVE A VIDEO RADAR RECORDING WITH REFERENCE OF A LARGE OBJECT WHICH APPEARED ON OUR SCREEN NO MORE THAN TEN MILES EAST-SOUTH-EAST OF OUR POSITION – STOP – DO YOU HAVE ANY IDEA AS TO WHAT IS WAS – STOP – THE BLIP WAS SHOWING FOR ABOUT THIRTY TO FORTY FIVE SECONDS – STOP – NO IDENTIFICATION WAS MADE AT THE TIME – STOP – THIS WAS DUE THE FACT ALL HANDS WERE UP

TOP ATTENDING THE FUNERAL SERVICE – STOP – WE ALSO HAD ANOTHER STRANGE OBSERVATION AT ABOUT THE SAME TIME – STOP – BRIGHT FLASHING LIGHTS FILLED THE SKY ALL AROUND US IN SAME DIRECTION OF THE RADAR SIGHTING – STOP – CAN YOU ASSIST IN ORDER TO CLEAR AWAY ANY THOUGHTS OF SEA MONSTERS OR MAYBE A PRESENCE OF ANY NASTY SEA BOGIES BEING UNEXPECTEDLY BROUGHT TO THE SURFACE – STOP – END MESSAGE – SIGNED COMMODORE BRAINSTON-GREEN HMS EXCALIBUR

Commander Thompson read the reply. Gradually the expression on his face changed from one of satisfaction to one of awe and he thought to himself, *Nothing seems to be right. What the heck was it out there in the Atlantic Ocean the Excalibur had picked up on its radar. Could the Russian sub be out there lurking, waiting to pounce?*

Thompson felt uneasy and was concerned about HMS Excalibur's last message.

Chapter Eleven

In Space

Thursday, 3 August 2017. It was nearing 15.00 hours. The Earth shone brightly beaming back a kaleidoscope of many different colours; there were reds, browns, all intermixed with the different and changing greens of fertile land. Yellow and orange areas of the hottest deserts glowed intermittently appearing through volumes of swirling cloud masses. The two huge frozen white caps of both polar-regions glinted as they reflected rays of the sun which seemingly bounced back far out into space.

The Russian space platform *Vostok* was slowly orbiting the earth with its two huge solar sun batteries splayed open like some strange giant albatross gliding about in infinite space. Inside the space station cosmonauts steadily monitored and watched the radar screen directed towards the North Atlantic. It was currently fixed upon a particular position. A second screen equipped with a rapidly revolving dial constantly maintained watch at close quarters for any intruder. The space platform's crew had been fully involved with the programme called Operation Invisible; they had operated it with total co-ordination and faultless precision. It appeared nothing would expose or jeopardise the carefully concealed plan.

"Submarine *Gorbachev* is now twenty miles from the American and British submarines. We will soon have it in radar contact so we can effect any modification or minor repairs," Major Chitov, the space platform Commander, said to his men while they were carrying out their normal daily duties. As he continued to speak a formation of dots appeared on the radar screen, and they appeared to be moving at great speed.

One of the operators spoke. "Commander, I believe we have a shower of meteors in our location."

"I see. Please keep me informed of their direction and progress."

The huge platform was fairly solid and capable of withstanding a certain amount of bombardment, but a shower of meteors could well inflict severe damage.

Major Chitov gave his men their instructions. "Just in case we have to cut back our inner power units, close the outer solar battery circuits. Activate this at once!"

Immediately, engines exercising the computer began a programme of withdrawal. Slowly the massive solar arms started to arch then fold in effecting the shutdown manoeuvre.

On the radar screen the little white dots now showed clearly.

"Fourteen I believe, sir," said Yuri, its operator.

"Are they going to miss us? Tell me that, man, not how many there seem to be," Major Chitov responded sharply.

The space platform's navigator interrupted. "Sir, if we maintain our current orbit I do believe they should pass us by, but, as yet, we've not been able to establish their speed. Therefore, we are unable to estimate the velocity of impact. At this moment the meteors are approaching us at a very steep angle."

Major Chitov looked again at the radar screen. He studied carefully the simulated video progress programmer. "I am also not so sure whether they will hit us or not. But I would say we have a fifty-fifty chance and, as a precaution, I think we had better lock tight all external emergency exits. Also, for our added safety, switch on the anti-magnetic force field shield. Hopefully, this should generate sufficient strength and have power enough to steer us away from any possible direct impact. Send a coded message to Moscow and Kapustin Yar. Advise them of all the emergency manoeuvres and urgent precautions we have taken. Made ready the laser missiles so we can take evasive action if necessary."

There was now a feeling of tension. An air of unexpected anxiety crept into the atmosphere surrounding the space platform's crew.

"We estimate possible impact in about four minutes, sir," advised one of the section crew operators.

"Arm the missiles!" came the Major's order. "Prepare to launch in three minutes from now!"

The radar clearly showed the grouped shower of meteors. All were approaching fast on a near collision course.

"Launch now the Red Army's orbiter space shuttle." Major Chitov, sensing the emergency, had prepared a skeleton crew to man the Russian military space shuttle. "Have it blast away from the space platform to a distance of safety." He hoped it would be able to get away in time.

"Two minutes and thirty seconds to go until possible impact, sir," came a voice from the space platform's operations room.

Major Chitov, together with the other crew members, watched the shape of the Russian space shuttle orbiter gradually distance itself from the space platform.

"One minute and thirty seconds until expected time of impact . Major, they seem to be on a course that could possibly strike us on our starboard side, sir."

"FIRE! FIRE!" came the Major's order.

There was a tremendous roar. A broadside of a dozen missiles raced off into space. Their heat-seeking laser beams quickly locked on to track the unseen targets. The seconds ticked by. Then, at what seemed to be a fairly close distance, a number of explosions erupted in space around the space platform sending orange and red molten fragments cascading in all directions. It was just like watching the climax of a massive fireworks display. Twenty seconds to impact was the recorded time when the laser rockets struck their targets.

"What does the radar screen show now?" Major Chitov asked.

"Nothing yet, sir. Twelve seconds to impact."

The radar still showed something approaching.

"There are still two unidentified objects approaching us at great speed. Five, four, three, two, one…

There was one tremendous explosion at a point of impact somewhere on the outer frame of the space platform.

Momentarily, all the lights dimmed.

An arm of the main solar battery system had been ripped away from the space platform's starboard side to become a distant satellite of space junk.

The radar still showed a single dot moving away earthwards which was eventually to burn itself up while entering the Earth's atmosphere.

"What damage to the platform do we have? Is there any leakage?" shouted the Major.

"No, sir. However, we have now gone on to auxiliary power as the main power supply has failed," came back the reply from the Chief Engineer.

"Is there anyone injured?"

"No, sir."

"Send a message to Moscow, also to Central Space Control. Confirm we have suffered major damage. Advise them that we have had to shut down the total system for emergency repairs. State we might be able to be operational on half strength but not for at least two hours." Major Chitov wasn't totally sure whether this could be achieved." Well, Chief Engineer, tell me how bad it really is."

"We'll recover, sir. But, all will take time. However, in order to quickly achieve the repairs you will have to shut down the radar screens operating Operation Invisible. If you don't we will not be able to generate enough supply for our mains power. I should state that when the men have altered the system to operate singularly from the port side solar battery arm, we should at least expect to be operating at about eighty percent our normal strength." The Chief Engineer continued to browse over his technical staff's hurriedly drafted details.

On looking at the man and not really knowing what to believe, Major Chitov said, "I see. Let us hope Moscow can contain whatever it is that has to remain secret under Operation Invisible. I do hope they accept that they will have to do this for a minimum of two hours. Order the shuttle orbiter to try and catch the lost solar battery arm, or should I say what remains of it. I'm sure we might be able to repair it if the solar cells have remained intact."

Throughout the emergency Major Chitov remained as calm as ever. He showed an air of coolness unprecedented amongst his fellow men. The whole crew respected him for his nerves of steel and perceptive judgement. Moscow also knew of his singular quality. The Major was the longest surviving astronaut of the space platform operational officers team, and was now in his seventh year of space service.

"Moscow is reporting, sir," advised the communications operator.

"Thank you, Grymikov. Please bring the message to me when you have deciphered it."

The time was 16.05 hours. The message read:

16.01 HOURS 03/08/17 MSCW TO VSTK –
PRIORITY ONE/TOP CONFIDENTIAL
YOUR EFFORTS ARE TO QUICKLY REPAIR DAMAGE AT ALL COSTS
– STOP – THIS ORDER IS PARAMOUNT – STOP – YOU HOLD IN
YOUR HANDS THE DESTINY OF OUR COUNTRY – STOP – WE
AWAIT CONFIRMATION OF YOUR TIME FOR RE-ESTABLISHING
OPERATIONS OF THE RADAR SCREEN – STOP – WE ARE PLEASED
OUR COMRADES HAVE ALL SURVIVED – STOP – YOUR REPORT BY
RETURN IS DEMANDED – STOP – END MESSAGE
SIGNED C-IN-C MOSCOW

Major Chitov knew High Command would obviously have problems due to the space platform's major malfunction. There was nothing else he could do for the moment other than have his crew work to quickly repair the damage.

Grymikov broke the silence. "We have heard from the space shuttle orbiter, sir. They are surprised to see we have survived. The Commander has stated, from where they were watching, it looked as though we had been blown to smithereens."

Major Chitov paused to think. "Well, I do believe that sometimes an extreme element of luck is held in all things. This time, I am happy to say, it was with us. Right, we must quickly get on with things. Please request that the shuttle orbiter immediately goes hunting for our missing power lifeline. This is imperative so we may continue the space mission and maintain our existence. Tell them we have to be operational and back at full strength as soon as possible. I just hope this will all be done within the next two hours."

Over the space platform's tannoy system, Major Chitov advised the crew of the situation. "Men, it is now a priority one order that we are back to operational power in under two hours."

The Major was agitated by Grymikov's slowness of instruction given to the space shuttle orbiter's captain. However, realising the difficulties of communication, he let it pass. He was more concerned as to why Moscow had advised it was so critical that Operation Invisible had to be back on stream.

With his mind trying to fathom out what really was going on back down on Earth, Major Chitov sat staring out into the black abyss wondering what he had been drawn into.

At Sea

The *Gorbachev* was progressing on its course at a depth of one hundred and seventy-five feet. The submarine was hastily beating a wider distance in order to diminish any possible chance of radar contact. At 13.03 hours, Moscow sent a confidential coded message for the attention of Captain Narodny. It read:

16.02:45 03/08/17 MSCW TO GORBACHEV
ATTN: CAPTAIN NARODNY – PRIORITY ONE/TOP CONFIDENTIAL
AT 15.45 HOURS VOSTOK BADLY DAMAGED – STOP – I BELIEVE YOU
ARE AWARE YOU ARE NOW EXPOSED – STOP – YOUR POSITION
INDICATES YOU ARE MAKING FOR OPEN SEAS – STOP – IT IS HOPED
AND EXPECTED OPERATIONS WILL BE NORMAL BY 18.00 HOURS –
STOP – YOU ARE THEREFORE ORDERED TO RUN SILENT AND RUN
VERY DEEP – STOP – END MESSAGE
SIGNED C-IN-C MOSCOW

Captain Narodny did not reveal the contents of the message to the crew. Only the team of privileged operators had any idea as to what the real situation was or meant. They were all sworn to total secrecy.

The Captain called the operations room from the bridge. "Radar operations, do we still have contact with the British and American submarines?"

There was a slight pause as the operator checked the screen. "We do, sir. But, I expect us to be out of their radar contact in about thirty-five minutes."

"Thank you," Captain Narodny replied. After a few moments of thought he gave further orders. "Engine room set all operations for silent running. Raise our speed to maximum thrust. Lower our depth to two hundred feet. For the next two hours we are going to make swift haste towards the open sea." Captain Narodny then turned and gave new instructions to his men on the bridge. "Officer of the Watch, set our new course south-south-east."

"Aye, aye, Captain," came the officer's response.

The ordered acceleration of speed took effect as the *Gorbachev* ploughed on. Nikita Narodny looked at his watch. The time was 14.15 hours. Whatever was going to happen, he knew his submarine could well have been located by any ship's radar in its current vicinity, or within a radius of sixty miles. Now with the submarine having been exposed for over thirty minutes, he hoped its distance was now greater than the eye could see. He hoped the *Gorbachev* was now out of any immediate danger.

On board the *Bowevil*, Captain Maxman had sent a message to Commodore Brianston-Green requesting a surface encounter take place within the next half hour. Each submarine gradually had eaten up the miles between them. It was over six hours since agreement for them to meet was cleared. *HMS Excalibur,* however, had maintained a very sedate pace allowing the *Bowevil* to increase its speed in order to meet with it.

At 15.46:17 hours, while logging a new radar position of *HMS Excalibur,* the *Bowevil* recorded the sighting of another large object about thirty miles south-south-east of the British submarine's position. At 15.51:10 hours, Captain Maxman received a message from Commodore Brianston-Green. The message read:

15.51 HOURS 3 AUGUST 2017
FROM: EXCALIBUR
TO: BOWEVIL
WE REQUEST YOU CHECK OUR POSITION – STOP – DO YOU READ

US TO BE AT 42.0 S – 25.9 SW FOR ENSURING OUR EXACT RADAR POSITION CONTACT – STOP – PLEASE ADVISE RGDS – STOP PS – WE WILL DISCUSS ALL MATTERS WHEN WE MEET – STOP – WE EXPECT TO SURFACE AT 16.21 HOURS – STOP – LOOK FORWARD TO MEETING YOU – STOP – END MESSAGE

While passing through to the bridge, Commodore Brianston-Green entered the communications room in order to see if Captain Maxman of the *Bowevil* had sent back an acknowledgement to his last message. As he did so he gave a quick look at the submarine's radar screen to see how close the US Navy submarine was. On looking he noticed there were six dots spaced across the screen. One he recognised as the *Bowevil,* three were listed as surface vessels – one of those being the expected Royal Naval Auxiliary vessel *HMS Geriant – and* the other two were logged as large container ships.

The Commodore enquired, "Have you got any idea as to what those other two sightings are?"

"No, not yet, sir," replied the operator. "We have been tracking both of them constantly since the time of our diving from the scene of the disaster area. However, one of them has maintained its course and position for a long time. The other object appeared on the screen just over half an hour ago. We are trying to make some sort headway on its identity from information taken from the data logged off the video recorder sonar scan which was covering the area and section sat the time. We hope to have some form of positive identification shortly."

"Good show," replied the Commodore. "How long do you think all this might take?"

"Sir, we should have the situation covered by about 18.00 hours. However, we're not quite certain how long the full scan recording took. To be on the safe side, I would estimate a result could be made ready in about one and a half hours."

"Please notify me as soon as you have clarified a firm identification and reading." The Commodore then made his way back to the bridge.

It was now 16.15 hours. Brianston-Green picked up the bridge telephone. "Good afternoon, Lieutenant Bergman." The Lieutenant had just come back on watch. "We are about to surface to encounter the United States Navy, Archie."

"Really, Commodore? Where the devil did they suddenly appear from?"

"No, no, it's their nuke submarine *SSN Bowevil*. Immediately after we have surfaced, please release an invitation for Captain Maxman to come aboard. I'd prefer that he get his feet wet rather than me. When we are up top prepare the crew to make ready. Ensure in your message you duly offer the Yanks the hospitality of our officers' mess."

"Aye, aye, sir."

"Do you know what I really dislike about all this stuff, Bergman?"

"No, sir. Please tell me."

"I hate being piped aboard by the sounds of a full-sized brass band. I suppose we shall have to suffer it if they do insist we go over and visit them. That's why it's imperative you get that message out first. Okay?"

Lieutenant Bergman gave the Commodore a polite nod.

Brianston-Green continued. "Anyway, let us wait and see. I'll wish to speak to Captain Maxman as soon as we get on to a one-to-one speaking frequency then quickly clear any dubious areas of security. I'll have each of us compare our independent information regarding these unidentified sightings as confirmed on each other's radar, and also any possible visual contact. I am sure we might get somewhere regarding this situation. Anyway, Bergman, see to it all is made ready. Are there any questions?"

Bergman gave a polite smile. "No, sir. I'll put all matters you have requested into action right away."

As Lieutenant Bergman left to carry out the Commodore's instructions, the submarine's tannoy sounded. "This is the Commodore speaking. We are about to surface to rendezvous with the US Navy. Please be informed, I do expect we are going to be receiving visitors. Therefore, men, your best behaviour please. That is all."

Within seconds the tannoy roared, "SURFACE! SURFACE!"

At 16.21 hours, somewhere in mid-Atlantic, the sleek shape of *HMS Excalibur* broke the surface of the ocean to greet a sunny afternoon.

It was a clear sky and a moderately calm sea. The hatches of the flying bridge and conning tower soon opened and the duty men of the watch quickly took up their positions. A breeze could be felt blowing in the warmth of the mid-afternoon sunshine.

"Sir, there's a submarine surfacing on our port side," a lookout shouted.

At that moment Commodore Brianston-Green stepped out from the conning tower hatch on to the top deck of the upper bridge. "Thank you, Able Seaman Spence. That should, I hope, be the US Navy's submarine the *SSN Bowevil*."

Brianston-Green looked about him then across the sea and out towards the horizon. He then turned to the men of the watch and said, "I presume there should now be a fanfare of trumpets."

Brianston-Green was never quite sure how to take or receive American hospitality. He had heard many stories from the past that had left him positively speechless. He hoped and trusted the Yanks' world would somewhat have changed since those far off days.

Slowly the greyish hull of the *Bowevil* levelled out on to the ocean surface.

Within minutes both submarines were stationed at close quarters.

Suddenly there was a loud high-pitched whining sound which seemed as if a tannoy system was being tuned in. After which a voice bellowed: "GOOD AFTERNOON HMS EXCALIBUR. GREETINGS FROM THE UNITED STATES OF AMERICA NUCLEAR SUBMARINE BOWEVIL. THIS IS CAPTAIN JACK MAXMAN SPEAKING. I WISH TO SPEAK WITH COMMODORE BRIANSTON-GREEN."

There was a slight pause then, a loudspeaker from *HMS Excalibur* gave its reply.

"I AM PLEASED TO SPEAK WITH YOU CAPTAIN MAXMAN. THIS IS COMMODORE BRIANSTON-GREEN SPEAKING. PLEASE KINDLY ACCEPT HER MAJESTY'S SUBMARINE'S INVITATION TO COME ABOARD AND CORDIALLY VISIT OUR OFFICERS' MESS AT YOUR CONVENIENCE. WE SHALL BE WILLING TO ESTABLISH A BREECHES BUOY IN ORDER TO FERRY YOU ACROSS."

There was a sudden silence.

After a pause of about a minute, the *Bowevil*'s tannoy again burst into life.

"YOUR INVITATION IS ACCEPTED WITH THANKS. A PARTY OF TWO WILL BE MAKING THE VISIT."

A dull thump of an explosion was heard after which a plume of white smoke was seen dissipating into the air from the deck of *HMS Excalibur*.

A signal rocket with a line attached swiftly raced towards the forward deck of the *Bowevil*.

Six seamen mustered in readiness each having quickly surfaced from a small forward hatch. The line passed about ten feet from the huge stack of the American submarine's conning tower. It was soon collected.

Some seamen began hauling at the main rope, which was to be made secure for connecting shackles, pulleys and the chair. Finally, the rope line reached the exposed deck of the *Bowevil*. It was quickly transferred and fastened from the deck to the conning tower.

On board *HMS Excalibur*, the same main rope line was fixed tight and the chair made safe for transportation.

Soon the figure of Lieutenant Douglas Odbie was seen gently swaying above the waves as each submarine maintained a slow but steady passage.

It was not long before Lieutenant Odbie arrived safely on the deck of *HMS Excalibur* to be greeted by Lieutenant Bergman after which the chair was whisked back to the *Bowevil*.

Within two minutes, Captain Maxman came over to start proceedings of the American Navy's cordial visit.

Commodore Brianston-Green joined the welcoming party on the conning tower bridge as the sound of the seaman's whistle piped aboard the US Navy.

For a brief moment, all parties saluted each other.

The Commodore then offered a handshake of friendship to the visiting Captain. It was not too long before the edge of nervous tension, often accorded to a first time meeting, soon disappeared.

Captain Jack Maxman was very impressed with all he had been allowed to see of the running operations of *HMS Excalibur*. He congratulated Commodore Brianston-Green and his crew on the efficiency of the British submarine. Furthermore, he respected how the British had reverently handled the difficult task of maintaining a house of mourning for the ninety-nine air disaster victims whose laying out had been hastily arranged in an improvised chapel of rest.

"Tragic circumstances, sir," remarked Captain Maxman.

"It is," came back the Commodore's reply. "I do think that we should first visit our communications centre. Thereafter, we can discuss the various matters that are currently unanswerable."

Jack Maxman nodded his head in agreement. He allowed the Commodore to lead the way.

Once or twice Captain Maxman stopped to observe little technical differences of construction between his submarine and that of the British vessel. Overall he was very impressed, and he made the occasional comment that he wished his command had arranged some of the basic elementary issues of storage and creature comforts he saw in the British submarine.

Soon, both officers arrived at the Commodore's quarters.

"Well now, Captain, let's get down to business."

The meeting and discussions covered every issue: the loss of the Russian submarine *Gorbachev*, the somewhat unusual circumstance surrounding the disappearance of the SS *Andros* and the air disasters.

Finally, they came to the sighting of the flashing lights which for now could only be described as unidentified flying objects. They also discussed coverage of the unexplained radar screen sightings. It was acknowledged both submarines had recorded these.

Commodore Brianston-Green spoke, "I am not at all convinced, Captain, the Russians and CIS have had no part to play regarding all these strange goings-on. One would not have thought it possible what with the world seeming to be such a peaceful place no more than two months ago. Now we have strange things supposedly going on in space, the surprise loss of that Russian sub, the disappearance of that freighter plus the air disasters. What do you think of it all, Captain Maxman?"

"Quite so, Commodore, and I do appreciate you're settling both myself and Lieutenant Odbie at ease with Her Majesty's hospitality." At that moment Captain Maxman opened his leather desk folder, and then continued speaking. "However, and as you have rightly pointed out, we do have a number of very serious issues to quickly cut through. Therefore, let's see if there's any real substance to come out of our government's investigations."

After nearly an hour of discussions, light refreshments were served in the officers' mess.

Both parties agreed the meeting was of significant importance. Each side now had sufficient evidence to forward to their respective Naval Headquarters; the matter of decision-making was not their concern.

"Well, Captain, I am sure we do agree on one thing."

"And what would that be, Commodore?"

"Whatever the two unidentified objects are, one of them is likely to be a piece of fuselage from one of the aircraft which came down in the sea."

"Yes, Commodore, I think you may well be right about that in my now having seen your sonar readings and observing the different radar positions. It's these additional radar readings of the other object which really puzzle me." Captain Maxman rubbed his hand over his chin while in deep thought.

"Why is that, Captain?" remarked the Commodore.

"If we were to consider the Russian sub, in fact, did not sink then our checking both sets of radar data might give us a clue as to what really happened to it. Or, is it possible this new Russian sub could have the capacity and speed to move as swiftly as it appears to have done. If this were the case, let us blatantly say it sunk the SS *Andros* and was then supposedly sighted about two hundred and fifty miles from the area of that sinking. All this after the whole world had been told that it had sunk on its maiden voyage."

Captain Maxman stopped for a moment and took a sip of water.

"If we are to take all our assumptions on spec, Commodore, do we really have any firm idea that the object currently moving south-south-east is in fact one and the same thing? If it is we must now ask ourselves if it had anything to do with that terrible air disaster."

Commodore Brianston-Green shook his head. "Captain Maxman, I must say I'm inclined to agree with you. However, I must also state a lot of our findings are inconclusive. I also think you have overlooked one or two other points the most significant of these being the appearance of those strange lights."

On hearing this remark, Captain Maxman shook his head in acknowledgement.

The Commodore continued, "Let us now view this particular point. Whenever these phenomenon, for the want of a better word, have been sighted there appears to be some terrible tragedy or disaster reported soon after."

"Rightly so, Commodore," remarked Captain Maxman.

Brianston-Green stopped for a moment to clear his throat. "And ironically, all of these happenings seem to point, in my opinion, to our connecting the recorded positions of those radar contacts we now have on record with those of the sightings of these strange lights. What do you think, Captain?"

"This does seem feasible."

"Come, Captain. Surely you agree that last blob we noticed on radar came from the area where the air disaster happened."

"Right you are, sir. I'll give you that one," quipped Maxman.

The Commodore smiled. "Oh, by the way do not forget our radar recorders, although unmanned at the time, also made record of all radar tracking. Well, whatever we think it is, the damned thing is now underwater at a depth of about two hundred and fifty feet, and is going away from us like the clappers. What do you think, Captain? Is it making a run for it or has something gone drastically wrong?"

Captain Maxman scratched his head. "Commodore, I don't really know where to start. Certainly I have never been one for starting rumours. It sure has a heck of a lot of speed, and I don't think I have ever heard of any sub pushing along at that kinda pace. I would also describe this submarine as a hostile object. Therefore, might I suggest that we both request to our High Commands that we go hunting for the hostile in question. Are you in agreement, Commodore?"

Both officers stood up and shook hands on the matter.

Each acknowledged they would give their respective Commanders-in-Chief the same recommendation.

"After all," the Commodore interjected, "we are here on the spot. And I don't know about you but I have that funny feeling I sometimes get when an enemy is close at hand. Do you understand what I mean, Captain Maxman?"

Captain Maxman looked at his watch. "Yes I do. However, I must be getting back. Oh, one thing more I must say, Commodore. It sure has been a pleasure meetin' up with you and having the chance to visit your sub. I might have to head back to home base soon, Commodore, but you have also got the *Intrepid* out here with you. In any event I'm sure one of our subs will be joinin' you. Well, I really must be gettin' along."

"Thank you for those kind words, Captain Maxman."

They both shook hands.

Soon the visiting party was making a move towards the ladder exiting up to the conning tower. Lieutenant Bergman ushered his counterpart Lieutenant Odbie to move first, while the Commodore and Captain Maxman stood talking.

It was nearing 16.45 hours when the breeches buoy began returning the officers back to the *Bowevil*.

The lines between the two submarines were soon released and hauled back to safety.

Not long after this three loud cheers echoed by loudhailer as each submarine crew gave a farewell salute.

Slowly the submarines began to distance themselves gradually to glide down beneath the ocean waves.

After everything had settled down, Commodore Brianston-Green read a message received from Northwood Royal Naval HQ. It advised the Royal Navy Fleet Auxiliary *HMS Geriant* would rendezvous with *HMS Excalibur* within three to four hours. His instructions requested he reset his submarines course east-south-east by six degrees. *Good*, he thought, *this would now give the Excalibur an opportunity to trail the unknown radar blob from its last given position.*

Brianston-Green entered the operations room and immediately checked the radar screen for an up-to-date reading. "Keep a close eye on that one, Jenkins. Do not on any account lose sight of it. If it should disappear call me immediately."

"Right you are, sir. By the way, what is it, sir? I'll have to register it in the log. Does it have a name?" Jenkins enquired.

"Not yet. We believe it's a large bulk carrier. One that's giving everyone a slight cause for concern." Commodore Brianston-Green did not wish to alert the crew to his own suspicions.

"I see, sir. No problem, I'll keep my beady eyes on it."

At 17.00 hours Commodore Brianston-Green cabled a highly confidential message to the Admiralty in Whitehall. It was marked for the attention of Admiral Raymond Marchant RN. It also advised a copy was to be made for the attention of Commander Derek Thompson RN.

At 17.23 hours came back a reply:

TIME: 17.23 HOURS 3 AUGUST 2017
FROM: NORTHWOOD HQ
TO: HMS EXCALIBUR
TO: CMDR B-G
PLEASE WITH ALL HASTE FOLLOW IT – STOP – STAY IN PURSUIT –
STOP – END MESSAGE
SIGNED: MARCHANT – ADMIRAL RN

For a further hour and twenty minutes the radar showed the unidentified object. Suddenly, at 17.45 hours, the blob disappeared. The Commodore was immediately advised whereupon he sent a cable to Northwood HQ.

At 17.53 hours a message came back. It read:

TIME: 17.53 HOURS 3 AUGUST 2017
FROM: NORTHWOOD HQ
TO: HMS EXCALIBUR
ATT: COMMODORE BRIANSTON-GREEN
CONGRATULATIONS ON YOUR JOINT EFFORT REGARDING
MEETING THE SSN BOWEVIL – STOP – YOU CAN TAKE IT FROM US
– STOP – WE NOW HAVE TWO NAVYS LOOKING – STOP – MAINTAIN
PRESENT COURSE – STOP – HMS GERIANT WILL RENDEZVOUS WITH
YOU AT 19.15 HOURS LCL TIME – STOP – IT WILL RELIEVE YOU OF
YOUR BURDEN – STOP – GOOD HUNTING – STOP – END MESSAGE –
SIGNED MARCHANT ADMIRAL RN

The United States submarine *SSN Bowevil* had requested leave to assist *HMS Excalibur*. With a sense and feeling of disappointment, although also somewhat relieved, Captain Maxman read the cable he had received. It confirmed his submarine was instructed to proceed back to home base. Captain Maxman was to advise Charleston, South Carolina, of the *Bowevil's* estimated time of arrival.

In Space

Major Chitov was relieved his engineers on the Russian space platform *Vostok* had been able to improvise and create a fully workable power support unit. Ingeniously, they had calculated that by engineering a reconstruction of single cell components in the remaining solar battery wing, it was found this would be capable of overriding the dual power control system which had originally maintained generating the total vital life support given to the electrical systems of the space platform.

It had been a harrowing task and had taken them two hours longer than was first thought. While the work was being carried out, Moscow had been totally blacked out from all communications. The first phase of repairs was an exceedingly dangerous operation as it meant that sixty percent of the space platform's crew were outside spacewalking. All were fully aware of the hazards. All knew that if they didn't complete their tasks of repairing the vital live dual battery terminals, all life support systems on the space platform would gradually fail leaving everyone to eventually suffocate from the failing air supply.

During the shutdown, and while working to divert and create a single power house support unit source, temperatures on the space platform fell below freezing. Now only the safety of thermolite space suits would ensure any warmth to combat the intense cold and keep everyone's body temperature at a level which would allow the repair operations to progress. It was an arduous task.

The space shuttle orbiter had twice passed the *Vostok*. Its crew had reported back that they had successfully captured the stray solar battery arm. However, due to the problem of there being no power available on board the space platform, it appeared the shuttle orbiter would be unable to dock because all outer door locking mechanisms were still out of action.

Finally, at 19.32 hours, all new outer casing wiring installations and systems were completed and the huge fuse links quickly set. The switches were thrown.

Just at that time the shuttle orbiter was returning from its third set orbit. The pilot smiled at his co-pilot when he saw the welcoming sight of the space beacon. Its flashing light was rotating.

The radio on board the shuttle crackled and burst into life.

"*Vostok* to orbiter, *Vostok* to orbiter. Well done! Well done! Return to base immediately. I believe we can now say, welcome home."

The message was hurriedly sent out and relayed to the stranded visitor.

Seconds later a reply came back.

"Orbiter to *Vostok*. Congratulations! We see your guiding candle and will be docking within seven minutes."

Major Chitov watched the outer long-range zoom cameras make contact. On the VDU he saw the distant shape of the shuttle orbiter cruising ever closer. The whole episode had been a close run thing.

Moscow received notice of completion of all works at 19.43 hours.

Moscow HQ immediately enquired if it were now possible for the huge discs on the space platform's underside to be opened.

At Sea

Captain Maxman had been completing a confidential report when the telephone rang.

"Yes! Oh, Lieutenant Odbie. What is it?"

"Sir! The object we have been monitoring has moments ago completely disappeared from our radar screen."

Captain Maxman didn't really want to be disturbed but, he knew this was serious.

"Oh hell! Confirm the situation in the log. Have the radar operator keep a watchful eye out just in case that darned disappearin' blob decides to come back again."

"Okay, sir, will do."

"By the way, Odbie,"

"Yes, sir."

"I'll require the report I am completing to be scrambled by code. It should be ready in about ten minutes. Will you please drop by and collect it. See to it that it gets sent out as quickly as possible."

"No problem, sir. I will be there in just a jiffy."

Captain Maxman replaced the telephone receiver then sat back in his chair deep in thought.

Commander Thompson was in his office reading a copy of the confidential report Commodore Brianston-Green had sent to Admiral Marchant. His eyes could hardly believe what they were reading. He knew that he could receive a telephone call from the Admiral at any time.

Raymond Marchant had been enjoying his early evening glass of gin and tonic when a special courier delivered a large envelope to him.

On handing the package to the Admiral the courier requested his signature. "Thank you, young man. I must say you lads make London traffic seem to appear like it doesn't really exist. Only twenty-three minutes from Northwood to here. That must be some kind of record."

The young man smiled. "Fank you, sir. I try to make sure me bike is always purrrrin' and up ter scratch."

Admiral Marchant smiled. Somehow the lad reminded him of Toad, a character from *The Wind and the Willows*. "Could you please bike this message round to Number Ten Downing Street. In the process, try not to get caught for speeding."

The bike rider gave the Admiral a smart salute. "Core blimey, sir! Do I get to see the Prime Minister?"

"I am not so sure about that, lad, but you might just ensure that I do get back the right signature."

The young lad again saluted then swiftly departed.

It was nearing 18.30 hours on Thursday, 3 August 2017 and it had been a very hectic day.

Admiral Marchant was busy clearing all matters concerning the proposed visit of the still unknown member of the Federal State of Russia's Naval Intelligence. With his desk now relatively clear he put down the confidential dossier and began comparing some of its content with that of a file regarding *HMS Excalibur*'s report. The Admiral's eyes were sharp and his face beaming as he thought to himself, *Well now, after reading all this lot, I wonder how many more people may also begin to suspect the Russkies. At least, we have a fairly substantial backup file. Boy! I can't wait to get John Kemp's reaction to all this. Yes, I think I'll call him.*

The Admiral got himself another drink, sat down, and began dialling.

"Good afternoon, is General Kemp available?"

"No, sir, I'm sorry. He's away right now but he should be back in about thirty minutes. Shall I get him to return your call?"

"Thank you. Please tell him Admiral Raymond Marchant called and that he urgently wishes to speak with him."

"Thank you, Admiral, sir. I'll do that."

Admiral Marchant paused. "Oh, by the way, to whom am I speaking?"

"Sergeant Lance, sir."

"Fine. Thank you, Sergeant. Do make sure that he does get this message."

"No problem, Admiral. The matter will be attended too right away."

Admiral Marchant sat back in his chair and took another large sip from his glass of gin. The telephone rang as he rested his glass back on the table. "Yes!"

"Good evening, Admiral. Thompson speaking."

"Ah, hello, dear boy. Did you get your copy of B. Green's report?"

"Yes, sir, I did. That's the reason for my call. I have been comparing this report against all information we have available. Sir, I do think the matter should be handled with great caution, but…"

Admiral Marchant interrupted him.

"Yes, yes, Thompson. What the devil is it you really wish to say?"

"Well, sir, I really wish to enquire if the matter has gone forward to the PM's office?"

"Thompson, be assured, I would not let something as urgent as this be left to rest in the out tray. Do not worry yourself, man."

"No, sir. Thank you, sir."

"Anyway, what do you now think about the Russkies? Do you now feel a little more assured the *Gorbachev* really is out there somewhere? I bet it's out there just waiting to exterminate some poor unsuspecting target. Well, Derek, do you think the same as I, or don't you?"

Admiral Marchant began to exert his forcefulness.

"Come on now. Where's your gut instinct and courage, man?"

Thompson knew he shouldn't really have called the Admiral. He felt before doing so, he should have laid low and waited. Now the Admiral's tail was up.

"Sir!" he yelled back, "Please allow me to advise you and to get a word in. Yes, I do agree with the observations the report is making, but…"

"Yes, Thompson?"

"Furthermore, I merely wish to point out and for you to know that a new report is just coming through which I am certain shows you something of even greater interest."

"I see. What is that then, Derek?"

"Our agents in Siberia have just confirmed the Russian space station was put out of action for nearly fours hours today by a shower of meteorites.

They advised the reason given for the malfunction appears to have been due to the destruction of one of the space station's solar battery arms. The report further states the arm was torn off during the bombardment. Notwithstanding that, the Russians have also confirmed that a military space shuttle orbiter is assisting with the rescue of the damaged solar arm." Thompson paused to catch his breath.

The Admiral was stunned to hear this news. "Great Scott! Those bloody Russkies! They have had that nasty little machine of theirs floating around up there all the time. Thompson, I thank you for the call and for advising me of this information. We must meet sometime tomorrow. The afternoon would suit me better."

"Why, sir?"

"Heavens above, Derek, to give me time to consider what these implications really are, man. Also, what international repercussions there will be from all this information; heaven knows what will come about when this has been released to the international news media."

"I see, sir."

"You should arrange to drop by here at about 14.30 hours. Will that be all right, Thompson?"

"Right you are, sir," Thompson answered, not really knowing what else to say. The telephone line then went dead.

Derek Thompson was still mopping his brow when Lieutenant Henderson and Staff Sergeant James Bluntly entered the office. Thompson quickly put his handkerchief away.

"Well, gentlemen, what can I do for you?"

They both looked at him then smiled. Lieutenant Henderson said, "It's your wife, sir. She has been outside waiting for you for the past ten minutes. I believe you had mentioned something to her earlier. An afternoon out maybe, or was it taking her out to dinner tonight?"

"Oh my God! It completely slipped my mind. Thank you for reminding me. Bluntly, thank you for collecting Mrs. Thompson and bringing her to Northwood. Please advise her I'll not be more than fifteen minutes. No, Ian, advise Mary I'm engaged with the Admiral. She will understand."

"Okay, sir. You can leave these matters with us while you go and change."

Thompson shook his head in agreement and then rushed off to his quarters.

Lieutenant Henderson and Staff Sergeant Bluntly showed the

Commander's wife into the office. They offered her a discreet tour of the operations room and a visit around the areas of Northwood that were unrestricted. Henderson advised they would end up at the entrance to the officers' mess.

The tour was soon over.

Mary Thompson was delighted to have seen something of the place her husband called his second home.

"Thank you very much, Lieutenant. I feel somewhat honoured to have finally been given the opportunity to see where the Commander works. Please could you let him know I am here waiting for him?"

Lieutenant Henderson acknowledged Mrs. Thompson's request. However, Staff Sergeant Bluntly had already rushed off in the car to collect the Commander.

Henderson spoke. "He shouldn't be too long now, ma'am. Unfortunately, Admiral Marchant can take a little longer than expected over a telephone call."

"Yes, Lieutenant, I think I understand what you mean."

At that moment the Commander's car pulled up outside the entrance leading from the main mess hall. Thompson got out. He briskly walked through the double doors to meet his wife.

"I am sorry, my dear, for the slight delay, but I believe you were advised that I was engaged with the Admiral"

Commander Thompson kissed his wife then escorted her to the waiting car.

Lieutenant Henderson called after them. "Enjoy yourself, sir."

The car slowly pulled away down the drive towards the sentry gate. A signal of release was given after which it disappeared away into the afternoon traffic.

Lieutenant Henderson turned on his heels and swiftly walked back towards the officers' quarters and then on to the operations room. Both he and Bluntly knew the whole thing had been a complete surprise to the Commander.

Henderson decided to ensure he had covered all the Commander's tracks.

"Hello, James. I thought I'd catch you on the car phone. If the Admiral just happens to call, tell him the Commander has gone out for a bit, okay?"

"Right you are, sir. I get the message. Anyway, I expect I'll have to pick 'em up later on."

Chapter Twelve

Just after 14.00 hours General Kemp's black limousine pulled up outside the entrance to his office building. Already the General had received copy of the Top Secret and Confidential File released by Captain Jack Maxman of the *SSN Bowevil*. He was pleased to see a message that Admiral Marchant had called.

Eager to hear from the Admiral as to what had transpired regarding the report, which had also been sent to British Naval Headquarters from the US submarine, the General settled himself down in his chair and considered whether to telephone right away, or should he wait to catch the Admiral just before he would leave for dinner.

Kemp picked up the telephone receiver and dialled the coded number. He could hear a loud hissing noise through the earpiece, then there were two clicks followed by a loud ringing tone.

"Yes, Admiral Marchant speaking."

"Good evening, Admiral. General Kemp here."

"Why, hello, John. Thank you for returning my call. I telephoned you earlier wanting to discuss the report I have just received. Am I to understand you also have a copy?"

"I do, Raymond. Did you also receive another file from our side concerning our findings by the *SSN Bowevil*?"

"Yes, I did."

"Well, what's your conclusion, or should I say comment regarding it?"

"John, I've not really had a chance to survey the document thoroughly as yet. What did you think of ours?" Admiral Marchant thought his soft approach would have Kemp spilling the beans.

"Well now, let's think back a little while. Somewhere, about the time when the *Gorbachev* had just disappeared, I was not quite certain then as to whether we might have been on the right track. But now…"

He paused, "Do you know, Raymond, now I'm even more sure that these strange and horrendous happenings are all part of a secret programme which has just gotta be something those Russkies have been dreaming' up for some considerable time. I'm a tellin' you, I really don't like it one little bit. Not one bit, Admiral!"

Marchant had read the report from *HMS Excalibur*. He was horrified as to what the implications might be, or bring forth. He was tending to fully agree with what Kemp had been advising.

"Well, John, I must also tell you something more. I have already released my own recommendations regarding these files to the British Government. I have, therefore, to consider that at this moment in time, it would be highly improper for me to continue to discuss the matter further with you. However, I will say just one thing."

"And what would that be, Raymond?"

"I am not entirely without supporting your theories. Also, I think your department has been far too easy regarding this situation. I trust my comments will not go unnoticed. Also, they will allow your anger to rise up and throw the book directly at those involved, and the circumstances which by now must surely be staring you right in the face! I hope I don't have to jog your memory again in respect of the joint findings made by both our submarines. However, I do expect our joint reports, if sighted by our governments in the same light, might finally get us sufficient support. I trust by then that it will be in order for us to be able to go off and find whatever it is, and hopefully eliminate once and for all what the hell it is that's been causing all of this dreadful destruction."

Kemp did not raise any sound or noise. Nor did he rise to Marchant's jibes. However, he was slightly amazed as to what the Admiral had said. He remarked quietly and with the utmost caution.

"I sure hope you, I mean we, are darned well right about all this, Admiral?"

"Damn it, John, don't start doubting the matter now. I must tell you there is still one thing which puzzles me."

Kemp couldn't resist interrupting the Admiral with a quip. "Oh yeah, and what may I ask could that be?"

"Oh, for goodness sakes, John. Surely to hell you can see what that must be?"

"Nope. Have I missed somethin', Raymond?"

Admiral Marchant roared back in reply. "Heavens above, man, it's to try and catch them doing it red-handed!"

In reaction to the Admiral's last comment, Kemp felt an ice-cold tingle go right down his spine.

He then lowered his voice and said, "Thank you, Raymond. I do think that I'm well aware of what my duties are in life, and emphatically where they truly lie."

Admiral Marchant calmly pulled back the sharpness of his tone. "Well, that's fine then. I trust we shall speak again about these matters sometime in the morning."

"You're right, Admiral, let's leave these issues pending until then. Allow me to say bye for now."

"Okay, John, thank you for the call. Do have a pleasant afternoon."

Marchant replaced the receiver. Sitting back in his chair, he looked through the first pages of the report he had forwarded to the Prime Minister's office and again began to read:

It is my very serious belief in view of the evidence, which has now come to light, matters clearly show that somewhere in the world's oceans there is an unknown evil aggressor at work.

The joint findings of our British Naval Department of Intelligence and with those of the United States Navy both condemn these vile acts of destruction and blatant international piracy.

I therefore wish it be suggested swift action be taken by both the British and American Governments. On this being done, and with total support of their joint intelligence departments, it is thought further there should be a pooling of all joint resources and information. Hopefully, this will lead to the exposure of the elusive and hostile renegade.

I do however stress, I do not think we have to look very far to find who the culprit is.

Evidence already received and confidentially put forward clearly shows a list of strange unexplained happenings. One cannot alter these facts placed before us. Clearly there is, and has been uncovered, a very grave problem. Whether it has been apparent in space or at sea, one thing for sure is that each time the Russians have had one of its units operating in the vicinity of each major disaster, something dreadful has happened.

Our department recommends a full-scale search over every inch of the world's oceans be made possible. We believe this should be achieved in order to expose what our radar has detected. Furthermore, it is requested that the world's space organisations duly reconsider assisting in this full-scale search programme in order we can rid ourselves of the space demons and of any supposed unknown sea monster that deems to lurk and kill without mercy.

Admiral Marchant having finished reading closed the file. For a moment, deeply immersed in thought, he sat quietly and finished his drink.

He then got up and left to have dinner with some friends.

It was now very late evening when the President of the United States of America made a call to the British Prime Minister.

Nearly an hour later, the joint decision made by each heads of state agreed to expose the international circumstance and dilemma; both premiers considered a joint statement being released in the form of a single *communiqué*. This was to be made jointly by the British and American Naval and Military Intelligence Departments linked with a press release by NASA. Thereafter, all concerned would make confirmations directly to the international press agencies.

The statement was to consider Russia be confronted with all the combined evidence then be challenged in so far as to determine whether it was attempting to enter the world into a new element of global warfare.

The statement text would be aimed as a direct attack against the Federal State of Russia for ignoring their policy of perestroika.

Further, it was suggested the Russian space platform, *Vostok*, may primarily have been studying atmospheric conditions of the world which agreeably were of real international concern.

It was respected this suggestion was made in regard to their country contributing a very valued analysis towards the world's daily weather pattern plus major growing problems concerning the now recognised greenhouse effect. Russia's intent in this field was considered in every way honourable. However, very strong allegations made in the statement, which duly centred on this absolute evidence, confirmed the Russian space platform was definitely involved in operating something which deemed to be that of an unlawful and sinister nature.

Constant vigilance of surveillance by friendly nations had collected very detailed reports which contained the evidence of dates and visual sightings of many unidentified flying objects.

All these records presented, now beyond all measure of doubt, the sole source of involvement did emanate from the Russian space platform *Vostok*. However, there was some conflicting evidence which was still unproved. It was suggested this evidence may well have had some indirect cause in regard to the hundreds of lives lost in the recent tragic air disasters over the Atlantic. The report stated that it was hoped a positive result would be achieved, whatever the outcome.

When the confidential statement reached NASA, within a matter of hours the world's space authorities utterly condemned the statement as an unprecedented international violation against the human rights of a peace-loving nation. It stated the Federal State of Russia had spread the tide of glasnost and perestroika across Russia and the CIS. Also, as a nation, Russia finally had cemented an all-time democratic world of friendship in the joint unification of their former Comi-Con satellite states. Not withstanding further similar comments made by the world's space authorities, NASA utterly condemned the proposed statement as an international violation. They stated the Federal State of Russia had themselves achieved the final completion with East and West Germany, the federation of a one united Germany, thus confirming their countries undying efforts to maintain a peaceful East/West relationship.

How on earth could the British and American Governments request NASA to put its neck on the line in agreeing with them on such utter nonsense?

America and Great Britain now stood alone; each nation isolated in regard to adverse world opinion which now duly scorned and vehemently rejected such blatant provocation made by each government's Department of Intelligence. World opinion suggested that it was they who were trying to effect world supremacy. Their governments were dictating an idealistic dominance against the rest of the world's peaceful nations.

Riots broke out in many capital cities. Crowds were seen protesting against Britain and America for making such wild allegations. Britain and America jointly stood aloof completely resigned to what had been stated by their intelligence departments.

Death threats were made against both the President of the United States of America and the Prime Minister of Great Britain.

Friday, 4 August 2017 was considered to have been one of the blackest days in the history of East/West relations.

Huge marches were held in many Middle Eastern and Far East countries. All were demonstrating against the imperialist attitude of the British and American Governments. Demands for aggression were being called for by all nations of peace to stand against such British and American defiance.

The world stood waiting wishing for a glimmer of hope.

The morning of Saturday, 5 August was bright and fresh.

General Kemp, staying at his office overnight, had followed closely the delicate circumstance, which had broadened on the international political arena.

After a day of expecting the worst, it now seemed the atmosphere had been manoeuvred into a national alert. Everything had been brought on to a state of amber at the American Military and Naval theatres of operations.

The world now seemed to wait held poised in a vacuum of its own mistrust and anger.

Only the United States of America and Great Britain, apart from both being put on a state of alert, seemed to treat life as if it was business as usual. All other nations of the world praised the Federal State of Russia for their reserve and cool constraint.

Lieutenant Logan arrived at the office just after 07.30 hours.

General Kemp greeted him. "Hi there, Smartie. Fancy some breakfast?"

Logan smiled back. "No thank you, sir. I'm in training for the US Air Force team's football season."

"Oh, come on now, that's not for a long hop yet. I'm darned sure you will have burnt away any extra calories long before the time you start playing. Come on, Smartie, look lively." Kemp was persistent. He knew the youngster had a big appetite.

"All right, sir, but only a small helping."

Both men considered it was appropriate to muster in the officers' service canteen. There they thought it would be safe and away from the press or any discord with the public. Kemp wanted to ask Logan something very important and he was sure this could only be done over a solid breakfast and a large cup of strong black coffee.

Both men sat down at a table. A serving conductor came over and they both ordered.

General Kemp opened the conversation. "Well, young man, I have to say I am very pleased with the way you have handled yourself since joining us."

Logan gave his commanding officer a very strange look.

Kemp ignored it and continued. "You have done your job well, and you have conducted yourself with the utmost professionalism, and, may I say, with the skill of a veteran. Amazingly, you don't appear to have been overawed by *G.O.D.* I congratulate you, lad!"

"Thank you very much, sir, but could you please tell me what this is all leading up to?"

Kemp looked up at Logan and grinned. He liked the lad for his cool directness.

Kemp eased back his friendly pace a little as breakfast soon became the centre of both their attentions. Finally, as the General sipped his coffee, he spoke.

"I am sure, Lieutenant, we both appreciate what's going on in the political power scene between the West and those Russkies. Well, to be a little more specific, I mean Britain. Our country and them! Life all of a sudden ain't so easy, and it don't look like it's goin' to get any better for the moment."

"Sure thing, General, but is it really going to get that bad in regard to what we all have been saying about the Reds?"

"Yeah! The hell it is! As sure as these are eggs on my plate, you bet it is!"

The General coughed to clear his throat.

"Our department is now linked up with the Brits, and we now have to prove all we have been spoutin'. Otherwise, Logan, there will be a lot of high and mighty heads goin, a rollin'."

Logan began to feel he was not going to be the one that was in the direct line of fire. He slowly relaxed.

"Now then, Lieutenant, early this morning I received instructions from HQ. They advised me the White House, in closed emergency session and cleared with Congress, has given full authorisation of the launching of the US Military's newest space shuttle, the *Liberty*, a manned vehicle derived from the concept of the X-37B. Now then, young man, I believe this has been considered and brought forward due to the immense public feeling quickly aroused by the rest of the world's opinion against us. D' you know, Smartie, what with the American press and the majority of the media harping on about so many of these 'unexplainables', I can quite understand why the President has authorised this measure.

"As to why he has requested it is under the utmost secrecy. In this regard this is where we come in. Our job will be to ensure that this one is pulled off with no major hitches. If this is achieved and the desired non-exposure effected then we'll have beaten the damned Russkies at their own game.

"The only difference, Logan, between them and us, is our true aim to control and maintain a strong peaceful existence, not one which is to provoke aggression as we now believe the Russkies are already doing."

Logan remained silent and continued to listen.

"Smartie, this job will demand every ounce of your self-control and absolute resolute stubbornness. If the outcome is positive, I can assure you I will no longer be talking to a lieutenant. Your promotion to captain would be guaranteed and fully in order."

Logan sat completely overawed by the unexpected gesture. He made no comment as the General finished his breakfast and drank his coffee. Kemp wasn't too sure as to what this silence meant.

In the past he'd noticed Logan was apt to be slow when responding to any direct questioning or advised reasoning.

The General began to make a move to leave whereby both of them rose from the table. As they started to walk away Kemp spoke. "Well, in due time, Smartie, I do expect to receive an answer to my request."

Logan cleared his throat. "Sir, I won't say I am not flattered by your request."

Kemp reacted inwardly. He was thinking to himself, *Jesus Christ! The sonofabitch is goin' to fail me.* His temperature rapidly began to rise.

Logan spoke. "Please tell me, General, will I still be remaining here with your outfit, sir?"

The General knew he couldn't really answer that. "I will see what can be done, son, but the matter may be entirely out of my control. However, I'll try and put a good word in and also my personal recommendation. How's that?"

"Fine, sir. By the way, isn't the US Military shuttle *Liberty* fitted out with the latest up-to-date surveillance equipment?"

"That's right, Logan, only the best!"

"Isn't it also armed with the latest type of combat armament, sir?"

"Your right again, young man."

"Aren't these something to do with a deadly new laser gun and laser assisted anti-rocket and anti-laser system?"

Jesus, the General thought, *what kind of person have I got working for me? Why won't he come out with a firm reply to my previous discussion? To hell with it,* thought Kemp. Was Logan just buttering him up in order to say no to his generous offer? Didn't the guy know, or even ' understand, you don't get something for nothing?

Kemp's patience finally gave in.

"Now look here, Logan. I am not here to be schoolmaster or nursemaid. Tell me! What in hell's name have you gotta say to my offer?"

The General wanted to know where he stood.

"Come on now, Smartie, let's have it. I want your reply NOW!"

Smartie Logan still said nothing. He merely acknowledged recognition to the General's line of questioning.

They both then left the mess hall.

As they walked down the steps towards the corridor that led to the General's office, Logan spoke.

"Sir, doesn't the *Liberty* have the ability to make itself invisible to any foe? You know, like what your report suggests the Russians are doing with that missing sub?"

General Kemp stopped in his tracks. "Say that again, Smartie! Please repeat what it was that you said about the Russians."

Logan repeated what he had just said.

"You're the greatest and the smartest arse in all imagination, Logan. I do believe you have just dropped in on the Russkies deal by a spot of sheer genius!"

The General paused for a moment.

"Now then, Logan, what's it to be? Are you in or are you out?"

Smartie stopped and turned to the General who by now was waiting with bated breath.

"Never said I wasn't in, sir. Anyway, what else could I do?"

They both laughed and entered the office.

Kemp felt very relieved but didn't want to show it. He immediately urged Logan back to work. "Smartie, get on to Professor Burston at NASA Tracking. I want you to tell him exactly what you just told me."

"Okay, General," replied Logan. He lifted the telephone receiver and began to dial.

Sergeant Lance sat at his desk listening to every word the two officers had spoken. His whole body remained motionless until he heard the click of the General's office door. His face then shone with a broad smile.

Lance thought to himself, *I can't wait to tell Liza about this shindig. She will wet herself for sure then laugh all the way to New Orleans. What a day this one's goin' to be!*

At that moment, Lieutenant Logan came out of the office.

"Sergeant Lance, could you please step in here for a minute," Logan said in an authoritative tone.

Yes, sir, make my day, the Sergeant thought to himself.

The General greeted Lance. "Ah, Sergeant. I am not too sure whether you might have overheard any of my discussion with Lieutenant Logan?"

Lance looked back at the General and kept silent.

"Come on, Lance, you know what I'm talking about."

Sergeant Lance stood absolutely still and showed no emotion.

"Well okay," said the General. "I just want to make the position quite clear. I have known you a long time and would not wish to lose you through my hearing any tails goin' a missin' out. Do I make myself clearly understood, Sergeant?"

"Yes, sir. I haven't heard nothin'. Nothin' at all, General, sir."

"That's okay by me, Lance. How about you, Lieutenant?"

Logan shook his head in agreement.

"Okay. You can go now."

"Thank you, sir." The Sergeant saluted then hurriedly stepped out.

Kemp leaned over to the intercom that was on his desk and clicked off the switch marked OPEN.

"Sorry about that, Logan, but we cannot have any eavesdroppin' goin' on around here."

Logan smiled. "You are right, sir. I'll see to it the matter goes no further."

"Thank you, Lieutenant. Let me know when you've been able to contact NASA Tracking."

"Yes, General."

Logan then left the office leaving the General to study further new details of the campaign.

About twenty minutes had passed by the time Logan called to General Kemp to confirm he had located Professor Burston.

"Sir, I have the Professor holding on for you if you want to speak with him right away."

"Okay, Logan, thank you. I'll do just that."

The switchboard lines clicked.

The Professor spoke. "Hello, John. What can I do for you? Was any of that information of any use?"

"Sure thing, Mac. Thank you very much for your kind assistance. It was much appreciated."

Professor Burston knew this was not just a social call.

"I suspect, General, the purpose of your call is still centred around the same subject, or is there now something new you wish to ask me?" Macdonald Burston smiled to himself. He was always eager to apply theory to practise regarding any new angle of scientific study or investigation.

Kemp replied, "Did Lieutenant Logan speak with you?"

" No, General, he just asked me to hold."

"Well, Mac, I am not quite sure how to put this, but I believe I've found out what we might be looking for and you're the man of the moment to talk to. "

"Okay, John. Shoot!"

"Well, you know the newest shuttle now out under US Military Operations, the *Liberty*?"

"Why, yes. What about it?"

"Well, the Lieutenant, the one who you met who works for me."

There was a pause as Professor Burston wasn't sure who the General was referring to.

"Come on, Mac, the young fellow you just spoke to."

"Oh yes," the Professor replied, still not really clear as to whom the General really meant.

"Well, I believe he might have tripped over something which could cause a major breakthrough regarding the yet still unsolved issue concerning that other major subject we have discussed."

"Which one was that, John?"

"The space tornados problem. Mind you, Mac, this is now only me puttin' two and two together. The figure may well turn up to come out as five. However, I would like you to take a look at all the stuff I've now put together. There is no harm in trying to see what you can make out from what the young man said."

"Okay, John," said Burston. "Run it by me. Just start talking and spell out all the facts. I'll stop you if it doesn't seem to stack up. Okay?"

Kemp knew if the situation in any way was woolly, Professor Burston would immediately shut him down. He began to relay the circumstance.

"Lieutenant Logan and I were talking over breakfast about a number of issues and subjects. It was when he just happened to say he believed the *Liberty* had the ability to become invisible to any form of radar tracking device.

"If this is so, Mac, I am sure the boys at NASA Tracking could somehow verify how this is done. Maybe the same theory can be applied to diagnosing these space tornados as being some kind of electronic field. If this is found to be the case could such a field be made sufficiently strong enough to probe any depths of our oceans? Surely such a field's strength could ratify this, or could such a beam be projected to go far enough and have strength great enough in order to effect the hiding or cocooning of something as big as a nuclear-powered submarine?"

There was a long silence. No comment was forthcoming.

Professor Burston continued to listen. He was fascinated although he had now become a little nervous when Kemp had described the supposed purpose behind his line of enquiry.

There was another pause as the General cleared his throat. "Well, what do you think, Mac? Has this idea got any mileage in regard to its concept?"

There was still no immediate reaction. Kemp was about to enquire if the subject might be boring the Professor.

Mac's soft voice broke its silence. "I would go so far as to say that your two plus two theory would never make a figure of five."

The Professor paused.

"Maybe I would say it could stick at about four and a quarter on light of what you have just said. Yes, I will go so far as to say I do think your lad may well have struck on something really worth looking in to. I'll have to get the boys to mull it over a little before we can place any greater credence on it, John. Let me get back to you as soon as possible. Is that goin' to be all right with you?"

"Okay, Mac, the ball's now in your court. Thank you very much for your time."

"Not at all, General. Thank you for the opportunity, my friend."

The telephone call closed.

Kemp began making a few notes in his desk pad when the telephone rang.

"Good morning. Is that General Kemp?"

"Yes, speaking."

"This is the office of the President speaking. Will you please hold for a moment?"

Only twice in his life had Kemp received such a personal call. Suddenly, just as before, his stomach was beginning to feel a strong nervous reaction.

"General Kemp?"

"Good morning, Mr. President."

"General Kemp, I am led to understand it was your department's joint report, together with that of the British Royal Navy, which appears to have placed both nations, America and Great Britain, into this state of isolation. Furthermore and personally, might I say it has placed us both not far short of the state of a war footing with Russia and the CIS.

"It's in this regard I am calling to request you please meet me at the Cape Canaveral launching sight in order to discuss various details pertaining to top secret discussions which have just been cleared by Congress. I'm requesting the meeting in order that my authorisation of the launching of the space shuttle *Liberty* will be seen to be a routine test mission. However, and based on our joint and confidential discussions, the shuttle will be directed to a yet unknown destination. Do you read me, General?"

"Yes, sir, Mr. President, I do."

"Good. Now, General, tell me, how do we really stand in these difficult times with all this supposed madness? What do you personally have to say about it?"

Kemp never ever wanted to discuss such matters of security on the telephone.

"Sir, Mr. President, I look forward to meeting you as requested and thank you for the invite. I'm sure, as and when we get together, we shall have a little extra time to discuss all current matters at that time. Please be assured, Mr. President, we will crack the problem, sir."

"General, I'm taking a tremendous amount of flak from the public lobbyists at the moment. They want blood, General. I do appreciate you may not totally be aware of all things, but these dreadful disasters and the loss of those civil aircraft in mid-Atlantic together with the news of these darned UFOs. The whole world appears to have got the damned jitters, General. I trust your department has got this one fully covered?"

The President paused for a moment.

"General, I'm sure I do not have to advise you as to where all this could lead. I hope you can see that the world's nearly at the point where known terrorists, adversaries or for that matter any aggressor may well at any time seek their chance to hit back at us and at Great Britain.

"At this moment of great exposure, I'm sure they'll try to hit us where it hurts."

General Kemp spoke. "I fully understand, Mr. President, sir. I hereby give you my fullest assurance we do genuinely have the situation fully under control."

"Fine, General, I do appreciate you telling me that. Okay, then I'll stick my neck out with you for the time being, but for God sakes, General, don't go and blow it. I look forward to seeing you later on to discuss matters further. My office will provide you with the schedules and times of our meetings."

"Thank you, sir. I'll await the call."

"Goodbye for now, General."

"Goodbye, Mr. President, sir."

Through the tension of the call Kemp found his mouth had parched dry. He took a sip from the glass of water he had picked up from his desk. In deep thought he lifted the intercom switch and advised Sergeant Lance he would be away from his desk for a little while. He was paying a visit to the men's room.

Back at Naval and Military Intelligence, it was 10.30 hours when Professor Burston called General Kemp.

"Well, John, the system on the *Liberty* is an inverted one. Technically, it screens the machine to maintain its radar invisibility. If sufficient power was to be generated by something strong enough to do it, plus the components set in reverse, then it would be feasible to transport a beam of some great force to lock on to its target, or maybe surround a chosen object.

"However, I must confess, I'm not totally sure whether this theory is the one that will solve your problem. Let us say, for example, a small nuclear reactor was installed to operate the concept. If this were possible, being the main device of power required as a fuel source, then I would certainly consider the position to be one of a distinct possibility. It could be one idea being based on a theory that your youngster's logic and proposed programme of practical disposition could be applied to."

Kemp's face slowly broke into a smile. "Say, Mac, would either you or NASA Tracking consider puttin' your signature to a statement confirming somethin' like what you have just said?"

"I don't see why not."

Kemp felt his fingers twitching. "Would you allow my limo driver to come over and pick up such a statement, let's say, in about two hours?"

"That'll be fine, John. I'll have it made ready for you in triplicate, as always."

Kemp's whole body had begun to tingle with the excitement of achieving what originally he thought was going to be a near impossible task.

"Thanks a million, friend. I do believe you have just gone halfway to making my day. Mac, I'll owe you for this one."

"Hey, what are friends for?" came back the reply.

"Okay, Old Buster. I'll say bye for now and thank you."

Kemp, still a little stunned by his success, slowly put down the receiver. He pressed the intercom button.

"Sergeant Lance, could you please see if Lieutenant Logan is busy at the moment? If not, ask him to drop by my office as soon as possible."

"Right, sir," the Sergeant replied, then made his way to the computer room. As he entered, Logan was in the middle of pre-setting G.O.D. for a major rechecking schedule.

Sergeant Lance spoke. "Lieutenant Logan, sir."

"Yes, Sergeant."

"Sir, General Kemp requests your presence in his office as soon as it might be convenient for you."

"Okay, Lance, could you let the General know I'll be with him in about five minutes."

"Okay, will do, sir."

The Sergeant then whispered to himself, "My oh my! How the gifted can make a General croon!"

The door of the General's office echoed as Logan gave it a sharp knock.

"Enter!" came the response.

Logan stepped inside.

"Ah, Logan."

"Yes, sir."

"Come in and sit down. It would appear matters have somewhat escalated since we met this morning. Firstly, I must put a feather in your cap regarding your mentioning that small matter concerning the space shuttle *Liberty*.

"All I can say is the matter has been given a definite plus by NASA Tracking. I now await my orders as to what goes on next."

"Why thank you, sir. What do you think is going to happen next?"

Kemp didn't expect such a direct line of questioning from the Lieutenant. "I am not sure as yet, Logan. Maybe you'll get to see the launching of the space shuttle while you're down here with me. It's more than anyone has achieved in your position."

Logan smiled. "My word that sure would be something. That's absolutely great, sir! Will I see it from here or from NASA?"

"Let's first of all see what comes round today, Smartie. Okay?"

"Yes, sir," came back the reply.

"That will be all, Logan."

In reply to the General's order the Lieutenant straightened himself. "Okay. Fine, sir. You will definitely let me in on it, won't you, sir?"

"I said that will be all, Logan. Be off with you now, and await my call."

The Admiralty — Whitehall, London

It was 11.15 hours when Admiral Marchant called General Kemp. Both officers chatted over the idea and concept NASA Tracking had given its credence to.

"Well, John, maybe the outcome of all this forecasting might not be so grim. Maybe Operation Ghostbusters is finally going to exorcise its supposed phantom. I wish you luck regarding the launch. Let me know how you get on."

Kemp felt pleased all previous indiscretions had seemingly been brushed under the carpet.

"Okay, Raymond, and thanks for all your input regarding operations involving Jodrell Bank."

"Not at all. Bye for now."

At Sea

HMS Excalibur had made her rendezvous with the fleet auxiliary *HMS Geriant*. Transfer of all the bodies from the aircraft disaster for forward shipment, identification and eventually land burial had been successful.

The *Bowevil* had made excellent progress on its homeward voyage. Captain Maxman advised US Naval HQ his sub would be docking at Charleston sometime early on the morning of 4 August.

The *Gorbachev* steadily distanced itself from the American and British submarines. Captain Narodny was well aware of the danger the power failure on board the space platform *Vostok* had caused. He hoped the *Gorbachev* would have no problems in making its escape.

It was a little after 13.00 hours when Commodore Brianston-Green received a coded message on board *HMS Excalibur*. It read:

TO: HMS EXCALIBUR
WE HAVE YOUR POSITION AS EIGHTY MILES SOUTH-WEST OF US
– STOP – WE RECEIVED A MESSAGE FROM HQ MSM VIA MAXMAN/
BOWEVIL OF YOUR FREQUENCY – STOP – WE WOULD BE HAPPY TO
JOIN YOUR PATROL MISSION – STOP – WE EXPECT TO BE IN YOUR
VICINITY NEXT FOUR HOURS – STOP – END MESSAGE
SIGNED: ADMIRAL GEORGE GRIFFIN- SSBN INTREPID

The Commodore was delighted. He copied the message forward to RN NORTHWOOD HQ for the attention of Admiral Marchant and requested further instructions.

HMS Excalibur had passed the position where the unidentified object had been pinpointed about six hours before. The British submarine Commander was pleased to have the company, strength and power of the US Navy's submarine flagship to assist.

Brianston-Green spoke. "Lieutenant Bergman, send a message to the *Intrepid*. State it was kind of them to let us know they are going to drop by and join the party. Also, confirm, as yet, we have still had no luck. Please remind them as of 16.00 hours we shall be running silent. Suggest if they would consider doing the same. We might just be lucky enough to get some sort of sounding from the UUO, or whatever this enemy is."

"Will do, sir. By the way, Commodore, it's just been confirmed over the wire. Britain and America have formally been challenged regarding their joint outrageous allegations of misconduct. This is in regard to both countries having stated that the Federal State of Russia had been waging its own world war on innocent unarmed civilian targets."

"Really, Bergman. Well, I'm now absolutely resolute in wishing to find and destroy whatever this unidentified thing is."

"I agree, sir. Another point you also might like to know which has just come over the wire: the US Congress has given clearance for a launch and test flight of the new US space shuttle, *Liberty*."

Brianston-Green looked at Bergman and smiled.

"That is interesting. I presume this is strictly routine of course?"

Both officers grinned.

Lieutenant Bergman spoke. "I wonder what Admiral Griffin will have to say about that, sir?"

"I expect we will hear in due course."

The bridge telephone rang. "Operations room to bridge. We have just marked a large object which has just appeared on the radar north-north-east of our position, sir."

"Thank you. Log its position and reference. I believe we will find out soon enough that this one has to be the *Intrepid*."

Chapter Thirteen

NASA Military and Naval Intelligence, Cape Canaveral
Information regarding Admiral Griffin's message was received by General Kemp and noted accordingly.

Kemp smiled.

He had already received another call from Admiral Marchant advising him the same information.

An hour had passed before his desk finally received news.

It was nearly time for some refreshment.

Lieutenant Logan requested Sergeant Lance to arrange a tray of fresh brewed tea and coffee to be delivered to the General's office. At the same time he requested the returned package delivered from NASA Tracking be presented.

"Come in," The General said in response to the door having been knocked.

"And when, Sergeant, am I to expect the pleasure of Lieutenant Logan?"

"I do believe any moment now, sir. He asked me to deliver this package to you which had just arrived from NASA Tracking."

"Thank you, Lance. Please leave it there on the table. That will be all."

Sergeant Lance saluted, stepped out and closed the door behind him.

The red telephone on the General's desk rang. Kemp lifted the receiver.

"Good afternoon, is that General Kemp?"

"It is."

"This is the President's office. I am instructed to confirm your meeting is arranged for 20.00 hours tonight. The venue is at NASA HQ."

"Thank you for your call. I confirm I'll be coming and will be bringing my *aide-de-camp* with me. Will that be agreeable?"

"Certainly, General. I trust you do have a mode of transport in order to get there?"

"That I do. Thank you."

"Fine. Please be advised we expect the launch of the *Liberty* to take place early tomorrow morning. By the way, I am instructed to ask is the further evidence you are providing sound? If so, the President will advise as to what is to happen from there on. Please come prepared, General. That will be all."

Kemp cleared the line then telephoned a bleeper message through to his driver. He instructed him to be available at 18.30 hours. He then called for Logan.

The internal telephone rang. "You wanted me, sir?" said Logan.

"Smartie, get on your best bib and tucker. Be ready by 18.15 hours. You're going out tonight, and remember you are on best behaviour from now on, young man."

Logan wasn't too sure what the General meant. "Sorry, General, but what's up?"

"I have kept my promise to you, Smartie. Now you are ordered to get into your gear so you can deliver your side of the package. Don't let me down."

Logan began to feel a little nervous. From that last remark he thought that Kemp was not his usual self. "Sir, are you sure you are feeling okay?"

"Never felt better, son."

"General, you do know 4 July passed us by nearly a month ago? Are you sure you're not goin' down with somethin' bad, sir?"

Kemp smiled. "Nope, I'm taking you out tonight as my official *aide-de-camp*. Young man, you're goin' to meet the President of the United States of America."

Logan nearly dropped the telephone. For a moment he completely lost his voice.

Kemp heard the crash and called out, "Logan! Logan! Are you still there?"

"I... think so, sir," came the reply.

"Okay, then jump to it!"

"You bet, sir."

Kemp could sense the youngster's excitement.

"Logan, you sowed the seed which has taken us this far. I believe we might now be about to take out the the face of the Russian bear."

Logan listened. By now he knew that Kemp really had got all his marbles together. Something big was coming up and he was invited to be a part of it. His response was not long in coming.

"Okay, sir, you're on. I'll be ready at a quarter after six. Thanks for the invite. By the way, do I have to supply the wheels, sir?"

The General smiled and replaced the receiver.

Professor Burston had laid out his report and findings in a first class manner. NASA Tracking fully supported the Lieutenant's chance theory and had backed General Kemp's idea of an enemy electrical force field being capable of reversing the components of an inverted radio beam force field. Professor Burston believed this was being done to project a major external beam that could well act as a screen. The Professor calculated that all matters would depend upon such a major power source being available. He had compiled a full dossier and diagrams to show how this theory worked. The diagrams showed the reality of what was available and what could be combated if the operational functions of the equipment on board the space shuttle *Liberty* could accommodate. He explained what an alien force might try to achieve. The Professor left only one comment hanging: why would anyone wish to achieve this situation? His theory could only draw one conclusion, and its implications were if an enemy needed to hide something surely this could be done in a more conventional manner. Certainly it should be considered as an alien threat, or it's to be treated as an enemy. In conclusion he had written, *Whatever the unknown force is, it has to be stopped. It must be completely destroyed.*

Kemp's limousine pulled up outside the entrance of NASA. There were many extra guards posted. An entourage of CIA and undercover agents were seen mingling around. The General and the Lieutenant produced their identity cards whereupon they were both frisked.

The security guard handed the briefcase back to the General. "Thank you, sir. Please proceed to the anteroom marked number thirty-seven. You will find it on the first floor."

Both men entered the building.

"Well, Smartie, are you okay?"

Logan was trying to take in all that was going on around him. "Yes, thank you, sir. Although, General, I do feel a little funny inside."

"Don't let that worry you. We're all apt to feel that sensation the first time. Treat it as an inner sense of the occasion."

Logan smiled at the General. "Thank you for that kind reassurance, sir. However, is there a rest room about? I sure could use one before we go in."

General Kemp grinned. He remembered a similar experience a few years back concerning his first meeting with a previous President. "Okay, Smartie. There should be one across from the elevator as we step out."

The lift stopped and the doors opened.

Kemp commented. "There you are, Logan. Over there on the left hand side."

"Fine. Thank you, sir."

Kemp stood and waited.

He glanced out of a window and looked across towards the vast area of the launching pad. Many memories from the distant past began to flash by.

Logan stepped out through the rest room door. He looked at Kemp and saw a strange glazed look. "Are you okay, sir?"

"Yes thank you, Logan. Are you now feelin' a little better?"

Logan felt himself blush. The General knew he was wound up with nerves.

"Take a deep breath, Smartie, then count up to ten. Here we go, lad."

Both officers entered the anteroom. It was filled with many personnel of mixed military uniforms. There were officers from the US Navy, Air force and Army, all being senior Chiefs of Staff.

"Good evening, General Kemp," said the President's aide as he greeted him.

"Good evening, Erwin." General Kemp then introduced his aide. "This is Lieutenant Logan."

"Pleased to meet you, Lieutenant. Will you both come this way please?"

Kemp and Logan moved forward. They entered through two large double doors into a large conference boardroom.

Mr. Erwin-Jones ushered them forward to their seats. "Please be seated here, General. Lieutenant, please sit over there." He then left them.

On closing the large doors behind him, Erwin went to advise the President everyone was now present. He requested if it was now appropriate to assemble the meeting. It seemed an age before the doors again opened. In filed the senior Chiefs of Staff to take their allotted seats. Shortly afterwards, everyone stood up as the arrival and entrance of the President of the United States of America was announced.

As he entered he moved forward and stood at the top of the table. "Be seated, gentlemen. Thank you all for coming and at such short notice. I'll not in any way beat about the bush. We are all aware of the implications of the past few days, and the occurrences of these separate disasters. On the face of it they all could be considered to be a natural phenomenon. However, our friends in Great Britain, like us, have concluded that these horrific occurrences are now becoming a regular thing. As always, a few people amongst our joint nations could not let matters simply lie down.

Therefore, and in my supporting such an insight, I requested the writer of a recently published joint nations report to be present here with us tonight. With this situation at hand, and these parties being present, I am sure the true facts to date will be advised to you all. May I introduce you to General John B. Kemp and his aide Lieutenant Logan."

Everyone in the room turned. General Kemp acknowledged the President's address and set about reporting the circumstance regarding the joint issued US Military and Naval *communiqué*. He confirmed all information from his department, in conjunction with the evidence given by the British Royal Navy, to be genuine.

There were considerable undertones and murmurs made when Kemp described details of the video recording concerning the sunken wreck of *SS Andros*. He showed his personal compassion towards the report made by Captain Maxman in joint collaboration with Commodore Brianston-Green, Commander of the British Nuclear Submarine *HMS Excalibur*. Continuing his address, he said, "Finally, Mr. President, gentlemen, I am sure all of this evidence has not totally convinced everyone that the Federal States of Russia possibly may be aggressively trying to achieve the waging of a war on all comers. One thing for sure, by whatever action this unidentified underwater object, we call it a UUO, has been doing these dreadful deeds of destruction, somehow it has always been able to hide away from any normal exposure. It is in this context, gentlemen, and with the facts being reported by our sub the *Bowevil* and the British sub *HMS Excalibur*, the evidence confirms that for over three hours on a particular date there was a large unidentified object on each of their radar screens. At the time, neither vessel had any way of visually checking after which the blip simply disappeared."

Kemp took a sip of water then continued giving further evidence in order to compound his theory.

"It was only this morning when my aide, Lieutenant Logan, came up with a possible breakthrough. This, Mr. President, gentlemen, leads me to request you all please observe NASA Tracking Institution's report which has been set out before you."

Each officer of the Chiefs of Staff and the President glanced at the report placed before them. They then listened intently as Kemp continued.

"As Lieutenant Logan has suggested, the space shuttle *Liberty*, our newest orbiter craft, has been fitted out with a new system that allows it to become invisible from any enemy who might wish to attack it. Myself being somewhat curious of the findings made by the Lieutenant, I contacted

NASA Tracking and asked for assistance of one of their best professors. Our department requested a full surveillance analysis be made available. Furthermore, we requested clearance and verification be given to confirm if the inverted system developed on the *Liberty* was in any way capable to be reversible by any enemy. At the same time, I personally requested further notification as to whether the latest technical apparatus on board *Liberty* could be capable of achieving a similar result. Gentlemen, kindly read Professor Burston's reply. You will see he confirms if a strong enough power reactor was available, this being even via a small nuclear reactor, one which might possibly have been installed somewhere on a space platform, a beam of immense strength could well be achieved. Also the possibility that it be could be directed thousands of miles in order to screen or cocoon such a desired object. He advises this beam, if created, could be strong enough to shield a plane or ship from any exposure of attack by a pursuer."

The conference room's reaction to this information was one of complete awe. The Air Force Chief of Staff interrupted General Kemp. "General, are you trying to tell us there probably is such an unknown enemy or hostile predator lurking somewhere out there in the great wide world? How absurd!"

Reaction from the conference table at this remark was one of tittering laughter. At least this seemed to break the high state of electrifying tension. Some of the other officers also rebuked and jested at the General's comments stating:

"Impossible!"

"That's just darn right ridiculous!"

"How on earth could something remain totally invisible for so long?"

"Surely there cannot be anything on record to justify this so-called myth really does exist!"

Laughter broke out everywhere.

"Gentlemen! Gentlemen, please!" called the President.

"It appears some of you do not seem to have been listening clearly. Allow me to remind you of certain facts some of which you appear to have forgotten.

"There is definitely something very nasty out there somewhere in the ocean. Whatever it is, it went and put that forty-foot-wide circular hole right through the hull of the cargo freighter *SS Andros*. I have yet to explore our records for any report which might relate to there being some kind of giant metal-eating killer whale.

"But this thing, whatever it is, did kill Captain Rossway and his entire crew. I ask you all again, therefore, to take this matter firmly into your consideration. Ask yourselves the questions regarding what General Kemp has said. Also, ask yourselves if it is possible that the same ghastly thing destroyed those two airliners?

"I'm sorry, General. I did not mean to break in like that, and I am not going to interrupt you again. I merely wish everyone else here to realise this matter is a very serious one. I do trust everyone around this table should button up and hear the General out. I also hope you will willingly acknowledge this threat to the world as being real."

For a moment there was total silence. Then a loud accord of respectful acknowledgement was heard in reply to the President's remarks.

The President again spoke. "Right then, General Kemp, please continue. This time I hope you will be allowed to proceed uninterrupted."

"Thank you, Mr. President.

"Gentlemen, whatever this thing is that made that hole right through the ore carrier still puzzles our department. It's got to be something which is very new in any field of up-to-date armament. In this regard, I've been requested to advise that both the US and British Naval Intelligence Departments strongly believe there's a very real connection concerning all this being linked to that missin' Russian submarine – the one Moscow recently advised had been lost while out on its maiden voyage. It's suggested this, most likely, is the culprit.

"Mr. President, gentlemen, the blip our subs recorded points very firmly towards it being some sort of very large submerged vessel."

"Okay, General," interrupted the US Army Chief of Staff, "how then do you account for this thing being supposedly visible at other particular times?"

After hearing this comment there was a disturbing murmur around the room.

"That's a very good point, sir," responded the General. "Please allow me to come to the three major discoveries our department has made during cross-checking all available evidence.

"At this point, if all parties present permit it, Mr. President, may I request my aide, Lieutenant Logan, now takes over? It was due to his efforts with *G.O.D.*"

There was a polite titter.

"In respect of such inferred deity, I refer to our computer system. It bears considerable credit for cracking the cross-checking of all our department's intelligence input."

The General then turned. Logan looked across at the General. Temporarily, the young man froze in his seat.

"Mr. President, gentlemen, please allow me to introduce you to Lieutenant Logan."

There was a considerable amount of muttering heard. Kemp seized the chance to whisper.

"Logan, take a deep breath and relax. The show's all yours, kid."

There was a moment of total silence as Smartie Logan stood motionless before the President and Chiefs of Staff.

"Mr. President, gentlemen, as General Kemp has already stated, many clear areas of evidence on record do positively prove this theory now checks out. Mind you, over a period of nearly ten weeks, a lot of recordings regularly started and then just fizzled out."

There were slight sniggerings. A voice said, "Ssssshhh! Give the youngster a chance."

"Regarding the three cases General Kemp stressed, plus one other which finally I only came across this afternoon. Gentlemen, please allow me to familiarise you all with certain new details, and some of the past basic facts.

"On the morning of 30 July, the *SS Andros* is recorded to have sunk due to a very heavy sea running at that time off the south-east coast of Iceland. It was at this time one of our submarine radar screen scanner recorders showed a blip between the time of 10:14:30 hours and 10:15:30 hours local time at the exact location of the sinking.

"Since then our department has received more information from an Icelandic listening post. The information and recording received, although very poor is believed to have been made by the *SS Andros* from its radio when sending out a Mayday distress signal.

"The signal lasted precisely eight seconds. It started at 10:15:00 hours, and continued presumably until the ship disappeared beneath the waves.

"Also at 10:15:08 hours, the US submarine's radar recorder showed that there were definitely two blips. At precisely 10:15:10 hours, there was only one. The US submarine confirmed its radar screen finally lost all contact at 10:16:45 hours.

"Whatever that blip was, it was very close to the *SS Andros* when it sank.

"Our department is certain the sinking of the *Andros* wasn't due to the vessel having foundered in the very heavy seas."

The conference room was filled with undertones of hesitant

murmuring. The meeting had been in session for over an hour.

The voice of one of the Chiefs of Staff interrupted the young man just as he was about to continue.

"Excuse me, Mr. President, could we please request a short recess in order a brief visit to the men's room could be made?"

"Yes, of course," the President replied. "I do believe this is a good moment for a brief pause. However, I wish to stress that this pause is to be only for five minutes, not a moment longer. This situation has to be completely wrapped up and as soon as possible. Gentlemen, I want a result tonight."

A short recess was granted.

As the President turned to leave, everybody rose from their seats.

In moving towards the door he called, General Kemp, may I have a word with you in private?"

The General nodded. "Certainly, Mr. President."

Soon the room cleared leaving Mr. Erwin-Jones and Lieutenant Logan.

"Nice goin', young man. Let me say you're sure doin' the General proud, son, truly proud. When you started you had a lot of angry disbelieving men in there, but I believe both of you have really begun to turn the corner."

Logan showed his modesty. He politely smiled at Erwin-Jones. "Thank you, sir. I had no idea what was going to happen when General Kemp asked me to address the meeting. I don't mind telling you, sir, I nearly died!"

Mr. Erwin-Jones placed his hand on the young man's shoulder. "You have begun mighty well, Smartie. May I call you by that name?"

"Sure, sir. I don't mind."

Erwin-Jones replied, "I only hope you have at least two or three aces up your sleeve for your finale."

He suddenly stopped talking.

The double doors opened and officers began to file in to reassemble the meeting.

Erwin-Jones spoke briefly and quietly to Logan. "Good luck, youngster. Go in there and get' em.

General Kemp reappeared through another door. His expression was one of cool reserve having had a long discussion with the President.

Erwin-Jones announced the President's entrance. Everybody stood and waited for him to be seated.

The President spoke, "Thank you, gentlemen. I trust you have all had time to ease your conscience?" There was an uneasy stillness in light of that remark. "Please continue, Lieutenant Logan."

"Thank you, Mr. President. As I have already stated, gentlemen, there were to be three more similar occurrences regarding these recorded and unusual events. The second one seems to be an oddity. It occurred at 17:29:50 hours on 31 July.

"Thankfully, I am able to say it appears no disastrous consequence came about, yet there has been recorded various listings of record breaking oceanic weather reports. These confirmations were received via our satellite *S.N.O.W.M.I.S.T. 'U'*, at the time a blip showed up on our submarine radar recordings.

"What occurred was a very strange major ice storm. It was experienced within the local vicinity where the unidentified object had briefly been recorded.

"Again, the same as before, the blip suddenly disappeared.

Our department is still checking out further data to see if we can trace any reason which might have caused this extraordinary ice storm."

Logan paused for a moment to take a sip of water.

"At 20:54:00 hours on 31 July, our submarine radar screens showed a blip reappearing. This time the location was registered to be two miles west of the last recorded position where both the British Airways and Air India airliners met their fate.

"Forensic reports suggested that terrorist bombs blew both aircraft out of the sky. Our department has since received further clarification which shows the wreckage of Air India's Flight A102 definitely had traces of high explosive burns.

"However, this was not so in regard to pieces of wreckage collected and examined from the British Airways Boeing 777. As yet, no trace of any bombing evidence has been discovered. The strangest comparison made so far are several very clean-cut circular edges.

"What's even more interesting, but yet still unresolved, these clean-cut circular edges seem to be very similar to those found on the *SS Andros*.

"Gentlemen, the submarine's radar recorders eventually showed the blip disappeared at 20:57:10 hours. I believe all of you have been made aware that US Navy submarine *SSN Bowevil* has successfully discovered and filmed the wreckage of the *S. Andros*. You will see in this report the submarine made good speed in order to meet up with the British submarine *HMS Excalibur*.

"It has been due to the kind assistance of the Royal Navy of Great

Britain that our department has been able to join a lot of the missing pieces together. I understand from General Kemp a great deal of this was co-ordinated through the British Royal Naval Intelligence Service HQ at Northwood, England."

The meeting echoed mutterings of approval.

Logan continued, "The final and longest period of radar recording our submarines made was when the blip of the unidentified object suddenly reappeared at 16:01:36 hours on the afternoon of 1 August.

"Our records show the blip remained for a considerable time. It appeared to move away from our subs at a great pace in a south–south-easterly course. We believe this to be an exercise of fleeing the disaster area and not wanting to be drawn into any involvement with the wreckage of the two aircraft.

"The blip finally disappeared from the screens at 19:23:18 hours.

"Gentlemen, may I stress, the Commodore in command of the *HMS Excalibur* also confirmed the discovery of this unidentified blip. Our department understands the British submarine is now in hot pursuit of the unknown blip.

"We are assured this is being achieved at a safe distance. We have received further reports from the *Intrepid,* by agreement of our Navy's General Chief of Staff, whereby we are advised our submarine has been commissioned to assist *HMS Excalibur* regarding any possible operation."

There was an immediate reaction from the conference upon hearing that comment, but it appeared it was not heard by everybody.

The President looked across the table. He put his hand up calling for order then passed forward an invitation for his Chief of Staff of the Navy to speak. "Alan, what was that I just heard you say? If you would be kind enough to repeat it so that everybody can hear what it was you said."

Admiral Alan J. T. Adams III paused. "Yes, Mr. President. I will do so if you so wish it."

The room fell silent.

The President replied, "Yes, Admiral. I do."

There was a soft murmur.

"Mr. President, sir, I myself issued this fully classified instruction so how on earth did these two guys get to hear of it? It was never released for any form of common conjecture, let alone for the ears of a mere lieutenant, and at that a freshman to this table."

Everyone had begun to mumble and gossip in utter amazement at the Admiral's revelation.

The President beckoned him to be seated. "All right, Admiral. Please, I do appreciate the information you are hearing is what we employ and pay these lads for. By that I mean if you put your name to it then you have got to ensure that you've got it right. Now, Lieutenant, please continue."

"Thank you, Mr. President." Logan took another sip of water.

"The only thing our department had still not questioned until this morning was what had given reason for that last recorded blip to remain exposed for a much longer period than before."

Again the soft noise of muttering could be heard.

"Well, as I have already stressed, we are still trying to see if this unknown object is mechanical or a living thing. I must advise, however, we do believe it is more likely to be mechanical. Please allow me to explain why. This morning our department received a vital breakthrough from one of our agents who is working undercover in Russia."

Logan picked up a leaf of paper from his portfolio. He read the message:

URGENT – VOSTOK – OUT OF ACTION FROM 16.00 HOURS 03/08/17
– UNTIL – 19.24 HOURS 03/08/17 – STOP – DAMAGE SUSTAINED BY
A SHOWER OF METEORS – STOP – END MESSAGE

"At first this message was not considered to be a significant piece of information. However, when the department's computer, *G.O.D.,* was fed the data it was left then for General Kemp to forward the co-ordination of the same data to NASA Tracking. Gentlemen, it's these results and findings that are now recorded within the classified dossier set before you. Thank you, Mr. President. That completes the updated report which is known only to those persons present in this room."

The President nodded in acknowledgement.

Logan again spoke. "The US Naval and Military Intelligence Department at Cape Canaveral wishes to extend its gratitude and thanks to all concerned throughout the world who have assisted us in this project. Only with their help has it allowed us to compile this dossier at such short notice. Mr. President, we are truly grateful for our having been given the chance to present the portfolio at this top secret meeting."

Lieutenant Logan sat down.

For a moment there was complete silence.

Admiral Alan J. T. Adams III broke the moment of peace by giving a resounding clap with his hands. Immediately, everybody, including the President, joined in.

After a minute the President raised his hand.

"Thank you, gentlemen.

"Well, General Kemp, I must say you certainly have trained him very well, very well indeed. May I say that my admiration goes out to both of you. At the beginning of this meeting I think everyone was ready to chop both your heads off. Well, now it's your turn to consider that to this meeting. You will now have to leave us in peace in order, hopefully, we may resolve a practical outcome to your department's invaluable support and assistance. On behalf of everyone present, I sincerely thank you both. Gentlemen, Chiefs of Staff, may I ask you all to stand and show your appreciation."

There was resounding applause in response to the President's request after which General Kemp and Lieutenant Logan were ushered from the conference room followed by Mr. Erwin-Jones.

As soon as the large doors had closed behind them Logan immediately made haste towards the men's room.

"He certainly did you proud, General," Erwin-Jones said after he had ensured both doors were firmly locked and barred.

"I know. He was even better than I thought he was going to be. Anyway, about the other matter. He doesn't know yet, but I am damned sure you're aware of things, Erwin. Isn't that why we've been asked to hang around for a bit?"

"Yes, General. I mean, I don't really know, sir. I was instructed to follow you both out, and then to ensure that you both wouldn't rush off."

The General answered, "If we are having to wait is there a place where we could go and grab a bite to eat?"

"Sure. There's a very good brunch facility on the floor below ground level."

"Excellent! You'll find us down there, otherwise expect us to be back here in about thirty minutes."

Erwin-Jones acknowledged, "Okay, General. I expect the President will want to finish with the emergency committee by about 22.45 hours. Please ensure you're back here before that time just in case the meeting happens to end a little earlier than expected."

"No problem, Mr. Jones."

At that moment Logan came out of the men's room.

"Feeling a little better, Smartie?"

"I don't really know yet, sir. Mind you, I wish you could have let me know what it was I was heading into."

"Hey! Come on now. You were great!"

Mr. Erwin-Jones acknowledged the General's sentiments.

Logan was relieved and felt an inner sense of elation.

"Well, General, can we now go and eat? I don't want my stomach playing me up again at such an important occasion."

Both Erwin-Jones and Kemp laughed. At that moment the elevator doors opened.

The General remarked, "See you shortly, Erwin."

"You bet."

After taking a little light refreshment both officers were back waiting outside conference room number thirty-seven.

It was about 22:40 hours when Mr. Erwin-Jones, followed by the President, came out of the conference room to meet General Kemp and Lieutenant Logan.

The President warmly greeted the General. "Thank you, General Kemp for bringing me all the way down to meet this youngster. I'm sure you're the one responsible for his turnout, plus the mainstay of support behind his youthful front.

"Congratulations, Lieutenant Logan. I'm certain you have the makings of a fine officer. I believe you have a very promising future ahead of you if this evening's performance was anything to go by. You've made a very positive start towards becoming a senior officer. See to it, General, that you continue directing him on the path that you started on."

"Thank you, sir. I'll certainly do my best."

"Well, Lieutenant, I understand it's Smartie Logan that you like to be referred as?"

Logan looked a little surprised, but before he could speak the President interrupted.

"Oh, do not worry about it on my account. Be sure, Smartie, a little voice has already filled me in concerning many matters in your regard."

They both laughed.

Kemp and Erwin-Jones also chuckled.

The President continued, "Well, Lieutenant, when all this emergency is over and settled down on the right side, I hope I'll have the opportunity and pleasure of meeting you again. That's of course when your official posting comes through confirming your new position and rank, Captain Logan."

For a moment Logan's expression froze.

"Congratulations, lad, you have earned it. America is very proud to have someone with your insight and calibre serving in the highly skilled field of your department; someone who is always working in the best interest of our country."

The President turned and faced everyone.

"Gentlemen, let me please tell you something that is highly important before I'm called back in."

All three men stood expectant but were not quite sure what the President might say.

"I have agreed to send up the space shuttle *Liberty*."

There was an air of surprise and excitement.

"Also, confidentially, I must say it will not just be a routine operation such as the rank and file will be led to understand. Of course the shuttle will be put into orbit, but it will be ordered to take a much closer look at that Russian space platform to see exactly what the Russians are getting up to. Gentlemen, I'm sure your report stands firm, therefore please be my personal guests at the shuttle's official launching which is to take place at 08:30 hours tomorrow."

Logan stood rigid as if frozen to the floor. He was speechless.

A little surprised with Logan's reaction Kemp answered, "Thank you very much, Mr. President. That's very kind of you, sir."

"Not at all, General. It's a tremendous job you've both achieved. Now, I'm fully resigned to believing those Russians really are up to something. For all our sakes, I just hope we're able to find out what the devil it is. Now, I must bid you both good night. We are deeply in your gratitude, and please continue to keep up the good work. By the way, General, don't be too alarmed about what Admiral Adams considers as law."

"I quite understand, sir. Good night, Mr. President."

They all shook hands and then departed.

Chapter Fourteen

NASA Military and Naval Intelligence, Cape Canaveral
Saturday, 5 August was a beautifully clear morning. A faint breeze was blowing off the coast of Cape Canaveral.

The time was 06:00 hours.

General Kemp's limousine had already collected Logan and now called back for the General who ordered his driver to quickly make best haste to the office.

"Good morning, Sergeant Lance."

"Good morning, sir."

"Bright and early enough for you, is it?"

"Yes, sir. Did everything go well for you both last night, sir?"

"It sure did, Lance. It sure as hell did!"

"Did the expected happen, sir?"

"You bet!"

"Well I do declare, now I'm livin' amongst the swells and toffs."

Kemp knew he'd made the Sergeant's day.

Logan entered the main entrance. "Good morning, Sergeant."

"Good morning, sir. I trust I'm still allowed to have the honour of speaking with you?"

"Why of course," Logan replied. "What's up?"

Immediately the Sergeant stood up, brought himself smartly to attention and saluted.

Logan braced himself against the unknown. He wasn't quite sure what was going to happen next.

Sergeant Lance relaxed. "Congratulations, Captain Logan, sir. I'll arrange for the change of nameplate on your door while you are out this morning."

Logan's face brought forth the broadest smile.

At that moment Kemp returned. "Did you catch him, Lance?"

"I sure did, sir. My Liza ain't goin' to believe this thing happened here today. The young 'un and our General both met up with our President! To top it all, the young Lieutenant that was, has now come back to us as a fully fledged Captain."

They all roared with laughter.

"Come on, Smartie, we mustn't keep the launch waiting," said the General.

Both the General and Logan turned to leave.

Lance bade them farewell. "Have a good time, gentlemen."

"Thank you, Lance. We should be back about noon time."

At precisely 08:30:09 hours, the majestic sight of the United States Military space shuttle *Liberty* slowly lifted itself clear of its launch tower. A gushing white-hot geyser of flame splayed its path across a parched launching pad. Loudspeakers bellowed a message that sounded the launch pad clearance: "WE HAVE A GOOD LIFT-OFF! LIBERTY YOU ARE GREEN FOR GO. YOU'RE LOOKING GOOD AND GOING UP! YOU'RE ON YOUR WAY AND LOOKING GREAT!"

Call sign F for Freedom responded.

"Thanks, NASA Control. All feels very well."

Within eight minutes the shuttle had reached a height of two hundred kilometres and was progressing into its first orbital flight. Soon, two rocket boosters (SRBs) fell away leaving the three main engines to continue.

After a further two minutes of flight, the SRBs could be seen by the naked eye falling away into the sea. The large external tank still continued to supply the shuttle's main engines. Finally, when these extinguished, the shuttle was just on the edge of space.

"Did you see that, Logan?" enquired the General.

"Truly magnificent, sir. I'm speechless."

"Yes, Smartie, I know the feeling. It still gets to me too, kid. Hey, look there, you see it? The external tank has just been jettisoned and is beginning to burn up as it hurtles back down through the atmosphere."

Logan looked up in awe.

"Do you see it, Smartie?"

"Yes, quite clearly. Thank you, sir."

"It's the only part of the shuttle that cannot be re-used."

Soon a large white vapour trail pillared upwards towards the cloudless sky. The vapour trail slowly began to arc. Finally, *Liberty* vanished from view.

Captain Logan continued to look up.

General Kemp turned and smiled at him. "It sure gives you one hell of a kick, don't it, Smartie?"

"Plus a grand sense of pride, sir."

The President's party began to disperse.

"Ah! General Kemp, Captain Logan." It was the voice of Admiral Alan J. T. Adams III. "Gentlemen, thank you for that very enlightening address last night.

We do hope this effort will solve this little mystery. By the way, General, I wonder if you would give me a call on my private line when matters have settled down?"

"Would be delighted, sir. By the way, Admiral, thank you for the compliment."

"Not at all, General. You have an outstanding team. Keep up the good work."

After the thunderous roar of the launch, peace came back to the launching pad. Slowly the white puffs of vapour cloud began to drift away.

"Come on, Smartie. Back to the drawing board. We'll have to sit this one out until the show's completely over."

"Okay, sir. I'm ready when you are."

Kemp summoned his limousine.

Soon they were being whisked away back to the Naval and Military Intelligence Department.

While sitting in the limousine, Logan suddenly thought of something that he considered was important enough to mention to the General. "Excuse me, sir. I'm sorry. Did I interrupt your reading?"

"That's all right, Smartie. Fire away."

"Well, General, I thought I should mention it just in case you might be speaking to NASA on our arrival back at the office."

"Mention what, Logan?"

"Well sir, I was just thinking back on certain things. Did you mention to anyone outside our reporting last night that a few weeks back the Russians launched a military space orbiter?"

"No, Smartie, I didn't. Why, should I have done?"

"Well, I just don't know, sir. I hope it's not going to be too important. But, it's in regard to this I thought you ought to know that late yesterday afternoon, just before our leaving, I believe I finally managed to break into the Russian's RIIC (Russian Intelligence Information Channel). You know, sir, the one that stores all past computer data of traffic movements to and from the Russian Siberian launch site Kapustin Yar."

"Holy cow, Captain! Why on earth didn't you split on this matter before now?"

"Sir, at first I wasn't really too sure what on earth it was I had rattled

183

into. Then by the time I'd begun to figure things out, we had to leave. I'm awfully sorry, General."

"It's okay, Smartie. No damage done, but what did you do when you got through? Did you begin to decipher anything? What the heck did you find out?"

Kemp was so taken aback with Logan's coolness he stumbled into his next sentence. "What bearing does it have in regard to this particular occasion?"

"Sir, I don't think Russia has returned that particular orbiter back to Earth. In fact, all my analysis decoding and information on checking the position firmly indicates the orbiter still has a launch/return facility. The computer sometimes shows this as uncleared. This was still coded as a positive return position. I have rechecked this. I found this still to be the case in the slot being left open as a confirmed order docking reference on board the Russian space platform *Vostok*."

Kemp put his hand inside a box. He drew out a large cheroot cigar and lit it. As he blew out the match his hand trembled slightly. "Good grief, Logan! You must recheck everything when we get back. Driver, step on it! If that sonofabitch of a Russkie is armed… Suffering marbles! Unknowingly, the *Liberty* could well have an unexpected reception committee waiting for it when it moves into a position to take a closer look at the *Vostok*."

"Okay, General, don't worry. I'll ensure everything gets done. I'll see to it. You'll have a full update as soon as I can get G.O.D. to put its brain back into action. I'll try to fill you in with any other stuff which might have come through on to the circuit overnight."

Both gentlemen nodded regarding the plan of action to be taken.

As the limousine sped along the interstate highway, the sun shone down from a cloudless sky. It had been a perfect morning for the trial launch of the American space shuttle.

Unknown to the public, *Liberty* was now further into space than any past shuttle mission had previously orbited.

NASA Control anxiously awaited the breakthrough of *Libertys'* long period of radio silence. All parties were poised ready to receive news of the space shuttle's flight progress. It seemed an age as the seconds slowly ticked away.

NASA Military and Naval Intelligence, Cape Canaveral

General Kemp sat on the veranda while enjoying his first cup of coffee of the day.

The morning's peace and tranquillity was soon interrupted when the house telephone rang. Kemp got up and answered it.

"Good morning, sir. Please excuse me for disturbing you so early but we have a report coming in from the *Liberty*. I believe it needs your urgent attention as soon as possible."

"That's okay, Sergeant Lance. I'm already up and under way. Send back a short message in reply. Say we will respond before 06:30 hours. I'll be there shortly to attend to it."

"Will do, General."

It had been nearly twenty-three hours since the US Military space shuttle was successfully launched. Everything had gone like clockwork. Even the national newspapers reporting on the previous day's events kept the whole thing observed as a low-key test bed operation.

A small footnote printed in the *New York Times* and *Herald Tribune* acknowledged the mission was a total success.

Kemp noticed it and hoped anyone reading the statement wouldn't feel too uncomfortable. He considered his department had always been a master of the understatement. It was not too long before he got himself ready and left the house.

Sergeant Lance was on the front step of the department as the General's limousine pulled up. He greeted the General as he opened the limo door. "Good morning, sir."

"Hi there, Lance. Everything okay?"

"Not exactly, sir. I'm afraid we've had a slight emergency since you left the house. The President's aide has been calling. Could you please call him back immediately?"

"Thank you, Sergeant, I'll do just that."

Kemp went straight to his office and picked up the phone. As he was dialling, Captain Logan knocked on the office door and entered.

"Good morning, General. Fine morning isn't it?" Logan saw that Kemp was on the telephone. He stopped sharp and sat himself down.

The General gave him a polite nod. He put his hand over the receiver and in a loud whisper said, "It's the President!"

A voice was heard on the line. "Good morning. Is that General John Kemp?"

"Yes, sir, Mr. President."

"Well, General. Sorry for the early start but I am calling to request you immediately put a complete blanket on any releases of information regarding details you will shortly be receiving. They concern reports just received from the space shuttle *Liberty*. I wish to advise you I am not in any way seeking to give any undue cause for concern. But, in regard to our operations possibly having entered into an undisclosed area of Star Wars, I've a nasty feeling, General. However, let me advise you, the *Liberty* has been fully programmed. It is armed and, if necessary, it has been ordered to take any desired evasive action. That is, of course, if encountering an attack from an enemy force."

Kemp gave a slight cough as the door of his office opened.

Logan entered and approached the desk carrying two large mugs of steaming coffee.

Under Logan's arm was a large envelope marked: FOR THE ATTENTION OF GENERAL JOHN B. KEMP VERY PRIVATE / HIGHLY CONFIDENTIAL.

The Captain put down the mugs of coffee and placed the couriered message in front of the General.

"Yes, Mr. President. We'll follow up everything very closely and indeed keep a close watch regarding the unauthorised release of any matters concerning the engagement of any unforeseen alien or enemy. I will notify your office immediately as and when anything has occurred."

"Thank you very much, General. That will be all."

"Thank you, sir. Goodbye, Mr. President."

Kemp carefully replaced the receiver. "Jesus! That was some call! What is that you've placed on my desk, Logan?"

"I don't really know, sir. It just came in by express courier. I picked it up as I was passing the front desk in order to come and see you."

"Well, I suppose we'd better take a closer look. By the way, has there been any news or information released concerning coverage of the *Liberty*?"

"Not that I know of, sir."

"Good. Any such information or news received concerning that department, Logan, is now to be completely silenced from the outside world. I trust I make my self quite clear?"

"Yes, sir."

Kemp looked down as he pulled open the red sealed tag. It was an emergency device, which ensured no booby traps or tampering had occurred during delivery. It first had to be broken so the envelope could be opened successfully.

"Jumpin' jellyfish! Who in hell has sent us this lot?"

Logan wondered what had upset the General so suddenly. "What is it, sir?"

"They look like some sort of first shots. I don't really know."

Kemp studied them for a moment.

"Maybe they're pictures taken from the *Liberty!*" said Logan.

"Who has done this? Who the devil has sent these here to me? After what the President has just said I don't want to be landed with this lot. Logan, see to it nothin' leaves my office."

"Yes, sir."

Kemp looked carefully over the package.

He then noticed a little card tucked in between some of the first photographs. It read:

FOR YOUR EYES ONLY AND NOT A WORD TO ANYONE EXCEPT TO THOSE IN THE RIGHT DEPARTMENT!

BEST REGARDS – MAC B.

"Good grief! Now I understand. Logan, hold everything!"

"Pardon me, General?"

"It's okay, Smartie. Everything's fine."

The General picked up the red telephone receiver and dialled a number.

"Could you urgently connect me to Professor Burston?"

The sweet voice of a bright young telephonist answered.

"Thank you, General. One moment please. I'll try to connect you."

There was a pause. A few clicks were heard then a familiar voice answered.

"Hi, John. What's up?"

"Mac, can you please call me back on my closed line? We need to talk urgently!"

"Okay. Did you receive the package, and…?"

"That's why I am calling you," the General interrupted sharply.

"Okay, John. I'll be right back to you."

A few seconds later the General's hotline telephone began to ring.

"You're a dark horse," said the General.

"Okay, John, tell me all about it?"

"Come on, Mac. Where on earth did you come by these pictures?"

"Simple, John."

"What do you mean simple? How on earth can you say anything like that as being just simple"?

"Just simmer down and stop huffin' and puffin' like that or you'll do yerself an injury. Just listen to me a mo' and I'll explain.

"NASA Tracking, unbeknown to a lot of high-up folks, decided to get in a first. We set up on board the *Liberty* a dual TV/Video camera just behind an unexposed infra-red heat shield. It's one with an undetectable internal screen. You see, John, in the past everyone here has got a little fed up havin' to sit and wait for clearance of the V.I.P. talk through. We only ever receive the still pictures of our organised space walks many hours later. Well, this time we decided to light our own fire. Therefore we arranged ourselves a little party, and we think a first. I don't mind tellin' you we have the whole launch plus a further twenty-nine hours of viewing for you. That is, of course, if your department wants to see it."

"Jesus, Mac! You bet we do!"

Professor Burston's tone of voice suddenly lowered and said coldly, "There's only one condition: this stuff leaks out to no one. Is that clear?"

"Now hold on, Mac. Nowadays I've got to report all matters to the big guy in person. What in hell's name do you think I am goin' to say to him about this lot? Sorry Mr. P. but NASA Trackin' holds the exclusive Film and TV rights to all video pictures of the *Liberty*? Sorry, Mac. No can do. And I mean NO!"

"Holy Smoke, John! I'm sorry. For a moment I had forgotten about that one." Burston's voice began to stutter. "Well, I suppose you could just show them to the President. Mind you, John, nobody else is to get a look. On no account are any copies to be made. Is that clear?"

"Okay."

While Macdonald Burston had been laying down his terms, Kemp had gone through the complete dossier.

"I must say they're really incredible, Mac."

"You bet!"

"Who made up the still shots?"

"I did."

"If ever you need a job change, Mac, I'd take you on right away."

"I'll bear that in mind. However, John, I think I'm best suited to the field I'm already involved in. So, my good friend, no stupid ideas. Okay?"

"Okay. Pity, Mac. Such a waste of good talent."

"Cool it, John."

Macdonald Burston was in no mood for any type of joke. His mind was purely directed towards the business at hand.

"Right then. If you accept we shall have these videos sent over to your department as soon as possible."

"Thanks again, Mac. I'll send over Rodney, my driver, with the limo if you so wish it?"

"No problem, John. We'll take care of the delivery. Have you seen the last three photos while you've been talking to me?"

"I have glimpsed through most of them." Kemp shuffled to the bottom of the pile. The first three photographs showed a picture of the Earth's curvature.

"Okay, John. Have you gott'em?"

"Yep."

"Right. Now take a look in the top left hand corner of the second one. Do you see something?"

"Yes, but I can't really make out what the thing showing is."

"Well, it may come as a surprise to you. That's the Russian space orbiter you can see."

"You've gotta' be kiddin' me. Surely they didn't build the thing looking like that, or did they?"

"No, John, they didn't. I thought at first the wrong shape might have foxed you. That little wasp has just gone out and captured, single-handed, one of the Russian space platform's solar battery arms. I can only presume it must have been in the process of trying to re-orbit in order repairs could be made."

"Now I see it, Mac. My, I wouldn't have relished the idea of steering that one back to base, would you?"

"Not really, John. Now, take a look at the next picture. *Liberty* took this one on its second orbit. We used the zoom lens in order to bring out a closer view of the damaged space platform."

Kemp perused over the picture for a few moments.

"It looks like an army of space spiders have set about re-spinning the main web."

"Yes, John, I suppose you could say it looks a little bit like that," Mac answered laughing.

"Right. Now take a look at the last picture. This one was taken on *Liberty*'s seventh orbit and from a different approach angle."

"It's comin' right out from beneath the space platform's belly. Holy cow! That's a green beam of spiralling light. Excuse me for a moment, Mac. Logan! Get hold of the Ghostbusters file."

Macdonald Burston could hear the sudden hive of activity taking place. "I thought you'd be most interested in that one, John. By the way, please remember the shuttle's pilot cannot see this himself. Only our complicated screening and sophisticated infra-red filter has been able to pick all this up. That was also just by chance. John, if *Liberty* had maintained its normal course we might never have discovered it."

"Mac, dear friend, I do sincerely owe you one. Thanks a bunch for this lot."

"Not at all, John. That's what friends are for. By the way, thanks for the special invite to the launch. I did see you, but you were too weighed down in rubbin' shoulders with the bigwigs."

"Okay, Mac. Nice one. What will all this cost me?"

"Oh, nothing, dear boy. Well, probably no more than a few days fishing on your boat."

"Mac, you're on. We'll fix it up sometime after the whole show's over. Is that okay?"

"You'd better believe it, John."

"Thanks again, Mac. I look forward to our receivin' the next lot of snaps. By the way, if anything else comes over that really does need swiftly watching."

"Don't worry, John, I'll give you a call. I'll ask you to come right over. Bye for now."

Kemp was gobsmacked. He could hardly believe his luck.

"LOGAN! Where's that file?"

Captain Logan entered the General's office carrying a large briefcase.

"Thank you, Smartie. Right, let's get things weavin'. Could you please get the President's office on the line? We've got some late diplomatic visiting to do."

"Why? What's up, sir?" Logan looked at the photographs laid out on top of the General's desk. He immediately recognised the Russian space platform in one of them. Then he noticed the thin green beam of fluorescent light arcing from beneath the platform.

"Kiss my arse! Hey, General, did you happen to see what seems to be showing in that picture?"

"Precisely, Logan. Precisely."

Chapter Fifteen

At Sea

Since being exposed by the breakdown of communication caused by the failure of Operation Invisible, it had been a nerve-racking time on board the *Gorbachev* for Captain Narodny. He was aware his submarine was now exposed to all radar contact. Also, it could have been attacked as an unknown enemy if caught within firing range of any pursuing predator. Luckily, the emergency didn't seem to show any immediate danger.

It was now late in the afternoon on 11 August. Captain Narodny stood on the bridge of his submarine studying the thin outline of the coast of West Africa.

With the extremely hot equatorial sun beaming down, the captain knew it would be very unwise to stay up top for too long. However, although the situation of exposure was critical, the submarine had surfaced in order to test its operational gauges and equipment for tropical conditions. *Only another hour at the most would be needed*, he thought.

Lying comfortably off the coast of Mauritania, Captain Narodny considered his position under cover of the heat haze would be fully screened and undetected from the shore. He even allowed some of the crew up on deck for a breath of fresh air.

The time was nearing 18.00 hours.

Just over twenty-five nautical miles to the north of the *Gorbachev*, and currently undetected by any of the Russian submarine's radar, France's latest type of super attack destroyer, the *Meridien*, was steadily cruising southwards. The French had been systematically patrolling the seas around Africa.

The French warship was just coming to the end of a courtesy patrol on behalf of the friendship pact that had been arranged between the governments of Morocco and Western Sahara.

As the French ship was beginning to make a one hundred and eighty degree slow arc to turn and head once again northwards, a lookout and duty officer of the watch were both making a final combing of the heat-hazed horizon through their powerful radio computerised binoculars. One of the lookouts made a visual contact with what looked like a large unidentified vessel on the surface.

At that distance it was very difficult to confirm what it really was. The duty officer of the watch verified confirmation of the sighting in his log. He then reported it to the bridge for the attention of Captain Charles de Mersinay.

The Captain received the message.

He read it and responded. "Thank you, Lt. Donat. Please have Sparks advise and notify all other shipping in our area of the position and sighting. Please confirm in the ship's log the circumstance of how it was sighted. Have it marked on our radar-scanning screen with a marker one that acknowledges the sighting is awaiting further surveillance. When you have completed these instructions, forward a copy of the recorded binocular computer sighting to central computer intelligence control immediately. They should be able to run the outline shape through the system in order to get a prompt positive match.

"If it simply goes away then all well and good, otherwise we might have to take a closer look at it later on. In the meantime, I suggest we steam as close as we can to the outer limits of Western Sahara and Mauritania territorial waters, but please ensure we stay just inside the limit in order we can keep our sovereign impunity."

Lt. Donat made careful note of what his captain had said. "Right you are, sir. I'll arrange release of your instructions immediately."

Captain de Mersinay acknowledged. "Be sure we do not expose our position and become a possible threat, or be treated as an unsuspecting target. We don't want a surprise attack emanating from local communist pirates or from the terrorists of these shores."

Lt. Donat answered, "I quite understand, sir. I have already posted a double watch. This was just in case of a possible night attack by gunboats or from any armed powerboat that might unexpectedly shoot out from Mauritania's darkened shoreline."

"Good," Captain de Mersinay acknowledged. "Lt. Donat, you had better sound the general alert. The crew will then be in total readiness if we are attacked."

"Very good, sir."

Gradually the glow of the sinking sun began to expand sending a carpet of red across the vast breadth of ocean.

Still the *Gorbachev* could not detect the *Meridien* on its close order radar.

As soon as a distance of eighty kilometres was reached, the French destroyer would be located and sighted on the submarine's radar.

The *Gorbachev's* position was about thirty kilometres due west of Nouadhibou, slightly north of Cape Blanc.

Captain Narodny knew that in the dimming light of dusk, the lights of the town of Arguin would soon be visible.

The French destroyer *Meridien* was just inside the three-mile limit of Western Sahara's coastal waters. Its distance from the *Gorbachev* was now eighty-six kilometres.

On board, Lt. Donat reported to Captain de Mersinay. "Sir, our radio message was received by the following ships: the *SS Koko Maru*, a Japanese freighter that is about forty kilometres north of our position who advised they would keep a constant watch on their radar for any unusual objects; the British nuclear submarine, *HMS Excalibur,* is somewhere west-north-west of our position and north-east of the British sub is the American strategic ballistic submarine, the *SSBN Intrepid*."

"It all seems like quite a party, don't you think, Lt. Donat?" Captain de Mersinay remarked.

"It would appear so, sir."

"One moment, Lieutenant, I'm not so sure. I think it could also be deemed as something very odd."

The Captain paused and thought for a moment: *Two major allied submarines being this far south, and roaming around off the West African coastline. I wonder what they are up to.*

Lt. Donat commented, "Maybe these subs are just passing through going southwards, and considered it was preferable to take this coastal route due to the favourable underwater currents, sir."

Captain de Mersinay wasn't too happy about it. "Lt. Donat," he called.
"Yes, sir."

"Kindly check on any of the latest international activity that concerns the USA and *Grande Brétagne*. Maybe it is something political which has brought these two ships together. Our mainstream link computer with HQ should quickly provide us with the answer. Please see to it right away. We should have the answer within a matter of minutes."

"Right you are, sir." Lt. Donat gave a salute then departed to the operations room.

The *Meridien* was the French Navy's most modern warship. Its keel was laid in Toulon in January 2012. In world ranking, the destroyer was one of the most modern surveillance detection vessels currently at sea. It had been acknowledged as the forerunner to the most up-to-date naval technology ships in any destroyer class, and had set the style of building under the French naval programme forward into the twenty-first century.

The French government had received many forward orders for building new destroyers of the same class from countries in the Middle East. The destroyer's most up-to-date armament included an advanced series of interceptor missiles based on the Harpoon Exocet MM40 block three and Arrow rocket-thrown weapons (*ASROC* and *Ikara*) missiles. This type and style of defence rocket had now been advanced to enable it to adapt itself to a strategic role of air-to-surface, air-to-air, sea-to-air or even to accommodate a surface-to-underwater encounter, the latter being specifically designed to be fired from a great distance and on impact would release a cluster of depth charges to explode at depths of between seventy-five and one hundred and thirty metres.

Lt. Donat called the bridge as soon as he had cleared the information. "Captain de Mersinay."

"Yes, Lt. Donat."

"Sir, as yet we have received no detailed report regarding the USA and *Grande Brétagne* subs. Also, in response to that unidentified ship, our intelligence links and computer references advise the description of our radio radar contact, as yet, has not been located. Nor has it been located or connected with any current logistics reference of all ocean-going vessels recorded afloat. Central Control advised they are now backlogging and checking all international and worldwide computer inputs, and all references that have been co-ordinated or altered over the past month. I will report to you as soon as anything is confirmed regarding the lookout's sighting that we transmitted."

Captain de Mersinay had listened to the Lieutenant's report and was pleased with its thoroughness. "Thank you, Lt. Donat. How long will this take?"

"I believe about five minutes, sir."

"Good. What is our current radar recording distance from the unidentified vessel?"

"Eighty-three kilometres, sir."

"Fine. Let me know when we are at eighty-one kilometres."

"Right you are, sir. May I ask as to why specifically eighty-one kilometres?"

Captain de Mersinay thought it was a reasonable request. "Certainly.

It is because we shall be in radar range if that unidentified vessel appears to be the type of vessel I think it is."

"What ship is that, sir?"

"Not a ship, Lt. Donat, not a ship. I believe it to be a submarine. Anyway, I would rather retreat into safer waters if we were unable to identify it at this stage.

"However, Lt. Donat, if the vessel does happen to be that elusive Russian submarine everyone has been carping about, we shall at least have enough time to surprise it."

Lt. Donat was not exactly sure what Captain de Mersinay meant. "But, sir, I thought I had read somewhere that the submarine had sunk on its maiden voyage?"

Captain de Mersinay remarked with some surprise. "Have you not read the latest reports circulating about the *Gorbachev*? By all accounts, Donat, it is now the most wanted ship, or submarine, in the world."

Lt. Donat felt a shiver go down his spine. "Goodness me, sir. Are you saying we have found it, or have we been looking at a ghost ship?"

"No, Lt. Donat, that object our lookouts picked up is no ghost ship. If it is the *Gorbachev*, I trust we will have a good chance to get a shot in first. We'll just have to wait and see, won't we?"

There was a pause as Lieutenant Donat slowly put down the telephone in order to begin reading a report just coming through on the printer.

Immediately he called back to the Captain. "An urgent identity information report is just coming though, sir."

"Right you are, Lt. Donat. Let's have it."

Lt. Donat began to read: "Type: Borei Buluva Class VI Nuclear Balistic Submarine. One only commissioned 2011. Name: *SSBN Gorba…*"

Captain de Mersinay suddenly stopped listening and looked up.

The sky was beginning to change colour. A series of flashes and bright lights engulfed the horizon.

Captain de Mersinay yelled at the top of his voice. "ACTION STATIONS! ACTION STATIONS!"

Lt. Donat's voice echoed back down the telephone. "We are at eighty kilometres, sir! I confirm again, we are at eighty kilometres!"

Captain de Mersinay snapped back. "Damn it, Donat, I specifically requested you to confirm and tell me when our position reached EIGHTY-ONE kilometres. I'm sure by now we must have been spotted!"

"But how?" Lt. Donat asked.

"Don't waste time asking me stupid questions! Order the launching crew to make the rockets ready for firing. Time them for one minute and thirty seconds. Fire both port and starboard Arrow (*ASROC*) rockets. Ensure they are fitted with underwater warheads for anti–submarine defence. For God sakes don't go making any further mistakes."

The French warship and its crew suddenly became aware they were on an unexpected war footing and were about to engage the most evil of opponents.

Lt. Donat calmly released his Captain's orders then replied, "Firing orders effected, sir."

On hearing this clearance Captain de Mersinay called to the engine room. "Engine room, we will be engaging an enemy in the next sixty seconds and firing two rockets. When completed, I will instruct that the *Meridien* is to go about one hundred and eighty degrees.

"Chief Engineer, I will want you to use all the power our ship can muster. I need us to proceed at full speed towards the coast of Western Sahara."

For a moment there was no response. Then a voice replied, "Right you are, sir. Who may I ask are we aiming at?"

The seconds ticked by then the Captain responded. "Do not worry, Chief. I believe you will know pretty soon."

"SIX, FIVE, FOUR, THREE, TWO, ONE…"

There was a terrific flash and roar as two Arrow (ASROC) rockets were launched. They gathered pace and had soon disappeared out of sight. All that could be seen were the long vapour trails vanishing into the dimming heat haze of a golden sunset.

On board the *Gorbachev*, Captain Narodny happened to be in the operations room when the position of a new small blip came on to the submarine's radar screen. Within seconds the lookout up top detected the ship to be a destroyer.

Captain Narodny ordered an immediate crash dive to a depth of one hundred and seventy-five metres.

For a few moments cheers from the crew rang out as the submarine plunged beneath the waves.

As the *Gorbachev* began to level out Captain Narodny spoke. "Goodness me, Number One. I think this is going to be a mighty close run thing.

"Our intelligence reports tell us it's the French destroyer, *Meridien*. If my memory serves me well, she is the…"

The Captain's voice was interrupted by a sharp very urgent retort. "CAPTAIN! CAPTAIN!"

Captain Narodny calmly flipped a switch to talk back. "What is it, Officer of the Watch?"

There was a distinct tone of panic in the voice that replied. "Captain, we have picked up a dual missile tracking on radar. Impact is expected in about twenty seconds, sir."

Captain Narodny knew his submarine's position appeared somewhat precarious.

His voice came calmly over the tannoy, "Secure all watertight doors. Seal off the nuclear reactor. All crew to battle stations. Sound the general alarm."

The *Gorbachev* had already dived to a depth of ninety metres. The effect of the 'G' force on its hull was tremendous. For the first time the submarine was beginning to groan.

Over the tannoy a nervous voice was heard, "Ten seconds to impact, sir."

Captain's Narodny said in a calm tone, "Hold on tight, everybody. I think we should be all right. Engine room, what is our depth?"

"One hundred and sixty metres, sir, and falling."

The officer of the watch called out the dying seconds before the expected impact. "FIVE, FOUR, THREE, TWO, ONE…"

Everybody held their breath waiting for the explosion and possible instant death.

Nothing happened.

Momentarily, an eerie silence engulfed the submarine.

Suddenly, right above them, a series of explosions was heard at a depth of one hundred metres. The *Gorbachev* shook violently.

A second lot of explosions then came at a depth of one hundred and twenty metres.

Everything aboard swayed and shuddered and the submarine lights flickered. Water suddenly spurted out from two fractured pipes.

Captain Narodny broke the ensuing deathly silence. "MY GOD! The French have attacked us."

His number one officer stood stunned.

On hearing his Captain's remark, he stuttered, "Sure…ly not, sir!"

Captain Narodny was incensed by this sudden unexpected outrage and roared, "Surely this must be deemed as an unprovoked cowardly attack? Number One, it is to be recorded as an act of aggression made against us and our beloved country Russia by another country's warship."

The Captain felt his pride had been seriously dented. "Number One, we are going to defend ourselves. Full speed ahead!"

As the noise and commotion died down, Captain Narodny pondered.

He thought for a minute then spoke, "I knew there was an outside possibility of a surprise attack. I knew it could happen at any time, but I never expected it to come from a puny destroyer, least of all one belonging to the French Navy!"

The Lieutenant, on listening to his Captain's mutterings enquired, "Are you all right, sir? Can I assist you in any way?"

Captain Narodny heard his most senior officer's enquiry and concern.

He responded abruptly. "I am quite all right. Just leave me alone and get on with your duties."

It was not long before things finally settled down in the Russian submarine. Captain Narodny wanted to settle any possible doubt in the minds of his crew that he might not retaliate.

The Captain moved quickly to glance at his charts. He made a few calculations. "Number One, what is the French ship's position?"

The Lieutenant quickly replied, "Twenty-eight kilometres north-east of our position, sir. Approximately six kilometres offshore. The French destroyer is just about to enter its authorised territorial waters between Western Sahara and Mauritania."

Captain Narodny quickly calculated the situation. "Good," he responded.

A telephone rang on the bridge.

The Lieutenant spoke. "Sir!" he called in alarm.

Captain Narodny abruptly responded. "Yes, Number One. What now?"

"Sir! We have a number of small radar sightings converging on the destroyer. They appear to be coming from the coastline of Mauritania."

Captain Narodny was not concerned about what was happening on the French warship. His mind was preoccupied with what he was going to do about the attack on his submarine. However, he didn't wish it to seem that he was to totally dismiss it.

His number one said, "I expect the previous action of firing those rockets by the French has sent the communist terrorists into some sort of panic."

"Good!" the Captain smiled. "Things should now heat up quite nicely."

"Yes, sir," the Lieutenant replied, hoping Captain Narodny was going to give some sort of lead as to what action might be pending.

Captain Narodny stood back from his desk which was now strewn with a number of oceanic depth ordinance charts.

"Number One, we shall attack the French destroyer from its starboard side. This should allow our submarine just enough room to manoeuvre in a depth of about thirty fathoms."

The Lieutenant at first hesitated then said, "Are we going to surface in order to commence our engagement, sir?"

"No. We will synchronise the firing of our armament with the sounding of the French ship's noise and screw revolutions. I want total precision to be maintained. We'll then prove the *Gorbachev* to be well capable of striking at an aggressive military target in self-defence from underwater. They will never know what hit them.

"Hold the crew ready for action, Number One."

"Aye, aye, sir," came the reply.

On board the *Meridien*, Captain de Mersinay, with some measure of surprise, was watching his ship's sudden change of fortune. Through his naval glasses he saw on his port beam, advancing at great speed, a flotilla of gunboats.

The Captain did not hesitate.

"FIRE! FIRE! FIRE!" He yelled the order for immediate action at the top of his voice.

He continued to shout until finally the forward gun turret opened up and engaged shelling at the oncoming flotilla of advancing enemy.

Large spouts of water began to erupt in front of the engaging armada. All of them landed very close to the first two boats of the enemy. Suddenly, there was a brilliant flash. An explosion ripped amidships of the leading boat. Another craft was instantly engulfed in a ball of flame; a huge fire of exploding shells and ammunition disintegrated the enemy boat sending a mass of debris showering upwards into the sky.

Now the guns on the remaining flotilla opened fire. These soon began to find their target.

Small explosions riveted the destroyer's port side, and then on bursting around the forecastle of the *Meridien* the windows on the bridge exploded and blew out. A shell burst immediately below. It exploded on the ships heavy superstructure causing very little structural damage.

"Bloody hell! Our fire is being returned. We are now being attacked," Captain de Mersinay said in amazement.

The Captain peered about him amidst the smoke and debris to see if anyone had been injured. As he glanced down he saw the blooded uniform of Lieutenant Donat. A piece of shrapnel had embedded itself into his neck severing the officer's jugular vein. Death must have been instantaneous. Another officer and two ratings were also caught by the force of an explosion from a direct hit of another shell.

Still the destroyer carried on firing. It was retaliating from every rocket launcher, gun turret and from any small arms defence weapon it could muster.

To Captain de Mersinay, it seemed the odds of survival were very heavily stacked against his warship.

As the battle on the surface raged on, below the waves clearance of all relevant instructions with the space platform *Vostok* had been made in regard to the *Gorbachev*'s time of operations.

Captain Narodny advised Moscow of the submarine's circumstances of engagement. He confirmed matters were one of self-defence.

Moscow responded noting the deemed action was to be done only in retaliation. He was told he was to proceed without there having been any further undue provocation.

Moscow acknowledged its acceptance in so far as such further action was solely at the discretion of Captain Narodny. To that extent, if any engagement was made, Moscow advised any retaliation necessary should confine itself to representing a show of strength. Thus, they allowed the Captain to proceed.

Captain Narodny carefully read the message he had received. He then quoted part of it to his number one.

"If it was found that the *Gorbachev* has to resort to defending itself."

The captain had very carefully considered the pros and cons of this statement. He then thought nothing else other than the position of his submarine and crew.

Again he spoke. "Well, Number One, in my opinion we have been victims of an unprovoked attack by the French. Remember that they surprised us. I do not intend to let them have a second chance."

"Yes, sir, I agree."

Captain Narodny said, "Sound action stations. We will attack in ten minutes."

It was 20.00 hours.

Captain Narodny had already preordained the time of the attack with the space platform *Vostok*. He announced. "We'll fire the atomic-powered laser gun underwater on a broad beam.

"As previously observed and proven, we will fire the gun blind. First, fix the range co-ordination and check the firing distance with our sonar sounding of the warship's radar position, engine noise and propeller's motion."

Slowly the minutes ticked by.

On the surface, the French destroyer had already sunk four terrorist gunboats and had badly damaged another.

Captain de Mersinay was now preparing his warship to make a full-scale rocket attack in order to try and eliminate the three remaining enemy ships.

The warship had not survived unscathed. There was a pall of dense black smoke belching out from its front gun turret.

The terrorist gunboats had finally silenced what they had considered to be their main opposition.

Captain de Mersinay gave the order to fire another rocket. With a blinding flash and immense roar, the weapon raced away. In a second it erupted on its target blowing the gunboat to smithereens.

The *Meridien* had gained another victory, but not without loss; twenty of its gallant crew had died and many others were injured.

Captain de Mersinay now gave very serious consideration to breaking off the engagement and retreating. He knew he was trapped in his own dilemma and unknown destiny.

The two remaining gunboats had now managed to outflank the destroyer. They had placed themselves into a position where they could easily attack the warship amidships.

Both enemy captains knew the danger it placed their gunboats in, but they knew it was the French warship's most exposed area where there was the least possibility of any strong gunfire or counter-attack being made.

Light armament from the destroyer continued to pepper the thin hulls of each oncoming gunboat. The two terrorist boats raced towards the destroyer.

Captain de Mersinay watched the enemy and waited.

He quickly viewed what action to take. Soon the enemy gunboats would be near enough and in range for him to allow his ship to release two Harpoon-Stinga defence rockets. These are not specifically designed for use in destroying any surface attack craft, but the French Captain knew he had to try throwing anything and everything that could be used in order to save his ship.

He knew his warship was exposed on one of its weakest flanks. His ship's position had been caught napping.

The time was 20.14 hours.

With all guns blazing the two surviving smaller craft were soon in range of the destroyer's rockets.

At a thousand metres orders for engagement rang out.

"FIRE! FIRE!" Captain de Mersinay roared.

At that moment a salvo of shells from the two oncoming gunboats splattered along the destroyer's port side. Two massive explosions ripped a huge gaping hole in the warship. The main Harpoon–Stinga rocket launcher's, for a split second, seemed to lift upwards. Both keeled over and disappeared, falling from the ship's side in to the sea.

Part of the destroyer's port deck yawned as a wide chasm opened up leaving a vast area of deck to tumble from the ship and vanish beneath the waves.

As the initial impact of the disaster died down all that could be seen remaining on board the French destroyer was a smouldering mass of burning debris.

A bloodstained carnage of human flesh lay across its decks. An acrid stench of toxic fumes from the burning hulk hung heavily about the ship.

Dazed and slightly bewildered, Captain de Mersinay knew the chance of his warship surviving were increasingly looking slim. He looked down at the total destruction about him.

In utter desperation and total despair, he realised his battle was soon going to be over.

Crestfallen and near to defeat, he leant against a rail on the bridge. He glanced out towards the rolling ocean and saw the enemy gunboats still coming towards his ship, advancing through the smoke and darkening light of dusk.

His expression froze.

In desperation he yelled to any of the crew that could hear, "*Sacre bleu!* They are going to commit suicide! They are bloody well going to RAM US!"

Within seconds there was a blinding flash. The French destroyer Meridien was instantly left as a pile of burning sinking wreckage. Both forward and aft sections of the warship were seen to gradually disappear beneath the waves. Two rapidly advancing gunboats also disappeared caught directly in the path of the deadly laser beam.

In the dimming light of dusk, the ocean was littered with a caboodle of flotsam and jetsam.

Almost silently, in the now calmed waters, the waves gently rippled over the upturned hull of an enemy gunboat previously hit by the French destroyer. It had caught fire and capsized earlier in the battle.

The *Meridien* was no more. The pride of the French Navy was gone.

Its survivors, although very few, would live to tell that the destroyer was suddenly and ferociously attacked, set upon by a bunch of war crazy communist terrorists.

Rightly or wrongly, the survivors stated the enemy was nothing but ardent battle-worn fanatics from Mauritania. The sailors were to give a very graphic account of how, in the destroyer's defence, the odds were just too great. Their story confirmed the destroyer's crew fought desperately in defending their ship against tremendous odds until finally its armaments were silenced. Also, how the two remaining terrorist gunboats proceeded, out of what appeared to be total fanatical desperation, to destroy them. They did this by ramming and sinking the destroyer in a horrific blinding flash.

The survivors stated it appeared the whole sky at the time was amassed with a series of recurring flashing lights. The lights remained until the moment of impact and then disappeared at the time of the *Meridien*'s death plunge, it's broken, sinking hull vanishing beneath the waves.

Captain Narodny looked through his periscope and saw the littered sea. He smiled, satisfied his submarine's task of engagement had been a successful one. His ship had rid the seas of a menacing aggressor which had wilfully unleashed two rockets to try and sink the *Gorbachev*.

On standing his crew down from battle stations, Captain Narodny announced his full approval of the victory. He congratulated and praised the crew for their success.

"The most important thing is that it was achieved without any unfortunate mishap or grave mistake."

Not long after the celebrations had ceased, Captain Narodny set the *Gorbachev* on a new course. His instruction echoed a now quietened operations room. "Proceed west-south-westerly. We'll make for the islands of Cape Verde."

On *HMS Excalibur's* radar screen, Commodore Brianston-Green had been watching the happenings which had taken place just off the most south-westerly tip of the coasts of Western Sahara and Mauritania.

He had watched the screen with great concern. Having now witnessed such tragic scenes, which recorded the loss of the French destroyer, it was obvious to him the French warship had tried desperately to defend its position to the last.

The whole matter came to light when the submarine's radar screen sensors picked up tracking of the *Meridien*'s two anti-submarine missiles. Having no knowledge as to why such an action should have been taken by the French captain, the matter became much clearer to him at the time of precisely 20.13.28 hours.

Suddenly, the radar screen showed another blip.

This appeared to confirm the presence of a much larger vessel. It was only in view and on the screen momentarily.

At 20.16 hours it finally disappeared.

Brianston-Green knew from past record what the blip might be. He made a very careful note of the blip's last recorded course marker. A message was instructed to *SSBN Intrepid*, marked for the attention of Admiral Alan J. T. Adams III. In it the Commodore confirmed what he believed had taken place.

It was not long before a reply came from the American submarine. It read:

TIME: 20:35:16 HOURS 11 AUGUST 2017
FROM: SSBN INTREPID
TO: HMS EXCALIBUR
ATTN: COMMODORE BRIANSTON-GREEN
REGRET NEWS REGARDING LOSS OF THE MERIDIEN – STOP – BELIEVE FRENCH WILL CREATE HELL AGAINST THE COMMUNIST TERRORISTS -STOP – KEEP ALL SILENT REGARDING THE SSBN GORBACHEV – STOP – WE WATCHED AND MONITORED THE SAME – STOP – AM SEEKING URGENT CLEARANCES TO TRAP THE ENEMY – STOP – WILL FORWARD THESE AS SOON AS RECEIVED – STOP – HAVE NOTED ALTERATION OF YOUR COURSE – STOP – PLEASE CONFIRM SOONEST YOUR NEW POSITION – END MESSAGE
SIGNED: ADMIRAL ADAMS – SSBN INTREPID

Admiral Adams gave instructions for the *Intrepid* to alter course towards the Cape Verde Islands. A further order was given for the *Intrepid* to increase its speed to full capacity.

News of the loss of the French destroyer *Meridien* soon reached Naval Headquarters in France.

The tragic loss began a vigorous campaign by the French government to finally put an end to the long outstanding problem.

It was agreed the French Navy would set about ridding the West African coast of its scourge of communist terrorist factions.

The three survivors of the *Meridien*, one officer and two ratings, were lucky to have been operating the rear anti-aircraft battery at the time the warship was hit.

All stated the *Meridien* suddenly seemed to glow red then disappeared into the sea, everything around them shining like a vivid bright torch. They were still suffering from the shock of what had happened.

Government helicopters from Western Sahara had managed to find the survivors and pluck them out of the shark-infested sea. The carnage of some areas of water around them had turned the beautiful clear blue water into a sea of crimson red.

The world was horrified by the blatant aggression shown by the terrorists. Both governments of the United States of America and Great Britain stayed calm and non-committal about the affair.

The *Gorbachev* slipped away unnoticed from the tragic scene of total devastation.

Captain Narodny, who completely unconcerned about all the hot air and veiled allegations being made by the French, wrote in his log:

> ..., *and in having been attacked without any provocation at the time of 19.15 hours on the evening of the 11 August 2017, by the French destroyer Meridien. I then took such steps that were deemed by me as necessary. I instructed my crew accordingly to ensure the safety of the Gorbachev. I hereby place on record that, in an unprecedented act of self-defence, SSBN Gorbachev defended itself admirably. No loss of life occurred to any of the submarine's crew in respect of such defence. The Gorbachev is now proceeding on a course south-south-westwards towards the direction of the islands of Cape Verde.*
>
> *The French destroyer, Meridien, sank without any trace of survivors. Time of sinking is confirmed at 20.16 hours.*

Chapter Sixteen

NASA Military and Naval Intelligence, Cape Canaveral

Shortly after 17.00 hours, news reached General Kemp's office regarding the loss of the French destroyer *Meridien*. Captain Logan had watched receipt in the general *communiqué* in the computer room. He logged the information into *G.O.D.* then proceeded to deliver the newsflash marked 'URGENT' to General Kemp's office.

On arriving, he knocked on the door and waited for a response. Nothing was heard so he entered. He saw General Kemp sitting at his desk, deeply involved.

Logan spoke. "Sir, a very important message just came through on the newscaster. I thought it best to bring it right away. By the way, sir, here are the files regarding the latest reports concerning the *Liberty*."

Kemp looked up. "Thank you, Logan. Please put them down over there."

He pointed to an empty space on the long glass table then realised Logan had said something else. "What was that again, Smartie? Did you say something about an important newsflash?"

Logan handed the message to the General. As he read, he suddenly shouted, "Holy cow! How in heaven's name could that have happened? Surely that cannot really be true, Logan?"

For a moment Kemp read on.

"Crikey! Gunboats operated by a bunch of bushwhackin' terrorists sink a fully armed destroyer. For God sakes, Smartie! It was the most up-to-date vessel in the French Navy."

Smartie Logan listened to what the General had said. He reflected, "What do you really think about the sinking, sir?"

For a moment Kemp gave no response to his aide's question. After pausing he said, "I just don't believe it, Smartie, that's all! I just do not goddam well believe it!"

With the Captain's inexperience of any combat, he unwittingly commented, "The ship's magazine could well have gone up, sir."

Kemp immediately retaliated. "To hell with that! Go and get me Admiral Marchant on the line."

"Under what number shall I find him, sir?"

"He will most likely be at the British Navy's HQ. Use any British Naval HQ code but not the one under the Northwood number. It should be the one referenced under the Admiralty."

"Right you are, sir. I'll put the call through right away."

"Also, Logan, will you fish out the last full intelligence survey report on the French Navy's destroyer *Meridien*."

"Do you mean the one that was just sunk, sir?"

Kemp was surprised by Logan's continued banter of inept comments and remarks. "Yes, Logan, that one!"

Captain Logan felt a certain uneasiness about the news. "Surely, sir, you don't think the Russians had anything to do with it?"

Kemp remained non-committal.

Finally the line connected.

Logan responded. "General, sir, I have Admiral Marchant on the line for you."

"Thank you," the General replied. He lifted the receiver. "Hello, Raymond."

Admiral Marchant had been sitting quietly reading a novel before having an early night.

"Hello, John. What can I do for you?"

Kemp did not preamble. He came straight to the point.

"Admiral, I have just received news about the sinking of the French destroyer *Meridien*. I thought I'd better give you a call to see if you might have any comment to make."

Marchant instinctively knew the General's call was a fishing exercise.

"Actually, John, I was going to call you regarding the activities of the *Intrepid* and *HMS Excalibur*. I think we had better put our heads together."

Kemp immediately rose to the Admiral's bait. "Why is that? Has something big come up?"

"No, John, you can ease yourself back and relax. It's nothing like that. Please listen." Marchant read Commodore Brianston-Green's report to Kemp regarding the action that had taken place off the coast of the Western Sahara.

Kemp commented, "I've not yet received a report about this from the *Intrepid*. It's our systems you know; sometimes everything gets terribly bogged down with red tape."

"I quite understand, John."

Kemp continued, "It was most likely those damned Russkies who put that French warship away. Moreover, it has been intimated they seemed to be using the terrorist gunboat skirmish as a form of cover. I suppose they will try to hoodwink the whole world into believing that the terrorists really did do it. Admiral, this is bad."

The General pondered for a moment. "Admiral, I believe you said that Commodore Brianston-Green had stated in his report he thinks the *Gorbachev* is now heading towards the Cape Verde Islands. Also that he advised both the *Excalibur* and *Intrepid* have altered course in possible pursuit."

Admiral Marchant acknowledged. "That's what I gather, General."

For a moment Kemp hesitated.

"Okay, let me think about that one. I may have an idea. Yes, I believe I could provide something that may prove to become an irresistible target for the Russians. I mean for the next time they might wish to try out their mysterious weapon."

"Are you sure about this, John?"

"Well, Raymond, we've certainly got to do something. Let's hope, for all our sakes, we can get lucky. Okay?"

"Yes, John. I fully endorse your line of thinking. By the way, I have sent an offer to the French.

"I have confirmed we are willing to send our diving team to assist in the investigation as to why the *Meridian* appeared to just blow up and disintegrate. Mind you, they have little knowledge as to our motive, but if we are to find traces of evidence that appear to be similar to those found in the underwater survey made by the *Bowevil* when investigating the loss of the *Andros*, we could well have a matching pair. With that I hope we will be able to convince the Russians, and their FSB, that their evil game of tricks has finally been exposed."

Kemp listened very carefully to what the Admiral had been saying. He was still not totally convinced his idea would be the answer. "I certainly get your drift, Raymond. Tell me, in all seriousness, how do you really think we are going to stop the bastard? Are we going to try and sink it or maybe capture it? Wow! What a prize that would be."

Marchant could not believe what he was hearing.

"John, for God sakes! How can you possibly think of trying to get approval for that sort of caper? Heavens above, man. How are we supposed to convince our people that our bunch are capable of capturing or sinking something that is already supposed to have sunk?"

"Raymond, maybe you're right, or, maybe not. Therefore, I think for the moment, we shall just have to play it by ear."

With that remark Marchant felt his frustration surfacing and decided to change the subject. "By the way, John, by tomorrow night I hope to have some more details regarding those elusive space demons."

"Oh, good for you, Raymond. I see you are also sticking to some of your own ideas. I understand from our boys currently up there that they are having a very interesting time. I hope I'll shortly be sending you a copy of all their up-to-date data."

"I'll look forward to it."

"By the way, Raymond?"

"Yes, John."

"What was the exact time your report states the unknown blip came up on *HMS Excalibur*'s radar screen?"

Marchant quickly flipped over the pages. "It was 20.14 hours, General. It then disappeared at 20.16 hours."

"Okay, that's fine. Thanks for all the news and for all your input."

"Not at all. I appreciate your calling. Glad to have been of some assistance. Bye for now."

Kemp's face looked a picture. Beaming with satisfaction he looked over at Logan whose nose was currently glued to the screen reviewing further details of the news report data.

The General interrupted him. "Smartie, I think it's all slowly coming together. Now please bring me those latest reports if you have finished them."

"Yes, sir." Logan collected the papers and handed them to the General. Both then set about the task of searching for more clues.

In Space

The Russian space orbiter had been out in space since early May 2017. Many times it had utilised the services of the space platform *Vostok*.

Major Chitov always welcomed the crew's visit. He recognised their task and respected that it was his emergency link with Earth, and a possible escape route at any time there might be any danger. When the shower of meteorites bombarded the Russian space platform, the immediate action was to rescue the solar battery arm that had been cut adrift. It was an important warning to everyone on board, and showed it was vital to have an operational rescue craft standing by in readiness to defend or engage in combat in an emergency. If necessary, the space orbiter was capable to assist in any rescue operation. In this respect the Russian space orbiter was now directed to collect another vital piece of the space platform's equipment which had also come adrift. It was an intergalatical radar monitoring system used for censoring any possibility of there being any life in space. It had broken free when the damaged solar battery wing came away.

Major Chitov was in *Vostok's* communications room. He had been assisting the crew in the monitoring, tracking and movement of the Russian spacecraft.

Each time the radar tracking arm rotated, a single blip lit up, then, for some unknown reason, a second blip appeared on the screen then vanished.

Major Chitov rechecked the situation. He had the video monitor replay the sequence.

One of the operation room's crew spoke. "Sir. Maybe, it was a stray meteorite?"

Again Major Chitov observed the radar screen, but after a few minutes he saw no showing of a second blip and said, "Log the sighting and any others as and when they occur. If at any time that blip comes back we may well have to consider having to move to the space station's position. Prior to doing so, I will have the space orbiter go and investigate."

"Right you are, sir."

Major Chitov then departed.

After a few minutes the radar screen again flashed showing a second blip. The crew operator obeyed his Commander's request and instructed the radar operator.

"You had better send a message out to orbiter control. Warn them to watch out for unsuspecting meteorites. Advise them that we have been receiving a series of intermittent unidentified radar contacts. Ask the Captain to keep a constant watch. Report back immediately if there has been any unusual sighting."

The US Military space shuttle *Liberty* settled itself into a very high orbit above the Earth. Equipped with a new type of anti-radar detection unit, the shuttle had successfully spent the last five days monitoring the Russian space platform, and had covered filming the rescue operation made by the Russian space orbiter.

Colonel Rose diligently logged everything and had watched the skill of the Russian astronauts carefully recapture the lost solar battery arm. Additionally, he thought he could see them catch back what seemed to be some kind of radar support unit. He continued to observe the complicated task of recovery being made by the Russian craft: the hauling back of the salvaged parts, then returning them safely back to the space platform.

Liberty maintained contact with Earth and had reported back to NASA Control everything that had taken place. Having constantly monitored the very heavy work schedule, Colonel Rose logged *Liberty*'s twenty-seventh orbit as the American space shuttle crossed over the Gulf of Mexico. *Liberty*'s radar again picked up the position of the Russian space platform.

This time, the Colonel noticed there was no tell-tale sign of the Russian space orbiter. *Curious*, he thought, *maybe it has finally docked.*

On board the *Vostok*, a full-scale general alert had been sounded.

Major Chitov was certain another meteor incident could happen at any time. He had sent a message to the Captain of the Russian orbiter requesting him to break loose from the rescue and fly in orbit around the Earth for a while until the pending emergency had finally passed.

Back on board the *Liberty*, Colonel Rose could not quite figure out, what the Russians were up to. Only when his radar picked up the Russian orbiter, seemingly trailing the *Liberty* some four hundred miles behind, did he know his blind flight position might well have been blown. However, it did seem a little unusual to him the Russian orbiter, as yet, had not made any attempt to intercept.

Major Chitov continued to advise the Captain of the Russian space orbiter of the continued intermittent radar blip sightings.

After a while Captain Rubicoff broke his radio silence. He acknowledged Major Chitov's communication and informed him of the current situation.

"Sir. As yet I have seen nothing which would endanger *Vostok*. Shall I continue to orbit, or shall I make a new course and return to the space platform?"

Major Chitov responded, "Good, Captain. I think you must make three more orbits. Yes?"

Captain Rubicoff acknowledged. "Okay, Comrade Chitov. We'll speak again when I have reappeared from behind the blind side of the Earth."

Major Chitov replied, "Understood."

Then he requested another confirmation. "Is our Earth beam good? I want you to check it regarding the force transmission of Operation Invisible."

"Yes, Comrade Chitov. Currently it is looking very good."

Back on board the *Liberty*, Colonel Rose carefully orchestrated the movements of the lens on the shuttle's rear video cameras. It was done in order to maintain good clear focus and correct the zoom lens beamed in on the Russian space orbiter.

Colonel Rose slowly turned the dials on the Earth receiver's switches.

He did this in order transmission could be monitored and checked by NASA Ground Control. As yet, the Colonel still wondered as to what the Russian orbiter Captain had in mind. He was frustrated as to why the Russian had not yet made any move to attack.

NASA Ground Control, Cape Canaveral

Professor Burston smiled as the pictures began coming through.

He was very pleased NASA Tracking's little extra addition to the *Liberty*'s payload had now begun to prove its worth.

As he watched he gave continuous instructions to his operators. "Make sure we have all these video recorders synchronised."

"Will do, Professor," responded one of the ground staff assistants.

It was just after 20.00 hours EST when NASA had begun receiving live visual communications from outer space. The Professor, with his colleagues, had waited patiently for this moment.

Macdonald Burston glanced up at the first of the *Liberty*'s transmissions.

Suddenly he noticed something. "My God! Look at those shots. General Kemp was right. He said we might well find the Russians had not after all sent back their military space orbiter to Earth. Great Scott! I must telephone him right now. I'll get him to come over right away. Hey, Mitch, hotline this number for me, will you?"

Professor Burston handed the assistant a piece of paper and waved his arm gesturing his desire for immediate attention.

While all this was taking place, a teleprinter began to receive the computer printout of *Liberty*'s latest intelligence report gleaned from the video camera recording statistics. They read:

VISION CONTACT CONFIRMS *****

INDENTITY:	SPACE ORBITER
ORIGIN:	RUSSIAN
DISTANCE:	7,900,000 METRES [APPROX 5,200 MILES]
ARMAMENT:	CONVENTIONAL PLUS LASER GUN
POSITION:	CENTRAL FUSELAGE, UNDERBELLY
CREW:	FOUR [4]
	CAPTAIN
	NAVIGATOR
	TWO [2] FLIGHT ENGINEER'S
SPEED:	16,000 M.P.H CRUISING
	25,000 M.P.H CAPABILITY ON RE-ENTRY

Professor Burston put the telephone to his ear; he heard there was a ringing tone, there was then a click.

"Hello! Who in hell's name is speaking?" came the General's retort having had his emergency line called.

Calmly the Professor answered, "Hello, John. Am I to understand from that answer that you are very busy right now?"

"You guessed right, Mac. There's a flap on and I've no time to speak."

Burston was not too sure how to take Kemp's remark. "But, John, I've gotta' speak with you. It's urgent."

The Professor didn't wait for a reply. He waded in to ensure he had a chance of getting his point across.

"General, I have just had the most exciting thing happen. It's a wonderful first. I just don't want to have to speak with you about it over the telephone."

The Professor was so laid back, but underneath all this he was boiling over with the amazement of his discovery.

Kemp acknowledged his friend's implied success. "Good for you, Mac. I'm pleased for you whatever it is you might have found, but what in hell has it got to do with me? What is it that is so important it requires you to call me on my hotline?"

"John, calm down a little. The matter does not seriously concern your department but could you possibly come over right away? Then you can see for yourself what it is I have on offer."

Professor Burston knew his long-time friend very well. He remembered he was always apt to cut and thrust first before considering any move being made.

By now Kemp was feeling tired. He knew he shouldn't have snapped at the Professor, but he had felt like calling it a day and putting his feet up. Easing back a little he replied, "Mac, is this thing really that important? Look, I have had one hell of a day regarding many international problems. Isn't there somebody else you can try? Surely to God you must have heard that this afternoon somebody went and sank the most modern ship in the French Navy."

Macdonald Burston had already heard the news. "Yes, John, I did hear something about it. What does..."

He paused. "Or should I say, how is that involving you?"

There was no immediate reaction to the Professor's question.

After a moment Kemp replied, "Mac, I am sorry. I am not at liberty to say anything about the subject. Even if I was, I would not talk about it on the telephone."

"There you are," Mac replied. "Surely we must have the same mentors."

General Kemp, slightly embarrassed in not being able to confide with a very old and close friend, thought he would shrug off the veil of secrecy by humouring the Professor. He pitched in saying, "Come on, you old dragonfly. What the devil is it you are keeping from me?"

Professor Burston was not going to be badgered. "Like I said, John, get yourself into your limousine and come on over to find out. You're missin' a great spectacle."

By now Kemp was intrigued. "Hell, Mac, what the heck is it you are up to over there?"

Burston replied, "By the way, do remember to come over alone. I've got classified clearance for only one party."

Kemp gave up. "Okay, Mac, you win. You have really whetted my appetite. I'll be there in about thirty minutes, okay?"

Professor Burston was pleased. "Fine, John. I'll see you shortly. Bye for now."

Immediately the call had finished, Kemp requested Sergeant Lance to get his driver, Rodney, to come over to the office building with his limousine. "And, Sergeant, do ensure he gets moving on the double."

"Yes, sir."

Kemp pressed the intercom button and yelled, "LOGAN!" As the seconds ticked by Kemp showed his impatience, and he began tapping his fingers on the top of his desk.

A minute or so had passed. A click was heard and a soft voice answered. "Yes, sir. How can I help you?"

Captain Logan had been taking things easy.

The General's voice snapped back. "Logan! You are in charge. Don't forget to have Sergeant Lance lock up everything and hand over to you the security keys."

"Okay, sir. Will do."

Kemp felt a little guilty at having groused at his aide. "Say, Smartie, do you fancy a late night?"

"I really don't mind, sir. What's it all about?"

The General was not prepared to give anything away. "Nothing really. I'll give you a call in about two, maybe three hours. I might have some good news."

"Right you are, sir. I'll wait here for your call."

Kemp flipped the switch off.

On stepping briskly over to his wardrobe and grabbed his jacket off its hanger. He then made his way over to meet his driver.

Rodney, who was busy wiping the front window, saw the General coming. Immediately he jumped up and opened the door. "Out somewhere special for the night, General?"

Kemp acknowledged his driver's alertness. "No, Rodney, just get in and drive. I'll tell you where we are goin' once we hit the highway. Make a right as you leave the main gate."

"Sure thing, sir. You just point the finger and I'll push the pedals."

The limousine departed.

Chapter Seventeen

In Space

Colonel Rose watched as the Russian orbiter began to close. It appeared to him to be in a lower orbit than the *Liberty* was. Gradually the small dot in the far distance began to enlarge.

It soon resembled the familiar shape of an American space shuttle. Far below them the Pacific Ocean showed a radiant blue, and Australia began to pass below them. The cloud formation towards the north west coast showed a deepening depression, and a growing tropical storm would become a devastating typhoon that would veer northwards to lash the southern shores of the Philippines.

NASA Ground Control, Cape Canaveral

The scene and atmosphere at Ground Control, NASA, was beginning to build to an immense tension.

A half an hour had passed.

A security guard handed General Kemp a security clearance disc then showed him the way to NASA's Ground Control and Tracking Centre.

Professor Burston, standing in the middle of his team of operators, was giving out orders.

As Kemp entered, the Professor looked up and called him over.

"Good evening, General. Nice of you to come along."

Burston greeted Kemp just as he was in the middle of finalising completion of a Ground Control instruction. He was making directions for a change of orbit manoeuvre to the *Liberty*. Again, constant monitoring distracted his attention.

Kemp waited patiently. He could see he had arrived in the middle of something. He called over to the Professor.

"Hey, Mac, you just stay there until you have finished. I'm okay here."

The main monitoring screen had remained blank for about ten minutes while certain adjustments had been made.

Professor Burston turned round to check on the General.

Kemp saw him looking and smiled back saying, "My word, Mac. You have got quite a show going on here." The General was well impressed.

Burston said, "Just hold on for one or two minutes more, John, then you will really see what things we have been brewing up here."

In Space

On board the Russian orbiter, the pilot, Captain Rubicoff, had just received a very firm radar reading of an unidentified flying object. It appeared to be some distance ahead of his spacecraft. As yet he could not see what it was nor from which direction it was coming from, or going to. The reason for lack of identification was because as soon as the blip had shown on the orbiter's radar screen, the UFO would then disappear. The orbiter's pilot radioed through to *Vostok* to speak with Major Chitov. He reported and confirmed the sighting.

Within seconds the Major responded. "Do not worry too much, Captain Rubicoff, these meteorites are always coming and then going away without trace. Remember that they are sometimes too fast to make a positive identification. We have also been picking up a number of unexplained radar sightings during the past two hours. Please proceed to dock with us in about twenty minutes."

Captain Rubicoff acknowledged his Commander's orders then continued to proceed.

The *Liberty*'s orbit was much higher than the Russian space orbiter. Colonel Rose realised he had to somehow glide past the Russian space platform *Vostok* without being detected. Also, following his orders and instructions from NASA, he had to try and angle his wing cameras to gain as much visual information as possible to enable a clear target reading. The *Liberty*'s main objective, however, was to remain unseen.

NASA Ground Control, Cape Canaveral

Back at NASA Ground Control Professor Burston pushed the computer button which switched on a giant television. For a moment the screen flickered, then cleared showing a very distinct image of the Russian space platform *Vostok*.

"Great Scott!" announced General Kemp. "Where the hell is that incredible picture coming from? How in the heck are you getting that shot back here?"

"It's okay, John," Professor Burston advised. "We have a video camera set forward and aft on board the *Liberty*. They are concealed and both are very functional."

"Well, stone the crows, Mac. Are those cameras really on board the *Liberty*?"

"Sure thing, General. You will recall you wanted a visual survey and report done on the Russian space programme. Well, here we have it. I considered, though be it on my department's head, in making the whole darned thing a mammoth picture show. I went ahead and authorised the fitment and installation of all the equipment. As you can see..."

Kemp looked at Burston in amazement; his face was one of near disbelief, but full of admiration.

His voice echoed as he interrupted the Professor. "WELL BLESS MY SOUL!" The General knew that if Professor Burston had failed.... "I trust that you know, Mac, you took one heck of a gamble and I think maybe pushed your luck to the limit. HOLY COW! What if the darned thing had failed?" Kemp was completely gobsmacked.

Burston could feel the tension rising between them. "What are you implying, John? Are you saying this action was supposedly some sort of spying trick? Surely you can see nothing has gone wrong and not a thing has been hidden from anyone. I invited you over here to be a witness to a first, but you are indirectly accusing me of blatant espionage. What crap, General."

Kemp knew he had riled his friend. He also knew he had to sit and receive what was coming at him.

The Professor continued, "So General, just you damned well sit and watch that screen for the next few minutes and shut your face. I hope I am able to continue operating the manoeuvre of these cameras. When we have gotten all the shots you need, then we shall talk."

Kemp, having been completely rocked off his feet, nodded his head in a sheepish manner. *Hell*, he thought, *I wish I had kept my mouth shut.*

Professor Burston, still seething about the whole incident, glared at Kemp for a full half minute. He then turned away and watched the screen with his colleagues. After a few minutes had passed the Professor broke the eerie silence. "Now, gentlemen, in a few moments we are going to try and get a shot from the zoom lens in front of the *Liberty*. We'll do this by aiming the lens away to face back towards Earth. Make any necessary adjustment for the take to then alternate back to the cameras astern. This should allow us to also see what the Russian orbiter has been doing. Have you got that, everyone?" The operators all acknowledged.

Meanwhile, Kemp had sat himself down in a comfortable seat. He watched the NASA Ground Control at work with growing admiration. Professor Burston could hardly believe what his eyes were watching as the camera slowly moved away from *Vostok* and began to focus earthwards. By now the American space shuttle was passing north of the Gulf of Mexico. It showed *Vostok* perfectly on the first shots. The second camera run then produced an unbelievable surprise.

"Heaven forbid! Have we actually gone and got one?" Burston turned round and beckoned Kemp from his seat.

"Look, John! Look closely at that picture!"

Kemp welcomed the sudden gesture. He felt, due to what he had previously done, he had been completely shut out. He moved forward to take a closer look at what Burston was trying to show him.

He then saw something and pointed.

The Professor responded. "Yes, you're right, John. There, that's it, a little to the left of the angle marker."

A computer cursor prompter came on to the screen to mark the point where both Burston and Kemp had sighted a space funnel cloud.

"There! There it is!" said the Professor. "That's got to be one of them. It's a space demon. What do you think, General?"

"It appears to be beaming right down towards the coast of West Africa, Professor," advised one of the technical operators.

Kemp was speechless. Burston wondered how long he could keep him in suspense.

The General then took a much closer look.

Suddenly he yelled, "Jumpin' jelly beans! Mac, are these pictures live or have they been recorded?"

"Precisely, General." Burston gave him a smile of reassurance which eased the tension between them. "I mean sure thing, General. These pictures are coming to us live and are very real. Now, I think we should both forget all about the previous personality skirmish, don't you, John?"

Kemp didn't catch what Burston had said. His eyes were still glued to the huge screen, and he was quickly making notes as matters progressed. He wrote: *NASA Ground Control estimates Earth contact should be made just off the coast of Mauritania. Movement suggests a south-westerly course to the next landmark –* CAPE VERDE ISLANDS.

The General had seen all he wished to see. He tried to catch Professor Burston's attention. "Mac, I think I had better be going."

Burston had heard Kemp's remark. He waited a few seconds before saying, "No! Not yet, General. The fun has only just started. I said we would speak when we had finished the programme."

The General knew he was not going to be allowed to just get up and leave. "How long will that be?" he enquired.

Burston looked at his watch. "I'd say about twenty minutes before Colonel Rose will be able to reset his cameras. Anyway, now for surprise number two." The Professor called for a change of picture.

"Can we have the last but one video replayed?" Professor Burston pushed a couple buttons and the screen blacked out. After a few seconds the picture returned. The video recording showed the Russian space orbiter passing slowly under the *Liberty* at a distance of about twenty miles.

Kemp's face was filled with awe. "Why didn't they see us, Mac?"

The Professor was enjoying himself and didn't hesitate to answer.

"Well, John, we have placed a blanket screening device that protects the *Liberty* from being seen on radar. Hold it. We should, I hope, be lucky enough to catch the Russian orbiter docking."

Kemp was sceptical about Burston's remark. "Mac, are you sure the Russians cannot locate the position of the *Liberty*?"

Burston realised he may have been a little over-optimistic. "Well, maybe it was about ninety-eight percent accurate. We have had one or two glitches on this run. However, I am certain we can iron them out before the *Liberty* goes up again."

Kemp was impressed. He held out his hand in a gesture of continued peace and friendship between them. "My word, Mac, that was quite a show. I am sorry about the few sharp words we had before you got started. Could you tell me how soon it will be before my department can have a copy of that first film?"

Professor Burston was suddenly very non-committal. "I really do not know, John."

The General showed his frustration. "Hell, Mac! It's very important!"

Burston replied calmly, "That may well be, John, but let me see what I can do. Okay?"

Kemp's face softened. He gave a slight smile and then shook his head in agreement. He realised there was really nothing else he could do about it.

Professor Burston didn't really want to upset his friend again. He looked at his watch and he said. "Okay, John. Will ten minutes suit you?"

"That's great! Can you really do it that quick?"

Burston knew he had scored game, set and match. "While you are at it, John, give my personal regards to the President."

Kemp was full of admiration for his friend and replied, "Don't worry, Mac. I'll certainly make this known to him, and where it has come from."

Burston gave Kemp a polite acknowledgement. "Well, I am sure you cannot have any better evidence than that, General. That's what this game is all about."

Kemp quickly recognised the angle his friend was aiming for.

"Sorry, Mac. I do have my suspicions, but for the moment I must keep them to myself."

Burston knew he could not delve any deeper. "John, happy hunting, my good friend, and I might just call on you again if anything else unusual turns up. I am very pleased to have been of help to you. It was a pleasure having you on board, General."

Kemp shook the Professor's hand. "Mac, I owe you one. So long for now."

Burston was pleased and said, "Not at all, John. I hope I'll be hearing from you shortly."

Kemp looked puzzled by what the Professor had hinted.

Burston saw the strange look on his friend's face. "I mean you letting me know what the President has to say. Also, what he thinks of NASA Tracking and Ground Control's newest toy."

Kemp accepted he had been well and truly drawn. "Okay, Mac, I will see to it. Bye for now." With that he departed.

It was shortly before 22.30 hours when Kemp left NASA's Ground Control Centre. Rodney was waiting for him with the limousine to drive him home.

"Good trip, sir," he remarked briefly.

"You bet," the General answered, "but I won't be going home yet, Rodney. Please drive me to the office."

Rodney could see another late night coming up. "Yes, General. Will you be very long, sir?"

"I think so. That all depends on how long it takes me to speak to the President."

Rodney could not contain himself. "My, oh my! Did you say the President, General Kemp, sir?"

"Yes, Rodney, I did."

"Wow! You must have had one hell of a good evening, sir!"

"You bet I did. I truly think this has scored the trump card." Kemp raised the video case up and brandished it at his driver.

Rodney realised the General was not kidding. "I bet that video must be some real hot potato, sir. My, oh my! The boss is goin' to call our Mr. President. Hell, sir, this surely' is the humdinger of them all. My lady, Liza, is goin' to love this one, boss."

Kemp had heard enough from his driver. "Come on now, Rodney, step on the juice. I want to finish before midnight."

"Okay, sir. I'll have you back at your office in a jiffy."

"That will be fine. I have to meet Captain Logan to process everything, and then I'll try and make contact with the President."

Rodney thrust his foot to the floor and the black limousine sped off into the night.

Chapter Eighteen

It was nearing midnight, 11 August 2017.

Normally, NASA Ground Control and Tracking would have scaled down its operation to a skeleton staff during the period astronauts took to sleeping.

Professor Burston had just taken his leave from the centre for a short break. He'd gone for some refreshment while the *Liberty* continued into another Earth orbit.

In the back of his mind the Professor knew it was going to be a long night.

In Space

During the evening, the Russian orbiter had successfully docked with the Russian space platform *Vostok*.

Major Chitov congratulated Captain Sukov for having successfully rescued the valuable solar power asset of the space platform. Surprisingly, the starboard solar battery wing showed little damage. The *Vostok* was now in the process of being repaired by an army of space robots.

Major Chitov requested Captain Sukov to report to him in the space platform's radar and observation room. It was still a mystery as to what had caused those momentary radar blips.

"Well, Captain, I had hoped you would have been able to allay my fears as to what the devil it was out there that has been making itself known to us."

Captain Sukov advised he was not in the least bit concerned about the matter. However, he did seem to appear to be somewhat puzzled.

"Yes, Major, the matter is all very strange. But I am sure there must be a very simple explanation. As yet, I have never heard of anything like space ghosts. Have you, Major?"

"Do not say anything like that, Captain. There is always a first time for everything."

Major Chitov replied, "Let me tell you what I would like you to do."

Captain Sukov answered, "Yes, Comrade Chitov. I am listening."

The Captain's eyes had been watching the radar screen. As he spoke it suddenly showed a small light start flashing.

"Just a moment, Major. We have another visit from our unknown celestial object. It's definitely with us again. Here, come take a look."

Major Chitov moved over to the radar screen.

He stood there watching for a moment.

The little light had again showed itself. It was situated at the screen's farthest direction point. For about fifteen seconds its signal flashed then disappeared.

"It's just like before. Mark that one down too, Captain Sukov."

The Captain did as he was ordered. "Yes, Comrade Major. Have you really any idea as to what all this might be?"

Major Chitov didn't wish the astronaut to think the sighting had in anyway been ignored.

"No, Captain. The problem is the blessed thing is never there long enough in order to get an exact fix on it. This is why we haven't been able to take any accurate reading. If we could achieve this then we could pick it up on the visual sighting screens."

Captain Sukov sighed. "I see, Major. That is a great pity. Maybe I should take the orbiter out there to investigate. I still have sufficient fuel that will allow me to do three orbits."

Major Chitov gave the matter some thought and said, "If I knew what is out there is not going to put at risk the repair work of restoring the solar power system to the space platform then I would consider it far better for you to stay."

Captain Sukov was inclined to agree. "I do well understand, Comrade Major. However, in the best interests of everybody's safety, I think I should go out and take a look into the matter more thoroughly. I'll take-off as soon as possible."

Major Chitov nodded his head. "All right, Captain. Then I leave the matter in your very capable hands."

Captain Sukov saluted his senior officer then made a move to depart.

Just as the Captain was leaving, Major Chitov stopped him and said, "Captain, do ensure the ground crew has preset the fuses of your armament. Also, see to it that you go under full cover of the space platform's battle station procedures.

"I have ordered and set its screen of enemy alert readiness procedure. Good luck."

Captain Sukov acknowledged Major Chitov's acute caution.

"Thank you, Comrade Major, for your very wise words. But, as I have already said, it probably is only another stray meteorite."

It was nearly 06.30 hours in Moscow when the Presidium received news that Captain Sukov had been instructed to take-off in the space orbiter to intercept and destroy a possible rogue meteor.

By 06.45 hours it was confirmed to Moscow that the space orbiter had been launched from *Vostok*.

Major Chitov watched from the space platform's bridge as the slowly diminishing shape increased its speed and finally had disappeared into orbit around the Earth.

"Sukov to *Vostok*. Do you read me?"

"Loud and clear, Captain. We also now have you on radar. At this moment we confirm you are entering Cosmic Atlas Map Sector W17."

"Good." Sukov replied. "I am now going to climb and proceed into Sector W14. This should place the orbiter well above the present Earth orbit of the *Vostok* space platform."

"Okay, Captain. Understood. But why are you going out so far?" Major Chitov enquired.

"Whatever that celestial being is, at that distance I should certainly be able to pick up some sort of radar contact or reading. If I do I will investigate and, if necessary, destroy it."

Major Chitov was pleased with the space mariner's logistics. "It is understood, Captain Sukov. Please proceed."

"Thank you, Comrade Major. Over and out."

The American space shuttle, *Liberty,* was proceeding at its farthest point of orbit. Captain Rose and his crew had been asleep for about two hours.

The time was 01.00 EST, 12 August 2017.

A little red light appeared on the shuttle's radar screen and began flashing. A buzzer alarm broke the flight deck cockpit's peaceful silence.

A small teleprinter began to type out the shuttle computer's report which had been deciphered from the *Liberty*'s sensitive surveillance equipment.

Soon a page of printed copier paper fell away from the machine into a tray near to the pilot's seat. The report read:

01.02 HOURS EST – LIBERTY INT – RDR SYSTEM REPORT

SE 04.15 SECS – STOP –VISITOR APPROACHING YOUR SECTOR W14 –

STOP – ORIGIN IND FED STATES OF RUSSIA – STOP – TYPE SX XL-

1934ER – STOP – ARMAMENT FUSES ACTIVE – STOP – VISIBLE SIGHT EIGHT MINUTES – STOP – ATTACK SEQUENCE WILL ACTIVATE NINE MINUTES FIFTEEN SECONDS – STOP – DANGER POINT COLLISION COURSE TEN MINUTES TWENTY-TWO SECONDS – STOP – ALERT NASA GROUND CONTROL AND TRACKING – STOP – FOR SELF SAFETY – STOP – ALARM – SYSTEM OF AUTOMATIC ENGAGEMENT WILL ACTIVATE IN EIGHT MINUTES THIRTY-FOUR SECONDS – STOP – NEED NO REAL ASSISTANCE – STOP – SLEEP ON BABY – HAVE LOTS OF NICE DREAMS – STOP – END MESSAGE

At 01.06 hours EST, NASA Ground Control and Tracking picked up the signal that confirmed the shuttle's automatic early warning alarm system had been activated. There was little anyone could do except wait and watch the video camera screens unfold what was about to take place.

The operators monitoring in NASA Ground Control and Tracking could see everything that was happening by the technology they had been able to build into the American spacecraft. What they could not do was to give an advance communication or warning by synchronisation of the cameras.

The operators had full visual control, but they had no way of effecting assistance backup control monitoring. For this, they had to wait for the *Liberty*'s crew to switch on the voice box links.

A faint buzzing sound woke Captain Rose from a restless and disturbed sleep. Slowly his arm rose and soon his hand was rubbing away the sleep from his eyes.

The time was 01.07.33 EST.

As he became aware of the noise of the alarm buzzer, the Captain quickly roused himself. He saw the message in the tray, picked it up and began to read.

"HOLY MACKEREL! Wake up! Wake up, everybody!" he yelled. "We are at RED ALERT minus one minute twenty-six seconds." Captain Rose switched on the scanning video screens that operated to cover sighting anything from the *Liberty*'s stern. They showed nothing. He immediately changed the viewing to cover the cameras scanning forward. Again, these showed nothing.

One of the crew having been roused by the sudden pandemonium asked Captain Rose, "What the heck is happening, Captain? We thought that Professor Burston had allowed us a six-hour break. We all thought we were in for some well-earned beauty sleep."

Captain Rose pointed his finger towards the radar screen, then to the video monitors. "Look there all of you! Take a look! Our AWACS, Airborne Early Warning and Control System has been out stalking an intruder. It's a Russian space orbiter!"

For a moment the crew felt an air of relief at having had on board such advanced technology.

"Nice work for a mechanical half-breed," Lieutenant Lottie Mason said. Her interest in the *Liberty*'s first test flight had been solely to collect information of any possible forms of plant life to be found in space. Until now she had wondered why she had been chosen for the test flight at all. However, her record and past history regarding her high velocity gunnery and laser gun practice was second to none. If it moved and it was instructed to be destroyed, then Lottie Mason was your 'man'.

Captain Rose spoke. "Lottie."

"Yes, Captain."

"I think we might well have found a job for you."

"Really, Captain? Well, what's on offer? I'll take just about anything right now."

"I'd say in exactly seventy-three seconds."

Lt. Lottie Mason always lifted everyone with her wonderful sense of humour. "What you got then, Cap'n, an alien Venus flytrap? One maybe that needs to receive a swat or a little pruning?"

Captain Rose smiled. "Not quite, Mason. All of you listen. That little blip on the screen has been identified by EWAS as a Russian space orbiter. We may not be able to see it but we certainly have it on our radar, and it might be a while before we can see it on the video. Assuming the *Liberty*'s reporting is accurate, Mason, it's up to you to be sitting there ready to fire our laser guns just in case the sonofabitch Russian is armed. For all our sakes you sure as hell better shoot at anything that looks like being hostile if it's comin' our way. Do not, however, fire at will at the Russian. I repeat, DO NOT FIRE at will. You will only shoot when I give you the order to do so. Is that clear?"

"Yes, sir."

"Okay."

A shot of adrenaline sent a feeling of nervous excitement right through Lt. Lottie Mason.

Great, she thought, *some solid action at last. Thank goodness for EWAS.* The Lieutenant turned on the space shuttle's armament automatic sensors that operate the laser guns.

The seconds ticked away.

It was now nine minutes and forty-six seconds since the first radar sighting.

There was a strange sort of expectancy on board *Liberty*.

On board the Russian space orbiter, Captain Sukov had taken his spacecraft into a much further orbit than he had first assumed. His position was about twenty-seven kilometres deeper into space than the orbit of *Liberty*.

Captain Rose with Lt. Mason sat watching the radar screen. Both were engrossed in monitoring the progress of the flashing red blip moving ever closer to the *Liberty*'s position. Both officers assessed the position of the Russian was definitely close, but still no visual trace had been made.

Captain Rose spoke quietly. "Hold your fire, Lottie. Ensure no mistakes now. Flip the auto firing switch into neutral."

Lt. Mason had already hyped herself in readiness. "Jesus, Captain, aren't we goin' to just blast that thing out of the sky?"

Captain Rose knew Lieutenant Mason was eager for action. "Wait for it, Lottie, just wait for it. If we were to fire first the blast would ricochet into our flight path. Not only that, we have no idea, as yet, if the Russian is going to fire at us."

Lt. Mason eased herself back into neutral. "Okay, Captain, I'll play it your way. Wake me up again if and when you think the excitement is goin' to start."

Captain Rose shook his head. He was slightly amazed at Lt. Mason's remark. However, with the alarm temporary over, he sat back watching his instruments.

As the Russian space orbiter neared the end of its first orbit, Captain Sukov checked his radar. There was nothing showing. With nothing to report he looked out of the orbiter's window at the curved shape of the world far below him. It shone a mixture of blues, whites and various shades of green and brown, reflecting the colours of the land, sea and sky.

The Captain turned on his radio. "Sukov to *Vostok*."

"Yes, Sukov, we hear you," Major Chitov advised.

"Nothing to report, Comrade Major. No sign of anything visual, nor has there been any radar contact made throughout our first orbit regarding our unknown celestial being."

Major Chitov responded, "Okay, Captain, you are clear to go forward for your second orbit."

Sukov acknowledged, "Thank you, Comrade Major. I will contact you again when I get clear of the Earth's blind side."

Major Chitov was pleased the first orbit had proved to be both negative and uneventful. "Fine. Keep searching and good luck."

Captain Sukov watched as the Russian space platform passed by. The *Vostok's* lights twinkled and flickered far off. It gave the appearance of a shining angel stationed motionless in the silent heavens. In no time at all the Russian orbiter began to distance itself from the space platform. Again Captain Sukov checked the radar screen. He then began to cover a full scan of the Earth's rim that would soon go dark as the orbiter passed out of sunlight to venture into night's darkness. As he looked down into the world below, he suddenly saw, at a distance of about eighty kilometres below him, the outline of another space shuttle. The Captain blinked his eyes in order to check that he wasn't seeing things. He then looked at the orbiter's radar screen. It was showing nothing. He checked again. Yes, he was not mistaken. He could clearly see the blackened shape of another craft that looked something like his own. *Whose is that,* he thought? Was it an American space shuttle? Captain Sukov knew he was badly positioned and could not really see too clearly. Gradually the Russian's orbit was now distancing the orbiter from the unidentified space shuttle. Soon he would completely lose his sighting and any chance to report back to *Vostok.*

Captain Sukov began transmitting, "Orbiter calling *Vostok.* Come in please."

Back on board *Vostok,* Major Chitov was not expecting a message from Captain Sukov yet. A transmission had begun to come through but was breaking up as it was received by *Vostok's* operations room.

> THIS ISC AP... OV. I HAVE... TEDSOME... IN A LOW... BITI BELIEVE
> THAT I MAY... ANOTHER SPACE S... MIGHT TRY TO... GATE WHEN
> COMING B...

From thereon the transmission cut.

Major Chitov was sure Captain Sukov had seen something, but whatever it was he couldn't decipher the message received. He requested the operations room to replay the tape back several times in order to try and piece the statement together. After a few minutes they contacted Major Chitov and advised what they assumed the message read:

> THIS IS CAPTAIN SUKOV I HAVE SIGHTED SOMETHING IN A LOWER
> ORBIT I BELIEVE THAT IT MAY BE ANOTHER SPACE...OR A SHOWER
> OF METEORS.

Major Chitov relaxed; he was not too concerned. Anyway, he would soon know the full story. In about twenty minutes the space orbiter would be back from the dark side of the Earth to start its final orbit.

Back on board the *Liberty*, Captain Rose bided his time. He had hoped by now the crew of the Russian space orbiter must have seen the *Liberty*. He manoeuvred the controls and fired a very quick burst of the craft's retro rockets in order to slow down the pace of the shuttle. Captain Rose wanted to achieve this manoeuvre for his craft to be in a suitable position to watch the Russian space orbiter re-enter from the dark side of the Earth.

Captain Rose broke the enforced silence. "Okay, Lt. Mason, let's show this Russian how we can really play hide and seek. Fire all the shuttle's thruster rockets for twenty seconds. Take the *Liberty* into a much higher orbit. Keep a full tracking mode on the Russian spaceship. At the same time keep the monitor recorder operational on the radar."

"Right you are, Captain," came Lt. Mason's reply.

Captain Rose issued her new orders. "Switch the laser guns back to automatic engagement. Set the firing button to co-ordinate its release of fire in response to any heat-seeking weapon attack from an enemy."

"Yes, sir," Lt. Mason responded excitedly.

By now both the *Liberty* and the Russian space orbiter were heading down towards the Earth's Southern Hemisphere. All around them was total darkness. Both spacecraft had just crossed above the south of Sumatra, and were heading towards the vast expanse of the northern most part of the great Australian Western Desert, which had begun to spread out far below them.

Captain Sukov received a full computer intelligence report with regard to the international launchings. He received this information just before entering the dark side of the Earth. After quickly checking it, Sukov considered the spacecraft he saw was none other than the latest American space shuttle called *Liberty*. He was sure it was out there somewhere, and possibly by now was very close to him. Also, he realised, it could only be a snooping intruder. It could be a great danger to the Russian space programme. Sukov was sure that if an outsider saw enough at this time then both he and his mentors would be exposed as being an enemy against humanity. If the changes that had been carried out on *Vostok* become known — Russia having virtually rebuilt its space platform — then a space Star Wars could certainly be deemed imminent. The Russian Captain knew there were no alternatives other than ensure the space platform's safety and protection. He checked to see that his armament was ready, set and primed just in case of an attack. *However,* he thought, *if I could just catch the Yanks with their pants down, safety for everyone would be assured.*

It wasn't too long before there was the ideal moment. Captain Sukov set the ignition timers and firing engagement of all laser heat-seeking missiles. Finally, he sighted the American space shuttle. Everything was co-ordinated and targeted. "FIVE, FOUR, THREE, TWO, ONE…" Captain Sukov pressed the red firing button.

Within seconds there was a blinding flash. All laser-homing missiles exploded having reached not more than half a kilometre from the Russian space orbiter. The force of the blast ripped the starboard control flaps away from the Russian spacecraft. It removed many heat protective squares off the fuselage. The orbiter's huge tail rudder disconnected itself in the blast; this fell away spinning into nowhere and disintegrating into millions of tiny fragments.

Sukov desperately fought to control his spacecraft to maintain its orbit. Unbeknown to him the orbiter was now in an uncontrollable spin. Because of this the Russian spacecraft's orbit was being pulled further and further out into space. The force of the explosion had accelerated the spacecraft's speed.

With no steerage Captain Sukov tried to seek assistance of the orbiter's re-entry retro rockets. He knew that these might be able to slow the spacecraft down. Hopefully, it would allow him to correct and control a rapidly increasing spiral roll. This action only further increased the orbiter's speed, and drastically changed the Russian spacecraft's course. It seemed that nothing was going to help its fate.

Captain Sukov now realised he was well beyond the point of no return.

On board the space platform *Vostok,* Major Chitov stood in stunned silence as he heard the repeated call for help made by the voice of Captain Sukov. It echoed throughout the operations room.

Captain Sukov continually uttered, "Be advised, the orbiter has suffered a major malfunction. I am spiralling out of control. THIS IS AN EMERGENCY!

"Please immediately send out a rescue craft to assist! Send out a rescue craft to assist! Send out a rescue craft to…" The message was now calm but kept on repeating itself.

Captain Sukov could no longer read his instruments well enough to determine where he was or what his course was. It was only when his spacecraft began to slow he got the chance to turn across the path of the rising Earth. It was then, when he saw the Moon was now much closer, he realised how small the Earth had become. With that he realised his fate and destiny was sealed.

Captain Rose sent a coded message to NASA Ground Control and Tracking. It read:

RUSSIAN SPACE ORBITER RELEASED ARMAMENT IN A DELIBERATE ATTACK AGAINST LIBERTY – STOP – AUTOMATIC LASER RETALIATED AND DESTROYED ENEMY MISSILE FIRE – STOP – ORBITER APPEARS TO HAVE SUFFERED DAMAGE FROM OWN BLAST – STOP – NOW OUT OF CONTROL AND SPIRALLING TOWARDS MOON – STOP – END MESSAGE

On board the Russian space platform *Vostok*, Major Chitov had no idea what had caused the damage, or how the space orbiter had gone out of control. He could only resign himself to knowing that he had sent Captain Sukov out on a normal mission to ensure the safety of the *Vostok*. *Unexpectedly, the orbiter had met with an unexplainable accident*, the Major wrote in the space platform's log. *A shower of meteorites striking the space orbiter probably caused the disaster.*

Moscow was sent full details of the incident.

The Russian press agencies published an account of the perilous journey made by one of Russia's heroic crew of space mariners. It told of great exploits that had been achieved. It advised the position of the disaster by notifying an ill-fated mission made by a space orbiter had met with disaster. The press confirmed all lives were lost when a shower of meteorites unexpectedly hit the spacecraft, and it was assumed that it was totally destroyed.

Slowly, still tumbling out of control, Captain Sukov sat and watched in silence as his fate came nearer to its end. The Russian space orbiter continued to hurtle onwards towards the Moon's cratered surface. Blindly, the orbiter spun and rolled. Pieces of debris fell away from it as its speed increased. Soon, the Moon's surface, somewhere in the vicinity of the Sea of Serenity became a crash site as the Russian space orbiter disintegrated on impact.

Chapter Nineteen

At Sea

HMS Excalibur had surfaced and rendezvoused about one hundred and thirty miles north-west of the Cape Verde Islands with America's nuclear ballistic submarine SSBN Intrepid.

On clearing operations in South Carolina after being relieved of duties under the *SSN Bowevil,* Captain Maxman flew to Tenerife in the Canary Islands to join Admiral Alan J. T. Adams III and the pride of the US Navy's submarine fleet the *SSBN Intrepid.*

The *Intrepid* had set sail the previous evening, and it was agreed everyone would turn in early in order to make a start at the crack of dawn.

Admiral Adams sent a message to *HMS Excalibur* marked for the attention of Commodore Brianston-Green requesting him to accept a visit on board the US Navy's submarine.

Commodore Brianston-Green acknowledged Admiral Adams' message and set a time for 06.00 hours.

At 05.15 hours, the sea was very calm. It was a beautiful clear morning. *HMS Excalibur* was cruising along at twenty-five knots. Thursday 12 August 2017 was going to be a memorable day for the sailors of the British submarine. Not one of them had ever seen an American strategic ballistic nuclear hunter-killer submarine of the supposed vast size of the *Intrepid.*

Shortly before 05.25 hours, the tell-tale sign of a rising periscope breached the surface about four metres astern of the *Excalibur.* The submarine's lookouts picked it up rising off the port beam. *HMS Excalibur's* radar immediately pinpointed a new blip showing on its screen.

"Commodore Brianston-Green, sir. Periscope sighted off our port beam. Range, four thousand metres."

"Thank you, Officer of the Watch. I'll be up on the bridge shortly." The Commodore had been changing in readiness for his journey by breeches buoy to visit the American submarine. He had spent a considerable time the previous evening checking depth of water around the islands of Cape Verde.

Lieutenant Bergman knocked on the door and entered the Commodore's room.

"Hello, Number One. Well, I wonder what it is Uncle Sam is planning. Having seen, although it was brief, their hunter-killer submarine *SSN Bowevil,* I am assured this one we are going to see makes the others look like toy models."

Slowly the massive hull of the US Navy's submarine began to break the ocean's surface. *Intrepid's* conning tower rose above its huge steel hull like a miniature high-rise building. As the submarine levelled out its turbine nuclear-powered engines turning four huge propellers made the sea boil and spit like white-hot molten lava which created a massive wake to emerge from the submarine's stern.

A message began printing out on *HMS Excalibur's* cable printer. It read:

FROM: SSBN INTREPID

TO: HMS EXCALIBUR

GOOD MORNING COMMODORE BRIANSTON-GREEN – STOP – WE AWAIT THE PLEASURE OF YOUR COMPANY FOR BREAKFAST AT 06.30 HOURS 12 AUGUST 2017 SIGNED ADMIRAL J.T. ADAMS III – STOP – END MESSAGE

The radio operator made contact to speak with the Commodore. "Operations room to bridge. Message from Admiral Adams on board the American submarine marked for your attention, sir."

"Fine. Thank you. Please read it over the ship's speaker to me."

Over the tannoy came confirmation of the pending breakfast meeting. It momentarily caused a stir. A member of the crew, a rating, assumed the word 'company' was meant to be considered an open invitation. A ripple of amusement let loose within the ranks due to the implied error made by the cable room operator; he had allowed the whole of *HMS Excalibur's* complement to hear the notice regarding the Commodore's breakfast invitation offered by the American Admiral.

"This is your Commodore speaking. I am sorry to dispel your hopes and wishful thinking into such disappointment. I am sure later on that you will all thank Mr. Miller for inviting the whole crew." Laughter was heard throughout the submarine.

Brianston-Green continued, "But, notwithstanding what you all might wish in the near future to consider doing to the young man, surely you are all well aware one single breeches buoy would take at least a whole day to get you all across to the *Intrepid*. Even those over-enthusiastic members of the crew who probably, if given half a chance, would have risked life and limb in trying to swim across for the prize of an American breakfast might think it not worth it."

The Commodore could hear loud laughter coming back from his remarks.

"I am sorry, gentlemen, but unfortunately the invite and request is for myself and my aide. Have the rocket party standing ready. I'm sure you wouldn't wish me to miss the party. Remember, I hope to be bringing back the intended battle plan so we can hopefully proceed to meet and silence our uninvited underwater guest."

Loud cheers were heard in response to the Commodore's advice. Several crew members, having grouped around the microphone in the cable room, roared back, "Hope we get the first chance to sink the blighter, sir." A loud cheer followed this remark.

On board the *Intrepid*, preparations for the visit were being made. The tannoy system was left on to allow the sounds of a brass band to play. The music drifted across the sea as a sound of welcome.

In reply, echoes of cheering from *HMS Excalibur* could be heard. On hearing the unusual sound, some of the crew of the American submarine looked at each other a little bewildered.

"Hey, guys, do you think the British are having some kinda all night party?" Another sailor quipped, "I could sure swallow a few cold beers right now." This was followed by one of the older crew members voicing, "Gee, I thought we'd got a pretty cushy number in this tin can, but after hearing that lot I reckon those Brits have got it made."

"That skipper of theirs, Brianston-Green, must be one hell of a guy."

"Say, what did you say his name was?"

"Commodore Brianston-Green."

"Awwww! Forget it. We're not invited. Let's not fret about it. They're just lucky fellars."

The tannoy on the *Intrepid* stopped playing the music.

The sound of Admiral Adams' voice began to boom. "Now hear this! We have a distinguished British officer coming on board at about 06.45 hours. No one, I repeat, no one is to fall out of line while this visit is on. Anyone caught doin' so will have twenty-eight days holiday in the brig. I trust this is clear. That will be all."

A crew member named Kelly murmured, "Dammit! This huge whale is big enough to support two bowling alleys, a pizza bar and a disco in its torpedo and reactor room."

By now all the banter and good humour was soaring and raising everyone's spirits. At that moment the officer of the watch entered. "Knock it off, you guys. Remember we have a full kit inspection in five minutes then the visit from the British officer follows." The officer didn't want Admiral Adams to show his lads up in front of any visiting British Royal Navy officer.

On board *HMS Excalibur*, the rocket carrying the line across to the *Intrepid* for the breeches buoy had already been fired. The American deck crew was in the process of hauling in the heavy rope that would carry the chair.

Soon, Admiral Adams and his number one, Lieutenant Timothy Mouse, were receiving their British guests.

"Welcome aboard, gentlemen," Admiral Adams said in greeting them.

"Good morning, Admiral," Commodore Brianston-Green responded. "Allow me to introduce my number one, Lieutenant Bergman."

"Pleased to meet the British Navy," Admiral Adams acknowledged warmly. "I must say that submarine of yours surely steals the best prize for looking the meanest piece of underwater equipment I have seen in many a day."

The Commodore was pleasantly surprised by the Admiral's remark. "Why, thank you for that compliment, sir."

Admiral Adams continued surveying the lines of the British submarine. "What speed will it reach, Commodore?"

"Official or unofficial, sir?"

"Come on, Commodore. What has that mighty beast given you while grindin' along in best conditions?"

"Nearly thirty-five knots on the surface, sir. Just under thirty when submerged," Brianston-Green said, smiling.

"My word! I think we'd have to go into dry dock and have a brand new engine refit if I tried to pull off a stunt like that on the *Intrepid*. What extra fuel ability have the British applied? By heavens, you make me feel like I have come out for a joyride in a military tugboat. I would surely love to have a fling in your British powerboat, Commodore."

"Certainly, Admiral. Maybe we could fix it for sometime in the future, when we have finished this little caper."

Admiral Adams was pleased with the British officer's spontaneous remark. "I'll look forward to it. Well now, how about havin' that breakfast

I invited you over for after which may be a quick tour of inspection. Then we can sit down and go through the plans and orders that I have brought along with me."

"That's fine by me, Admiral," Brianston-Green replied.

Admiral Adams smiled. "Good. I've not long come over from Washington. We, I mean the US Navy's bigwigs, had recently been watching the launch of our newest space shuttle *Liberty*. It was a fine show. The craft was off on its first base-to-base trial. A grand splash had been laid on for the President."

Brianston-Green was impressed. "That must have been quite something. I hope I might have the chance to see a launch during my lifetime."

Admiral Adams was somewhat surprised. "Are you sayin' you ain't seen a launch yet? My, my, Commodore, leave it to me. I'm sure I can put somethin' together to sort that one out for you. Let's say the next time round, okay?"

The Commodore was elated. "Thank you very much, Admiral. That is most kind of you. I'll look forward to it."

Lt. Mouse had already escorted Lt. Bergman to the officers' mess hall. They were in the process of pouring themselves a fruit juice when the room was brought to attention. Admiral Adams and Commodore Brianston-Green entered and were ushered to their places and seated by the mess hall staff. Steaks, eggs, Canadian bacon, cereals of every type, mushrooms, tomatoes, hash browns, grits, waffles with maple syrup were listed on the menu. Some of the dishes were already prepared on the serving tables.

"My word, what a spread, Admiral," Brianston-Green remarked.

"I think if you particularly wished to name any of your favourite food I would say we'd probably got it."

"I know I have a fairly good appetite, Admiral, but this spread amazes me. Do you really sit down to this sort of thing every morning?"

"Sure do. I believe that breakfast is the best meal of the day." There was a resounding, "Hear Hear, sir," which came from other American officers who had joined the Admiral's company.

"Thank you for that, gentlemen," Admiral Adams replied.

Soon the general crescendo and noise of cutlery intermingled with clashing china plus the day to day chit-chat being voiced by all filled the air. After half an hour Admiral Adams and Commodore Brianston-Green, followed by the two lieutenants, made a move to depart. Everyone in the mess hall stood up as the Admiral and guests departed.

The tour of the American submarine and ship's company was soon completed.

Such immense space and the quiet running of the *Intrepid* impressed Commodore Brianston-Green.

Lt. Mouse, slightly ahead of everyone, checked that everything ahead was in apple-pie order.

Finally, all parties reached the Admiral's quarters and stopped at the door of the conference boardroom.

"Please enter, gentlemen. Is there anything I can get you before the meeting starts?" Lt. Mouse requested.

"Maybe a cup of coffee wouldn't go missing," Admiral Adams said. "What would you say to one, Commodore?"

"Thank you very much, Admiral. That would be splendid."

"Fine. Please sit down, gentlemen. Coffee will be delivered to us shortly."

For a brief moment Admiral Adams slipped out with Lt. Mouse. He ventured to the operations room to collect data of the latest radar checks and weather report.

As Commodore Brianston-Green sat himself down at the boardroom table, he drew out from his *attaché* case a waterproof protected file. Looking across at Lt. Bergman he said, "What did you think of that breakfast, Bergman? Splendid, wasn't it?"

The Lieutenant smiled. "Yes, sir, it was quite something, although I'm not exactly sure whether I would like that sort of thing every day of the week."

The Commodore agreed. "I can understand that you being a bit of a sports enthusiast. I suppose it could very quickly begin to increase the waistline if one had to tackle that challenge daily."

Just as the Commodore was about to say something else Admiral Adams and Lt. Mouse stepped into the room.

"Sorry to have kept you waiting, gentlemen. I thought before we got started it might be handy to have the latest data reports and readings."

"Fine, Admiral," the Commodore responded.

Everyone took their seats.

Admiral Adams opened the meeting. "Well, Commodore, let's get down to business and hit it from the baseline. As you are already well aware both our governments have been hankerin' after this unidentified radar blip for some time now. You yourself have had some first-hand experience of possibly seeing the damned thing. I'm sure you will recall this happened when your submarine, *Excalibur,* was in close session with Captain Maxman of the *Bowevil.* Since the tragic loss of the French destroyer, *Meridien,* I believe your sub again picked up a similar radar reading of this UUO."

Brianston-Green, a little surprised by the use of the new abbreviated term, responded, "Please excuse me, Admiral, for interrupting. Would you mind advising me as to what is meant by the term UUO?"

Admiral Adams somewhat taken aback by the British officer's comment responded, "Haven't you heard that one before? That's an unidentified underwater object."

"Thank you, Admiral."

Admiral Adams continued, "As I was sayin'. I believe, Commodore, you found a similar UUO on your radar screen at the time of the *Meridien's* sinking. Correct me if I'm wrong, but I think you had recorded and reported that the UUO was now heading in the direction of the islands of Cape Verde."

"That is quite right, Admiral."

On receiving such a direct and positive reply Admiral Adams felt very reassured. "Fine. Mighty fine. In that case I'd like you to take a look at this chart. We have labelled it 'Operation Overview'. It is run in conjunction with another programme called Operation Ghostbusters. Please have a good look at it."

Admiral Adams moved the chart across to Commodore Brianston-Green.

"Based upon your clarifications and comments, Commodore, I'll now proceed to outline what I believe should be put into action. Please take your time."

Lt. Bergman motioned to join the Commodore. As he did so he looked across at Admiral Adams as if to beckon an informal clearance.

"Yes, Lt. Bergman, go ahead. Please also pitch in," the Admiral advised.

"Thank you, Admiral Adams," Lt. Bergman responded.

On receiving the US Navy's chart, Brianston-Green took out from his waterproofed pouch a chart which he had received clearance from Royal Naval Intelligence, Northwood. It was titled Operation Blindfold. As he presented it to the table he said, "Here, Admiral. Please kindly study this chart. After quickly checking yours I am sure you may well find that there are some very accurate comparisons to be found in conjunction with Operation Overview."

"Thank you kindly, Commodore. I'll do just that," Admiral Adams responded.

All parties spent many minutes perusing the separate charts. Brianston-Green said, "Admiral, I think we can definitely say our operations have been independently compiled, but surprisingly they do have an awful lot in common."

Admiral Adams studied the British Naval Intelligence chart in great depth and interest. After a few minutes he said, "Well, boys, I think I have to hand it to you British. Your operation is slick and appears to be about ten hours ahead of ours. Do you agree with me, Commodore?"

Both British officers smiled at the Admiral's remark.

Admiral Adams glanced at them for a moment then looked back down at the charts. His voice was much softer when he next spoke.

"Okay, take out five hours for summer time and the difference in time changes. Yep! I must agree you boys do certainly have the edge on us. I will confirm this when I report back to Washington. Congratulations, Commodore."

Brianston-Green was pleasantly surprised. "Why, thank you, Admiral. It is nice of you to say so."

"Not at all. Credit is given where credit is due. That's what my Grandpappy always said," Admiral Adams responded.

Everyone smiled.

The Admiral continued, "Right then, let's see what we can make of all this information. You British seem to be in the swim of things. How about it then, gentlemen? Shall we get the British Navy to get the show cracking along? What do you say to that?"

Brianston-Green nodded in response to the Admiral's address and advised, "If you are in agreement together with your staff, Admiral, we will go along with that."

Admiral Adams looked around the table for a firm response from his officers. There was no objection and he nodded his head in joint approval. "Yes, Commodore. You have a deal on that."

"Thank you, Admiral. We accept your invitation to start and thank you for the privilege for being able to do so."

Admiral Adams began to follow up the path of past events that were marked on the chart. His staff started from the first known sightings of the so-called space demons.

The Admiral then moved on to the pattern formation that seemed to coincide with each known marker point ratified as a presumed position of the Russian submarine *Gorbachev*. He noted down the facts from the time of its last recorded position – just off the most northerly point of Norway.

From thereon he saw each marker on the chart co-ordinated the joint readings and sightings with those of the supposed positions of the UUOs.

Both the Admiral and Commodore carefully noted each position following all events from the loss of the *SS Andros* through to the sinking of the French destroyer *Meridien*.

Admiral Adams congratulated Commodore Brianston-Green. "Well, Commodore, that just about covers everything up to the date of 13 August 2017."

He looked around the boardroom table. "Do you have any questions, gentlemen?"

Brianston-Green interrupted, "No, I don't think so, Admiral. I believe we are both now of one accord."

Admiral Adams stopped and beamed at the Commodore. "Okay, Commodore, let's now have a look at what our mentors currently propose and compare it with what we already now have underway."

The Admiral produced the *Intrepid*'s latest radar report. It clearly showed the position of *HMS Excalibur*. There were two ships marked well to the north-east of the American submarine's position. One was very near to the coast off Western Sahara; the other was south of the Canary Islands.

To the surprise of Commodore Brianston-Green, since leaving his submarine he noticed that a new object now showed. It had just entered radar contact and was north-east of the *Intrepid*'s position.

He said, "What in heaven's name is that monster object? That wasn't on our radar screen prior to my coming over here."

Admiral Adams replied, "You're absolutely right, Commodore. We were at first a little concerned that we were too early with our surprise than we had anticipated. However, please let me reassure you all. That grand monster object of a blip is a friend, not a foe."

"What the devil is it, sir?" Lt. Bergman enquired.

Admiral Adams appreciated the response. "Believe it or not, that gigantic radar blip is a very large crude oil supertanker. She is a very old ship, but excellent for her age. It is the sister ship of the *SS Globtik Moyo* named the *SS Globe Kobe*. Its size is about four hundred and eighty thousand tons. Normally, and until recently, it had been used for oil storage. It was lying idle so our governments agreed to charter it for assisting our purpose. Gentlemen, we are to use it as a decoy to attract as bait the UUO. Does anyone have anything to say about that?"

Lt. Bergman was eager to check. "Sir, I trust that the ship isn't going to be carrying millions of gallons of crude oil?"

Admiral Adams had begun to enjoy the British youngster's keenness. "You are right to assume that, Lt. Bergman. No, it will be full of water."

Brianston-Green enquired, "Why is it in this area, sir? And what is its present course and destination?"

"Good question, Commodore. That's what we are all here for. I mean, so we can determine what its role will be."

Everyone shook their heads in agreement.

As time went on the meeting cleared many issues and doubts.

Commodore Brianston-Green knew well the capabilities of his submarine. He studied at some length the difference of the charts that the US Navy had of the islands of Cape Verde with those the British Navy were using. He knew from past experience the waters around the area were never pleasant. Swift underwater currents and strong winds were a major hazard.

The Commodore looked across the table at the American officers and said, "I trust, Admiral, we are going to decide to place that huge decoy in sufficient depth of water?"

Admiral Adams was waiting for such a comment.

"Commodore, we are. More likely it will lie west of the main island group. The ship will be kept well away from any danger to local shipping."

Brianston-Green posed another question. "Am I led to understand, Admiral, there are about four hundred thousand inhabitants spread out all over these islands. My information states some are separately scattered about on the islands of Santo Anlao, Boa Vista, Sao Nicolau, Maio and Sal. We are advised that very few are living on the island of Fogo; this due to the fact the volcano there is apparently still very active. What are we going to do about this situation, Admiral?"

"A volcano that's still active? How big is it?"

"Two thousand eight hundred and thirty metres, sir."

Admiral Adams could see that the British officer had done his homework.

"Is that rightly so, Commodore? Also, you say most of the Cape Verde Islands inhabitants are housed on Sao Tiago. Yep! You're right there too. We register that they live around the colony's capital called Praia."

Brianston-Green interjected, "I believe, Admiral, the Portuguese have survived there for many generations."

"Precisely, Commodore, ever since one of them found the place in about the year 1460. Who was it, Mouse?"

"Diago Gomes, sir."

"That's right, Lieutenant. He's got a very good brain, Commodore.

I mean for names and dates. Does this place, if we happen to run into a little trouble, have any defences or armament?"

"Yes, sir. The Cape Verde Islands' Navy has proud possession of four high-powered gunboats."

"Is that all?" Adams retorted.

"Not quite, sir."

"What do you mean, Lt. Bergman? There's more?"

"Yes, Admiral. They also have twenty-four torpedo boats."

Adams smiled back at Lt. Bergman. He then looked across at Brianston-Green. "My lucky day, Commodore."

"I'm sure we will manage, Admiral. We, I mean the British Navy, by tradition have always managed to survive against vastly adverse elements, and history shows sometimes tremendous odds," the Commodore responded.

"I do sincerely hope so", replied the Admiral, "because I have a sneaky feelin' this operation isn't goin' to be a pushover. I have an instinct which tells me there's goin' to be one hell of a loss of human lives concerning this proposed shindig before it's over."

Seeing, for the time being, the discussions had stopped, Commodore Brianston-Green gave the matter several moments of deep thought.

"Admiral, I can well understand your statement and its concern, but in war I have always believed if your number is up then so be it. In this day and age you really only have to worry if you happen to be left behind as a survivor."

Deep down, Adams was aghast at what the Commodore had indicated, but equally he was pleasantly surprised at the Englishman's practical approach.

"I'll live with that, Commodore. Right! Let's get down to the meat of the problem. We have got to find out, and as soon as possible, whether or not that blip is a damned UUO or the missing Russian submarine, *Gorbachev*."

Brianston-Green responded, "Admiral, might I suggest instead of placing all our thoughts into the realms of supposition, let us take the matter at face value."

"I'll buy that. Okay, shoot!"

The Commodore addressed the meeting and checked back through every conceivable piece of evidence.

"Therefore, gentlemen, based on all intelligence information and reports received to date, I believe we should set our course to a positive approach. We should all firmly agree that the UUO is really none other than the missing Russian sub."

"Thank you, Commodore," Admiral Adams remarked, "So, gentlemen, can we all agree the Commodore is right? If so, where do we go from here?"

For a moment Admiral Adams digressed.

"Point one: We all know at sometime the Russian sub should become visible, yet we still find that we cannot see it. Correct, gentlemen?"

Everyone agreed. "Correct, Admiral."

"Okay then. Point two: We are now only left with a decision of how we are goin' to nail the enemy. Is this agreed, everyone?"

Admiral Adams looked up to see all heads were nodding in agreement.

"Fine. Then jointly we have to work out the routing and course of the *SS Globe Kobe*."

Again the Admiral received the room's agreement.

"Excellent. What's next? What's goin' to be our final angle?"

Lt. Mouse piped up. "Check matters regarding the position of the Russian space platform *Vostok*, sir."

"Goodness me, Lt. Mouse! Finally, you have surfaced. Anyhow, that's a good point, Mouse, a very good point. Why did you say that?"

"I'm not exactly sure, sir. I just thought it seemed the most logical thing to say. Sorry, sir, I guess it was just a hunch." Lieutenant Mouse sheepishly sank back in his chair.

Admiral Adams was pleased that his aide had not totally vanished.

"Well, Lt. Mouse, that ain't altogether such a bad hunch."

By now Admiral Adams felt his throat drying up. "Would anyone like a cup of coffee? I could sure do with one myself. How about it, gentlemen?"

"Thank you very much, Admiral," came a resounding reply.

Admiral Adams considered now was the right time to take a break.

"I think, everyone, for now that just about wraps things up. We'll exchange verbal orders shortly and put everything into action as and when the supertanker reaches its point of rendezvous."

Everybody acknowledged their approval after which Lt. Mouse vanished to organise refreshments.

Before the meeting became somewhat informal, Commodore Brianston-Green passed a comment.

"Admiral, should we not be exchanging each other's written agreement to these plans? I do think we should have a written record of them."

"Good thinking, Commodore," Adams replied.

"I'll have them drawn up prior to your departure."

"Thank you, Admiral."

"Splendid, Commodore. Then we are all agreed."

Everyone shook hands.

However, Brianston-Green and Lieutenant Bergman were not really quite sure as to why this celebratory function was being enacted or performed. Neither British officer was certain as to what the implied agreement really was, or by what rules of conduct any action would be staged.

The Commodore began to feel restless.

"Excuse me, Admiral, I think we should shortly be getting back to our normal duties, sir."

This was duly accepted and the meeting was brought to a close.

As everybody stood up Brianston-Green spoke. "Thank you very much, Admiral Adams, for a superb breakfast and morning coffee. I do hope we may have an opportunity, sometime in the coming future, to extend the same pleasure to you, sir. I duly trust that this will not be too long."

"Thank you, Commodore. I will hold you to that and hope you will keep that invite open-ended for me."

"Certainly, Admiral. It will be a pleasure."

Soon the British officers were on their way back across to *HMS Excalibur*. It was nearing 09.30 hours by the time both officers were back settled in familiar surroundings.

"Well, Lt. Bergman," the Commodore said, "I think we have a very busy day ahead of us. Please proceed to advise the operations room the details and identity of that large blip on the radar, the one currently well north-west of our position.

"Have a message sent to Northwood HQ. Confirm in the message the main details regarding the outcome of our visit and meeting to *SSBN Intrepid*. Please ensure that you forward everything under coded transmission. After you have done that forward a simple message of thanks to Admiral Adams and his crew. In it, duly extend an invitation to Admiral Adams and Lieutenant Mouse to visit the *Excalibur*. Acknowledge this should be done when a suitable moment or convenient time arises. Suggest we all meet up in Tenerife or somewhere similar when this caper is done with."

Lieutenant Bergman hurriedly wrote down all that was instructed. "I think I've got everything, Commodore. Is there to be anything else, sir?"

"I don't think so, Lieutenant. You had better be off sharpish and get those messages away."

"Right you are, sir."

Just as Lt. Bergman was about to leave, Brianston-Green commented, "I trust you enjoyed your little excursion, Lieutenant?"

Lt. Bergman turned and looked back at the Commodore. He said nothing but beamed a very broad smile. That said it all.

Meanwhile, aboard the Russian submarine, Captain Narodny had steered the *Gorbachev* on a course that was to go well south of the islands of Cape Verde. He had given considerable thought to various matters of operations. After the sinking of the French destroyer, *Meridien*, he knew attempts would be made to try and track down the *Gorbachev*.

Over the past days the *Gorbachev*'s operations room had plotted the steady progress and different courses made by the British and American submarines.

Captain Narodny followed the movements with great interest. However, he could not quite understand as to why, at one particular time, both submarines seemed to spend nearly three hours locked together. He assumed one of them must have had some sort of mechanical or technical fault and had sought the other's assistance.

Shortly after 11.00 hours, the special operations room on the *Gorbachev* picked up a new very large radar contact.

Captain Narodny requested full details and confirmation as to the position of the unknown contact.

When he had received the information he said, "Well, Number One, I just cannot imagine what that huge blip could be. It's much larger than anything we have been informed to expect. Have you got any idea as to what it might be?"

Captain Narodny's second in command was very cautious by nature.

"Not really, Comrade Captain. I do not believe it can be one of those massive cruise liners on which the decadent western countries flaunt their time-wasting rich people, sailing them from ocean to ocean."

For a moment Captain Narodny paused. "No, this ship is much too large to be anything like that."

"Maybe, Comrade Captain, it is something like a western supertanker, one that could be full of crude oil," the number one said. "Heavens! If we deem to consider destroying something like that, it could have catastrophic consequences for the world and create unknown depths of disaster."

Captain Narodny checked his charts. On making accurate calculations he advised, "Number One, we shall now proceed on a new course. Steer north–north–east at a speed of twenty-five knots. We are going to investigate what that big blip really is. How far away are the American and British submarines?"

"They are positioned about a hundred and forty-five kilometres east of the unidentified radar contact, Comrade Captain."

"Fine, then we shall again alter our course in order to make time, and pass between the two most westerly islands of Cape Verde. What is the ocean's depth at that point?"

"Four hundred and thirty metres, Comrade Captain."

"Excellent! That means we should be sighting this large radar contact in just under three hours while running against this current."

On board the *Intrepid*, Admiral Alan J. T. Adams III had received an urgent message relayed from the NASA Military and Naval Intelligence Department signed by General John B. Kemp. It read:

FROM: NASA M/N DEPT INTELLIGENCE
ATTN: ADMIRAL A. J. T. ADAMS III NAVAL CMDR IN CHIEF – SSBN INTREPID
BE ADVISED – STOP – LIBERTY DEFENDED AN ATTACK MADE BY RUSSIAN SPACE ORBITER – STOP – RUSSIAN CRAFT WENT OUT OF CONROL – STOP – IT CRASHED ON MOON – STOP – RUSSIAN SPACE PLATFORM IS TRANSMITTING MAIN RADIO MAGNETIC BEAM – STOP – AT PRESENT BEAM LOCATION IS CENTRED APPROX EIGHTY MILES SOUTH-EAST OF YOUR PRESENT POSITION – STOP – BELIEVE DECOY COULD BECOME VERY VUNERABLE AS TARGET – STOP – FULL CLEARANCE TO ENGAGE IS GIVEN BY BOTH US AND BRITISH GOVERNMENTS – STOP – REQUEST YOU PROCEED AND INVESTIGATE – STOP – ENSURE TOTAL PROTECTION IS GIVEN TO DECOY – STOP – END MESSAGE
SIGNED GENERAL JOHN B KEMP CHIEF OF STAFF M/N INT

As soon as the message was received, Admiral Adams requested it be immediately relayed to *HMS Excalibur* marked for the urgent attention of Commodore Brianston-Green.

He was very concerned regarding the news about the *Liberty*. Was all this space action something to do with what was happening on Earth? Now, with NASA advising that the Russian space platform had something to do with it, it appeared in some way to be connected with naval operations near to where they were heading. *By golly,* he thought, *this one definitely has to be sent out marked* URGENT. The message read:

FROM: INTREPID

TO: HMS EXCALIBUR

ATTN: COMMODORE BRIANSTON-GREEN

DECOY ON STATION – STOP – HAVE RECEIVED FIRM ADVICE FROM OUR SIDE THAT INTRUDER COULD BE SET TO TAKE BAIT – STOP – PLEASE PROCEED SOUTH-WESTERLY – STOP – PASS THROUGH CHANNEL BETWEEN TWO MOST WESTERLY ISLANDS OF CAPEVERDE – CONTINUE TO INVESTIGATE REGARDING INTRUDER – STOP – ENSURE PROTECTION OF DECOY/BAIT – STOP – END MESSAGE SIGNED: ADMIRAL A J T ADAMS III C-IN-C US NAVY OPERATION BLINDFOLD

On board *HMS Excalibur,* Commodore Brianston-Green looked at Admiral Adams' cable. On reading it he gave a smile in regard to the US Admiral's instructions. When he'd finished reading he showed the message to Lt. Bergman saying, "Well, Roy, what do you think of that?"

Lt. Bergman read the message. He paused a while before he replied. "Do you want my official opinion, sir, or might I have the opportunity to pass it to you on a silver plate?"

The Commodore had expected an air of sarcasm. "Ouch, Roy, I can see you and I obviously are thinking the same. In that case, what would you consider doing?"

Lt. Bergman was pleased with his Commander's response. He respected his senior officer's frankness and enjoyed the open consultation offered in friendship. However, what he really wanted was to see something positive finally happen. "Well, for a start, sir, the American submarine *Intrepid* in no way should sail in to those waters. Its draught is too deep and it would surely bottom out. In my opinion, it would be too risky for it to try."

"Good point, Roy. What else?" the Commodore enquired.

"I also feel Admiral Adams wishes at all costs to protect the *SS Globe Kobe,* but…"

"Yes, yes. What else?" Commodore Brianston-Green interrupted.

Lt. Bergman remained calm. "Sir, if the UUO intruder turns out to be none other than the *Gorbachev,* I believe, if the Russian Captain was to be cunning, he would possibly choose to hide himself away somewhere in the islands' shallow waters.

"At least if I were he, I would select a spot that could give me sufficient room to achieve periscope depth, and just enough to complete a crash dive. I think he would then sit on the bottom of the sea and wait for his quarry to arrive."

"Very good, Lt. Bergman, very good indeed," said the Commodore. Now let's look at things from another angle. What would you do if you happened to be in command of the *Excalibur*? What would you suggest was to be done next, Lieutenant?"

Bergman did not hesitate. "Sir, I would immediately head southwards at very high speed. I would then set a course in order to pass between the two major islands of Cape Verde before exposing us to the Russian sub after which I would then say that it had acquired a problem."

"I see, Bergman, and what would that problem be?"

"Sir, let me put it to you another way. With our submarine running this gauntlet, we would have blocked off the Russian submarine's only possible plan of escape. We would have stopped it from being able to run straight and free."

The Commodore listened with great interest. "Hmmmm. Not bad, Bergman, not bad at all. Then what?"

"I'm not quite sure as to what you mean, sir?" Bergman hesitated for moment.

"Oh, yes! Please excuse me, Commodore, sir. Don't we have to get our battle station clearances before engaging?"

Brianston–Green knew he was pushing his man.

"Oh, Roy! Slow down, man, slow down. I'm not suggesting you go out and start a war, but let us say what if you had already received such confirmations of battle clearances for engagement. What then?"

The Commodore eagerly awaited his Lieutenant's reply.

"I would release one of our main defence missiles and hope to score a direct hit in order to sink the damned coward, sir."

An expression of surprise showed on the Commodore's face. He knew in theory the young man was right. However, he knew he had to get Bergman to realise that the *Gorbachev* was no ordinary foe.

"Mmmm, most entertaining and interesting, Bergman."

"Why thank you, sir, the Lieutenant responded.

The Commodore was pleased with the Lieutenant's sense of naval ability and that his insight of positive thinking of naval battle strategy clearly showed. However, he realised the basis of such advice the young man had given in respect of this situation may prove to be not good enough to succeed.

"Lieutenant, as much as I do applaud your suggestion we do still have one major problem."

"What would that be, Commodore?" Bergman eagerly answered.

"Well, as yet, Lieutenant, we have no radar contact with the enemy. We need this in order to get a fix and lock on to a target to enable our rocket system firing. This is essential in order for us to engage any enemy."

"Sorry, sir. I thought it all seemed too easy," Bergman replied.

The Commodore smiled. "Do not feel depressed about it. You have to learn. You did very well for your first try. Let us now try to construct something else."

He paused for a moment.

"Right. Now, in order we can effect the locking process to ensure destroying our target, we shall have to go and rewrite the book of rules."

At first the Lieutenant looked somewhat puzzled at the Commodore's remark. He gave a polite smile.

"Don't be alarmed, dear boy. I'm very pleased with the practical knowledge and common sense you have shown. In respect of my latter comment, I wish you to proceed and continue to deal with that side of operations. Let me try to work out how we are going to get a shot at this confounded enemy. Is that alright with you, Lieutenant?"

"Yes, sir!" Bergman was pleased by the Commodore's remarks. They gave him confidence, but he also knew he had no time to stand about reflecting on what might have been.

Brianston-Green spoke and gave the Lieutenant an order. "Please send a copy of the message the *Intrepid* sent to Commander Derek Thompson at Northwood HQ.

"Remember to mark it for the attention of Admiral Marchant."

"Yes, sir, I'll do it right away," replied Bergman.

On board the *Gorbachev*, Captain Narodny was pleased with the progress of his submarine. In just under three hours it had made all its planned speed targets and had arrived at its destination by 12.50 hours.

Soon he was making preparations to raise the periscope in order, hopefully, to get a first glimpse at what the massive radar blip might be.

Captain Narodny called out an instruction from the bridge.

"Special operations room. What is the latest radar position you have regarding that large contact?"

"Position, north–north–west on our port beam. Distance, ten thousand metres, Comrade Captain."

Captain Narodny's face showed no emotion. "And the position of the two western submarines?"

There was a slight pause before an answer came back.

"Comrade Captain, we only have one radar contact at the moment. Its position is forty-five kilometres due north–north–east of our position, and now appears to be bearing westwards."

"Fine. Thank you, Comrade Chervisky. Keep up the good work."

"Thank you very much, Comrade Captain."

Captain Narodny desperately wanted to surface but knew this would increase the chances of possible detection. He gave the orders, "Up periscope and apply zoom focus."

Once everything was in order, Captain Narodny leant forward to take what he had hoped was to be the first view of what had been intriguing him for the past few hours.

Slowly turning the periscope, he saw the sea swell appeared to be moderate. However, to his disappointment, the weather was not so good. To the west of the Russian submarine's position heavy fog was blanketing the sea's surface like a thick woolly carpet. There was no sign of any visual contact of the radar blip. To the east, Captain Narodny could see heavy low cloud which predicted that more fog banks would be probable. Still no visual sighting of the huge radar blip was evident.

Captain Narodny stood up and moved back from the periscope. He was in deep thought; calculating and weighing up the odds. He looked across at his first officer.

"Number One, I think that right now we have a very good chance to surface. Up top there are many thick fog banks. We can possibly hide ourselves in the shadow of one of them after we have seen what the devil that monster contact is."

His first officer nodded in agreement.

Again Captain Narodny placed his eyes against the aperture of the periscope lens. This time he considered he would move the lens sight clockwise when traversing the sea surface. Still there was no change.

The fog bank to the west hung like a thick white wall. To the east, the low cloud had sunk down to the sea surface and was beginning to form another huge fog blanket. Directly ahead the sea was shimmering like a Golden Fleece.

Still observing the ever-changing weather patterns, Captain Narodny considered it was the very dense weather conditions that could be creating the huge radar contact. He kept viewing the ever-closing white blankets. Suddenly, his thoughts were instantly changed. From out of one of the huge white walls of fog slowly appeared the massive bows of a huge supertanker.

With great excitement Captain Narodny yelled out, "We've got it, Number One, we've got it. My God! What is that great big ship doing crawling about in these seas?" The air was filled with tension created by what the Captain had shouted out so suddenly. Everyone was now poised in trepidation.

"What is it, Comrade Captain?"

"Just a minute, Number One. Hold on a second or two then I will tell you. *Globe Ko... be.* That's it! A super VLCC, a very large crude oil carrier! We would certainly start one hell of a bonfire if we were to use the atomic-powered laser gun on that. Mind you, I very much doubt if we could ever get Moscow to give clearance for us to destroy it. My, but what a prize! A five hundred thousand ton fully laden supertanker."

Captain Narodny's nerves and adrenaline were pumping. He wanted that ship. He wanted to prove that his submarine was capable of sinking and destroying anything. He kept thinking of the size of the ship. *No*, he thought, *I can't give up the chance of destroying such a wonderful target.*

"Number One, get a message off to Moscow right away. Request clearance is given for us to engage. Advise them we shall set a time for firing. We will do this after I have again studied the changing prospects of this weather pattern a little more thoroughly."

"Right you are, Comrade Captain."

Chapter Twenty

A message was soon received from *HMS Excalibur* at Commander Thompson's office. It was immediately faxed through to the office of Admiral Marchant at the Admiralty.

Not long after the Admiral had read it he telephoned General Kemp.

"Good morning, John. I see you must have had a very busy night?"

"Sure have, Raymond. Things appear to be hotting up here."

"John, I telephoned because I've received a message from our submarine the *Excalibur*."

"Okay, Admiral. Shoot!"

Admiral Marchant took a sip of his drink. "Right, General, in order to ratify its contents I want to see if all matters tie up with what your department may well have already issued."

Kemp quickly got the gist of what he thought the Admiral was up to. "Come on then. Let's have it on the nose, Admiral."

Marchant read Commodore Brianston-Green's message to Kemp. There was a moment of silence from the General. "Hold on a minute, Raymond. Are you reading me only part of the message?"

"No, John, all of it."

"Well, how does anyone expect matters to be fully understood when only half the information is passed forward?"

"What seems to be the problem?"

"Let's put it this way. It's nothin' that can't be corrected."

Marchant paused. "Is the matter serious?"

Kemp was surprised by the Admiral's manner. "Hang it all, Raymond. If you and I weren't such telephone buddies then, I…"

The General stopped himself from saying something that could be taken out of context.

"Yes, Admiral, this whole matter could become very serious and have far-reaching consequences."

Marchant heard the change of tone in the General's voice.

"Okay, John, what part is missing?"

There was no reply from the General.

The Admiral persisted. "What is it that's so important that I should have received it?"

"Jesus Christ, Admiral, it's only what I'd considered to be the best part."

"Tell me more, John," the Admiral replied.

Kemp proceeded to explain. "Sometime during the early hours of this morning, those damned Russkies tried to take out the space shuttle *Liberty*."

"WHAT!" Admiral Marchant exclaimed. "Did they succeed?"

"Yep! I mean no to your question. And, yep, they went and pushed their firin' buttons. Raymond, this is now being treated as a total act of war. There was warning. Just, ZAP!"

Marchant was completely taken aback by it all. "John, what happened to the *Liberty?* Is this really happening?"

Kemp realised how he must have sounded and quickly responded.

"Hold it, Admiral, do not alarm yourself. There was no damage done to our lot. Our boys had it all set up just in case something like this could happen."

"I see. Thank goodness for that. What happened to the Russian space platform *Vostok*?"

"Nothin'!" Kemp advised. "It wasn't the space platform that was involved. The Russians had one of their military space orbiters up there. God only knows where they hid the darned thing."

"A space orbiter? Up there?"

"You know, Raymond," the General said, interrupting, "the one they sent up last June and said they had successfully brought back to Earth after. They didn't. Jesus, they really are a bunch of conniving polecats!"

"Knock me down with a feather," Marchant responded, showing his surprise.

Kemp replied, "Admiral, I'll probably do just that. Let me tell you what we received from the *Liberty*. Categorical evidence by video recording of, wait for it, space demons."

Marchant was amazed. "Good Lord! Now that's more like it. Where at present are the blighters beaming them down to Earth?"

Marchant hoped that the General might be squeezed into giving him the answer he had wished to hear for such a long time.

"Well, Raymond, now we come back to that message you received.

Let me tell you in confidence that all of what I have told you was said in a message sent to Admiral Adams. What I cannot comprehend is why he didn't send confirmation of the whole shootin' match through to your sub *HMS Excalibur.*"

Kemp was pleased that Admiral Marchant had clarified the circumstance that had occurred regarding this situation. "My, my, Admiral, talk about the blind leading the blind. Mind you, I still can't understand how all of this happened."

"Well, John, I sincerely thank you for all the updated information. By the way, what did happen to the Russian space orbiter?"

"Shucks. I am sorry, Raymond. Did I not tell you? The darned thing was blown out of control by its own armament. It disappeared out into space. NASA followed the craft to its destiny. They tracked the flight path through to its tragic end. Apparently, it smashed itself to smithereens when crashing into the moon's surface. I am led to understand that this happened somewhere in the Sea of Serenity."

"Good heavens, John, maybe somebody was trying to tell the Russians something?"

Both General Kemp and Admiral Marchant laughed.

"Thanks again, John, for the information. I trust I may call on you again if I find matters here don't really add up?"

Kemp chuckled. He felt somewhat relieved.

"Feel free, Raymond. It's been nice talkin' with you. Bye for now."

Admiral Marchant sat for a moment in deep thought. He was trying to think of a reason why Admiral Adams had done this. After a while he picked up the telephone and called Commander Thompson.

"Good afternoon, Thompson. Thank you for your message." The Admiral then acknowledged to the Commander all the information he had gleaned from his sources.

"Derek, I want you to send a message to Commodore Brianston-Green. Please advise him of the points I have just told you."

"Right you are, sir."

"Send the message by special code and decoder. Please add to it the following: 'WE CAN ASSUME THE RUSSIAN SUB IS CLOSE AT HAND – STOP – TRY NOT TO ENDANGER THE DECOY – STOP – AT ALL COST EXCALIBUR MUST GET ITS DESERVED PRIZE – END MESSAGE'."

It didn't take Thompson long to get the message compiled and coded.

It was 14.06 hours when the coded text was dispatched.

At 14.20 hours, Northwood HQ received a reply from the British submarine. It read:

FROM: HMS EXCALIBUR
TO: NORTHWOOD HQ RN INT
ATTN: CMDR THOMPSON FOR ADVICE TO ADMIRAL MARCHANT
THANK YOU FOR MESSAGE RECEIVED – STOP – HAD READ INTREPID's
DETAILS WELL – STOP – TOOK ALTERNATIVE ACTION – STOP – OUR
POSITION NOW READS 14.2 N 28.0 W – STOP – INTREPID's POSITION
NOW READS 18.0 N 23.2 W – STOP – DECOY POSITION READS 16.1
N 26.4 W – STOP – BELIEVE UUO TARGET IS POSSIBLY POSITIONED
AT 16.0 N 25.4 W – STOP – WILL COME UP AND PROCEED THROUGH
SHALLOW WATERS FROM SOUTHEAST – STOP – IF CONTACT WITH
ENEMY IS MADE – STOP – WILL REQUEST PERMISSION TO ENGAGE
AND ATTACK – STOP – END MESSAGE
SIGNED COMMODORE C. BRIANSTON-GREEN – HMS EXCALIBUR

Immediately the message was received, Northwood Royal Navy HQ, Naval Intelligence operations forwarded it to Admiral Marchant at his Admiralty office in Whitehall.

Just after 14.30 hours, Admiral Marchant called Commander Thompson.

"Thank you for that last message, Thompson. I think that one firmly settles matters. We can hazard a guess that confirmation sets the Royal Navy to be first in line for a crack at whatever the unidentified underwater object is. Don't you think so, Derek?"

While Thompson was listening to the Admiral's conversation, he again read the message received from the *Excalibur.*

"I would hope so, sir, but it could turn out to be a tricky business. I just hope the decoy doesn't get caught in any crossfire."

Marchant checked what Thompson had observed and was not in the least concerned. "Thompson, I think the decoy may well have moved on by the time any real action begins. Still, we shall see as operations develop."

Admiral Marchant picked up the message and placed it into the red file on his desk marked 'Classified'.

"Now then, young man. At present we have far more urgent matters to attend to. The committee handling the recommendation for the proposed political asylum of Lt. Commander Ivanov began sitting at 14.00 hours."

Thompson acknowledged the Admiral's comment.

"Yes, sir, it has been at the back of mind. However, what with all this other stuff and the nuke sub action going on, the matter had been somewhat put into second place."

"I fully understand, Thompson. I would have done the same thing myself although we must still make a point of consolidating the control of our affairs on the home front. This you have to cover as well as the very serious matters currently happening abroad."

"Yes, sir, I fully agree."

On hearing Thompson's response, Admiral Marchant felt reassured. "I would expect to be hearing of the outcome from the board of interrogation at about 17.00 hours. Why don't I give you a call at that time? I'll let you know all of what has transpired and we can then organise what it is we are expected to do with the Russian chappie. We'll take up all matters from thereon. Is that all right with you, Thompson?"

"Right you are, sir."

"Fine. Until I speak with you later. Bye for now."

"Goodbye, sir," Thompson put down the receiver.

In Space

Captain Rose and Lieutenant Lottie Mason, on board the *Liberty*, had circled the Earth seven times since the unprovoked attack made by the Russian space orbiter. NASA Ground Control and Tracking Centre had received a full account of the incident. All military departments and the President were notified. The whole matter had been completely screened by the release of 'D' notices to both the American press and television news media.

Russia's news agency printed an article that confirmed there had been a minor incident in space involving the space platform *Vostok*.

It advised: *With great sadness we announce the loss of Captain Sukov and his survey crew.* The press statement advised all parties had been working on the *Vostok*, and that they were repairing part of the outer superstructure on the space platform when a shower of meteors inflicted some damage. Tragically, the incident caused the unfortunate deaths of the five crew of the space orbiter who at the time were assisting as the repair survey team. The paper continued to report that there would be a period of official mourning, and in due course a service of remembrance would be announced.

NASA Ground Control and Tracking, Cape Canaveral
US Military and Naval Intelligence Department

Professor Macdonald Burston received a call from General Kemp.

It was a little after 08.20 hours EST, 13 August 2017.

"Mornin', Mac," said Kemp. "How are you doin', buddy. Progressed any further?"

"To put it mildly, I'm feeling a bit shattered, John. It has been one hell of a night. For a moment I really thought we had seen the last of Captain Rose and his crew. To think those Russians had the balls to open up their space orbiter's main armament at the *Liberty*.

"Shucks! I'm pleased that Captain Rose, as a precaution while he was sleeping, turned on the Automatic Retaliation Sensor Equipment. Didn't it work like a dream, General? A real gem of an invention that turned out to be."

"Well, Mac, that's what *Liberty* stands for – Freedom!" Kemp said firmly.

"I think our space shuttle has now added an extra bit to the meaning of the word."

"John, we gather that the Russians are planning to try and make a moon landing in the near future."

"Oh, yeah!" the General barked. "I wonder what they want to go and do that for."

Burston replied, "We gather that it might have something to do with a plan to begin work on preparing ground clearance for a cemetery to be constructed somewhere in the Sea of Serenity."

"By heck! What was that you said, Mac?" Kemp wasn't too happy with the Professor's wry sense of humour.

"Hey, John, I was only kiddin'," the Professor replied grinning like a Cheshire cat. He was thankful the conversation was over the telephone. He knew Kemp would have blown his top if he had seen him laughing."

"Thank goodness for that. I thought for a second that I hadn't been forwarded any intelligence on it. Mind you, tell you what I did receive."

"What was that, John?" the Professor enquired.

"Those sneaky Russian polecats have gone and released a report in one of their national newspapers. It states there had been a minor accident on board *Vostok*.

"It further advised five persons had perished. It would seem they don't wish to expose the truth of what happened. Moreover, they haven't mentioned anything to back up what they had already stated last June. Did you know that it was nearly two months ago that the Russians reported their military space orbiter had returned to Earth safely?"

"How can they do that? They always seem to get away with it."

Kemp knew exactly what his colleague was hinting at.

"Mac, they must have done it a thousand times. However, I am pleased to say that Uncle Sam, and some of our allies, finally seem to be getting the better of a lot of their games and surprises.

"Mac, I'm now sure that in some way all this is connected with the disappearance of that Russian nuclear submarine *Gorbachev*. Give me a few more hours, let's say, twenty-four hours in your trackin' room, linked with Captain Rose and *Liberty*. After that both the American Navy and the British Royal Navy will have bagged their prize."

Burston didn't understand what the General was referring to.

"Sorry, John, you're way above my head on this one. However, I'd be very pleased to welcome you over for the viewing and communication time you have suggested. You can bring one of your lads with you and have the run of the place for as long as you wish. Do you need any special clearances for that?"

Kemp's mind was already racing way ahead of the Professor's suggestion.

"Leave that one to me, Mac. Thank you very much for the kind offer. Give me an hour or two to make the necessary arrangements. I'll get back to you as soon as possible. Okay?"

Professor Burston was delighted to be of assistance.

"Fine, John. I look forward to hearing from you a little later on."

The General was very pleased. Now he thought he had a real chance to get to grips with the whole situation, which had been bugging him for so long.

"Thanks for the invite, dear friend. I'll give you a call later. Bye for now."

Kemp requested Sergeant Lance to contact, through classified security channels, the confidential communication numbers for knowledge and the whereabouts of the President.

"Right you are, General, sir. I'll fix that up for you immediately."

"Thank you, Lance. As soon as you have obtained them, place a call for me with the 'Big White Chief' himself."

"Yes, sir. Wow! What a wonderful start to my day," Lance replied.

Kemp couldn't help but laugh. He wondered what would happen if Sergeant Lance were no longer about to bring a little humour into his day.

Ten minutes had passed before Kemp's red telephone rang. "Hello," the General said answering it.

"Sir, I have the President on the line for you."

"Thank you, Lance." Kemp heard the line connection change, then silence. At first he wasn't sure if he was through but the sound of a click came and a noise of faint background movement.

The General spoke. "Good morning, Mr. President."

"Good morning, John. What can I do to assist your day? It sounds as if it might be very important." The President always respected Kemp's interruption to any part of his day. Whenever it occurred, he knew it meant action.

"Mr. President, thank you for calling me back so promptly."

"Not at all, General. So, what's happening in the world at present that appears so urgent?"

Kemp pulled out a cigarette and lit it. "Mr. President, I'm sure by now you have heard the news concerning the *Liberty* and the Russian space orbiter."

"Yes indeed, John, but I have received only a few details. Why? What have you heard?" the President replied.

Kemp opened the page of the file that revealed the latest pictures taken by the *Liberty*.

"Well, sir, I believe a whole picture regarding the intelligence of this situation is finally coming together. I think I can safely state, sir, the matter leads towards possibly exposing a connection with the Russian space platform *Vostok*, and linking it with the long outstanding file concerning the space demon saga."

The President listened carefully to what Kemp said.

"Why is that, John? What do both operations have in common?"

"That's the reason for my call, Mr. President. Currently, I have to obtain full security clearance in order my department can officially enter NASA Ground Control and Tracking. If I were to gain official special clearance, I would be able to spend a few hours checking with Captain Rose the position of the *Vostok*. With this purpose in mind we will be able to survey the discovery of radar beams currently being emitted from *Vostok* towards Earth."

The General waited to hear the President's reaction.

"I see, General. What then do you expect to achieve? I mean, having found out exactly where the position of this beam is centred."

"Sir, I sincerely do believe," the General said, "in possibly being able to connect all of the co-ordinated readings together, our department will be able to successfully expose what this wretched unidentified underwater object really is."

The President showed an air of surprise. "Good grief, General! Do you firmly believe you could crack this mystery?"

Kemp felt a softening in the President's tone. "Yes, Mr. President, I most certainly do."

The President paused for a moment.

It appeared to Kemp that he was home and dry.

The President spoke. "Let me dwell on the matter for a little bit, John. Mind you, if I do say yes…" the President stopped again. He seemed not too sure of what he should say in response to Kemp's request.

"John, if you should let me down, you are aware the least you can expect to receive will be a massive amount of flak flying your way; most of it will come from your most senior officers, and that's apart from what I might have to say."

The General was well aware of the intimated caution he would have to show. "I do well understand and thank you for your advice, Mr. President, sir."

The President again pushed home the point. "Even if it means you may be put in front of a major board of investigation to denounce and ridicule your actions. That's, of course, if you happened to be found to have violated any of the standard codes of practice."

Kemp stood firm. "Sir, Mr. President, if your permission is granted then I will hold my head up with honour and pride knowing that I have done my duty in offerin' nothin' but my best efforts in serving both you and the United States of America."

The President knew Kemp's past record was impeccable. "All right. Like I said, General, leave the matter with me a little bit longer. You shall hear from me within the hour."

"Thank you, Mr. President."

"Goodbye for now, General. Nice talking with you."

Smartie Logan had just come into the office as Kemp was finishing his telephone call.

"Hi there, General. Everythin going okay?"

Kemp looked up. His face showed no emotion.

"Hopefully, Logan. We'll just have to wait and see what comes round in about one hour."

It was just after 09.00 hours.

Kemp felt it was time he replenished some of his energy.

"Say, Smartie, how about my treatin' you to a late breakfast?"

Logan was ravenous; he hadn't had time for a bite to eat before leaving.

"Thank you, sir. That would be great."

"Okay," the General said. "Tell Sergeant Lance we are both goin' to the canteen for about thirty minutes. Advise him that if there are any messages or important calls to pick us up over the internal tannoy."

"Right you are, sir."

Logan then left the General's office to speak with Sergeant Lance.

Sergeant Lance made note of Logan's details. "Okay, Captain. Will, do. Say, what if it's the President callin'? Do I let the General know as he has requested?"

"I suppose so, Sergeant. Orders are orders," Logan advised.

At that moment, General Kemp stepped out of his office.

"Is everything all right, Sergeant?"

"Just fine, sir, the Sergeant replied. "By the way, sir, if that last caller you had should happen to call back on the hotline, what do you wish me to do, sir?"

Kemp realised what might have happened if the Sergeant's voice had bellowed across the internal tannoy with such confirmation.

"Good thinking, Lance. Nope, you will have to come down and get me to come back up top. That's if any calls happen to come in on that line. Thank you, Sergeant, you were right to put that one over."

"Why, thank you kindly, sir. I was just recheckin' things, General."

"Okay. Stand easy, Sergeant. Stand easy."

As Kemp and Logan made their way upstairs, the smell of freshly made waffles and the sweet aroma and fresh scent of rich maple syrup caught their nostrils. Kemp looked at Logan. "Gee, that sure smells good, Smartie."

Logan couldn't wait to get stuck in. He was famished.

After about fifteen minutes a facsimile message began to print through on to the tray beside the General's desk.

It was headed with a big seal that encompassed the words: FROM THE OFFICE OF THE PRESIDENT OF THE UNITED STATES OF AMERICA. It was marked: TOP CONFIDENTIAL. The message read:

ATTENTION: GENERAL JOHN B. KEMP

CHIEF OFFICER, NASA MILITARY AND NAVAL INTELLIGENCE DEPT

PLEASE BE ADVISED FULL CLEARANCES HAVE BEEN GRANTED TO YOU AND CAPTAIN LOGAN TO PROCEED TO NASA GROUND CONTROL AND TRACKING CENTRE IN ORDER THAT YOU COMPLETE YOUR MISSION AS DISCUSSED.

SIGNED: THE PRESIDENT OF THE UNITED STATES OF AMERICA.

Shortly after 10.15 hours, General Kemp returned with Captain Logan back to his office.

As the General walked past Lance he enquired, "Any calls, Sergeant?"

"No, General, sir. The wires ain't been burning at this end."

There was a look of disappointment on Kemp's face.

"Okay, Sergeant."

Both Logan and the General laughed as they entered a peaceful office. A red light was showing on top of the small facsimile unit which sat on a low shelf beside the General's desk. The light registered to show that a message had come in.

As the General sat in his chair, he picked up the two pages and read the text. On finishing he looked across at Logan who had paused to study a huge sea chart Kemp had laid across his glass table.

"Smartie, tell Sergeant Lance to get the car and driver out right away. Have him send it round to the front door, pronto."

"Okay, General."

"Young man, it looks like finally we are in business."

The General stood up, crossed the room and showed Captain Logan the message.

"Why, congratulations, sir. When do we leave?"

"I'd say in about ten minutes if that's all right with you, Smartie?" said the General, smiling.

"It's mighty fine by me, sir. Just mighty fine."

Chapter Twenty-One

At Sea

The towering island of Fogo lay in the distance. Its volcano, still active, left a trail of sulphurous steam dissipating into the heavens. Soon it began to grow smaller as *HMS Excalibur* continued its progress westwards.

Commodore Brianston-Green had instructed his crew to operate full radio silence and arrange for a system of radar jamming be put into effect.

The British submarine's position was now at 25.0 W 16.0 N Time: 17.23 hours, Monday, 14 August 2017.

On looking northward, the distant outline of the islands of Slo Antao and Mindelo appeared. They looked like a couple of thimble tops just noticeable way off on the horizon.

The weather forecast for the evening was for good visibility. However, on checking the submarine's weather charts the radar showed very deep fog banks centred about eighty miles north of *HMS Excalibur*'s present position.

Sometime around mid-afternoon, Admiral Alan J. T. Adams III advised before the agreed communications blackout that the *Intrepid* would remain positioned about thirty miles north-west of the island of Slo Antao and would, for the time being, carry on observing the *SS Globe Kobe*.

On board the *Gorbachev*, Captain Narodny had twice tried to get a fix on the great prize in his sights. Each time the fog had come to the huge tanker's rescue.

Captain Gladstone Tremaine had reduced the supertanker's speed down to ten knots. He was not really sure as to what his ship's purpose was in constantly having to sail a course of a huge square, or why it was to be filled with a cargo full of seawater. All he knew was the Joint Chiefs of Staff of both the United States of America and Great Britain had instructed the ship's owner. They had seconded the ship under a time charter; the purpose of the charter was listed as 'Extraordinary Naval Training Exercises'. Captain Tremaine checked his charts. It would not be too long before he would have to change the tanker's course to proceed northwards.

As midshipman Luke Applebury entered the bridge he handed the Captain a cable message received from the *SSBN Intrepid*. It read:

TIME: 17.50 HOURS 14 AUGUST 2017
FROM: INTREPID
TO: SS GLOBE KOBE
ALTER COURSE 180 DEGREES – STOP – STEAM WESTWARDS AT SIX
KNOTS – STOP – END MESSAGE
SIGNED: ADMIRAL ADAMS

Slowly the huge tanker, using the strong current's assistance, began to turn to starboard.

On board the *Gorbachev*, Captain Narodny had noticed the change of the tanker's course and decided also to alter his submarine's course. He ordered that the *Gorbachev* make headway west-south-west to enable it to follow the huge vessel.

Captain Narodny hoped the severe fog conditions to the north would soon begin to lift.

"It doesn't look like we are going to become too involved in trying to capture the superb prize today, Number One. However, I would like to shadow it for a little longer; maybe its Captain is not so silly. He could be trying to sail out of the huge fog bank and take up a different course. I presume he is also hoping the weather will improve."

"Could be so, Comrade Captain. It could be so," the first officer acknowledged.

"Fine, let's leave all this for now. I think maybe it's in order for us to break for an early evening meal. We can come back and check everything a little later on."

"Right you are, Comrade Captain. I'll inform special communications to have them acknowledge us in the mess if there happens to be anything changing under our present circumstance."

"Thank you, Number One."

Both Captain Narodny and the officer of the watch left the bridge. The time was 20.10 hours.

NASA Ground Control and Tracking, Cape Canaveral
US Military and Naval Intelligence Department

General Kemp had just returned from a meeting of the Joint Chiefs of Staff. He had fully reported the findings regarding the *Liberty*/Russian space orbiter, the result of which meant that the NASA US Military and Naval Intelligence Department had been given clearance to investigate and examine the yet unknown position regarding the Russian space platform *Vostok*. This clearance was allowed in order to determine its current purpose and role in space regarding Russia's last update and report issued during July 2017.

As the General stepped back into his office he called Captain Logan in to join him.

"Good trip, sir?" Logan asked.

"Do you know, Smartie, I do believe we are gradually coming closer to finding out what these darned space demons really are. Hell, it sure makes me feel a whole lot better to know that the headman at the helm of our country is now backin' the department all the way down the line."

"That sure feels great, sir. Please allow me to say, General, a lot of credit personally goes down to you. Also, your close friends in the UK for stickin' their necks out on something everyone believed was a real patsy."

Kemp grimaced at Logan's remark. "Why, that's real nice. Thank you very much, Captain. Let me also say somethin'. Young man, you also deserve a major piece of everyone's gratitude. Your help has been invaluable for this department. Anyway, let's not get too complacent; we still have one very important matter to resolve."

"What's that, General?" Logan remarked.

"Well, Smartie, actually there are two. The first thing to find out is what those spirals in space are, and what they are being used for. The second is to find out if there's any connection with the first situation. We need to do this in order to help resolving the matter of that unidentified underwater object. Let me say, Logan, privately, I still believe that UUO is that goddam'd Russian submarine."

Logan soon got the General's drift. "Yes, sir. I'll go along with that."

Kemp continued, "Well Smartie, right now we need to have a breakthrough. Somethin' has got to snap, and soon."

"Sure thing, General. That's a sure thing," Logan said in full agreement.

By now Kemp was feeling tired and a little out of sorts.

"How about a quick snorter, Captain, before we cut loose for the night?"

As the General made a move towards the drinks cabinet, the red telephone sprang to life. He quickly moved back to his desk and picked up the receiver.

"Why, hello, Raymond. What's the matter? Can't you sleep?"

Admiral Marchant had poured himself a stiff drink in order to settle himself down.

"Hello, John. I think you had better brace yourself for this one."

"Okay, Admiral, I'm game. Shoot!"

"I should really say, John, that last remark of yours is the operative word. Sometime during the late evening, the Russians had two of their FSB hitmen kill one of their own. He was the envoy who, you may recall, had come over to collect the parcel of butchered remains of the two senior FSB officers who disappeared some time ago in the States. By some strange quirk of engineering, one of the officers in my department, a certain Commander named Derek Thompson..."

"Oh, yes. I remember you mentioned his name sometime before. I believe you told me he was the guy who played a major part in monitoring the breakout of that Russian sub the *Gorbachev*."

Marchant was never too happy at the best of times if anybody interrupted him. "John! One moment, please!"

"Okay, okay, Raymond. I'm sorry I butted in. Please continue."

"Well, you may already know what I am going to say. If not, allow me to tell you. As yet, I am certain the Russians do not know the full implications of what they have done. Let me explain why."

There was a slight pause as Admiral Marchant took another large sip from his glass.

"When the Russian came over to England to do his job, he applied for, and received, clearance of political asylum. On receiving such immunity he became a British subject. As yet, John, I have not received all the specific details, but I am sure by midday, my time, a lot more information will be coming into my hands. Anyway, General, I would like you to address your thoughts to assessing the implications of the FSB needing to silence this fellow. By the way, John, I'm led to understand that the FSB may have lost one of their best hitmen in the process. Apparently, Commander Thompson's aide saw the Russian off."

"Great Scott! My goodness, Raymond. I should think the fellow must get a gong for that."

"Okay, John. Nice talking with you. Bye for now."

Marchant put down the telephone receiver, turned off the lamp, rolled over and shut his eyes.

Kemp replaced the receiver. As he did so, two clicks were heard just as he put it down. The General noticed them but made no comment to either Logan or Sergeant Lance both of whom had just stepped into the General's office.

"Yes, Lance, what can I do for you?"

"Sir, I have just received a message for you from the President's office."

"What does it read?"

Sergeant Lance went to hand the message to the General.

"No, please, Sergeant, go ahead. You read it," Kemp said, knowing the message was of great importance to everyone present.

The Sergeant's voice boomed out: "FROM THE PRESIDENT OF THE UNITED STATES OF AMERICA. FOR THE ATTENTION OF GENERAL JOHN B. KEMP – NASA MILITARY AND NAVAL INTELLIGENCE DEPARTMENT.

"YOU ARE HEREBY ADVISED TO PLACE ALL MATTERS OF COMMUNICATION AND OPERATIONS FROM THE NASA BASE AND LINKED AREAS ON TO A STATE OF FULL ALERT AT GRADE 'AMBER'. WE HAVE BEEN LED TO UNDERSTAND FROM OUR FRIENDS AND ALLIES IN THE UNITED KINGDOM ACCUTE SUBVERSIVE ACTIVITY BY RUSSIAN FSB AGENTS HAS BEEN UNCOVERED, OPERATING WITHIN LONDON AND THROUGHOUT ENGLAND. A FULL ALERT THEREFORE IS TO BE MAINTAINED UNTIL FURTER NOTICE IN ORDER TO PROTECT ALL STRATEGIC OPERATIONS OF THE STATE DEPARTMENT AND ALL MILITARY UNITS BASED ON LAND, SEA OR AIR THROUGHOUT THE UNITED STATES OF AMERICA. SIGNED: THE PRESIDENT – END OF MESSAGE."

"Holy cow! Sergeant! Captain Logan! Neither of you have read, or heard any of this message. Do you hear me? I'll be issuing my instructions to you both in due course in compliance with this message. Okay?"

"Yes sir, General, sir," Lance replied.

Logan stood still and said nothing.

Kemp responded to the security officer's answer. "Thank you, Sergeant Lance. That will be all."

The Sergeant turned and left the General's room with a broad grin beaming across his face.

Captain Logan looked very keenly at the General then said, "What do you think is up, sir?"

Kemp sat down.

"I'm not exactly sure, Logan. It seems very odd this message from the President didn't come in over the security fax line."

Kemp stood up and began to pace the floor.

"When Admiral Marchant's telephone call finished up, I'm darned well sure that I heard the tell-tale clicks of a listening bug, or possibly it was some kinda' mole unit that was cancellin' out."

"Good grief, sir! You can't be serious saying that we are being listened to at this moment."

"I don't know, Logan. I don't even know why."

"But, sir, don't you think we have been laid wide open for someone to be spying on us? Jesus Christ, if they have managed to have gotten through to the UK, maybe a damned renegade Russian FSB unit has also managed to get itself planted into our system. Maybe even inside our operations at NASA Military and Intelligence."

Kemp's face now looked very tired and drawn.

"Logan, to hell with it! I don't know what to believe except there seems to be somethin' mighty queer goin' on. Smartie, go and get me a very strong black coffee. I sure as hell may be bushwhacked, but I ain't goin' to be beaten by it yet, either."

"Okay, sir, one strong coffee comin' up."

Logan departed leaving Kemp to forward a copy of the message directly to the President's private office to his dedicated facsimile line.

Within thirty seconds of the message being sent the red telephone on the General's desk began to ring. The General answered it.

"This is the office of the President speaking. General Kemp, sir, please hold for one moment."

"Thank you, I'm holding."

Kemp lit himself a cigar and then eased back into his chair.

Soon a deep voice came on the line. "Good evening, General. Still working late I guess?"

"Yes, sir, Mr. President."

"Now then, John. Thank you very much for sending me that last message. It was right of you to inform me as soon as you had received it. Please, General, I beg to warn and caution you most strongly about the message and its contents. In respect of our nation's security, John, I hereby confirm to you that I was not the writer of the message."

"Good Heavens!" Kemp retorted. "Am I right, Mr. President? You did say you weren't the writer?"

"That's correct, General. I was not the writer. Moreover, and what's more astounding, part of the detail of that message has reported something which has only just happened in the United Kingdom."

"Good grief, sir. Do you mean to say that…" General Kemp gulped then took a deep breath. "God almighty! Those renegade goddamned FSB Russkies. They have now infiltrated into our own operations. It would also appear, sir, they have done this at our highest level of security."

"I'm afraid, John, it would certainly appear to be so. From now on I suggest that you and I keep in very close contact over the next few days."

"Okay, Mr. President."

"Thank you again, General, for contacting me so promptly. By the way, was there something else you wished to discuss with me?"

"Well, sir, actually there is."

Kemp notified the President regarding the events and circumstances revealed from his sources from over the pond. He confirmed the matter which had occurred in the UK regarding the death of the FSB officer and the assassination of the Russian naval officer, and advised that prior to his death the officer had already defected.

"I must say, General, you are extremely well informed. I congratulate you and your department for being so prompt in notifying me of these matters. Is there anything else?"

"Mr. President, the defector who was released into the charge of a British Naval Intelligence Officer gave a full report that could very well determine and be officially placed on record that the Russian submarine *SSBN Gorbachev* really does still exist."

"What was that, General?"

"Furthermore sir, there may well be a definite link somewhere that exists between the submarine and the Russian space platform *Vostok*."

"Good Lord! Really?" the President remarked.

Kemp continued, "I'm being led to understand, sir, that some highly sophisticated operations room up there in space seems to be handlin' and co-ordinatin' operations. I wish an immediate order be made for the US space shuttle, *Liberty,* to go and investigate further into the mysterious sightin's of those fluorescent spiralling lights. It appears the *Vostok* has been beaming these signals earthwards. Sir, I strongly believe that these beams have a direct bearing in connection with some sort of screening cover that somehow must be shielding the Russian submarine."

"General Kemp, these are very serious revelations and the implications of which, if found to be true, will indeed reveal a very grave situation. Have you considered the circumstances if you find you have made a terrible mistake?"

"I have considered that position, Mr. President. I also realised during our recent meeting of the Joint Chiefs of Staff at the time of my showing the pictures of the so-called space demons. Do you happen to recall, sir, what I said regarding the loss of the *SS Andros* and the two civilian aircrafts, then, a little later on, about the unbelievable loss of the French destroyer *Meridien*."

"Yes, John, I do believe I do. Anyway, what does this have to do with all you have been saying?"

"Well, sir, at the time of that meeting, all of what I then stated, you may remember this was advised as not being of any significance."

"That I well recall, General."

Kemp was pleased to hear the President's answer. "It's in connection with these past findings, sir. I really do believe, and now beyond all doubt, that the Russian submarine *Gorbachev* is still with us. Moreover, Mr. President, may I respectfully suggest that the submarine has on board a sinister secret weapon. I believe the sub destroyed those ships and planes killing hundreds of innocent people."

Kemp paused to take a sip of water.

In reply, the President's voice was calm.

"One moment, General."

The President paused to reflect.

"Well, John, that is an extraordinary conclusion for anybody to make. I would go much further than that to say it's so ridiculous that it's inconceivable for the rest of us to try to believe it."

The President stopped for a moment and took a handkerchief from out of his pocket. He mopped his brow. He took a sip of his coffee and again paused for a moment in deep thought.

Kemp waited in silence.

"General, I trust that you will be able to corroborate everything you are stating?"

Kemp was slightly alarmed by what was just said.

"Mr. President, sir, I do fear that by the time we would have convened all the necessary committee meetings it would be much too late. Mr. President, sir, this situation needs action now. This must be considered in order to prevent any more events of such dreadful destruction. I beg you please to consider my request, Mr. President. Currently, off the islands of Cape Verde, Joint Chiefs of Staff of our country and the United Kingdom have mustered a formidable force. They have placed a decoy in order to have the unidentified underwater object, or the Russian submarine, lured into believing the thing has another handsome prize to destroy. I personally advise to you, Mr. President, we do have our submarine, *Intrepid*, and the British Navy has their submarine, *HMS Excalibur*, on the spot. They are waiting to intercept the UUO. Mr. President, I need your due attention and consideration to give me a full clearance to shut down the space demon file. By you granting this, the UUO, or if it is the Russian submarine *Gorbachev*, will either be exposed or we will have found another enemy. Please, sir, do I have your permission to do this? Can I proceed and engage all parties dealing with this task?"

Kemp fell silent and waited.

The President had long respected Kemp's intuition and foresighted projections towards world events. He had always keenly acknowledged the General's very cautious judgement.

"Well, John, I do trust you know what you're doing. By the way, what's going to happen if that UUO turns out to be the missing Russian sub? Then what, General? Are you suggesting that we sink it?"

Kemp did not hesitate in answering.

"Sir, as yet I have no idea as to what the overall decision is going to be. Both of the submarine Commanders will be advising me of that circumstance in due course. One thing is for sure, Mr. President, if it does turn out to be that Russian sub there sure is goin' to be a lot of explanations demanded from some very high-up people sitting in the Kremlin."

The President interrupted, "General, as I have already said, I hope that you know what you could be letting yourself in for. Remember if everything turns turtle…"

Kemp interjected, "Sir, I am well aware of the steps that will be taken if in any way I have misjudged this situation."

With that very direct resolve and response from General Kemp, the President gave his consent.

"Okay, John. So be it. You will have your clearance as requested."

Kemp's heart began to pound.

The President again spoke. "By the way, John. May I personally wish good luck."

"Thank you, Mr. President. I'll instruct NASA Ground Control and Tracking as soon as I have received your written authority. By the way, sir, I would strongly suggest you instruct a turnover of the joint USAF and Military Chiefs of Staff be done, and put into action right away. I have very firm reasons to suspect one of their senior staff is involved, and is engaged as an active member of the FSB. Please, Mr. President, throw a security blanket over the whole of these organisations immediately."

The President appreciated Kemp's advice.

"Will do, General. Let me have your progress report soonest."

Kemp felt an air of pride and personal achievement in what he had been able to accomplish.

"Sir, I'll certainly advise you as and when any progress in made. Or, alternatively, may I call you over the next two or three hours?"

"That will be fine, John. Just make damned sure your plans finally get those space demons. Bye for now."

"Goodbye, Mr. President. Once again, thank you for the chance, sir."

The time was nearing 21.30 hours when Kemp called Professor Burston. He formally requested the Professor begin programming the space shuttle *Liberty* to move on to the same orbit as the Russian space platform *Vostok*.

In Space

The space shuttle *Liberty* had begun moving into a closer orbit to pass by the Russian space platform *Vostok*.

NASA Ground Control and Tracking had ordered this be done to enable Captain Rose make a more accurate fix on the fluorescent spiralling beam. The fixing was clearly showing to be emanating from somewhere under the lower section of the twinkling space city.

After having readjusted the zoom cameras on board the shuttle, Captain Rose could see the thing more clearly on the video screen. By now he had locked all the cameras to zoom in on the *Vostok*. He did this in order to achieve sending an accurate information report and reading back to Earth. Everything was geared and synchronised to be set under the same time slot advised by NASA Ground Control and Tracking for a joint live transmission.

The Space Control Centre had already acknowledged to the *Liberty* confirmation that NASA had successfully received all previous data transmitted.

Captain Rose heard clearly the voice of the ground controller state, "This is NASA Control to *Liberty*. We advise you are looking very good, Captain. We at NASA confirm your pictures are great, but are you able to get any closer shots of the space platform?"

Captain Rose immediately responded, "I'll try to adjust the cameras during *Liberty*'s next orbit."

"Okay, Captain, that'll be fine. Please advise us if and when you see anything that finally pinpoints the whereabouts of these strange beams. Please double-check to see if it is emanating from out of the base of the *Vostok* space platform."

"Will do, NASA Control. Roger and out."

Captain Rose fully understood his task. Gradually the *Liberty* manoeuvred into its next orbital course. He had estimated the space shuttle would pass within four miles of the Russian space platform.

"*Liberty* to NASA Ground Control. Do you read me? Over."

"We read your signal loud and clear, Captain."

As yet, Captain Rose was still not too sure whether NASA Ground Control had been able to get a fix back on Earth of the exact position of where the beam of fluorescent spiralling light was hitting the Earth's surface.

He called back and asked for verification.

Moments later the response came. "The exact position of that beam, Captain, is being worked on at this moment. We will report back to you when we know."

"Okay, fine," came Captain Rose's reply.

NASA Ground Control then gave Captain Rose a new instruction. "Captain, we have been requested you now proceed and break the seal of your classified operation orders. We have been instructed to notify you, when Ground Control and Tracking confirm full clearance of the fixed position, that you are hereby ordered to complete this instruction, then report back."

Captain Rose broke the red seal on the black folder. His face showed no emotional change as he read through the various detailed orders. When completing his reading he passed the folder over to Lt. Lottie Mason. He then prepared himself to verify matters with NASA Ground Control and Tracking. "This is Captain Rose. Affirmative, Ground Control, I confirm the *Liberty* stands ready to action operations as instructed."

While waiting for further advice, Captain Rose checked that all of the space shuttle's anti-radar detection and missile defence systems were functioning properly. As the *Liberty* approached the space platform, he could now see very clearly on the video screen the sophisticated communications section beneath the main structure of the *Vostok*. Captain Rose marvelled at the incredible advancement in technology the Russians had made.

On board the space platform, Major Chitov had been communicating with Moscow on various matters regarding the disappearance of the space orbiter.

Suddenly, something triggered off the space platform's emergency automatic alarm sensor. It set all the sirens off, wailing and howling, echoing eerily far into space. All personnel were called directly to action stations by the automatic computer-controlled announcer which constantly repeated itself. This ordered everyone to rally round in defence of an approaching alien or UFO.

On board the *Liberty*, unbeknown to Captain Rose and at a distance of five thousand metres, the American space shuttle had penetrated the Russian space platform's outer defence shield and had been detected. However, the highly sensitive radar shield on board the *Vostok* failed to break through the *Liberty*'s anti-radar screen thus halting the UFO's identity from being revealed.

In *Vostok*'s communications and control centre, operators were frantically trying to detect who or what the invading UFO was. Their detection screen and locator board merely showed a red light flashing. Within ten seconds of any unauthorised contact being made, the space platform's anti-alien defence system automatically fired a salvo of short-range heat-seeking missiles.

On board the *Liberty*, its laser gun sensors instantly detected the oncoming danger. As soon as the sensors locked on to the target the guns fired returning a laser screen barrage of fire in effecting a counter-attack. Within a split second each rocket exploded as the laser guns' beams located and destroyed the attacking enemy.

Captain Rose immediately opened radio contact back to central control advising details of the unprovoked attack.

"NASA Ground Control. NASA Ground Control. This is *Liberty*. We have been located by the space platform *Vostok*. I confirm some sort of short-range missile has been fired at us from the space platform. In retaliation I took immediate evasive action and engaged *Liberty*'s laser gun defences. I report all enemy missiles have been destroyed. I request permission to engage a counter-attack and require central control's clearance to fire at a specific authorised target."

For a moment there was total silence. It seemed as if the shock of the unprovoked attack had stunned everyone.

"NASA Ground Control to *Liberty*. NASA Ground Control to *Liberty*. We hereby confirm under the authority of your classified orders. Please proceed and direct your fire at the enemy in self-defence."

Captain Rose steadied the *Liberty* in order to set all the instruments of the shuttle to manual control and target co-ordination. As soon as this was achieved he reset the space shuttle's laser firepower to be programmed. He directed it to lock on to the specified target set out in *Liberty*'s confidential classified battle mission instructions. The Captain rechecked and verified his target as being the lower section of operations at the base of the space platform *Vostok*.

Suddenly, another bright flash lit up the darkness as a second barrage of rockets was fired from *Vostok*. Again the space shuttle's automatic defence and laser counter-attack system protected *Liberty* against the angry wrath of the cosmic giant.

The force of the explosion shook Captain Rose. The spacecraft buffeted and rocked as the shockwaves vibrated past the *Liberty*. Once again Captain Rose rechecked all his target readings. He then made contact with NASA Ground Control.

"NASA Ground Control, this is Liberty. Do you read me?"

"We read you loud and clear, Captain. Please go ahead."

Captain Rose gave his report. "The *Liberty* has just sustained another hostile attack from *Vostok,* and reports no damage. I confirm all is prepared and set for the space shuttle to fire its main laser gun to action a counter-attack. Countdown is starting now!"

On board the *Vostok*, Major Chitov still had no idea as to what or who the alien UFO was. He was concerned as to the ease with which it had destroyed two dozen of the space platform's heat-seeking defence missiles.

"Operation control, prepare to transmit a message back to Earth to Moscow and to the submarine *Gorbachev*."

At that moment there was a blinding flash. Instantly, many instrument panels, conduits of electric cables, transformers, large computing and transmission consoles all exploded, disintegrating in a cascade of white-hot embers. Satellite chambers each containing a number of operational cells, all having been built and attached to the space platform's main housing frame under the high-tech expansion scheme and of which housed highly skilled teams of transmission operators, were gone. Within a split second the majority of these cells decompressed resulting in bodies being sucked out and being jet propelled into space like unexploded shells due to the sudden loss of pressure.

Automatically, at the time of impact from the *Liberty's* counter-attack, the airlock docking doors on board the space platform tightly closed. All internal airtight door systems slammed shut and sealed themselves. If ever these doors were to be opened again they were only operable by manual release and were controlled by individual code numbers.

The force of the blast knocked Major Chitov on to the floor of the main flight deck. It also put out of action all the internal links to the main operations control room. The room was centred above the outside satellite cell position from where all the newest transmitting equipment had recently been built and installed. The main frame superstructure was now a mass of burning entangled metal.

At the time of impact from the counter-attack the whole of the space platform was plunged into darkness. Major Chitov and other senior officers that were on the floor of the space platform all now slowly got to their feet.

Still very dazed, the Major struggled over to where an emergency panel of interlinked unit switches were housed. As he began to throw some of the switches, these re-engaged many of the emergency backup services, and auxiliary power units. In the murky dimness around him, he could gradually see certain areas of the space platform's electrical power system were again restored.

As Major Chitov began to look around him he felt a slight air of relief. On glancing over his shoulder he could see that one of the large viewing screens had come back to life. In order to try and ascertain what damage could be seen of the space platform, the Major began to operate the visual display unit [VDU] that co-ordinated the picture viewed by an external security camera. As he slowly turned the camera projection vertically the picture began to veer off out into space due to one of the dislodged tracking rods being forced out of line by the explosion. The picture instantly picked up a movement and locked on to something which gradually began to disappear as it moved away from the space platform.

To the Major's horror it showed the diminishing shape of the US space shuttle. His faced grimaced. "Oh my God! Why on earth didn't Moscow warn us that the Americans had put a space shuttle up into orbit?"

"Pardon me, Comrade Major. What was it you said?" one of the platform operators remarked who had begun handling another of the external vision cameras for further expansion of the screen tracking system.

"It was nothing, Comrade. I'm just shocked that we are still here and alive to tell the tale."

"What was it that hit us, Comrade Major?"

"At the moment, Comrade I'm not exactly sure. Whatever it was it could only have been something that was done in retaliation to the *Vostok* automatically firing two salvos of missiles at it. Or, by some strange quirk of fate, it could have been an undetected rogue meteor. How bad is the damage? How many men have we lost?"

As the control operator was trying to obtain readout from the computer another senior officer came into the flight deck in a very great hurry. "Comrade Major! Comrade Major!"

"Yes, what is it?" Major Chitov responded calmly.

"Sir! We have completely lost our aerials, antennae and transmission discs for sending to Earth the radio beams controlling Operation Invisible."

Major Chitov's face looked grimly back at his officer. "Have we no communication at all back to Earth? Nothing at all back to Kapustin Yar or Moscow?"

"No, Comrade Major, not for at least three or four hours. By then an emergency rescue repair team should be able to go and establish a full report of the outside damage. Certainly enough information by that time will allow us to effect immediately any emergency repair work to be undertaken."

Major Chitov hesitated for a moment then replied, "I see. Then we shall just have to hope that somebody down there on that little blue and golden ball wishes to speak with us before they realise the true aspects of our predicament."

Only Major Chitov really knew of what the implications could be. He was very aware of what the position on Earth was if the radio beam was down and not working for any long period of time. *God*, he thought, *surely the Gorbachev would become totally exposed now the screen was down. Every radar screen within one hundred nautical miles of its position would soon pick it up and be in radar range. Heaven knows what might happen next.*

Having just received the first details of the space platform's damage and its list of casualties, Major Chitov read that six men were dead and thirty-nine were missing. The main damage was confined to most of the outer platform that had contained the communication transmitting centre.

Major Chitov felt empty and alone. He was the most senior officer of a force of seventy-five men all of whom were now completely cut off and marooned in space.

"We... I'm sorry," Major Chitov said trying to regain his self-composure. "We had better start programming a service maintenance schedule and a roster of small teams of men to action any rescue. Those not involved with internal damage control will be expected to venture outside for a spacewalk to survey and inspect the damage to the space platform. After this we shall have to see what work can be done to repair the damage immediately or what can be improvised so that we can communicate with Earth. We must try and increase the level of our operational power output in order to bring it back to full strength. First things first. I would suggest two maintenance repair teams begin tackling the local damaged areas around us. We can then re-establish power back to the circuits. Thereafter, you will all work at full pace to bring the power supply back to full strength and, if successful, hopefully it will be sufficient to allow re-commencement of the space platform's transmission programme."

"Very good, Comrade Major. I confirm this will be started right away," advised one of the senior repair technicians.

Major Chitov stood in silence as he listened to the proposals of rescue and repair planning. However, his eyes were trained in looking far away past everybody standing about him. He was looking way out into space watching for sight of the American space shuttle reappearing as it gradually came into view approaching on a new orbit.

"This is NASA Ground Control calling to *Liberty*. How do you read us? Over."

"Loud and very clear," Captain Rose responded. "We are proceeding on our first orbit since completing our strike at the target. We advise we can no longer see any trace of a fluorescent spiralling beam of light that previously had been emanating from the *Vostok*.

"NASA, I believe we can happily say, well at least for the moment, the file regarding Operation Ghostbusters should be considered closed."

Captain Rose, through his headphones, could hear the sounds of jubilation.

"This is NASA Ground Control. Thank you, *Liberty* for that confirmation. Nice goin', Captain. By the way, are you still fully intact and free of any damage?"

Captain Rose turned and looked back at his crew. All shook their heads in agreement. "NASA, I confirm we are all looking good and have a clean bill of health."

"Good for you, *Liberty*. Please proceed and prepare all systems in readiness for a homeward routing. We estimate your journey back and re-entry is looking good. The weather at the landing strip is clear. Set your timing forward to read — FOUR HOURS AND FIFTY-TWO MINUTES — to touch down.

On hearing the announcement there was immense cheering from the staff of NASA Ground Control and Tracking.

"Thank you very much for that news, NASA," Captain Rose replied sporting a very big smile. He turned to the crew and gave them the thumbs up sign.

At that moment NASA Ground Control responded, "You're very welcome, Captain. We hope you have a nice flight back. Over and out."

NASA Ground Control and Tracking, Cape Canaveral
US Military and Naval Intelligence Department
General Kemp together with Captain Logan had received from NASA Ground Control and Tracking the completed recordings of the attack made by the Russian space platform on the *Liberty*. Additionally, the data

contained a full record of the space shuttle's defence. It also showed the skilful counter-attack which resulted in inflicting serious damage to the communications centre on board the *Vostok*.

The General looked at his watch. The time was just after 03.15 hours. A new day was dawning. His gold Rolex watch, now nearly ten years old, had served him well since receiving it from his wife on his forty-fifth birthday.

"Well, Smartie, we have finally got the information we have waited a very long time for regarding the space demons."

Captain Logan had been hard at work for nearly fifteen hours. With little time for a break he had persevered at his task. Now, finally having the chance to stop, he said, "Hell, sir, I'm totally bushed. How about another cup of coffee?"

"That'll be fine, Captain," the General remarked. "But don't you go and relax just yet. We still have to programme the exact position in relation to the last point of entry given on Earth regarding those goddamned spirallin' lights. Smartie, how long do you reckon it will take *G.O.D.* to do all that?"

Logan wasn't too clear as to what Kemp had said. "Just a moment, General. Did you just say you wanted the computer to give out the exact geographical map reference?"

"Yep! That was what I asked for, and I want it as soon as possible. Okay?" The General yawned. He was also feeling the pace of the night's work.

Captain Logan briefly stepped back into the computer room. He called back to the General. "One moment please, sir." Seconds later he walked back into the General's office. "Here you are, sir. I am sure this should hold your operations together for a while." Logan passed to the General one of the steaming hot mugs of coffee he was holding.

"Sir, you can now transmit to all concerned the logged position as follows 10.5 N 30.7 W. General, this was the last entry made by NASA Ground Control and Tracking at 02.36 hours. The *Liberty* received it at 02.41 hours. I have rechecked this data with *G.O.D.* I have estimated this should pinpoint the place of entry. It's approximately thirty-five to forty miles south-west of an island called Sto Antao. Sir, that is the most westerly island of a group called the Cape Verde Islands."

"Are you absolutely sure, Captain?" the General responded with an air of excitement.

"You bet I am, sir. *G.O.D.* has just confirmed it!"

Kemp knew by Logan's remark that there was no way he could doubt such information.

"Okay, Captain, I'll go along with that."

"Are you sure, sir?" Logan asked.

"Right, lad. Now I'll tell you why that reading had better be correct."

"Okay. Fire away, sir. I'm ready."

"The *Liberty* has just busted a great big hole into the underside of the *Vostok*. In doing so, Logan, it has completely wiped out all of its communications."

"Crikey, General, surely that must be going a bit too far?"

General Kemp didn't bat an eyelid. "I have just heard that Captain Rose had a darned good reason for kicking the shit out of that space platform."

Logan stopped pacing about and looked at the General. He was slightly stunned by his angry tone of voice.

"And another thing you didn't know you bloody smartarse is that those damned Russkies only went and fired twelve heat-seeking missiles at the *Liberty*. This was before Captain Rose stood to lose the shuttle's total firepower. I'm pleased to state not one of them got anywhere near its target. Well, Smartie Logan, it seems that the *Liberty* scored a bullseye!"

Logan felt relief come over him. "That must have been some deal, General," Logan said, smiling.

By now Kemp was exhausted. "Okay, Smartie, now you can at least do somethin' useful. Tidy up a bit in here, and in the meantime I'll send all the coded messages away to the *Intrepid*. I'll copy the same to the British Navy's HQ at Northwood. When we have finished all that then I think we can get off home."

Logan looked absolutely shattered. The General said, "Say, Smartie, if you happen to be ready within the next ten minutes I can offer you a lift. Is that okay?"

"Sure thing, sir. I will be clear and ready by then."

"By the way, Logan," the General said, "not a word about this operation to anyone outside this office. I trust you read me well, Smartie?"

"No word will pass my lips about any of it, sir. Of that you can be sure."

At Sea

At 06.45 hours, Lieutenant Bergman wakened Commodore Brianston-Green. "Good morning, sir."

"Good morning, Number One. What is it that is so important that you decided you can rob me of another hour's sleep?"

Bergman's voice was full of excitement. "Commodore, our operations room have just reported a very large unidentified underwater object has suddenly appeared on our radar screen."

"Good Lord, Bergman, I wonder. Could we just possibly have hit the jackpot?"

"Could be, sir. Mind you, the course you set has resulted in our position ending up on the blind side of the Yank sub and decoy. May I offer my congratulations, sir. It certainly looks like we might have scored one."

Brianston-Green respected the Lieutenant's judgement and the implied caution veiled in his remark. "Why thank you, Bergman. By the way, do you think it might have been due to the teeniest stroke of luck? Or, did it happen to be a complete coincidence? Maybe there's something else we don't as yet know. Something else might well have happened to cause the exposure of the UUO."

Bergman didn't mind either way.

"Maybe you're right, sir. I just can't get over how exciting the situation all seems to be getting."

"Calm down! This could be just what we have been waiting for, Lieutenant. Let us therefore not lose the chance of such a great opportunity. Okay, Bergman?"

"Right you are, sir."

Brianston-Green was pleased. In the past he knew Bergman had been quite capable of exceeding all expectations by engaging operations well before considering what the outcome might be. Luckily, he seemed to recall. it was always when a practice run was in progress. However, Bergman had never missed his target yet. The Commodore trusted that if ever the chance came again his Lieutenant would not let him down.

"Good, Number One. Now then, where at this moment is the decoy, and what is the position of the *Intrepid?*"

"Sir, the decoy *SS Globe Kobe* is forty-five miles directly north of us. The *Intrepid* is seventy miles north-west of our position. Also it is still north of the island of Mindelo."

"Right, Bergman. What is the reading of the unidentified underwater object?"

"Sir, the UUO is about ten miles south-west of the island of Sto Antao, heading northwards."

"Mmmmmmm! That's most interesting," the Commodore advised quickly comparing the status of where everyone appeared to be situated.

"This then means our position puts us, at a guess, currently at about 28.5 W and 6.00 N."

"Not very far off the mark, sir," Bergman remarked. "I would say we are less than twenty-five miles west-north-west of whatever that UUO is."

Brianston-Green paused to recheck a small chart he had left on his cabin table. "Bergman, has there been any message come in from RN HQ this morning?"

"Not that I know of, Commodore. I'll have to go and check, sir."

"Right you are, Number One. Please report back to me immediately something comes through. I'll quickly get dressed and come and join you on the bridge shortly."

"Very well, sir. Any cable that may have been received, I'll ensure it will be awaiting your attention."

It was not long before Brianston-Green appeared on the bridge. As he stepped in Lt. Bergman handed him the message which had come through moments before. It read:

FROM: RN HQ NORTHWOOD

TO: HMS EXCALIBUR

ATTN: CMDORE C BRIANSTON-GREEN CY MSSGE RCVD FROM US MILITARY DEPT NASA – STOP – REF GEN J B KEMP NAVAL/MILITARY INTELLIGENCE – STOP – ATTN: SSBN INTREPID – ADMIRAL ALAN J. T. ADAMS III – COPY – SSBN HMS EXCALIBUR ATTN: CMDORE C BRIANSTON-GREEN – STOP – GENTLEMEN AT 02.45 HOURS EST – STOP – US SPACE SHUTTLE LIBERTY IN ITS DEFENCE COUNTER-ATTACKED AN UNPROVOKED ATTACK MADE BY RUSSIAN SPACE PLATFORM VOSTOK – STOP – IT IS BELIEVED THE LIBERTY'S COUNTER-ATTACK MAY WELL HAVE TERMINATED ALL COMMUNICATION SYSTEMS OF VOSTOK REFERENCE OUR KNOWLEDGE OF THE OPERATION REFERRED TO AS OPERATION GHOSTBUSTERS – STOP – NASA GROUND CONTROL AND TRACKING CONFIRM SPACE DEMONS ARE CURRENTLY NO LONGER TRACEABLE – STOP – LAST UUO ORDINANCE READING AT 02.36 HRS EST READ 25.8 W – 07.8 N – STOP – PROCEED TO LOCATE UUO – STOP –VERIFY THEN ENGAGE – STOP – END MESSAGE -ORDER DISPATCHED UNDER THE FULL AUTHORITY OF THE PRESIDENT OF THE UNITED STATES OF AMERICA – STOP NO REPLY NEEDED SIGNED: LT HENDERSON – OFFICER OF 'C' WATCH PP CMDR D THOMPSON – STOP – CC: ADMIRAL MARCHANT – ADMIRALTY OFFICE – WHITEHALL

Commodore Brianston-Green read the message very carefully. "Damned that for a bunch of rotten garlic and onions!"

"Why is that, sir?" Bergman asked.

"Well, for a start, Lieutenant, I think we are being asked by the Yanks to consider performing the slightly eccentric deed of the impossible."

"And what would that be, sir?" Bergman asked.

"Well, let me put it to you this way. If the Americans seriously believe that we, or for that matter Admiral Adams of the *Intrepid,* are simply going to hang around and wait for them to verify and authorise all manner of things before our submarine engages then they must have gone and lost their marbles!"

The Commodore's temper began to rear itself on one of its rare occasions. Certainly he wasn't going to just hang about like some sitting duck.

"Bergman, send a message back to RN HQ Northwood immediately. Mark it for the urgent attention of Admiral Marchant and Commander Derek Thompson. Please put in the message an acknowledgement that reads the following: 'FROM WHAT WE HAVE JUST RECEIVED – STOP – WE ARE TRULY THANKFUL IN RESPECT OF SUCH INFORMATION – STOP – HMS EXCALIBUR HEREBY CONFIRMS WE HAVE LOCATED AND HAVE DIRECT RADAR COMMUNICATION REGARDING THE MISSING UUO – STOP – ITS POSITION READS 25.8 W – 07.1 N – STOP – WE WILL NOT WAIT IN ORDER TO ACHIEVE ANY VERIFICATION FROM THE AMERICANS – STOP – OTHERWISE WE MAY NOT BE AROUND IN ORDER TO TELL THE TALE OR RETALIATE – STOP – I WISH AT ALL TIMES TO MAINTAIN THE TOTAL SAFETY OF BOTH MY SUBMARINE AND CREW – STOP – HMS EXCALIBUR REQUESTS PERMISSION TO ENGAGE ITS COMBAT OPERATIONS AT A RANGE OF SIXTEEN NAUTICAL MILES – STOP – WE CONFIRM WE STAND READY AND REQUIRE YOUR RESPONSES BY URGENT RETURN DURING THE NEXT HOUR – END MESSAGE'."

"Yes, Bergman, that sounds like it should do the job intended. I just trust that Admiral Marchant is on good form this morning."

"Right you are, Commodore. I'll see that it goes off right away. Mind you, sir, if someone has already upset the old boy this morning then I think we should stand a jolly good chance in getting a response."

They both laughed.

"Thank you for that, Lieutenant. I duly trust you will not in any way disclose any of this conversation to any other members of the crew."

"Certainly not, sir. Absolutely, not at all!"

"Fine. Please process that message immediately and have it forwarded under HMS Excalibur's urgent coding call reference. Mark it with the following footnote: 'FOR YOUR EYES ONLY – STOP – WE AWAIT YOUR VERY PROMPT REPLY SOONEST – STOP'."

Not more than fifteen minutes had past when Bergman called from the submarine's operations room asking for Commodore Brianston-Green to come down to sign off an urgent response coming through in reply to the last message transmitted.

"What the devil is it, ops?" Commodore Brianston-Green said, as he paused at the door. He saw his Lieutenant standing holding a piece of paper.

"Oh! I'm sorry, Bergman." Brianston-Green took the message off him. It read:

REF YOUR MESSAGE TIMED 07.42 HOURS – STOP – RECEIVED AND UNDERSTOOD – STOP – TWO FSB OFFICERS INTERCEPTED AND FINISHED OVERNIGHT – STOP – IN SAME ACTION UNFORTUNATELY DEFECTOR DISPOSED OF – STOP – BELIEVE ALL VERY GENUINE RE: UUO – STOP – SUBJECT IS DEFINITELY NOW BELIEVED TO BE THE GORBACHEV – STOP – DO NOT WAIT TO VERIFY – STOP – AS SOON AS BATTLE RANGE REACHED – STOP – CONTACT FOR ENGAGEMENT – STOP – PLEASE PROCEED AND GOOD LUCK – STOP – KINDLY ACKNOWLEDGE TO INTREPID DETAILS OF YOUR ACTIONS WHEN CARRIED OUT – STOP – END MESSAGE
SIGNED: ADMIRAL MARCHANT RN ADMIRALTY

"Thank you very much for that, Lieutenant. Immediately sound the crew to battle stations. What range do we have on the target now?"

"Twenty-one miles, sir."

"Fine. We should be at sixteen miles by about 08.15 hours."

Soon the sound of a deafening klaxon alerted everyone from a quiet breakfast into a state of instant nervous excitement."

Quickly, the crew hastened to don their special clothing; each and every one of them now stood ready for action.

On board the *Gorbachev*, Captain Narodny had been studying the overnight position of the VLCC *SS Globe Kobe*. He had taken some considerable time and thought, finally, that the prize was well worth having. He didn't really wish to sink the huge tanker. He was trying to work out how the crew of the *Gorbachev* might be able to try and seize it.

He felt there must be a plan that could be conceived which might threaten the tanker's crew to abandon ship.

It was to be a very delicate and cautious operation.

He also wished it to succeed without causing any bloodshed or damage to the huge tanker. Everything had to be carefully planned down to the very last detail. *After all*, thought Captain Narodny, *time is not of the essence.* It appeared to him that there was no real threat from either the American or British submarines.

Captain Narodny checked again and found both were still well over twenty-five miles away and without any knowledge of the *Gorbachev's* presence.

"Yes, Number One, we will try and steal this one right from under the noses of the British and American capitalists."

"That would certainly be quite an achievement, Comrade Captain. Do you as yet have a plan of how we are going to achieve this?"

Captain Narodny spoke softly. "No, not as yet, but certainly I think I'll have a plan hashed in about an hour or so. Firstly, I'll put such a plan to Moscow so they can clear up any matters of the current position concerning the *Vostok*. Secondly, I'll be in my quarters if you should need me for anything."

Captain Narodny's first officer knew by the Captain's arrogance he was very near to completing his plans. "Thank you, Comrade Captain. If anything should alter, I will contact you immediately."

On board the *Intrepid*, Admiral Adams had seen the dramatic change of circumstance.

It was just before 03.30 hours when he received the first notice of his instructions regarding events concerning the space shuttle *Liberty*.

Unlike Commodore Brianston-Green on board *HMS Excalibur*, the Admiral had been notified regarding the message from NASA Military and Naval Intelligence through US Naval HQ at Charleston. The Admiral had also sent confirmation of *Intrepid's* radar sightings of the unidentified underwater object in order to clear notification of the same.

"Do yer know, Lieutenant Odbie, we shall have to get our skates on if we are goin' to get a fair crack at this UUO before the British. Instruct an immediate course change. We'll run our submarine through that passage between them there islands of Sto Antao and Mindelo. That should just about bring us out at a range of ten to twelve miles directly due east of that darned underwater object."

"But, sir!" Odbie exclaimed.

"Yes, Lieutenant, what the devil is it?"

"Sir, it's the depth of water in the channel between the islands."

"Why, what about it, Odbie?"

"Admiral, the chart only shows a mean depth of two hundred feet."

"Don't worry about it, young man. I am quite confident we shall have ample free water to get this sub through that gap. Now then, go forth and have our speed increased to thirty knots.

"Get a move on, Lieutenant. As I have already said, I don't want us to miss out on any of this action. Okay?"

"Okay, sir, but…"

The roar of the Admiral shouting his name drowned the Lieutenant's voice. "ODBIE! Don't argue with me, man. Just go and get the job done."

Lt. Odbie knew he couldn't disobey the Admiral's orders. However, he knew deep down something felt dreadfully wrong. As he delegated Admiral Adams' orders to the engine room, Odbie could feel his stomach begin to take a turn for the worse. He very carefully advised all of the course changes and speed directives. "That's right, engine room. Increase our speed to thirty knots. Please ensure you ratify that both speed and course changes are entered and logged as and when completed."

"Aye, aye, Lieutenant, sir."

In the meantime, at a depth of one hundred and thirty feet, *HMS Excalibur* forced a massive bulge and huge headwave of water as the submarine surged its way forward at a speed in excess of thirty knots. By now, Commander Brianston-Green had begun to consult the submarine's computer memory bank searching for any updated information and detail regarding a Russian Type Borei Buluva class VI nuclear ballistic submarine. He requested for the availability of any special classified record or details in regard to the *Gorbachev*. The Commodore wished to try and ascertain where and how *HMS Excalibur* should proceed in carrying out its attack on the Russian submarine.

"That's it, Bergman! At least by doing that we might possibly achieve taking on board a few survivors."

"By doing what, sir? Bergman replied. "I'm sorry, Commodore. I don't quite follow."

"Maiming the damned unidentified underwater object, that's what! Then, if we are lucky, we might get the darned thing to come to the surface."

For a moment the Commodore paused to think a little more on what he had said.

"Yes, that's when we shall try and take survivors on board, Bergman. After that we will bloody well sink it, or kill it. Whatever the flaming thing is."

Lieutenant Bergman was somewhat alarmed by what he had heard Commodore Brianston-Green say. "Surely not, sir. Whatever it is? If it still remains firmly afloat hadn't we better think of capturing it, Commodore?"

Having pondered on the matter long enough Brianston-Green replied, "Bergman, I really don't think there is anything else further to say on the subject, do you? By the way, what in the devil's name is the time?"

"It's 07.50 hours, sir."

"Thank you. Right! I want you to go and send a message off to RN HQ Northwood. Ensure a copy is advised to the Admiralty.

"Now then please make note as follows: 'FROM: BRIANSTON-GREEN COMMODORE HMS EXCALIBUR. FOR YOUR EYES ONLY – STOP – TOP SECRET – STOP – ATTN: FIRST SEA LORD – ADMIRALTY – STOP – REQUEST PERMISSION TO LAUNCH ATTACK ON UUO – STOP – METHOD OF ENGAGEMENT IS TORPEDO ATTACK – STOP – STATUS NON-NUCLEAR WARHEAD – STOP -CONVENTIONAL WEAPON ONE TIGERFISH MARK MU92WIRE/GUIDED/ ACOUSTIC HOMING TORPEDO – STOP – INTEND TO COMMENCE ATTACK AT 08.45 HOURS – STOP – REPLY REQUESTED SENT BY RETURN – STOP – PRESENT POSITION SEVENTEEN POINT FIVE DEGREES DUE WEST OF TARGET – STOP – END MESSAGE. SIGNED: COMMANDER OF SEA OPERATIONS OPERATION BLINDFOLD'."

Lieutenant Bergman quickly read the message back to the Commodore.

"Right, that will do nicely. Thank you, Bergman. Please have it sent off immediately."

"Yes, sir."

As the news leaked from the operations room it was passed around the submarine's crew. There was now an air of excitement as the tension buzzed throughout the *Excalibur*. Everyone now had some idea that an attack was pending. Everyone waited excitedly for a reply to come back from the Admiralty or the Royal Naval Headquarters at Northwood.

"This waiting can certainly get to you, Bergman," the Commodore said while looking at his watch.

"How long does it normally take to come through, Commodore?" Bergman enquired.

"We shall have to see, Lieutenant. We shall just have to wait and see."

It was at 08.10 hours BST when Lt. Henderson forwarded the message received from *HMS Excalibur* through to the Admiralty marked for the attention of Admiral Marchant.

In Whitehall, when Marchant finally received and read the message, he allowed Commander Thompson to briefly see it.

Thompson smiled at the Admiral as he entered the Admiral's quarters.

Only minutes before, Miss Penny Hardcourt had woken him from his forced sleep having heard that Admiral Marchant was beginning to rant and rave about the Commander's absence.

"Derek, please excuse me. I must get the Commander-in-Chief, the Minister of Defence and the Prime Minister on the hotline for a conference call. You will have to sit and wait for a bit."

Commander Thompson nodded then sat in silence. As the time passed he began to remember when it was that those Finnish intelligence agents had informed the operation's office at Northwood. It seemed a long time had past since the Russian submarine had sailed from the Russian naval base in Severomorsk. As his mind continued to reflect, his thoughts drifted through some of those first days of the operation. All now seemed so far away from what was currently happening. As his mind continued to interpret, Thompson could hear the Admiral talking in his private office.

"Yes, Prime Minister. We are absolutely sure beyond all doubt that this unidentified underwater object is definitely the Russian submarine *Gorbachev*."

"I see, Admiral," the Prime Minister replied.

"But wasn't this submarine reported by Russia to have sunk on its maiden voyage?"

"Quite so, Prime Minister. We believe that may well have been a cover-up and the reason as to why Russia chose not to disclose full details of the real position. We further believe such a cover-up was put into action by their naval department and possibly the FSB. We understand this supposed plot became reality under a certain strategic classified reference known as Operation Invisible, or Blindfold. We have deemed to give it the title of an unidentified underwater object. This UUO is, in fact, the Russian submarine. Most certainly it was the source that caused the recent air disaster destroying one or more of the wide-bodied jets which crashed into the Atlantic Ocean."

The Prime Minister listened intently. In near disbelief he responded, "Admiral, I do sincerely hope that your advised brief is correct. I was led to understand all these losses were caused by terrorist bombings."

"Quite so, Prime Minister." Marchant paused for a moment then said, "At the time, diplomatically, it was thought at best to keep this very sensitive and delicate matter veiled under a 'D' notice, and as far away as possible from the popular press."

"I see," the Prime Minister said interrupting the Admiral. "So do you now actually have firm knowledge as to which aircraft the Russians supposedly shot down?"

"Yes, Prime Minister, we do." Admiral Marchant knew his neck was on the line. He felt he was slowly being edged out in walking a plank towards possible disaster.

For a moment both men paused.

The Prime Minister then spoke in a calm voice. "Which plane was it, Admiral? Come on, which plane was it that you and your department believe the Russians were supposed to have shot down?"

With a slight croak in his voice Marchant responded, "Unquestionably, Prime Minister, it was a Boeing 777-300ER, a British Airways plane, Flight BA182, which on that fatal day took off from New York bound for Manchester Ringway. There was also an Air India aircraft. The only information known at that time was that the planes were hit by something, or by some form of weaponry, which as yet has been totally unexplained. Certainly, it was hit by something so devastating that the aircraft was completely and utterly destroyed into millions of pieces. Exactly by what method of destruction this was achieved, Prime Minister, we still don't know."

The Commander-in-Chief and Minister of Defence who had listened in near astonishment at what Admiral Marchant had revealed stayed silent as the telephone call progressed on the open telephone hotline.

The Prime Minister continued to question various aspects of information that had been received. "Speaking about doing things, Admiral, how on earth did the Russians manage to conceal the whereabouts of their supposed lost submarine for so long?"

Marchant felt slightly relieved by this comment; it appeared the subject was now beginning to receive considerable attention.

Admiral Marchant spoke. "Prime Minister, apparently there was also some sort of involvement regarding a highly intensified radio beam. We are led to understand this beam was supposedly transmitted to Earth and was some sort of veil of transmission from the Russian space platform *Vostok*. It has been advised from very reliable sources that it was this veil, or beam, which somehow could have shielded the submarine from any form of radar detection."

All who had listened to the Admiral were still not convinced.

The Prime Minister interjected, "I see. So, Admiral, we are now being asked to accept something that really is still assumed to be undetected." The tone of the Premier's voice lowered. "Gentlemen, it would appear we are to assume we now have a ghost Russian submarine which appears to be running around the high seas acting as some sort of pirate. Come, come, Admiral Marchant. Surely you cannot seriously be asking all of us to give you our vote of credence for you to engage in your incredible venture. Also, your message appears to ask us to sanction this venture and engage ourselves in some sort of open warfare in order to rid the seas of this unidentified underwater object which you cannot as yet confirm you have been able to detect."

There were strong murmurs of disapproval which were now followed by jested laughter from others involved in the conference call.

Marchant began to feel the dampness of perspiration forming under his arms. Had he got it so terribly wrong? Was all that his department had been working on for so long finally going to be given the thumbs down? He also wondered if he was going to be made the laughing stock of the Admiralty. As he listened to the Premier's ridicule, he could hear a voice speaking somewhere in the background of the Prime Minister's voice.

"One moment please, Prime Minister."

It was one of the PM's private secretaries advising that the President of the United States of America was waiting to speak with him on another telephone line.

"Kindly excuse me for one moment please, gentlemen. Admiral Marchant, please hold for a while. I have to take this other telephone call. I won't keep you waiting for very long. Everyone, kindly hold matters for a moment."

Everyone acknowledged and remained silent trying to listen to what was being said.

"Really, Mr. President, and you say that the space shuttle *Liberty* was attacked without any warning or prior provocation to which it admirably defended itself. In the process you say it knocked out all the space platform's communication, which somehow has resulted in exposing the whereabouts of an unidentified underwater object your Navy happened to be shadowing. Just one moment please, Mr. President." The Prime Minister quickly changed telephone receivers. "Please excuse me, everyone. I'll not keep you waiting much longer."

Everyone acknowledged the Prime Minister's request and waited.

"What was that, Mr. President," the PM said in astonishment. "Your Military Chiefs of Staff have every reason to believe that the unidentified underwater object is none other than the Russian submarine *Gorbachev*."

The Prime Minister paused as the President advised the list of recorded losses attributed to the renegade actions of the cowardly pirate. "I see, Mr. President, so, you have your best and biggest submarine down in the area taking care of matters. I wonder can you possibly advise me as to what these matters might consist of?"

The President then elaborated on what plans had already been put into action to which the British Premier responded, "Oh, I see, you are going to blow the goddamned thing right out of the water. Well then, Mr. President, let me wish you good luck."

The American President interrupted the PM and said something that received an apt reply. "Yes, life does get more and more interesting every day, doesn't it? Thank you again, Mr. President, for calling."

The Prime Minister paused for a moment to think then slowly he replaced the receiver back on the hotline telephone. On lifting the other receiver, which was holding the conference call, the Premier said, "Gentlemen, I'm so sorry for that slight interruption."

"Not at all, Prime Minister."

Marchant had been quite taken aback by the previous negativeness. He was ready to argue any point that needed questioning, or was in need of strengthening of reason.

The Prime Minister spoke. "Well, Admiral Marchant, after my interrupted telephone call I now truly understand the meaning and extent of your department's request. Gentlemen," the Premier said with an air of positive defiance, "I hereby confirm I'll take full responsibility, Admiral, for any action caused by our boys. That is if, in what you have stated, it happens to be in any way erroneous. However, please try to ensure that we have a minimal loss of life. I am led to understand our allies in America are considering, as their President has just put it, TO BLOW the unidentified underwater object right out of the water."

There were many undertones, murmurs and guttural retorts in response to the Prime Minister's revelation. "Please, Admiral Marchant, send a reply back immediately to the Commander of *HMS Excalibur*. Instruct him to proceed under the orthodox rules of conduct and engagement which are those that might concern any act of provoked war in supporting our allies. I request the Commander is to ensure that any attack be conducted in the manner that for centuries has been the steadfast style of the Royal Navy.

Please confirm when the cable is ready. I'll acknowledge and endorse your instructions to the full. The Minister of Defence will also countersign this message as soon as we have finished this telephone call. That will be all, Admiral Marchant. Now then, everyone. Are there any questions?"

"No, Prime Minister," was the resounding response that came back.

"Thank you. I then consider this conference call at an end. Oh, one moment, please. Naturally, I would like in due course, Admiral, to receive a full account of any action. This is to be advised to me as soon as possible."

"Yes, Prime Minister," came a single answer.

"Gentlemen, I bid you all goodbye, and you, Admiral Marchant, may I offer you and your men the best of good luck."

As Marchant put down the telephone he checked the time on his desk clock. It was 08.35 hours.

Derek Thompson had nearly fallen asleep waiting for the Admiral to finish his call. When he heard the shouting he awoke with a start.

"Thompson! Thompson! Here! Come quickly! Come on, man, jump to it!"

Thompson sprang to his feet; he was ready to fight and defend anything. He rushed into the Admiral's office with his arms waving to strike out at the unknown assailant. To his surprise he confronted Raymond Marchant whose arm was outstretched waving a piece of paper. He instantly checked himself. "I'm so sorry, Admiral. I thought…"

For a split second, Marchant was somewhat surprised by such an unorthodox entrance. He could hardly control his smile. "Err, excuse me, Derek."

"Yes, sir."

"Please have this message coded immediately then send it off right away marked 'TOP PRIORITY, EXTREMELY URGENT'. Send it to the *Excalibur*."

The message read:

TIME: 08.40 HOURS 16 AUGUST 2017
FROM: ADMIRALTY RN HQ
TO: HMS EXCALIBUR
ATTN: SEA COMMANDER OF OPERATION BLINDFOLD.
REQUEST GRANTED – STOP – ATTACK AT YOUR LEISURE – STOP –
SAVE LIVES AT ALL COST – STOP – EVEN CAPTURE UUO IF ABLE –
STOP – GOD SPEED AND GOOD LUCK – STOP – PM C-IN-C MINISTER
OF DEFENCE AND GOVERNMENT STAND BY THIS ENGAGEMENT –
STOP – WATCH OUT FOR THE YANKS – STOP – END MESSAGE

SIGNED: ADMIRAL MARCHANT – BY ORDER OF THE PM AND
BRITISH GOVERNMENT

Derek Thompson knew in his heart that this message would be
the start of something big, and that it could foretell the outcome
of a possible Third World War. As he handed the message to the
coding cable operator, he gave him a very long thoughtful look.
He then took a deep breath and said, "I hope that one goes out
without any hiccups."

Chapter Twenty-Two

At Sea

Stealthily and almost silently, the *Gorbachev* moved through the depths of the southern Atlantic Ocean. Its titanium hull and liquid nuclear-cooled engines made it virtually undetectable.

By now Captain Narodny had nearly completed his plan for submission to Moscow. He had to put one or two finishing touches to it. Its acceptance, he hoped, would allow him to handle the capture of the massive oil tanker.

Shortly after 08.50 hours, the *Gorbachev*'s special operations room announced that *HMS Excalibur* was now only about fourteen miles away. It was confirmed the *Excalibur* was on a course due west of the Russian submarine's present position.

Unperturbed, Captain Narodny said, "That's quite all right, First Officer, we are still very well protected and cocooned. Mind you, if that British submarine is still around in one hour then I think we may well have to contend with the matter. We'll just have to wait and see what they are going to do next. Let us now concentrate on the big prize that awaits us thirty-five miles north of our present position."

"Right you are, Comrade Captain. Shall I, for the moment, hold back this morning's transmission to Moscow?"

"Yes, Number One. We'll transmit the message sometime around 10.00 hours. That will be all."

On board the American submarine, *Intrepid*, Admiral Adams observed that his submarine had just begun to enter the waterway channel between the two most westerly islands of Cape Verde. The wall of water that headed the huge submarine's thrust constantly reduced the submarine's depth between the surface and ocean bed.

The submarine's massive hull, travelling at near maximum speed, pushed a huge head of sea as it drove its way forward. Gradually the immense force of downward thrust drew the submarine perilously close to the seabed of sand and silt. Beneath the sand lay a bed of jagged granite rocks.

Soon, the *Intrepid* approached the midway point of the channel. Changing currents had formed a sand bar which ran ahead for nearly two miles. At first, a soft scraping was felt as the submarine's hull slipped headlong into the rising sand then, as *Intrepid*'s speed forced the submarine's bow deeper, a horrendous grinding noise was heard. It was just like the sound of metal being relentlessly stripped and cut. A noise of continuous jarring echoed the ocean depths. The scene could be visualised like when schools of bloodthirsty Mako sharks pounce and attack an injured whale. Razor-sharp tips of pointed granite rock severed and split open the hull. Like shark's teeth they cut long and deep into the nose and belly of the huge submarine's whale-shaped titanium steel hull.

About thirty-five miles due west of the American submarine, *HMS Excalibur* had received the awaited cable message from Admiral Marchant. It was immediately decoded and Commodore Brianston-Green read the text.

Upon finishing he looked up at Lieutenant Bergman. In a soft dulcet tone he calmly said, "Load the forward torpedo tubes with two Tigerfish Mark MU92 torpedoes. Prepare *Excalibur* for firing the forward tubes one and two. Our battle engagement plan should be recorded as being set to commence exactly on the dot of 09.00 hours."

"Aye, aye, sir!" came Bergman's sharp response.

Within seconds the instruction echoed through the British submarine. The sound of klaxon sirens wailed continually for two minutes then there was an eerie silence. In the forward torpedo room both armourers and able seamen went about their task. They began moving and then loading the deadly tin fish.

"Where are these two destined for, Bosun?" enquired one of the seamen.

"I'm not too sure, son, but there's one thing for certain I'm pleased about."

"What's that then?" came back the young seaman's reply.

"We're not the ones who are going to be on the receiving end of this lot, that's what, youngster!" the bosun remarked.

Again, the young man spoke. "Why is that?"

The bosun knew the lad was eager in his constant desire and quest to learn. He liked him for that.

"Well, young un', over past years the Tigerfish has acquired a brilliant record for being a highly effective weapon. It is deadly accurate in finding its target."

The rating listened, fascinated. However, the bosun realised he had little time to chat. "Now then, boys. Are we ready?"

"Aye, aye, Bosun."

"Thank you," the armourer replied.

The bosun then spoke to the officers on the bridge. "Torpedo room to bridge."

Lt. Bergman acknowledged the call and passed the telephone to the Commodore.

"Sir, torpedo tubes one and two are ready for firing," the bosun advised.

Brianston-Green responded," Thank you, Bosun." He then turned to the Lieutenant.

"What time is it, Bergman?"

"08.58 hours and thirty seconds, sir," came his reply.

"What's our present speed and course?" the Commodore rattled.

"Thirty-four knots. Course 0.28 degrees and thirty seconds, sir."

"Fine. We will fire the first torpedo at exactly 09.00 hours. Start counting at ten seconds, Lieutenant."

"Yes, sir."

The tension on board *HMS Excalibur* was electric. In the forward torpedo room all waited for the firing instruction. Everyone stood ready.

The bosun spoke. "Blimey, you could split the atmosphere with a carving knife down 'ere. I wonder how long it's gonna' be before they let fly of this lot?"

Up on the bridge, "Nine…Eight…Seven…Six…" Lt. Bergman counted the seconds through as they ticked away, "Five…Four…Three… Two…One," he then pushed the ignition button.

The sound of jettisoned and escaping air was heard. The force of pressure thrusted the Tigerfish torpedo out of the number one torpedo tube at great speed. Fifteen seconds had past. Commodore Brianston-Green then instructed for a second torpedo to be fired. With the same procedure completed, again there was an eerie silence.

"Torpedo running smooth, sir," the torpedo room operations officer advised the bridge.

"Thank you for that, operations."

Fourteen and a half miles was a long distance to cover. There would be a few agonising minutes before the crew of *HMS Excalibur* knew if their submarine had been lucky enough to affect a strike on the unidentified underwater object.

Everyone stood in silence listening for any distant sound of an explosion.

The voice of Lieutenant Bergman broke the peaceful atmosphere. "Four minutes and ten seconds."

Everyone then heard a soft muffled explosion. It was nothing like what was expected. Moments later there came another one.

"Congratulations, sir." the Lieutenant remarked. "I think we might have got it."

"We'll soon see, Bergman. We'll soon see," the Commodore advised.

Everything for the moment seemed to have gone very quiet and had fallen into a lull.

The whistle phone to the bridge broke the silence. "Operations room to bridge."

"Yes, ops, what is it?" the Commodore requested.

"Sir, We have just received a Mayday signal," came back the reply.

"Fine, operations. Please have it sent up right away," advised Brianston-Green. He then turned and spoke to the Lieutenant.

"Well, well. I must say, Bergman, their radio room was quick off the mark."

Only seconds had past when a seaman came clambering up the ladder to the bridge. He quickly passed the message to the Lieutenant who in turn handed it to the Commodore. He opened it and began to read:

MAYDAY! MAYDAY! TO ALL SHIPS IN VICINITY OF 23.0 W MINUS 10.0
N – STOP – THE SSBN INTREPID REQUIRES URGENT IMMEDIATE
ASSISTANCE – STOP – REPEAT URGENT IMMEDIATE ASSISTANCE IS
NEEDED – STOP – SEVERLY HOLED AND TAKING IN WATER FAST –
STOP – END MESSAGE

Commodore Brianston-Green yelled, "Good grief, we have gone and hit the American flagship!"

"Bloody Christ! Surely not, sir! How on earth could that have happened?" Lieutenant Bergman screamed.

For a moment a state of panic ensued. Again the operations room rang through to the bridge. "Sir! Sir! We have another Mayday message coming through."

The Commodore snapped back, "Thank you very much, operations. We have already received the news regarding the American submarine *Intrepid*. You had better bring it up anyway."

"Right you are, sir," Sparks replied.

As the rating ordered to deliver the message to the bridge received the signal, he briefly studied it.

He then looked blankly at the radio operator and said, "Blimey! You would have thought 'earing the news about the Yankee sub's Mayday was blummin' well enough. What the heck are they ruddy well doin' up there? It seems like they're shootin' at anything and everything in sight. Crikey! I just don't understand it, Sparks. First the *Intrepid* and now we've gone and bloody well hit a Russian submarine as well. I'm certain that the Admiral ain't going to like this next one, not one little bit."

Sparks had briefly listened to what the rating was saying. He interrupted him. "Wait a moment. Did you say a Russian sub?"

"Yep. That's wot it says down 'ere."

The radio operator snatched back the cable slip and read it. When he had finished reading he shouted out, "Good grief! We've gone and finally got the bastard! We've gone and hit the bloody *Gorbachev*!"

As the cable message was delivered to the bridge, news spread through the submarine like wildfire. Soon, cheers were heard coming from the crew's quarters, both fore and aft.

When Brianston-Green received the message. He opened it and began to read:

09.02 HOURS 16/08/2017 FROM: SSBN GORBACHEV ✶✶✶✶✶✶ U R G E N T ✶✶✶✶✶✶MAYDAY✶✶✶MAYDAY✶✶✶ – STOP – HAVE BEEN ATTACKED – STOP – HAVE LOST TOTAL STEERAGE – STOP – BOTH PORT AND STARBOARD PROPELLOR SHAFTS HAVE SEIZED – STOP – WE HAVE A FIRE IN THE MAIN REACTOR ROOM – WE ARE SLOWLY TAKING ON WATER AND SINKING – STOP – MAYDAY✶✶✶MAYDAY✶✶✶MAYDAY✶✶✶ – ANY SHIPS INVICINITY OF 24.5 W AND 09.06 N – STOP – PLEASE COME TO OUR ASSISTANCE – END MESSAGE

The Commodore spoke. "Well now, Lt. Bergman, it would appear we now no longer have an unidentified underwater object to worry about. Please convey full details in regard to the combat to RN Northwood HQ. Kindly request that a copy is sent through to a certain General John B. Kemp at NASA Military and Naval Department of Intelligence."

"Nice work, sir," the Lieutenant remarked.

Commodore Brianston-Green gave Bergman a smile. "Well, I think we can now break radio silence. Request the decoy to proceed as fast as possible in order to offer what help and assistance it can give to the *Intrepid*. Amazing! How on earth did Admiral Adams go and do that to his submarine?"

"At the moment, Commodore, I couldn't even hazard a guess," Lt. Bergman replied.

"I do think we should send a cable to Admiral Adams. Confirm to him all we are arranging. Ask him to advise to us a full report. Enquire as to whether he can hold on until the *SS Globe Kobe* arrives. We will follow up in order to assist his sub's unfortunate plight."

"Right you are, Commodore," Bergman responded. "By the way, sir, what is the *Excalibur* going to do now?" The Lieutenant was hoping that the Commodore was not going to just let the Russian sailors drown.

The expression on his commanding officer's face told him nothing.

"We'll wait for a little while. Possibly take our lead and instructions from RN HQ. Bergman, I'm quite sure the Admiralty will come up with some idea that will be satisfactory. In the meantime we shall go over and see what condition the Russian submarine is in. Then we shall see what can be done."

On board the *Gorbachev* a state of total shock had taken over. The harsh sounds of klaxon horn fire alarms rang. Both crew and sub-officers ran and scrambled about the submarine trying to control the sudden change of events.

A ripple of fear now ran through the spines of the whole ship's company. Fire, the most deadly enemy of any submariner, must not be allowed to gain control. In such confined quarters oxygen is very quickly depleted.

With the build up of smoke and toxic fumes, it was becoming difficult to breathe. Captain Narodny had never expected to receive any form of attack. He now had to make a decision that meant he would either have to scuttle his ship, which he knew could further endanger the world through possible leakage of radiation, or have the crew try to put out the fire and leave himself and them to the mercy of the unknown aggressor.

The Captain placed himself on the control deck of the submarine's special operations room. He was checking the instrument consoles and soon saw that the fire had spread. It had now broken out in compartments five and six. It was quickly reported back to him the fires were sparked off by a nuclear turbine seizure which had caused a major electrical short circuit. In horror he watched the instrument panel show the temperature gauge in compartment five soar way up past the danger mark of one hundred and sixty degrees centigrade.

At that moment Captain Narodny was alerted by one of his officers. "Comrade Captain! Comrade Captain! We must now turn on the LOK system," the officer shouted. "Otherwise, Comrade Captain, surely we will all perish!"

Captain Narodny hesitated to answer. He was well aware that LOK, a form of freon gas designed to smother any fire by depriving it of oxygen, could still save his sub. However, it could also endanger his entire crew. Certainly he knew if the young officer switched it on it should see matters hopefully improve. He thought carefully to himself. The timing of this had to be right.

"Well, Comrade Captain?" the young officer asked. "I do hope we don't experience anything in the way of cable or pipe fractures due to the build up of such immense heat. Nor, I hope, do any freak electrical fires break out like what happened on board the *Komsomoltes* way back in April 1989."

Captain Narodny's voice calmly spoke, "I think at present, First Officer, we are going to be all right. However, we must try to surface as soon as possible. This must be done to try to release the smoke."

"Comrade Captain, I believe most of the firefighting crew have donned their protection masks; these will have been connected to the submarine's compressed air supply."

"Well, First Officer, things will have to accelerate regarding extinguishing these fires. This must be done as soon as possible if we are to have any chance of survival."

HMS Excalibur acknowledged to the *Intrepid* that it had arranged for the supertanker *SS Globe Kobe* to steam southwards in order to assist a rescue attempt.

Nineteen seamen had died in the American submarine's forward torpedo compartments when it grounded. Only immediate evasive action and quick thinking by Lt. Odbie had secured any chance of saving the American submarine. Apparently, as soon as he realised what was happening, he instantly instructed the closure and locking of all watertight doors.

It was hoped that Admiral Adams would soon try to bring the damaged submarine to the surface.

On board *HMS Excalibur*, Commodore Brianston-Green had sent out a cable in response to the Russian submarine's Mayday message. It read:

TIME: 09.15 HOURS 16 AUGUST 2017

FROM: HMS EXCALIBUR

TO: SSBN GORBACHEV

WE HAVE RECEIVED YOUR MESSAGE – STOP – WILL ASSIST RESCUE
EARLIEST BY 10.00 HOURS – STOP – EXPECT TO BE DETAINED AND
ARRESTED FOR CRIMES OF INTERNATIONAL PIRACY AND WILFUL
DESTRUCTION OF HUMAN LIFE – STOP – SURFACE IMMEDIATELY
AND WITH DIGNITY ACCEPT TO OFFER A TOTAL UNCONDITIONAL
SURRENDER – STOP – OR WE SHALL BE FORCED TO TAKE ACTION
ACCORDINGLY IN OUR DEFENCE – STOP – END MESSAGE

SIGNED: COMMODORE BRIANSTON-GREEN C-IN-C OPERATION
BLINDFOLD

Captain Narodny read the message in total disbelief. He knew in his heart
that he would never surrender his beautiful submarine.

"The gall of this impudent British commander," Captain Narodny
said. "In fact, First Officer, let me tell you that I will make the decision
to destroy him and the British sub. Our submarine will never surrender.
We have the biggest and best sub of its kind in the world. We shall not
simply beg, nor shall I give it to them as they have suggested. We'll fight
to the last!"

Captain Narodny's first officer listened in total amazement. Shocked
by what his commander had said he replied, "But, Comrade Captain, we
are not in any fit state to launch a counter-attack."

Captain Narodny swung round on his heels and retorted, "Whaaat!
Are you saying, Number One, you do not wish to fight? I suppose you are
wishing everyone to be branded a coward!"

The first officer stood his ground. "Captain, I merely wish you to
recognise the state we are in. It should not be necessary to throw away the
lives of our gallant crew when our submarine is no longer fully operational
to defend itself. I do think you should at least give our crew a chance."

Captain Narodny wasn't sure what his officer was implying. Was he
experiencing a mutiny, or had his first officer taken leave of his senses?

"Are you in effect deeming to take charge, First Officer? Or, do I take
it you mean that our men should now abandon their ship?"

Captain Narodny didn't allow the young officer from the Crimea to
respond. "You swarthy young pup, Number One! Your insolence has been
tolerated long enough! For the moment I'll overlook it but, if you should
consider to stage something against my orders, I'll have you immediately

arrested and shot! I trust that I make myself clearly understood! Now, instruct the men to have the submarine surface at once. See to it that the *Gorbachev* is prepared in readiness for a counter-attack."

The first officer, with a sullen expression, looked straight at Captain Narodny. His face showed an inner fear of horror and total disbelief.

Captain Narodny saw there was no sign of any movement from his first officer in reaction to his order. "Don't just stand there! Do it, man! When I say do it, do it NOW!" Captain Narodny roared.

The young officer knew if he didn't obey the order Captain Narodny would pull out his revolver and shoot him. On fearing the worst he picked up the tannoy speaker and issued the Captain's orders. "Surface! Surface! All available crew not involved with firefighting are to go to battle stations immediately."

The general alert was then sounded.

Sluggishly, the *Gorbachev* began to surface.

On the bridge of the British submarine, Commodore Brianston-Green had been considering all matters of extreme caution when arriving at the spot where the torpedo explosions were recorded. He was in deep thought. *What if, when they arrived, there was only wreckage and very little possibility of finding any survivors? Yes,* he thought to himself, *The Excalibur will have to approach the area where it was believed the Gorbachev had stopped with great caution.* He pushed the communications button on the telephone. "Operations room, do you still have that large blip on the radar screen?"

A voice came back, "Yes, sir, we do. We advise its position hasn't changed, nor has it moved very far over the past twenty minutes."

"Thank you, ops. Please keep me informed if there is any change."

"Aye, aye, sir," came the reply.

The telephone line went dead.

Brianston-Green paced up and down by the bridge console. He looked over and said, "Well, Lieutenant Bergman, I do think we had better go and take a look up top for ourselves. Don't you agree?"

"As you wish, sir," Bergman responded. "I have already placed four lookouts up there to see what's about. As yet, they have sighted nothing in the way of any wreckage, Commodore."

"Thank you, Bergman. By the way, before coming up top to the flying bridge, could you please have the following message sent to RN HQ Northwood. I have written it to report *Excalibur*'s current status."

The Lieutenant viewed the text of the message. He knew the next hour or so was going to be a little circumspect with everyone still not knowing what condition the Russian submarine was in.

"Right you are, sir. I'll get this message sent," the Lieutenant said. The message read:

TIME: 08.45 HOURS 15 AUGUST 2017
FROM: HMS EXCALIBUR
TO: ROYAL NAVAL HQ NORTHWOOD
ATTN: ADMIRAL R. MARCHANT RN
BE ADVISED AT 09.00 HOURS HMS EXCALIBUR ENGAGED ATTACK – STOP – 09.10 HOURS RECEIVED STRONG ACOUSTIC RESPONSES CONFIRMING TWO TIN FISH MADE CONTACT – STOP – ENEMY STILL POINTED ON RADAR – STOP – HAVE NOW MADE DEFINITE SONAR CONTACT – STOP – AS YET NO SIGN OF WRECKAGE ON SURFACE – STOP – PROCEEDING SLOW AHEAD WITH CAUTION – STOP – END MESSAGE
SIGNED: COMMODORE BRIANSTON-GREEN C-IN-C OPERATION BLINDFOLD

Slowly the bow of the Russian submarine gradually broke the ocean's surface. As soon as the conning tower had cleared the waterline, its huge black shape levelled out. Immediately, the deck hatches were thrown open. A dense cloud of acrid black smoke poured out from each hatch. The smoke from the extinguishing fires soon began to mingle with the lifting banks of fog and dissipating mist. The submarine's internal auxiliary motor units continued to turn in supplying compressed air to the firefighting crews.

In very foggy conditions, and at a distance of about six miles, *HMS Excalibur* continued to make slow headway. The lookouts up top were totally oblivious of the awesome sight ahead; the huge Russian submarine having emerged from the ocean's depth now began to settle motionless on the surface of the sea.

On board the *Gorbachev*, Captain Narodny, in studying the circumstances of what had happened over the past hour, as yet had not broken radio silence with Moscow. He thought to himself, *What on earth has gone wrong? Something else must have happened to enable this submarine's exposure to the world to have been so complete.* He decided it was now time for his sub to make contact with Moscow. From the bridge the Captain contacted the special operations room and requested them to try and start communicating.

Soon the radio operator was heard calling, "This is submarine *Gorbachev* calling Moscow. Lubyanka Control, come in please."

After ten minutes of trying there was still no response to the special operator's call. Only a constant sound of radio interference and continuous crackling was heard. The operator tried again to make contact. This time he retuned the radio frequency to try contacting the headquarters of the Russian Navy at the naval base in Severomorsk.

The room remained calm.

For a long time only an echoing sound like rushing wind was heard. As the minutes ticked by, tension mounted.

Suddenly, the radio receiver began to make a very faint sound.

The room's stillness was broken by what could faintly be heard to say: "We hear you, *Gorbachev*. Please clear your call sign for verification and identity."

Immediately, the operator called Captain Narodny to come from the bridge and make the response. Within seconds the Captain stepped into the special ops room. As he entered the radio operator handed him the microphone speaker. "This is Borei Buluva class V1 six slash zero one X calling," the Captain said as he released *Gorbachev*'s classified code call sign. "We appear to have lost all the shielding cover made by *Vostok* under Operation Invisible. Please advise why. Over."

"We now hear you loud and clear Borei Buluva class V1 six slash zero one X. We confirm *Vostok* ceased communication with ourselves, Moscow and Kapustin Yar at 02.46 hours. We have received no instructions for your file."

Captain Narodny's face showed little emotion to the advised remark. He merely kept on listening as the radio speaker repeated the same instruction. "Go deep. Go very deep. Go deep. Go very deep…"

Captain Narodny raised the microphone to his lips. "Thank you very much for that advice HQ. Unfortunately we cannot do this. We have been exposed for too long. We have sustained an attack by a submarine. We believe it to be a new type of submarine known as an Astute Super class. I have checked and believe its name is *HMS Excalibur*. We have no steerage or drive operational. We still have minor fires on board caused by the attack. We wish clearance to be given to enable our responding a counter aggression. Please acknowledge to us by cable forthwith. Over."

"Your message is fully understood Borei Buluva class V1 six slash zero one X. How many dead are there on board?" came back an immediate response.

Captain Narodny answered, "We have eleven dead and nine seriously injured. Over."

"Await our response. Keep this frequency open at all times in case we cannot send a cable. Over and out."

The operation's room on board the American submarine *Intrepid* had listened to the surprise call of desperation made by the Russian Captain. Admiral Adams knew how serious his own submarine's predicament was. However, he also was well aware the British submarine possibly might not have such a sophisticated monitoring system as did his submarine.

"Lieutenant Odbie," Admiral Adams called. "Please send the following message by coded cable to *HMS Excalibur*. Head the message with our normal formalities. Then say this: 'NICE SHOOTING COMMODORE – STOP – TRICKY BIG FISH TO HIT – STOP – CONGRATULATIONS – STOP – NOW HEAR THIS – STOP – HAVE INTERCEPTED AND TRANSLATED RADIO MESSAGE FROM GORBACHEV TO RUSSIAN NAVAL HQ AT SEVEROMORSK – STOP – GORBACHEV SKIPPER IS REQUESTING PERMISSION TO ATTACK YOU – STOP -SUGGEST YOU TAKE ALL NECESSARY ACTION TO PROTECT YOURSELVES – STOP – REMEMBER WHATEVER THE RUSSIAN SUBS FIREPOWER IS – STOP – IT DOES NOT SEEM TO LEAVE MUCH EVIDENCE – STOP – WE HAVE CONTAINED OUR FLOODING – STOP – ARE NOW WAITING FOR DECOY TO ASSIST – STOP – SORRY WE COULD NOT JOIN THE PARTY – STOP – GOOD LUCK AND GOOD HUNTING – STOP – END MESSAGE'."

"There, Odbie, that should do it. Have it scrambled into code and send it off right away."

"Aye, aye, Admiral."

Admiral Adams now felt he had something real to contribute to the battle scene even though he had managed to put his submarine out of commission.

It was not too long before a reply was received. It read:

TIME: 09.52 HOURS TUESDAY 15 AUGUST 2017
FROM: HMS EXCALIBUR
TO: SSBN INTREPID
ATTN: ADMIRAL A. J. T. ADAMS III
THANK YOU FOR WATCHING OVER US – STOP – PLEASED TO SEE YOU ARE STILL SEMI-OPERATIONAL AND KICKING – STOP – THOUGH IT BE COMING FROM WAY DOWN IN DAVY JONES LOCKER – STOP –

WILL WATCH SURFACE MORE DILIGENTLY AGAIN AND OBSERVE
ACTIONS OF TARGET – STOP – HOPE TO BE ASSISTING YOU SOONEST
– STOP – END MESSAGE
SIGNED: COMMODORE BRIANSTON-GREEN C-IN-C OPERATION
BLINDFOLD

Admiral Adams read the message and smiled. He was pleased the British
Commander showed he had a sense of occasion and good humour.

Another message was passed on to Lieutenant Odbie. He advised
Admiral Adams, "Sir! It's from the decoy. The tanker confirms it has
released a lot of its water ballast. It will be entering the island's channel
sometime within the next hour."

Admiral Adams was very pleased with that advice. "Why, that's truly
great news. Any longer and the air down here will begin to smell of old
rotten socks." They both laughed then waited for the next news from *HMS
Excalibur.*

Commodore Brianston-Green climbed up the conning tower steps and on
to the flying bridge. The British submarine was dipping and rolling in the
moderate swell.

The mid-morning sky had now begun to clear, and the heavy sea
fog of the previous twelve hours had started to disperse. Brilliant beams of
sunlight began breaking through the thinning fog and clouds of thick mist.

Lt. Bergman joined the Commodore. He handed him a set of
binoculars. The Commodore turned to the lookouts and enquired if
anything had been sighted.

"No, not yet, sir," came back the word. "We have seen only a few
playful porpoise and flying fish."

"Thank you," Brianston-Green replied.

The time was 10.08 hours.

"Well, Bergman, we advised we would assist in a rescue operation
as from 10.00 hours. I don't think the Russian Captain can complain or
criticise us for being a tiny bit late. What do you think, Lieutenant?"

"Not really, sir. The *Gorbachev* is certainly out there somewhere. We
are now receiving very strong sonar responses. The radar shows a blip and,
if it is the Russian submarine, it's out there at about six thousand metres off
our starboard beam. With the visibility over that way being steeped in a
heavy mist, one cannot make out any surface contact as yet."

Brianston-Green could sense the frustration. "Lieutenant, have the engine room increase our speed to thirty-five knots. Alter our course by steering six degrees to port."

"Port, sir?" Bergman exclaimed.

"TO PORT, Bergman!"

"Aye, aye, Commodore."

On board the *Gorbachev*, Captain Narodny promptly received notice from the special operations room that confirmed the British submarine had altered course.

"This is now becoming very interesting. Comrade First Officer, I sense an act of good fortune. We might have just acquired a lucky break."

The first officer had been busy rechecking the perilous position of many of the dials, having been shouted at to promptly advise and update the situation regarding the state of the fire.

"I beg your pardon, Comrade Captain? I'm sorry, sir, I didn't quite hear what you said. I was in the process of receiving details concerning our fire damage and the current position of its control."

Captain Narodny shook his head. "I was saying that now the British submarine has altered course we may be lucky enough to rid ourselves of this aggressor."

The Captain showed his first officer the position of the *Gorbachev*. He then advised his calculation of the suspected course and passage he hoped that *HMS Excalibur* would be taking.

"You see, Number One, that would be it if the British submarine's current speed and course is maintained. In about twelve minutes we will have the chance to sink the scourge of our present dilemma."

"But, Captain!" the young officer shouted.

"No ifs or buts, Number One! Please sound ACTION STATIONS!" the Captain roared. "Prepare to engage the atomic-powered laser gun for firing. Time the shot to be set for precisely 10.20 hours."

"Aye, aye, Comrade Captain," the first officer responded, fearing that if he didn't obey he would not be given any chance of survival.

On board *HMS Excalibur*, Commodore Brianston-Green had gone below to forward another message to RN HQ Northwood. He left Lt. Bergman up top to command the flying bridge, and control the continued watch.

The time was 10.14 hours.

The distance between the two submarines had closed to five thousand metres. The heavy mist was now beginning to quickly rise. Brilliant sunlight above it had been gradually burning the mist away allowing its radiant beams to break through and glitter upon the ocean.

Suddenly, sunlight reflected a quick flash of light that caught the eye of one of the lookouts on the conning tower of the British submarine. "Ere! What in ell's name was that?" the rating shouted.

"Don't know as yet," said another lookout that had been watching the sea with his naked eye. "It appears to be some sort of glinting. You know, like yer get from the surface of shiny metal."

The first lookout trained his powerful computerised naval field glasses in the direction of where the bright flash had been seen. As he panned the sea towards the spot, his eyes again soon picked up the glint from where the flash of light was coming. Through the thinning mist he could now make out the dark outline and shape of a vessel that appeared to be stationary on the sea surface. He pushed the field glasses' magnification button to achieve a better sighting.

"We have visual contact, sir. A very large submarine is sighted bearing 024 degrees off our starboard bow."

Everyone on the flying bridge turned their field glasses towards the advised direction.

Lieutenant Bergman immediately pushed the button of a klaxon horn siren. He then yelled into the submarine tannoy microphone, "Action Stations! Action Stations! Man all surface-to-surface missile launching units. Hold your fire until fully instructed."

Brianston-Green quickly ascended to the flying bridge. "Well, Bergman, where is the UUO? What in the devil's name, man, does it look like?" The Commodore had not heard the lookout's previous advice and notification.

Lieutenant Bergman pointed in the direction of where he had seen the flashing glint of light.

The Commodore raised his heavyweight video recorder computer naval field glasses and started to scan the sea. As the lenses began to focus and zoom, a close-up of the distant object came into view. He looked in awe.

The camera lens unfurled the sight of the Russian submarine. He viewed its huge sinister black shape, and then picked out the high column conning tower bristling with communication antennae. Three tall steel masts stood protruding from the top of its flying bridge; each supported a duel periscope and an array of sophisticated communication and radar systems.

"Good grief! What a monster of a submarine that is," the Commodore said taking in the incredible sight.

His eyes then followed the huge submarine's contour. He watched in near disbelief as the *Gorbachev* appeared to be turning towards the *Excalibur*. Staggered by the sudden change of events, he now saw before him what appeared to look like two huge black jaws opening. It was just like the aperture of a camera. "Oh no! Oh my God! NO!" Commodore Brianston-Green yelled. "Bergman! Bergman! Here, quickly. Take a look at this!"

The Lieutenant took a very quick glance and replied, "Good grief, sir, what in hell's name could that thing be?"

The Commodore suddenly felt very exposed. "One thing for which I'm certain, Bergman. I sure as hell don't wish to stay around here one second longer in order for us to find out. Order the helmsmen to turn our rudder a full ninety degrees. Let's get the hell out of here! Warn the crew to stand ready just in case any evasive action is to be taken."

"But, sir!" Bergman shouted.

Brianston-Green roared back, "JUST DO IT! THAT'S AN ORDER!"

Instead of obeying the order of his commanding officer, Lieutenant Bergman yelled at the top of his voice to his rocket crew, "FIRE! FIRE! FIRE!"

Two Tomahawk heat-seeking cruise missiles, preset for the desired track and course of the Russian submarine's position, left the decks of *HMS Excalibur* with a flash and sheet of flame.

At that moment there was a blinding stream of light that appeared to exude from the barrel protruding out from the upper deck gun turret on board the *Gorbachev*.

A tremendous explosion was heard. All around *HMS Excalibur,* flames and smoke belched out, and spread out across hundreds of feet of ocean. An ear-shattering roar then followed.

Suddenly, the sky was lit up as explosion after explosion ripped the air asunder.

A huge column of smoke pillared into the sky, and the scene was of burning twisted metal and mass destruction.

The lookouts on the starboard quarter of *HMS Excalibur* lay bleeding from their ears, nose and mouth.

Two of the deck crew were struggling to swim having broken several limbs, their injuries caused by flying shrapnel. Both of them had been thrown far out to sea by the huge blast that followed the firing of the *Gorbachev*'s atomic-powered laser gun.

Commodore Brianston-Green was laid out flat on his back still holding on to his naval field glasses. Lieutenant Bergman was nowhere to be seen.

An able-bodied seaman rushed up from down below in order to assist in any rescue; in seeing his commanding officer lying spreadeagled on the deck, he set about checking if he was seriously injured. He carefully helped him to sit back and rest against a deck board.

"Sir! Sir, are you in any way hurt?" the young rating asked anxiously.

"No! No, thank you, young man. I think I'm okay. Maybe just a little shaken. By the way, who the devil are you?"

"Leading Seaman, Archibald Smith, sir," came the reply.

"Well, lad, what does it feel like to have your first bit of naval action?" the Commodore said while brushing dust off his uniform sleeves.

The youngster looked blankly back at his commanding officer then answered, "Well, at least I can say I've lived to tell the tale, sir. And I'm sure you will be very pleased to see that one of our missiles got the blighter!"

At first Brianston-Green wasn't sure if he had heard right. "What was that you said, Smith?"

The rating spoke again. "We got the bloody Russian right on its snout, err, I mean its nose, sir."

"Here, let me see," Brianston-Green said taking a look through his field glasses. His face showed no emotion.

Then he smiled. "Good Lord! How did that happen? How did we make that come about?"

Suddenly he was conscious that someone was missing. "SMITH! Where the hell is Lieutenant Bergman?"

"Who, sir?" the seaman replied.

"Lieutenant Bergman, man. Dammit, Smith! Surely, by now, you must know whom the devil your number one is. Or don't you?"

Leading Able Seaman Smith looked the Commodore straight in the eye. "Sir, I trust it wasn't that poor fellow who came reeling head first down the hatch ladder at the time of the explosion. It happened just as we were all trying to get up top to see what was happening."

Brianston-Green's face went pale. "I suppose it could have been, Smith," he said, now worried that his closest colleague and first officer, might well have met his worst.

By now one of the lookouts was just beginning to come back to his senses. He had been easing himself up into a sitting position in order to make things a little more comfortable. He began to wipe the blood from his mouth. He happened to have overheard part of the Commodore's conversation and interrupted, "Sir, I'm sorry. It was Lieutenant Bergman who disappeared down the hatch."

The Commodore's jaw sunk. "God! I hope he's all right. What do you know about it, Smith?"

"When I saw him last, sir, he was lying flat on his face in a pool of blood."

"He isn't, is he, Smith?" asked the Commodore.

"I'm very sorry, sir, I really do not know."

Commodore Brianston-Green, now back on his feet, stood on the conning tower. Totally stunned he looked out to sea. His submarine was miraculously still intact and was now surging through the sea back to the scene of the battle.

It had sailed what was soon to be considered one of history's tightest maritime arcs.

A huge white wake of bubbling foam covered the submarine's tight course of turning. Its set course had taken *HMS Excalibur*, at a speed of thirty-five knots, right back round to the scene of where the explosion of one of its missiles had occurred.

The firing had been triggered off on having received the full blast of the beam from the Russian submarine's atomic-powered laser gun when the *Gorbachev* fired it.

"It could so easily have been us, sir," the familiar voice of Lieutenant Bergman said as he reappeared bloodstained from the hatchway of the conning tower.

In hearing Lieutenant Bergman's voice, Brianston-Green turned to see where it was coming from. "Bergman! It really is you. By Jove, dear chap, you really don't look the best of sights."

The Commodore realised how tactless his remark may have sounded. "I'm sorry, Lieutenant. Are you in any way injured, dear boy?"

Bergman had already realised what a sight he must have looked, but he didn't concern himself with that. "Sir, I think I have a severe crick in the neck and some bad bruising, that's all."

"Well, I think we had better have the sub go round again so we can pick up our two gunners. Don't you agree, Bergman?"

Lt. Bergman nodded although he was still unaware as to what really happened. On trying to collect his thoughts he began to scan the sea aft. As he did, he saw two sailors trying to tread water.

"Thank goodness for that," he said, and then asked the Commodore, "What caused them to be in the drink, sir?"

"It appears, Bergman, contrary to my orders and somehow in line with your actions, miraculously one of our missiles met with the full force of whatever the *Gorbachev* had unleashed at us. It was the force of that explosion that apparently threw our gunners way out into the ocean.

"Might I say, Lieutenant, thank heavens they are both alive, although possibly injured. Otherwise, I must tell you, certain circumstances regarding your past actions could well have been viewed very differently."

The Lieutenant turned and gave the Commodore a cheeky smile and then winked.

Brianston-Green continued speaking, "I am sure by now, Bergman, you must understand that I am fully aware of your actions. However, this does not remove the fact of your disobeying my orders. I must say your action, against all odds, showed great perception and courage. Therefore, I might be convinced into maybe considering that some great power above had somehow directed matters."

Bergman smiled. He felt the Commodore was trying to tell him something but he just couldn't put it into words.

"Therefore, Bergman, the matter will rest there for the time being. I'll have to find the time to discuss it with you at a later date. Let us now get this task finished and our two men back on board. We can then get *Excalibur* over to see what's left of the Russian renegade."

"Aye, aye, sir," Bergman responded.

He then stood to attention and gave the Commodore an official salute.

As Bergman was about to leave, the Commodore responded, "Oh yes, Number One. I nearly forgot to mention it. Nice shooting, Lieutenant. Nice shooting."

Lieutenant Bergman felt somewhat relieved. His cheeks bloomed red with the compliment. Underneath, he felt a slight embarrassment for all that had happened.

On board the *Gorbachev,* there was now a gaping hole where the atomic laser gun had been. The British submarine's missile, on sensing its heat source, had found its target and blown it into a red-hot framework of bent and twisted scrap iron. Flames and smoke belched out of the inferno that was raging beneath the deck.

The twin nuclear reactors had both been shut down to minimise the risk of any radiation fallout and threat of contamination. The fires had taken a strong foothold in the submarine's forward sections. Temperature gauges now began to pass the danger limit of one hundred and sixty degrees centigrade.

In total desperation, junior officers were trying to ensure if the movement to safety of many of the wounded could be achieved. Breathing apparatus was issued to all that were still standing. Captain Narodny was asked if the LOK should now be turned on. He had resigned himself that all must be done to try and save his ship.

"Yes, you must now turn on the freon gas. But make sure all of the crew are adequately protected otherwise they shall die a very cruel death."

As time went on, the situation worsened. Cable lines had begun to melt. Then, by some sheer quirk of fate, a sudden power surge swept through the submarine's electrical system. More fires started. Then, to add to the increasing problems, instrument panels and wiring casings began to explode.

Captain Narodny entered the special operations room situated well aft behind the two shut down nuclear reactors. He placed the *Gorbachev*'s log and documents on the radio operator's desk and spoke.

"Do we have any word yet from Moscow? Have we received any instructions from the naval base at Severomorsk?"

"Not as yet, Comrade Captain," the operator advised. "Sir, you will recall they did schedule us to link up with them at 10.30 hours. There are only two or three minutes left for us to have to wait for this communication."

Captain Narodny knew the feelings of his men. He could sense an air of acute desperation setting in. In a soft voice he said, "Thank you, thank you all, every one, of you. You have done a fine job."

Soon a crackling sound was heard over the radio. A voice spoke, "This is Chublavitch speaking from the FSB Headquarters, Lubyanka, Moscow. Can you hear me, *Gorbachev*?"

"Yes. This is Captain Narodny answering."

"Good, Comrade Narodny. We were led to understand your submarine was sunk on its maiden voyage. I have been instructed to notify you, you are deemed a traitor to Russia also the illustrious name of your submarine. But, in view of the circumstance you are in, you will no doubt be greeted back in our country like a hero."

Chublavitch coughed and cleared his throat. "I have been advised by our agents in Europe that your so-called friend, Lt. Commander Ivanov, has been assassinated while trying to defect. I duly trust, Comrade Narodny, you will not consider taking a similar route. On my having heard how bad your situation is I would further suggest you try to save yourself and your crew. How long do you think you have got left, Comrade Captain?"

Captain Narodny felt as if a knife had been thrusted through him.

What friends he thought he had left in high places had suddenly vanished.

"Comrade Chublavitch," Captain Narodny replied, "I really do not know currently what our present position is. Since speaking with you a British missile has hit us. The *Gorbachev* tried to defend itself. I believe we might have hit the British submarine, but as yet I cannot confirm this."

Captain Narodny paused. He hoped he was making sense. He then went on the offensive. "What happened to the *Vostok*? Why were we not pre-warned of our acute exposure?"

A loud crackling sound was heard after which the line went dead.

At first a loud roar momentarily engulfed the air. Then an explosion rocked the Russian submarine from end to end. A high-pressure air pipe had been ruptured by the intense heat and now began fuelling the flames with pure oxygen.

A third class officer entered the special operations room.

He looked exhausted. "Comrade Captain, compartments three and four are now well ablaze. We really cannot hold out much longer. Comrade Captain, if the bulkhead leading to compartments two and one are soon exposed then this intense heat will definitely further increase the chances of the forward torpedo chamber and ammunition store exploding.

"Comrade Captain, we are nearly completely finished."

Captain Narodny leant forward and rested his arms on the radio operator's desk.

The officer spoke again. "Comrade Captain, what are your orders, sir?"

The Captain stood looking aimlessly at the young officer. At that moment a junior captain, first class, came hastily through the entrance of the special ops room.

"Comrade Captain, sir, there are now flames everywhere. The crew are desperately trying to extinguish them by ripping the cables and cases off the wall brackets with their bare hands. The situation is near hopeless."

The despair and desperation of the young officer showed as tears streamed down his cheeks. "Comrade Captain! Sir! These cables are now exploding everywhere!" the young officer roared. He waited hoping that some sort of instruction would be forthcoming.

Dense smoke began pouring from the hatch of the *Gorbachev*'s conning tower. It was spewing out through the gaping hole just forward of the huge steel tower. In places the submarine's decks had begun to glow red. Inside, some areas of the now stricken vessel were reaching temperatures of nearly one thousand degrees centigrade. The bulkhead of compartment three was beginning to melt away.

A warrant officer and his fire crew gallantly stood their ground to operate the fire hoses.

All seemed now useless and a lost cause.

News gradually spread across international networks of both television and radio. Press releases gave little account of the action but notably mentioned that the Russian submarine had been found, somewhere near the islands of Cape Verde.

The American news media released another bulletin of how their gallant space shuttle the *Liberty* had defended itself against an unprovoked attack. At this moment, however, no precise details were given as to what had caused this act of aggression.

As *HMS Excalibur* came within a mile of the heavily smoking hulk of the pride of the Russian Navy's submarine fleet, the British submarine further reduced its speed.

On the flying bridge of *HMS Excalibur,* many stood watching in awe.

The sight of such a huge vessel lying helpless, slowly dying and burning in such a terrible way, caught the two officer's emotions.

Commodore Brianston-Green broke the silence. "Bergman, send a message to the Captain of the *SSBN Gorbachev.* Acknowledge we stand ready to assist rescuing the wounded and survivors. Advise we are prepared to receive a Russian crewmember and officer if they can swim or arrive by inflatable life jacket or rescue dinghy."

"Aye, aye, Commodore!"

The Commodore's message was transmitted at 10.56 hours.

The crew of *HMS Excalibur* waited anxiously for a reply.

The Russian submarine received the message but there was no reply.

On board the *Gorbachev* many of the injured crew were horribly burnt. Their hands were raw where they had desperately tried to beat out the flames. A junior officer's oxygen mask had melted to his face. Medical officers in the sick bay tried to gently remove it. With it, the poor man's skin came off too.

Again, a loud internal explosion was heard. Compartment two's bulkhead had melted and disintegrated. Captain Narodny expected his submarine would not last much longer. He recorded and placed the *Gorbachev's* latest position into the ship's log.

He had previously done so at the time of the first torpedo strike.

After having had the radio communication he now knew there was

316

bound to be a full investigation and enquiry. He sat at the radio operator's desk and continued to write:

10.56 Hours. Message from the hms excalibur received. Have no ability to respond any message back. Fire continues to rage. Compartment two now exceeded over four hundred degree…

The time was one minute after 11.00 hours.

More violent explosions rocked the Russian submarine. Pressurised oxygen tanks now began to explode. The upper outer seals in the hull above compartment three began to break. Fire could be seen burning through the ever-increasing gaps. Soon the danger of incoming seawater would become apparent.

What exactly happened next, to this day, has never been known or understood. After the series of explosions, Captain Narodny went up top and appeared standing on the lower bridge or deck area. He appeared to be organising everyone to escape the horror that lay about them. Each crewmember, wounded or otherwise, was being personally asked by him to abandon the submarine. Many of the crew seemed to have suddenly come on deck from somewhere aft from a stern hatch. Some helped as the wounded were lowered into four large rescue dinghies. It appeared, by now, more than thirty of the Russian crew, wounded or still able to swim, had got away. They were either afloat or trying desperately to swim away from the burning deathtrap. It is believed that the forward torpedo room and ammunition store suddenly exploded. There was a tremendous flash followed by a huge explosion.

The *Gorbachev* seemed to frantically shudder. It was as if the Russian submarine, having struggled to survive for so long, finally began to die. First it lurched to port as it sucked up shockwave after shockwave. Then its bow rapidly began to disappear beneath the waves.

Captain Narodny could be seen handing a waterproof bound package to his number one officer, Bischoff, who then leapt into the last dinghy. As he turned and looked back he watched as the seawater rose over the burning holes above compartments two and three, covering the now white-hot glow.

It seemed the end was only moments away.

Captain Narodny was last seen standing as a solitary and lonely figure on the flying bridge of his submarine. Then the sea reached the gaping molten hole made by the British missile. The *Gorbachev* shook violently as the sea cascaded in. Shrill screams and cries of desperation echoed as the Russian submarine's hull dipped suddenly and began disappearing under the rising water covering the lower bridge, then the conning tower.

Some of the surviving crew believed they saw their gallant Captain jump in order to try and swim to safety. The *Gorbachev*'s stern then lifted in a bubbling mass of water. Defiantly, for a moment, it stood upright. The survivors watched in awe as the submarine's remaining hull and stern slipped deeper and deeper into the sea. The sound of crashing bulkheads deafened the ears of those survivors drawn nearer to the dying hull by the sudden pull of the ocean. The Russian submarine made its final dive deep down to its place of rest.

The supposed unidentified underwater object now took up its new place of detection by automatically releasing an international distress wreck marker buoy.

In seconds, *HMS Excalibur* picked its signal up first. Thereafter, it was picked up by the *Intrepid*.

Incredibly, from that horrific inferno and death of the Russian submarine, over a third of the crew who could swim had clung to the sides of inflatable dinghies. Most of the wounded crew now on board the *Excalibur* lay motionless, numbed by shock and suffering in pain.

The Russian sailors, burnt, exhausted and frightened, soon saw sight of their enemy through the lifting smoke and mist. The outline of *HMS Excalibur* gradually came into view. The British submarine had proceeded forward to the place where the burning hulk had been moving forward at a speed of about five knots. As the *Excalibur* approached, Lieutenant Bergman thought he could see several seamen bobbing about in the water, but he wasn't too sure.

Four orange inflatable dinghies became visible floating in the midst of a cloud of dissipating smoke. All around the seamen a layer of thick black oil still covered the water's surface. Sporadic pieces of flotsam and jetsam plus other wreckage littered the sea. Occasionally a sudden thrust and an explosion of bubbles would bring to the surface canisters of something or other which the dying submarine had unleashed in its final death plunge.

"Stop engines! Stop engines!" came a cry from the *Excalibur*'s flying bridge.

Soon the noise from the turning propeller screws gradually diminished. At first it seemed only the sound of lapping water could be heard splashing against the hull of the British submarine. The *Excalibur* grew closer to the scene.

Voices calling for help and sailors crying in agony now echoed the air. Moans and groans chilled the inner senses of one's mind. It was as if the ghosts and spirits of those gallant sailors, all who had lost their lives, had now come back, crying, demanding peace, pleading that all that was done was not of their doing.

As the British submarine drifted closer the eerie sounds grew louder. It was as if the spirits and souls of the dead from the aircraft disasters, in addition to those who had lost their lives on board the French destroyer *Meridien* and the *SS Andros*, all seemed to have come back to haunt and torment the scene.

For the second time in less than three weeks, Commodore Brianston-Green had ordered his crew to perform and assist in rescue work. This time, however, the feeling felt different. It was probably a sense of knowing that the final piece of the jigsaw puzzle, one that represented the closing of a book, had taken place. The ghastly sight of dismembered and terribly charred corpses together with those unlucky seamen who lay in the sick bay tortured by horrendous burns received from the worst enemy of any submarine were dreadful sights, and were to stay scarred in the minds of the *Excalibur*'s young crew for a very long time.

Commodore Brianston-Green sat at his desk. He began to compile some messages for sending to Northwood RN HQ and to the *Intrepid*. The first message read:

TIME: 12.15 HOURS 15 AUGUST 2017

FROM: HMS EXCALIBUR

TO: NORTHWOOD RN HQ

ATTN: ADMIRAL R MARCHANT RN

SURVIVED AN UNPRECEDENT ATTACK FROM THE GORBACHEV – STOP – IT APPEARED TO COME FROM A NEW EXPERIMENTAL WEAPON – STOP – OPINION CONSIDERS IT WAS A TYPE OF ATOMIC LASER GUN – STOP – SUFFERED MINOR CASUALTIES – STOP – NO FATALITIES – STOP – REPLIED BY FIRING TWO MISSILES – STOP – ONE WAS EXPLODED BY ENEMY FIRE POWER – STOP – SECOND ONE SCORED DIRECT HIT ON UNKNOWN TYPE OF GUN – STOP – RUSSIAN SUB GORBACHEV SANK AT 11.06 HOURS – STOP – THIRTY-ONE SURVIVORS FROM COMPLEMENT OF EIGHTY-TWO ON BOARD – STOP – REQUEST HONOURS BE EXTENDED WITH UNPRECEDENTED PRIDE AND VALOUR TO THE FOLLOWING – STOP – LIEUTENANT BERGMAN WITHOUT WHOSE QUICK THINKING AND

UNNERVING RESOLVE – STOP – WE MOST PROBABLY WOULD NOT
STILL BE AROUND TO SEND THIS MESSAGE – STOP – I TRUST THAT
THE BLINDFOLD CAN NOW BE PUT AWAY FOR GOOD – STOP – END
MESSAGE
SIGNED: COMMODORE BRIANSTON-GREEN C-IN-C OPERATION
BLINDFOLD

The second message read:

TIME: 12.18 HOURS 15 AUGUST 2017
FROM: HMS EXCALIBUR
TO: SSBN INTREPID
ATTN: ADMIRAL ALAN J. T. ADAMS III
THANK YOU FOR YOUR WELL TIMED WARNING – STOP – WE WERE
VERY LUCKY – STOP – GORBACHEV SANK AT 11.06 HOURS BY ONE
OF OUR MISSILES – STOP – THIRTY-ONE SURVIVORS NO CAPTAIN
AMONGST THEM – STOP – SHOULD BE WITH YOU BY 15.00 HOURS
TO ASSIST IF NEEDED – STOP – HOPE YOU CAN SURVIVE AND STAY
THE COURSE – STOP – YOU ARE WELCOME FOR DINNER IF YOU
CAN HOLD YOUR BREATH A LITTLE LONGER – STOP – TELL ALL
CONCERNED THE GHOST HAS FINALLY BEEN BUSTED – STOP – END
MESSAGE
SIGNED: COMMODORE BRIANSTON-GREEN C-IN-C OPERATION
BLINDFOLD

Slowly, the compassionate task of the victor in bringing home the dead or
injured, whatever their colour or creed, was finally underway. Out of the
total crew complement of eighty-two men, the British submarine accounted
for only thirty-one survivors. The reality of what fire can cause when
happening in such a confined space had become a most dreadful experience
for the young crew of the *Excalibur*. Most of the injured had received ninety
percent burns. However, it was well appreciated the facilities in the sick bay
of the *Excalibur* were able to cope. The gruesome sight of some of the badly
injured made many a young crewmember physically sick.

Diligently, *HMS Excalibur* remained in the area for a long period
having offered to assist in the rescue. The submarine continued a zigzag
course covering the whole area scattered by the Russian submarine's flotsam
and jetsam. Captain Nikita Narodny was never found amongst the debris,
or with any of the survivors.

On the deck of the British submarine those Russians who had escaped serious injury were the last to be assisted by *Excalibur's* crew. While waiting, everyone received a lifeline just in case a sudden sea swell or rogue wave was to sweep them off the submarine and out to sea.

Lt. Bergman looked down from the flying bridge. He watched as the last remaining survivor was lifted to safety. As the aft hatch closed he said, "What is the final count, Smith?"

"Thirty-one survivors and sixteen bodies, sir."

"Thank you, Leading Seaman," the Lieutenant acknowledged, then advised, "Please dismiss the deck crew then muster below."

"Aye, aye, sir." Smith responded.

Commodore Brianston-Green came up on to the flying bridge. He stood beside Bergman for a moment surveying the scene. "How are things, Lieutenant?"

"The crew are just finishing up, sir." Bergman responded. "We have a total of forty-seven of the Russian crew accounted for, Commodore."

"It's a dreadful shame, Bergman. So many of the *Gorbachev's* gallant crew seemed to have perished," the Commodore said, on seeing the Lieutenant's note of tally.

"I agree, sir. It has been a very nasty business."

"Well, Lieutenant, we had better set our new course for the southern entrance channel between the islands of Mindelo and Sto Antao," the Commodore said. "Now we will have to go and see what we can do to assist operations with the *Intrepid*."

Bergman gave the Commodore a polite smile. He felt the instruction was like a breath of fresh air. "Right you are, Commodore."

Bergman spoke into the bridge telephones. "Bridge to engine room. Full ahead, both engines. Speed thirty-five knots. Set our course bearing zero three four degrees north-eastwards."

Slowly a ripple of water began to splash against the bow of the British submarine. Once again, the shiny hull of *HMS Excalibur* began to cut through the ocean waves.

Apart from the constant attendance made to the sick and injured sailors, memories of the engagement and battle had now become history.

The weather had cleared and the sea was a deep indigo blue. The sun, now shining high in the heavens, was warming into a beautiful afternoon. Anyone suddenly appearing on the scene would never have suspected that not more that two hours previously, the world had rid itself of a most notorious vehicle and evil weapon of carnage and horrific destruction.

Chapter Twenty-Three

NASA Ground Control and Tracking, Cape Canaveral
US Military and Naval Intelligence Department

On having made an early morning appearance at his office, General Kemp received a notice from Sergeant Lance advising that a call would be coming through from the President at 08.00 hours. The time was now 06.00 hours, 16 August 2017.

The General had risen at 04.00 hours. He had already been over to NASA Ground Control and Tracking to speak with Professor Burston. At the same time he collected the latest video recordings of the attack made on the space shuttle *Liberty,* and also the counter-attack and destruction of the Russian space platform's communication centre.

As the General was about to enter his office, Captain Logan popped his head from out of the computer room. "Good morning, General," Logan said, feeling the day had seemed to start well for him. "Fine morning isn't it, sir?"

"You can say that again, Smartie. The sun is shinin', there are no clouds in the sky and the *Liberty* has gone and smashed the Russian's communications on board their space platform." The General felt good as he began to reel off all the day's plus signs. "Our boy's and girls in space should be coming home today. So, Logan, what else is going to be good?"

"Well, sir, let's hope we shall be hearing some good news from our submarine. Maybe Admiral Adams will finally make our day, sir."

Kemp was non-committal. "We'll see, Smartie. One thing for sure, that damned Russkie sub ain't got any protection any more. It shouldn't, I hope, be too long now before we hear somethin' that's gonna be real positive."

"What time does the *Liberty* touch down, sir?" Logan asked.

"In about three hours," said Kemp, looking at his watch. "I believe, Smartie, that Macdonald Burston has received a confirmation which sets the shuttle's landing time for about 08.55 hours EST."

"Gee, that's fine, thank you, sir. By the way, have you had breakfast yet?" Logan enquired.

"Nope. Why is that, Smartie? Are you feelin' hungry again?" Kemp laughed. "Do you know, Logan, if I didn't know better I'd say that you had an appetite of a Colorado vulture."

Logan gave Kemp a very strange look then burst into laughter.

The General could see that the young officer was amused so he didn't wish to disappoint him. "Okay, Smartie, I'll join you but please give me a moment as I first need to clear down a few things in my office. Then we can go and eat to celebrate *Liberty's* successful mission."

"You bet, sir. See you in the canteen, General, in about ten minutes? Captain Logan then departed.

Kemp walked over to the safe and opened it. He placed the digital recordings inside then carefully locked the door and moved back to his desk. As he sat down he noticed that a facsimile message had been sent through. Having bent down to pick it up he began to read:

TIME: 11.03 HOURS 15 AUGUST 2017

FROM: SSBN INTREPID

TO: UNITED STATES NAVAL HQ CHARLESTOWN S C

TO: NASA MILITARY AND NAVAL INTELLIGENCE DEPT

ATTN: GENERAL JOHN B. KEMP

RELEASED MAYDAY CALL 08.58 HOURS – STOP – SUB HIT A SUBMERGED OBJECT WHILE PASSING BETWEEN MINDELO AND STO ANTAO ISLANDS OFF CAPE VERDE – STOP – NINETEEN DEAD – STOP – FIRST TWO COMPARTMENTS FLOODED – STOP – DECOY SS GLOBE KOBE ON ITS WAY TO ASSIST – STOP – CURRENTLY MAINTAINING ALL OTHER FUNCTIONS – STOP – AT 09.08 HOURS LOCAL TIME HMS EXCALIBUR TORPEDOED UUO – STOP – HAVE RECEIVED MAYDAY FROM RUSSIAN SUB GORBACHEV REQUESTING IMMEDIATE ASSISTANCE – STOP – RUSSIAN ACCUSES ALLIES FOR STARTING ATTACK STATING IT WAS MADE TOTALLY UNPROVOKED – STOP – AT 09.45 HOURS LOCAL TIME HMS EXCALIBUR CONFIRMED WOULD MAKE ARREST OF THE GORBACHEV AND CREW – STOP – HAVE CURRENTLY NO FURTHER NEWS – STOP – WILL REPORT BACK EVERY HOUR – STOP – END MESSAGE

SIGNED: ADMIRAL ALAN J. T. ADAMS III C-IN-C OPERATION GHOSTBUSTERS

In near total disbelief General Kemp shouted out aloud, "BLOODY HELL! What in God's name was Adams tryin' to do? JESUS! It sounds like a case of very bad driving to me."

Sergeant Lance heard the General shouting. He quickly came into the office. "Say, General, what's all the noise about? Is somethin' wrong, boss?" Sergeant Lance beckoned seeing the General standing in the middle of the room holding a piece of paper.

"Kemp looked at the security officer. He heaved a big sigh. "Oh, it's really nothing, Lance. It's nothing that can't be put right!"

The General felt slightly embarrassed. He hadn't realised that the noise of his ranting had carried so far. "Sit down will you, Sergeant."

Lance acknowledged the General's request.

At the same time, Kemp sat himself down in an easy chair next to his long glass table.

"Well now," said Kemp. "Lance, let me see how I can set this out and tell you. First of all, we will have to see how long the darned news is goin' to remain an absolute secret, especially around here."

"I'll buy that one, General," Lance replied.

"Okay," Kemp responded with an air of unexpected caution.

"Right sir, shoot for the stars. Let the chips roll. Come on now, General, spill the beans."

The General smiled. "Well, Sergeant, if I was to tell you how good the day was at the start you might not seriously believe me. There again, if I was to say that somehow one of our Admiral's had missed a golden opportunity and has gone and sunk his sub, you wouldn't necessarily believe that either. Or would you, Sergeant?"

The Sergeant shook his head as if to say no.

"Well, Lance, I'm afraid it's true," the General snapped back.

Sergeant Lance's face was a picture. "Why'd he go and do that, sir?"

"It beats me, Sergeant. Sure as hell it beats me!" Kemp retorted.

"Maybe, somehow, he went and got lost, sir. Moreover, General, he could 'ave tried to take a short cut."

"Sergeant Lance!" the General roared, "there are no short cuts to be had in the US Navy, nor, for that matter, in any of our military forces!"

With that forthright reaction Sergeant Lance responded immediately. "Yes, sir!" He then jumped to his feet, stood to attention and saluted the General.

For a moment Kemp was without words. After the Sergeant had stood rigid and silent for nearly half a minute, Kemp realised his security officer might have taken the remark as some form of reprimand.

"All right, Lance, I didn't really mean to snap like that."

"No, sir!" Lance responded.

Kemp asked the Sergeant to stand easy. "It's like I said, Lance. At first the day looked so good. Now, it's just turned into a very bad start. Oh, by the way, there was one bit of good news. The British sub, *Excalibur*, has sunk the Russian sub, *Gorbachev*."

Sergeant Lance wasn't too sure if that was supposed to be good or bad news. He thought he'd take the chance to enlighten the heavy discussion. "Well, I do declare! Sure as hell, General, that has gotta' be some good news, sir?"

"Maybe, Lance. Maybe. I suppose I really must be gettin' too old for this sort of stuff. Could I be losin' my touch?"

The General crossed the room and sat down at his desk.

Sergeant Lance knew he was worrying about something. "Hell's bells, General, sir. I'd even go and telephone the President on that one if I knew it would help. Mind you, I'd laden the call with lots of the purest maple syrup then merely go and do it. I'd do that to cheer myself up a little. Come on now, General, let's have a smile coming on that little old grouchy face of yours." The Sergeant knew his comment would certainly bring something back as a reaction.

"That's enough, Sergeant," the General said, knowing that if he didn't try and brighten up Sergeant Lance would hover over him for the rest of the day. "Okay, okay! I'll go and do it, and right away. Only please stop sayin' I'm old and grouchy. Do you hear?"

On hearing the General's reply Lance chuckled and then said, "You bet, sir. I'll wait and see what you are like after you have made the call."

Kemp knew the Sergeant well enough and he often had a way of softly winding him up. He immediately retorted, "Heavens above, Lance! Now just you go and haul the butt of Captain Logan from out of the canteen. Do you hear me?"

Sergeant Lance gave the General a look of surprise. Kemp saw the Sergeant's expression and retaliated, "I know I promised him a breakfast but it's too late for that now."

From that remark the Sergeant knew that Kemp was back on stream and ready to pounce. "Ride on, General, ride on!"

Kemp looked across at Sergeant Lance and glared at him.

"Okay, sir, I'm off," Lance said, not wishing to take any further chances. As he opened the office door to leave he quipped, "Now don't forget to make that call."

Finally, as the security officer left, the General produced a very broad smile. He always knew it didn't really matter what else was bad in the world.

Somehow, Sergeant Lance would eventually jog his sense of humour.

The General picked up the telephone receiver of his hotline and began dialling the President's private telephone number.

"Good morning, John," the President answered. "Somehow I guessed that I'd receive an early bird call from you, General. I believe that congratulations are in order on the success of the space shuttle mission."

"Why thank you, Mr. President, sir," the General acknowledged.

"I do believe that I can now say, John, America duly owes you a tremendous debt of honour. We are all very proud of you, General. Personally, I must say your ESP in regard to the space demons and the exposure of the Russian submarine is quite something."

Kemp was quite taken aback by the President's comments. "You have heard about that, sir?"

"Yes, John, I have."

Kemp's brain immediately flashed signs of alarm and fear of exposure. He knew then what he might have done.

"Oh! I am sorry, John. The British Prime Minister telephoned me a short while ago. It was in order to verify and confirm one of the British submarines had torpedoed and eventually had sunk the Russian sub *Gorbachev*."

Kemp felt a little reassured by the President's statement. However, he still felt uneasy. "Sir, I wonder… Could you advise me of something?"

"By all means," the President responded. "That's, of course, if it is in my power to do so, General. Fire away."

In regard to all past record with his department, the General felt he should enquire. "Mr. President, has the US Navy's HQ confirmed to you any details concerning the most recent activities of the *Intrepid?*"

"None that I know of, John. Why? Should they have done so?"

"I certainly do believe so, sir."

The President was not too sure what the General was leading up to, and commented, "General, please tell me more. Come on, man, hit me with it."

The President sat and listened in silence as Kemp reported all the facts known to date that his department was aware of. As Kemp finished the President could be heard breathing heavily.

After a lengthy pause the President's spoke calmly, "Thank you very much, John, for that most detailed report. I suppose that such things cannot be helped. However, I must admit the loss of nineteen of our boys because of what surely must be deemed as bad seamanship… There will have to be an investigation regarding this matter. John, please see to it as soon as possible. D' you know, General, I seem to get the sneaky feeling that someone in the General Chiefs of Staff appears to be holding back on me."

As the President spoke he felt his spine tingle. *Who on earth might it be?* he thought.

"Could you organise a witch-hunt for me, John? See if your department can somehow bring out in the open why this very important information appears to have been held back from me. You alone, I believe, can understand what I am getting at. Let me say that I have been led to understand you already have had some sort of past experience and a track record regarding this sort of thing. I seem to recall that the past exposure revealed the guilty had a very grave connection with the FSB. I should like to see a copy of that file, if I may, in order to privately study it a little more. General, could you please see to this as soon as possible?"

Kemp had been most attentive. "Right you are, Mr. President, I'll get that seen to right away." The General had noticed that the tone of the President's voice clearly showed his despair regarding the loss of life. He was sure the great man's heart wore the heavy burden and responsibility of it all.

"John, I am sorry," the President said wearily. "There's a lot more I would wish to say, but there is nothing more at present that I can do about it. We'll speak later. I now have to make a call and I want you to listen in on the linked extension in your office."

"No problem, Mr. President."

Kemp picked up his extension and heard the President's brief instruction given to his private secretary. He listened carefully as the President put down his telephone receiver.

The General paused for a moment before replacing his and listened. Sure enough, as previously heard once before, there was a pause, then a click.

Kemp was now almost certain someone was bugging the President's private telephone line. *Who the devil was it? And why?*

There was no time like the present to find out. Kemp replaced the extension receiver and returned to his other telephone.

The President spoke. "Well, John, I leave the matter in your capable hands."

"I'll get back to you soonest, Mr. President. Thank you very much for listening to me. Goodbye for now, sir."

Kemp sat for a moment pondering over what to do next. Then, on opening one of the drawers of the left side of his desk, he pulled out a small box. He opened it and took out what looked like to be a small compact black box. It had a little screen on it at the top and wiring attached to it.

The General leant over and plugged in a power line. He then inserted two small attachments into a scrambler device connected to the hotline telephone. With everything having now been set up, Kemp redialled the President's private office line.

"Good morning again, Millie."

"Why? Hello again, General Kemp."

The General needed to find time to prolong his call being held. "I wonder, Millie, could I please have another brief word with the President?"

"Just one moment please, General. I'll see if it's possible for him to take your call."

"Thank you."

While waiting for reconnection, Kemp watched as the numbers dialled display on the little screen began to show. The first number showing was the one he had dialled, and then there were six other number slot spaces below this one. These were there to register any further numbers that might be traceable.

Soon, noticeable against the little screen's black background, the computerised red number digits began to roll. The General's telephone spy had now begun its task of searching.

"Hello, General?"

"Yes, Millie, I'm still here."

"Oh, thank you, General, for waiting. The President will take your call in a moment. Please kindly hold the line."

"Thank you, Millie." *Great,* thought Kemp. It was just the stroke of luck he required, but he would need a minimum of two or maybe three minutes if he was to have any chance of getting a firm registration back.

As the General sat waiting, watching for any movement on the small screen, he knew the seconds were ticking away. He smiled to himself as the first set of red digits locked on to the top line showing a Washington number. Still there remained five blank lines waiting for new digit numbers to show. As the second line reached halfway to revealing its secret, a third line of numbers began to roll. To the General's amazement, a fourth line had begun to start. Still Kemp waited for the President's secretary to respond. At that moment the line clicked and opened.

"Hello, General Kemp," Millie said, having just sneezed and blown her nose. "Oh, please excuse me. I appear to have a touch of the summer sniffles. I am sorry, General, the President's still talking. Would you like to try and call back later? Let's say in about five minutes, sir?"

"That's okay, Millie, I can hold out for a little bit longer. That's, of course, if you don't mind."

Millie knew very well that she shouldn't allow any caller to hold on a line for more than a minute. "Okay, General, I'll give you a few moments more, but please remember, sir, it sure is busy around here this morning."

"Why, thank you, Millie," the General answered, feeling relieved. "That's most considerate of you."

Just as Kemp had finished speaking Captain Logan entered the office. By now little beads of perspiration were beginning to form on Kemp's forehead.

Logan stood for a moment staring at the strange position his commanding officer was sitting in. "Say, what's up, General?" Logan said, seeing his commanding officer was somehow nearly bent double. He couldn't reason why his boss was leaning over the side of his chair and peering in to one of his desk drawers.

As Kemp moved it was then that Logan saw the jumbled apparatus of the telephone spy. Logan also noticed that it had begun to rattle its way towards an unknown target.

Smartie Logan watched intently as a fifth line of numbers had begun to roll. "Jesus, General! Who on earth are you about to chop in half this early in the morning? Golly, it sure must be a bad one."

"Why should that be, Captain?" the General snapped back.

Logan looked at Kemp's stern face. "Heck! Come on, sir. You haven't even had breakfast yet and already you are goin' for some poor bastard's blood."

"LOGAN!" General Kemp roared. The General knew he didn't want Logan or anyone else nosing around him at present. "Actually, you're right on that one, Captain. Come to think of it, Smartie, you are absolutely correct. I am feelin' famished. Say, how about you goin' and being a good chap and fetching me back here a large mug of hot strong black coffee, plus a large Canadian bacon buttie?"

Logan immediately acknowledged General Kemp's request. He promptly turned and departed on his errand.

As Logan closed the office door, he had a distinct feeling that the General didn't want him to see anything of what he was up to. He thought to himself, *No doubts about that one. The boss will probably tell me all about it later on.*

Kemp's heart had begun to pound strongly as the second line on the telephone spy finished, and the third line had only two digits to achieve its completion. The General's eyes watched without flinching as the fourth line showed it now needed only four numbers more. Soon a fifth line was rolling well. As yet, the sixth line had not moved. "Good grief!" the General said to himself. "Holy Moses. There are now FIVE BUGS on the President's personal lines. HELL! God only knows what he would do if he knew."

Millie, the President's personal private secretary, came back on the line. "Again, General Kemp, I am so sorry, but he is still not free. Sir, I think you are going to have to hang up. He's on one hell of a long one, General, and I don't really know how much longer he is going to be."

Kemp looked at his watch. Nearly two minutes and thirty seconds had passed. He only needed a little luck and a few seconds more. "Millie, the matter I am wishing to convey to the President really is one of great urgency. It is regarding details of my previous call. Please, be a darling, could I possibly ask you to put a note under the President's nose? I'll be very quick and dictate the text to you. One moment please…" Kemp said, trying desperately to extend the time of his call for as long as possible.

"Okay, General," Millie replied, "but, sir, please make the message as brief as you can. I really cannot hold this particular line open for much longer. It just ain't normal."

Kemp looked at his watch. By now two minutes and fifty-one seconds had passed. He also saw that digit dials two, three and four all had one digit of the expected telephone number taps to clear.

The palms of the General's hands had begun to sweat and feel sticky. He found he was having difficulty trying to write. His pen kept slipping from his grip. *Jesus Christ! What on earth can I say?* he thought. It was then that he considered the position didn't bear thinking about regarding what might happen next. If the President knew that the NASA Military and Naval Intelligence Department was checking up on his private lines, the General, through past experience, was well aware the man would blow his top. After that, well, it would be anybody's guess. Kemp shook his head. No, he didn't wish to give the matter any further thought or consideration.

After a few more seconds had passed the President's personal private secretary came back on the line. "Come on now, General, are you ready for me? If not I'll have no more time left to let you continue holding on, sir. I'm sorry but rules are rules. I'll have to shut you down. That's if you don't give me the President's message right away."

Three minutes and twenty seconds had passed.

Kemp replied, "It's okay, Millie, here it is. Please have the following delivered to the President right away."

He then read the message: "'*Your eyes are good but your ears are needing either filling tight with wax or you will have to face a complete clinical surgical syringe.*' There you are. Did you get all of that, Millie?"

"Yes, thank you, sir," came the reply. As she wrote down the message, Millie could not believe what she had written. "General, is this some kinda joke or something?"

"Nope, Millie, it ain't. Just hand that message to the President and advise him I'll be flying up to see him in about an hour. Have you got all that? Oh, by the way, have him return my call as soon as possible. Is that clear?"

"Yes. That's fine, sir. Thank you, General."

"Not at all, Millie. Thank you very much for the kindness you have shown me. Goodbye for now."

As Kemp replaced the telephone receiver back on the hotline both Captain Logan and Sergeant Lance entered the General's office. They stood in silence, patiently waiting for further instructions.

Kemp had not noticed them. He continued to shuffle a few papers about on his desk. He was still keeping his eye firmly fixed on the small screen.

Under the President's private number, the General saw that four completed numbers now showed, and these flashed in red illuminated digits. Line five showed nine figures out of a possible ten figure number.

As he sat back, Kemp took a handkerchief from out of his trouser pocket and proceeded to mop his brow. It was then that he noticed the two men looking at him.

Sergeant Lance spoke. "Hey, General, sir, Are you feelin' okay, boss?"

Kemp looked up at him and said, "I think so, Lance. Might I enquire as to why you have asked and why both of you have entered my office unannounced?"

The security officer had been waiting for the General to pounce. "Well, sir, for the past five minutes the switchboard has been goin' at me like a bat out of hell. Maybe, General, sir, you have gone and got all the lines crossed and darned well near blocked the whole thing off."

Sergeant Lance had been looking straight at the General as he spoke. It was only when he had finished that he saw the telephone scrambler on the General's desk.

"Say, General, sir, what on earth's been goin' on in here?"

Kemp knew that he couldn't possibly have any chance of hiding this one. "Please, both of you, sit down."

"What the devil is it, General?" Captain Logan remarked, who by now had begun to realise something nasty was coming up. Whatever it was he knew it was serious, and was worrying his boss.

"Gentlemen, I won't beat about the bush regarding what's been goin' on in here."

"Heck, is this one goin' to be a serious problem for us all, sir?" Lance said, feeling a little uncomfortable.

Kemp spoke very softly. "I wish to confirm to you both, I have just violated the privacy of the lines of the President of the United States of America."

"HOLY COW!" Lance roared, although he did not believe what the General had just said.

The General continued, "As I was saying, the two of you are fully aware of what I have just stated. It is a complete breach of our rules and codes under the constitution. However, and in my blatantly doing what I have done, I hope that my instincts are not letting me down."

"FOR GOD SAKES, GENERAL!" Logan shouted angrily. For a moment the Captain's loud reaction completely silenced the room.

Kemp ignored the young officer's outburst. "It's because my having done this thing that I wish both of you to bear witness to my honesty and integrity. Furthermore, and in return, I'll jointly want you both to swear a pact of the utmost secrecy regarding what I have just found out. Do I have your word on this?"

Both Lance and Logan looked at each other then replied, "Yes, General."

"Thank you. Well, gentlemen, in all there are a total of five telephone tappings which are bugging the President's most personal and classified telephone lines."

Both Sergeant Lance and Captain Logan's faces were a picture of stunned silence.

"Gentlemen," Kemp advised, "here are the numbers I have just recorded."

Both men looked at the piece of paper the General had laid out on his desk. On it, clearly written, were five sets of numbers bearing a Washington telephone prefix.

"Jumpin' Jiminy Crickets," Lance responded. "I just knew it! I really doggarn knew that a stupid thing like this was goin' on in here. My God, General, sir, why on earth is it I can't leave you alone for one teeny weeny second?"

Logan began to feel that they needed to shape up. "Come on, General, sir, we had all better get a grip on things around here otherwise, when the shit hits the fan regarding this dirty mess, as sure as eggs is eggs we'll all be getting some of it back in our faces."

Lance smiled. He just knew Captain Logan would bring them all back to sanity.

With that Kemp sat speechless.

Smartie Logan spoke again. "Hey, General. Is all of this really true?"

"Fraid so, Logan. But don't you go worrin' yerself about it. You just try and get yerself back to thinking straight."

Logan could feel something was brewing.

Kemp spoke softly and calmly. "'Cause, I'm telling you, boy, from now on we all have got a real and vital job on our hands to contend with."

The room fell silent on hearing the General's last remark.

Logan eyed his boss with a look of cautious apprehension.

Kemp ignored the Captain saying, "To take immediate effect, I will want a full clampdown on all communications to and from our offices to be actioned for a period of twenty-four hours from now. This is also to be done in every one of our departments. IS THAT CLEAR, LOGAN! At least this should minimise the slightest suspicion of any leaks coming from our side."

Kemp hated the effrontery of doubt he had now made towards his own department, but he knew it had to be done. "Now then, both of you, I will only say this once. On my taking these actions you must ensure that all personnel are made fully aware. The enemy, whoever they are, isn't going to take too kindly to this."

An hour had passed since the finding of the telephone leaks.

Kemp sat in silence. He was reminding himself of the words Admiral Marchant had uttered the night before. He recalled in his thoughts the Admiral saying, *Somebody across the pond, I believe, knows a lot more than any of us about what is really going on. Now, Kemp, if you were to arrange or at least devise the doings of a quick and silent pounce?* The General sat holding his head in his hands. It was the thought of such a thing that made him think of how the exposure of this crime could be achieved.

Captain Logan, having now calmed down regarding the hiatus that General Kemp had uncovered, entered his boss's office and sat down to look at one of the General's charts. On finishing, he looked up and eyed his boss with reserve. "General, might I enquire as to what you might be thinking?" Logan asked, hoping that he could repair the pensive atmosphere he felt was between them.

On hearing Logan's voice, Kemp dropped his hands.

"Oh! Sorry, Smartie, I didn't realise you had come by. I must have been miles away."

"Really, sir?" Logan said, trying to get a feeling of how things stood between them.

"You know, Logan, my mind was all blank. I was thinking about a conversation I recently had with a very important friend and close colleague."

"It must have been pretty deep, sir." Logan said, feeling a little more comfortable about the situation.

"Yes, Smartie, the gentleman in question advised me to look more closely into things over here. He seemed to be sure somebody, someone whom we all know, a person of whom it was thought and was assumed to be totally sound and trustworthy, was involved. Apparently, a person who is deemed to be completely above any suspicion who might know more about what's going on than the President himself."

Logan's mouth fell wide open. "HOLY MACKEREL! What on earth is this world coming to? Could that really be true, sir?"

"Well, Logan, at first I began to doubt the person's sanity for even thinking it. Now, after what has happened, I really don't know. However, I will say that I'm being drawn, minute by minute, a little closer in having to appreciate what has been said to me. In that respect, Captain, my close friend's statement could well be much nearer to the truth. Certainly much closer than I had first realised."

"What is to be done about it then, General?" asked Logan. "Where, if anywhere, do you think our department can assist?" Logan showed he was agitated and concerned of there being any exposure.

"As yet, Captain, I'm not exactly sure about how we are going to play this." The General thought for a moment. "Right, Smartie, I want you to go and get your wings on right away. We are going to make an unscheduled spot check on certain things after which we will then head to the White House."

Logan felt as if a great weight had been lifted off his shoulders. "Okay, General. It won't take me a moment to put everything into good order."

Kemp quickly stopped the young man in his tracks. "Nope, Smartie, just leave everything as it is. Sergeant Lance will do the necessary. I want you to get used to being as close to my side as you can possibly get. Also, you are to cover my flank at all times."

Captain Logan gave the General a look of reassurance.

"Now then, Logan, we take-off in about twenty minutes," the General said, stepping away from his desk.

Logan felt relieved and said, "That's okay by me, General."

They both then made a move to depart.

At that moment the office door opened and in walked Sergeant Lance.

"You timed your entrance well, Lance, " Kemp commented as he picked up his briefcase.

"Why is that, General? You going somewhere?"

The General didn't reply to the Sergeant's remark. He proceeded to issue him an instruction. "Sergeant, I want you to put a security lock on everything we have that's lockable in here. The same with G.O.D., okay? Do this while we are both away. You are to keep these rooms out of bounds to anyone, and guarded day and night. Is that clear?"

"Clear as mud, General, sir," Sergeant Lance responded.

"Sergeant, you may consider joking about this matter, however, in our absence from the department, see to it that nothing in it is changed, altered or unlocked by anyone else."

Kemp was not amused by the security officer's light-heartedness.

"Yes, sir, I read you loud and clear," Sergeant Lance said in coming to attention.

Kemp gave Sergeant Lance a long hard look.

Lance's expression changed. He suddenly realised how serious the situation was, and its implications. "Ain't your car ready yet, General?" Lance said, wishing to change the subject. "I believe, sir, Rodney is waiting to take both of you to the heliport."

"Thank you for that advice, Sergeant," the General acknowledged. Kemp now relaxed his forthright approach. "You take care now, Lance, keep a very sharp eye on things, okay?"

"You likewise, sir," the Sergeant responded. "Remember, man, somewhere out there, General, there's gotta' be a big bad wolf. Don't let him get too close to either of you. Is that clear?"

Kemp knew the Sergeant was only kiddin', or at least he hoped he was. "I'll try not to, Lance. Now, you hold the fort and keep everything safe. Be off and do what I've instructed."

That was the last conversation that either General Kemp or Captain Logan was to have with their security officer and friend. Within an hour of departing it was reported that both were cruelly blown to smithereens. Their deaths were caused by a PETN bomb that had been timed to explode moments after their taking off from the local United States Air Force base.

335

Chapter Twenty-Four

At Sea

By now *SS Globe Kobe* had arrived and anchored in deep water. It was near to the buoy marking the spot where the *Intrepid* lay in approximately one hundred and eighty feet of water.

The American submarine had survived the worst. Although heavily laden and with extra water contained in compartments one and two, also in the forward torpedo room, Admiral Adams had ensured the excess weight of water, and the levelling of air ballast, had stabilised his submarine. This was done so huge steel hawsers could be attached to the submarine's hull enabling the supertanker to pull the giant vessel from off the seabed.

The team of divers and engineers had successfully secured the lines, and the attempt to pull the American submarine free was to be made at 09.30 hours on 17 August 2017.

During the previous evening *HMS Excalibur* had joined the supertanker. The submarine was positioned about a mile off the leeward side of where the *SS Globe Kobe* was anchored.

Commodore Brianston-Green had been receiving numerous messages via Northwood acknowledging congratulations.

During the period of waiting, the Commodore had ordered the transfer of the survivors from the *SSBN Gorbachev* to much better accommodation aboard the supertanker. He instructed that the transfer was to take place only after operations with the American submarine had ceased.

A message had come through to the *Intrepid* from General Kemp marked for the attention of Admiral Adams. It read:

TIME: 03.00 HOURS AUGUST 16 2017

FROM: NASA MILTARY AND NAVAL INTELLIGENCE

ATTN: ADMIRAL ALAN J. T. ADAMS III

PRIVATE AND VERY CONFIDENTIAL

ALAN WE NO LONGER HAVE ANY SPIES IN THE HOME CAMP –
STOP – OUR PRESIDENT EXPOSED THE MASTER – STOP – AIR VICE-

MARSHALL GOODHOUSE TO BE SURE – STOP – SORRY FOR MESSING
UP YOUR GOLFING PARTNER – STOP – GOOD LUCK WITH THE PULL
– STOP – HOPE TO SEE YOU SOON IN CHARLESTON SC – STOP – END
MESSAGE
SIGNED: GENERAL JOHN B KEMP C-IN-C NASA MIL/NAVAL
INTELLIGENCE

Admiral Adams read the cable. He was gobsmacked. "Holy smoke, Odbie!"
he roared.

"What's up, Admiral?" Lieutenant Odbie replied, having been
surprised at the Admiral's sudden outburst.

"Suffrin' meatballs! We really have been a missin' out on all the
action," the Admiral remarked. "Maybe, Odbie, when all this is over I
should go and take up clay pigeon shootin'."

Lieutenant Odbie looked at his commanding officer then considered
that the Admiral's comment was some sort of passing dream.

It had been nearly two days since the *Intrepid* had become embedded in
the ocean floor. Odbie had just come back from checking that all operations
were set in readiness for the attempted pull. "Well, sir, our engineers have
confirmed that all systems are set in readiness to go forward and attempt the
pull. Are we all set, Admiral?"

"Okay then, let's do it. Lieutenant Odbie, ensure the crew are all
dressed in life jackets just in case we hit some kinda unforeseen snag. I'll
make an announcement at 09.20 hours and I will want every man to be
standing ready by then."

"Aye, aye, sir."

Lieutenant Odbie spoke calmly over the submarine tannoy to the
crew. "Every man is to go to his position immediately. At 09.29 hours, all
watertight compartment doors will be sealed. This will be done to prevent
any possible loss of pressure. It will also assist any rescue attempt if a mishap
might occur. That will be all, gentlemen."

The submarine became silent and the tension began to mount.

It seemed an age had passed as the seconds ticked away.

On the surface, the crew of *HMS Excalibur* had been allowed to
muster on deck to watch the spectacle. The *SS Globe Kobe* sounded its deep
booming horn. Slowly the huge propeller screw at the supertanker's stern
began to turn. Gradually, the huge ship's hull started to slip backwards. The
steel hawsers tightened as the supertanker moved.

Underwater, groaning noises of the straining metal hawsers pulling on heavy steel shackles echoed throughout the depths and stillness of the darkened sea. Admiral Adams knew his submarine would either survive the ordeal or be ripped apart. If all failed its belly would be torn to shreds on the razor-sharp granite rocks that lay hidden beneath the mud, silt and sand. No movement from the submarine was felt in the first few seconds of the pull starting.

Back on the surface, as the Captain of the SS *Globe Kobe* ordered the speed and thrust of the supertanker's engines to be increased, greater motions of straining were heard deep down in Davy Jones's locker.

Suddenly, and quite unexpectedly, the tanker seemed to quicken.

A huge mass of bubbles broke from beneath the forward part of the American submarine's hull. At first there were tremendous crashing sounds then a spate of torturous grinding noises. Finally, there was a large explosion. A mass of bubbles and debris floated upwards to the surface.

The crew of *HMS Excalibur* watched in horror.

There was an eerie silence before a huge turbulence of water thrust itself above the surface of a very calm sea.

Lieutenant Bergman, having looked in awe at the sight, turned round to speak to Commodore Brianston-Green. "I don't like the look of that at all, sir."

"It's early days yet, Lieutenant. Maybe something had to give before *Intrepid* could free itself."

Down below in the American submarine, first the tremendous noise, then the shuddering of a massive vibration, plus the force of the explosion sent some of the *Intrepid*'s crewmembers falling over in all directions.

Fearful screams and yells were heard. All were made in terror of what might happen next.

"It's the end, fellars," yelled one of the ratings.

"We are all going to die, "shouted another.

After the big bang nothing else happened.

There was now a very strange silence on board the submarine. Nothing seemed to be moving.

Outside on the ocean bed, the *Intrepid* lay upright. It was about sixty metres from the point of impact where it had first met with disaster.

The blast and explosion had somehow shortened the rounded nose of the submarine. It appeared that some of the torpedoes had exploded against the rocks when *Intrepid* was hauled free.

On the surface of the now calm sea, debris appeared from the murky depths showing a more gruesome sight. Slowly appearing from the deep

338

came the bodies of some of the nineteen seamen who lost their lives when the disaster happened.

The crew of *HMS Excalibur* were ordered to lower life rafts to begin a thorough search for any survivors. However, by now it was believed *SSBN Intrepid*, like the *Gorbachev*, had perished. It appeared that the American submarine had sunk with a total loss of all hands.

The steel hawsers on the supertanker hung lifeless and limp. As soon as the *Intrepid* had freed itself the shackles automatically released themselves from their hold.

HMS Excalibur flashed a message in Morse code to the supertanker. It read:

WHAT DO YOU THINK HAPPENED – STOP – HAS THE YANK SUB GONE – STOP – OR IS LAST SUNDAY'S DATE OF THE THIRTEENTH GOING TO BE INTREPID'S LUCKY NUMBER – STOP – END MESSAGE

Soon a reply came back:

HAVE NO STRAIN OR HOLD ANY LONGER – STOP – CANNOT TELL – STOP – WILL HAVE TO WAIT A BIT – STOP – END MESSAGE

Admiral Adams spoke softly and quietly over the tannoy to his crew. "Men, do we have water coming in anywhere since that explosion? Please clear down and advise back, compartment by compartment."

The first responses came back from compartments three and four. Then gradually the remainder reported to the bridge their watertight doors had held.

"Not a sound has come back from compartment number two, sir," Lieutenant Odbie advised.

Admiral Adams was concerned. "What in hell's name could that explosion have been?"

"I don't rightly know, Admiral. The only thing I can think that might have been possible was…"

Admiral Adams interrupted, "Well, Odbie, and what might that be?"

"Well, sir, I believe that the torpedo detonators and explosives in the sub's arsenal were somehow triggered when *Intrepid* broke free."

Admiral Adams gave the suggestion some thought. He considered the Lieutenant possibly to be correct. "Maybe, Odbie, your thoughts could be right. Go forward and check."

The Lieutenant was surprised at the Admiral's proposal. "Sir? Are you saying you wish me to break the current safety of our submarine? Endanger its survival by opening all the watertight doors?"

The Admiral looked over at the Lieutenant. "Do I take it, Odbie, that you are questioning my judgement?"

"No, sir, not in the least. I had merely considered the safety of the submarine and the crew, Admiral."

Admiral Adams didn't say anything in response to the Lieutenant's comment. He turned away and asked another officer to make a check on the pressure of the forward bulkheads. He also further enquired if an individual test could be made on each ballast tank.

Lieutenant Odbie stood in silence and waited for further instructions.

On the surface *HMS Excalibur's* crew had picked up eleven bodies. It was then that everyone realised from the state of the corpses that the bodies had been trapped underwater a lot longer than just a few minutes.

"Bad show, Bergman," Commodore Brianston-Green commented.

Bergman's face grimaced at the awful sight. "It looks like these poor fellows must have died when the Yankee sub struck the sea bottom, sir."

"I think that your assumption, Lieutenant, could well be right. But what about the rest of *Intrepid's* complement? Well, Bergman?"

Every few minutes further wreckage continued to burst out on to the sea surface. Flotsam and jetsam now littered the waters around the British submarine.

"The poor bastards," one of the *Excalibur's* crew commented as another body was hauled on to the aft deck.

The *SS Globe Kobe* signalled a message to *HMS Excalibur*. It read:

STILL NO SIGN OF ANY LIFE – STOP – WHAT ARE WE GOING TO DO –
STOP – END MESSAGE

Commodore Brianston-Green knew it was probably too early to organise an inspection dive. He requested that a message be sent back. It read:

WAIT ANOTHER HALF HOUR – STOP – END MESSAGE

Down in the murky depths, *Intrepid's* Commander had sent out two divers to inspect the hull of the American submarine. The divers found the smooth round hull at the front of the submarine had been transformed into a gaping mass of twisted metal and jagged steel. The whole of the torpedo compartment had been blown away. Part of the bulkhead of compartment one was severely fractured.

On swimming closer both divers saw there was a hole just big enough for a diver to squeeze through. They needed to do this in order to check whether the American sub had sustained any further serious damage.

The leading diver pointed. He indicated that he was going to attempt the difficult and dangerous task of entry. His diving partner watched as the light of his colleague's torch flickered. Then there was total darkness.

Two minutes had passed. There were no signs of any reaction, nor could the waiting diver see the flashing torchlight. He was becoming very anxious. He was concerned for the safety of his partner and decided to swim closer to the breached bulkhead. Suddenly the swiftness of the current drew him directly into the bent and twisted aperture. As the diver tried to correct himself his air pipe became caught, and severed on a jagged steel edge. In desperation the diver ripped off his rapidly filling mask and grabbed the broken air pipe. At that moment the first diver reappeared. On swimming back through the channel he had come, he saw his colleague struggling. He instantly realised what had happened and the acute danger his partner was in. He grabbed the severed air pipe and tied a knot in the tube. He then helped to secure his partner's mask back on to his head. The rescuing diver then shuttled a supply of air back and forth. He transferred enough air until his panicking partner started to calm down. There was no time to lose. As soon as matters became clearer the first diver helped his colleague from out of the forward wreckage. He eventually managed to make his way back to the safety of the *Intrepid*'s decompression chamber.

Inside the American submarine an undercurrent of tension had risen as precious minutes ticked away. The crewmen in compartment three had heard a faint knocking sound coming from the forward section of the hull. They had assumed the two divers had reached the damaged area.

Now there was a different sound. A dull noise like distant heavy thumping was coming from the watertight door that led to compartment two.

"What the hell is that?" remarked one of the crew.

"It sounds like someone's alive in there," another crewmember said.

"Let's try and knock out a message to them. Try and ask them to advise what state things are in," a rating said.

"Jesus! How on earth did someone manage to survive all of that lot?" came the comment from another seaman who immediately telephoned through to the bridge to advise them of the situation.

It was not long before one of the divers came through to the bridge to meet with Admiral Adams.

"Well done, Lt. Sampson," the Admiral said, having been concerned regarding the reports he had received advising that the diver's companion had met with a problem.

"I'm sorry to hear that Leading Seaman Thrush had a spot of bother."

"Yes, sir, he's now recovering in the sick bay."

"Well now, Sampson, how do we look from the outside?" the Admiral asked.

Lieutenant Sampson didn't quite know how to respond to the Admiral's question. "Do you wish me to report regarding those parts that are there, sir, or advise you as to those which have gone?"

The Admiral gave Lieutenant Sampson a strange glance.

Lieutenant Sampson continued, "Sir, those parts that are missing do leave us in a state of being a little light, and looking somewhat naked up front."

Admiral Adams thought it wiser to request details of what was remaining rather than to embark upon hearing how bad the destruction of the bow section of *Intrepid* had been.

"Sampson, before you go and give me an account of either of those matters, please tell me, did you get far enough into the front section to examine whether or not the main bulkhead between compartments one and two was still intact?"

"Yes, sir, I did," Sampson replied, now feeling somewhat surer of himself as to what it was the Admiral was asking for.

"Well, thank heavens for that," Admiral Adams remarked in expectancy.

"It certainly does appear to have held firm, sir. However, it was very difficult to see if the explosion had in any way weakened it. I could not see if the bulkhead wall had a bow in it or not."

"What was that, Lieutenant?"

"Well, sir, it was about the time when I realised Leading Seaman Thrush was missing. I was concerned as to whether he may have got into difficulties. I'm sorry, Admiral. I considered that having made safe inroads in order to check that the bulkhead was still intact, I would swiftly retire to assist Leading Seaman Thrush. Otherwise, I'm certain we would have had another death on our records."

For a moment Admiral Adams cringed. He felt his conscience prick him.

"Okay, Sampson, I'll buy that. But, Lieutenant, why didn't you go back having established the safety of Thrush?"

"Pardon me, sir?" the Lieutenant said in surprise.

"I'm sorry, Lieutenant, maybe that was a little out of order. I'll duly retract that last remark." The Admiral knew he had stepped heavily on the Lieutenant's toes. "Well, what damage have we sustained, Sampson? How do you view our chances of getting out of this mess? Will we be able to get ourselves up top?"

Lieutenant Sampson could not really believe what he had been hearing. He felt it was as if Admiral Adams was pointing the finger at him.

He felt that somehow he was being made responsible for having got the submarine into this precarious position in the first place.

"Admiral Adams, sir! Contrary to what your thoughts, beliefs and personal views might be, I do not wish to be involved, nor do I want to seem to be implicated in any way as to how this submarine met with its unfortunate circumstance.

"My report will show that I carried out my instructions as ordered. Anything else you may wish to contrive me to state will only evade the real issue. However, sir, I'm sure the situation and conduct of the real circumstance will forever keep coming back to haunt you."

"Why, you impudent young pup!" Admiral Adams roared.

"That's okay with me, sir. And, just for the record..."

"Yes, Sampson? Now what?"

"There were six recognisable bodies trapped up front in amongst the wreckage. I fear there must also have been a seventh which could have been blown to smithereens by the explosion in the torpedo room. The poor bastard's remnants were scattered everywhere. By the way, Admiral, regarding your enquiry as to the status of the torpedo room and armoury; these were no longer there for me to survey.

"In all, Admiral, you have the first operational flat-nosed sub in the US Navy. The rest of the bow looks something like a spray of daisy petals except for being all disfigured and twisted, plus, a damned great hole up front. One thing is for certain, Admiral."

"Yes, Sampson, and what's that?"

The Lieutenant felt he was obliged to state another observation, if only to rub salt into the wound. "At present you sure as hell ain't going upwards, nor front ways, Admiral."

On hearing that remark Admiral Adams had heard enough. "So, Sampson, apart from diving, you think you can also advise me how to run my sub. I suppose you'd be thinking we couldn't even raise a peep of sunlight between ourselves and the seabed?"

"No, sir. That's not so. However, what I would advise you to do…"

"Yes? Please, do go on," Admiral Adams interrupted.

"Sir, I would advise you to simply slowly level the air compression ballast. This should allow you to let *Intrepid* float up gradually. Or, alternatively, give a quick burst on the engine's reverse thrusts. I'm sure this should put us in with a good chance of making it to the surface. However, if there is a sign of the slightest adverse vibration, this could split the sub apart and finish us for good."

Admiral Adams eyed the young Lieutenant up and down for a moment.

He knew what the young man had said was probably true, but he didn't like hearing it all the same.

Sampson knew by the Admiral's look that if he stayed any longer the tension now festering between them could well explode.

"Admiral, a copy of my written report will be on your desk in the next ten minutes, sir." The Lieutenant didn't wait for a reply. He stood to attention, and then departed.

Admiral Adams stood in silence.

Lieutenant Odbie entered. He placed the logbook down in front of the Admiral.

"Sir, I have come to have the bridge report signed."

"Thank you, Odbie. That will be all."

On board *HMS Excalibur,* Commodore Brianston-Green had issued instructions to his operations room. He had requested they try and send a message through to Admiral Adams. It read:

TIME: 11.30 HOURS 16 AUGUST 2017
FROM: HMS EXCALIBUR
TO: INTREPID
ATTENTION: ADMIRAL ADAMS
IF THIS MESSAGE GETS THROUGH TO YOU – STOP – DINNER IS AT
EIGHT SHARP – STOP – TRY NOT TO BE LATE – STOP – IF IN FACT YOU
ARE EARLIER YOU MIGHT WISH TO STILL CATCH LUNCH – STOP –
END MESSAGE.
SIGNED: COMMODORE BRIANSTON-GREEN

Back on board the *Intrepid*, a message slowly tapped itself out on a telex receiver. When it had finished Admiral Adams read the text and smiled. He then thought to himself, *Well at least somebody has still got a sense of humour around here.*

The morning slowly dragged on. Three hours had passed since the rescue operation started.

The sea was calm.

Lookouts on board *HMS Excalibur* would occasionally report sighting further wreckage and masses of bubbles still surfacing.

By 12.30 hours, Lieutenant Bergman had relieved both the watch and Commodore Brianston-Green from the conning tower bridge. In passing, the Commodore enquired to see if there had been any reply from *Intrepid* in response to his message.

"Nothing as yet, sir," Lieutenant Bergman replied.

Brianston-Green was concerned that there had been no response.

"Bergman, do you think, or expect there will be some sort of answer?"

"It's difficult to say, sir. Things are still thrusting themselves up to the surface. Maybe someone is trying to tell us something. However, as yet, it could still be quite dangerous for divers to go down in order to take a gander."

"Okay, young man, you know your apples. I trust your judgement, Bergman, but I'll want to see some action shortly. That's if no more wreckage is sighted. Do you hear me?"

"Aye, aye, sir."

"Thank you, Lieutenant. That will be all. Oh, by the way, call me immediately if anything breaks. I'll be in my quarters."

A message flashed from the *SS Globe Kobe*. It read:

DO YOU WISH US TO STAY – STOP – OR SHALL WE PUSH OFF – STOP
– END MESSAGE

Lieutenant Bergman could not quite believe what he was reading. "Signals! Hear this. Look sharp now. Send this reply in answer to that message and on the double. Just say the following: STAY OR ELSE. I'm sure that should get its Captain to think again."

On board the *Intrepid*, Admiral Adams had by now fully assessed the report that Lieutenant Sampson had compiled. He also knew that the feeling of his crew was running high. After some considerable thought, the Admiral decided to make an announcement: "To all crew members of the *Intrepid*. Now hear this! Contrary to what some of you might be assuming, my command of this submarine is not in doubt.

"I wish to make it known to all men of the *Intrepid* that the events that recently happened were not contrived, nor were they miscalculated in order

345

to purposefully endanger our submarine. The circumstance of these events has been recorded in the ship's log. To all concerned it reads as, 'accidental misadventure while actioning and carrying out *Intrepid*'s battle duties'.

"If any man here wishes to challenge this, let him please now come forward and speak out."

There was no movement from any member of the crew.

Admiral Adams continued, "Gentlemen, thank you. Please be advised that I requested this matter be known, as I believe it is a matter of honouring my duty and total commitment to you all as my crew, thus ensuring those of us who have survived will all see daylight again. It is in this respect I will now explain what it is I propose to do."

The Admiral then set about advising the orders and tasks he wished each man to accomplish. He then made a further address.

"Naturally, like you all, I am very saddened and aggrieved at the tragic loss of nineteen fellow members of our crew. But, being ordered to be at a state of war *is war.*

"Maybe worse things would have happened if we were amidst the thick of things. I do not mean by that statement that we got off lightly. The loss of life, at any time, is answerable by ones own conscience. I know I will live the rest of my life remembering the lives lost of the nineteen crewmembers and fighting men. No man amongst you should ever forget them.

"Men, I require you to stick steadfast to the duties that I have ordered you all to carry out. Each of your individual actions, when carried out, will ensure the *Intrepid* pushes itself to its limits. I ask you all to see that everything humanly possible is carried out in order to save our submarine. I wish you all God speed and good luck. We start our road to survival in two minutes and thirty seconds from now.

"That will be all."

The tannoy went silent.

A sound of cheering began throughout the submarine. Its echo soon spread upwards through the silent waters.

The men who were on duty in the operations room of *HMS Excalibur* sat quietly going about their business.

A strange sound of distorted cheering began to be heard, and then the noise of hand clapping followed by cheering applause.

Each operator looked at one another. One of them pushed a button on the sonar sound recorder.

At the same time another rating rang through to the bridge. "Operations room to bridge. Please could Commodore Brianston-Green and Lieutenant Bergman report to the operations room. Urgently!"

On the surface the sea was nearly as smooth as a millpond. It was the moment of the day when the sea's current and tide began to change.

A slight breeze left a tranquil ripple on the water which glistened in the brilliance of the sun. By now the temperature was very warm and the sun's heat had begun beating down upon the steel hulls of the vessels lying at anchor.

A shimmering haze lifted from the metal changing its natural lines and contours into irregular shapes.

Suddenly, and quiet unexpectedly, an uneven turbulence began to boil up from the deep. Its ferocity broke upon the sea's surface not more than five hundred metres from where the British submarine was moored. The water began to erupt like a river breaking into rapids, cascading and raging on its course. Within seconds a huge churning sea began to reveal two thin periscope masts. Then, totally unexpectedly, two stern propellers emerged. To all men watching it seemed as if the American submarine *Intrepid* was about to make its final bow to the living world. The huge hull hung in that position for at least two minutes.

On board *HMS Excalibur*, both Commodore Brianston-Green and Lieutenant Bergman scrambled up the conning tower ladder on to the flying bridge.

"Good God," Bergman shouted.

"Great Scott! Not another *HMS Truculant!*" the Commodore yelled.

"Oh hell! I certainly hope not," the Lieutenant shouted, not that he was even born at the time the British submarine was lost many years previously while leaving the River Thames and striking a war time mine.

Escaping air from *Intrepid*'s stern ballast tanks hissed and spat as, very slowly, the submarine began to sink beneath the waves. For a moment everyone was completely speechless, while gazing at the sea's empty surface. It looked like total disaster was surely imminent. The watching sailors were amazed when the two periscopes reappeared. Soon afterwards the American submarine's conning tower gradually came into view.

Finally, the *Intrepid*'s huge hull eventually struggled to raise itself. The protruding sight showed the severely damaged bow. It also revealed the horrific sight of the torso of a dead seaman still held firmly in the jaws of the vast gaping hole.

The *SSBN Intrepid* was not going to die though it was struggling to keep an even keel. With its nose blown off, it no longer looked the most serene sight as it did when leaving the United States Naval Base at

Charleston, South Carolina at the beginning of its voyage. Miraculously, the submarine's huge frame had held itself together.

Admiral Adams had calculated everything. Even to the extent that the submarine's new trim was sufficient enough to ensure the aft section would lie deeper in the water; this was done by easing any weight of water pressure on the bulkhead of compartment two.

Once the *Intrepid* had finally settled, the crew that was housed in compartment three initiated a quick emergency rescue. All who attempted the mission knew they risked certain death if it was found that compartment two was totally flooded.

Slowly the wheel on the watertight compartment door gently turned. It clicked as the locks released. There was a sudden rush of air as the door swung open. Five crewmen lay unconscious having suffered shock, concussion and lack of oxygen.

The force of the impact and blast of the explosion had completely knocked out all the main internal communications. It had damaged electrical equipment that operated the contact services between each compartment. The injured sailors were swiftly transferred into compartment three, then the watertight door was slammed shut and compartment two was rendered out of action.

On board *SS Globe Kobe* and *HMS Excalibur,* the crews all mustered on deck. Each gave resounding cheers of relief and delight as the emerging American seamen finally came out on deck.

Admiral Adams requested a message be sent to both *SS Globe Kobe* and *HMS Excalibur.* It read:

TIME: 13.25 HOURS 16 AUGUST 2017
FROM: SSBN INTREPID
TO: SS GLOBE KOBE and HMS EXCALIBUR
THANK YOU ALL FOR YOUR KIND CONSIDERATION – STOP – YOUR PERSEVERENCE AND HELP WILL NEVER BE FORGOTTEN – STOP – WITHOUT WHICH WE ALL KNOW WHERE OUR LIVES WOULD BE – STOP – WE ARE ALWAYS IN YOUR DEBT – STOP – END MESSAGE
SIGNED: ADMIRAL ALAN J. T. ADAMS III

Soon afterwards, *HMS Excalibur* received a separate message. It read:

YOUR KIND INVITATION FOR A LATE LUNCH IS ACCEPTED – STOP – HOPE 13.45 HOURS WILL NOT BE TOO LATE – STOP – END MESSAGE

Admiral Marchant and Commander Thompson had flown up to Scotland on the Monday night. Both men knew that certain formal celebrations would be in order. Staff Sergeant Bluntly and Lieutenant Henderson had left early on the Tuesday morning and arrived late in the afternoon.

It was now early evening on 20 August 2017, and everyone was assembled relaxing in the officers' mess. Commander Thompson noticed Bluntly was alone and went across to request he join the party.

After opening the conversation he said, "Rumour has it, Staff, that you may well be getting some sort of a gong for your amazing exploits."

"No, sir, not me. It's not my sort of line, Commander. I'm just an ordinary guy doing his daily job. Nope, they won't want to decorate one on me, sir. Anyhow, who would I go and leave it to when I retire?"

They both laughed.

"Let me buy you another drink. Surely you will consider moving on to something stronger?"

"No thank you, sir. I'll have a J2O. That will do me fine."

"All right, James, but remember the Admiral might order you to drink a stiff one. That's if he thinks you have darned well deserved it."

Bluntly smiled. "I quite understand, sir. I'll tackle that one as and when the situation arises."

"Well, we had better turn in early. I have a sneaking suspicion it's going to be a very long day tomorrow."

"Right you are, sir."

Both gentlemen departed and went their sep2arate ways to their temporary quarters.

Early on Monday morning, 21 August 2017, at 03.30 hours, *HMS Excalibur* had reached the point of entry into home waters. Commodore Brianston-Green sent a coded message to Northwood and to Farslane in Scotland. It read:

TIME: 03.35 HOURS 21 AUGUST 2017

FROM: HMS EXCALIBUR

TO: HOLY LOCH-FARSLANE/NORTHWOOD ROYAL NAVY HQ

PLEASE BE ADVISED SSBN INTREPID IN TOW – STOP – POSITION NOW SOME SIXTY MILES DUE WEST OF THE AZORES – STOP – DESTINATION US NAVAL BASE HQ CHARLESTON SC – STOP – WE SHALL WAIT UNTIL DAYLIGHT BREAKS – STOP – THEN WE WILL REQUEST TO ENTER HOME WATERS AND BASE – STOP – LOOK FORWARD TO HAVING A

BUCKS FIZZ UPON ARRIVAL – STOP – END MESSAGE
SIGNED: COMMODORE BRIANSTON-GREEN C–IN–C OPERATION
BLINFOLD [NOW UNCOVERED]

At 05.30 hours, the still waters of the deep water channel off Holy Loch began to ripple and churn as a bow wave broke and disturbed the calm, glassy surface. Dual periscopes emerged followed by the black conning tower and finally the long shape of the top of the submarine's hull.

A few moments passed.

Soon the full serene lines of the Royal Navy's pride and joy glistened and gleamed in the first rays of the dawn's sunlight.

The date 21 August 2017 was to be a memorable day in the annals of history of the Royal Navy.

The military honours list was to award a Victoria Cross to Lieutenant Bergman and Staff Sergeant James Bluntly for their extraordinary actions and unselfish valour. Each had risked certain death or injury in their unyielding bravery. By their separate brave actions, both had ensured the safety of fellow officers and men.

Distinguished Service Orders were awarded to Commodore Brianston-Green RN and Commander Derek Thompson RN, and other well-deserved awards were bestowed upon many of the crew of the British submarine whose diligent and brave efforts against all odds ensured the world was rid of an evil aggressor.

Her Majesty's Naval Base (HMNB) Farslane, Clyde

A large crowd gathered by the quayside to watch as *HMS Excalibur* slowly and gracefully approached. On the submarine's mast was fixed an upturned besom. Tradition signified that a broom attached in this manner confirmed that the submarine had recorded the successful completion of its campaign or mission.

Cheers rang out as the submarine's crew, in full dress, came out on deck to receive a well-deserved and honourable welcome. They returned the cheering with equal gusto. The roar of a resounding 'three cheers' echoed through the harbour area as thick heavy ropes and steel hawsers were moved to make fast, and secure the submarine's stern and bow.

At 07.00 hours, the sentry on duty at the harbour gates checked his watch as the pips of seven o'clock heralded the morning news, noisily coming from the guardroom radio.

The newscaster had begun to read:

"Good morning. This is BBC Radio Five Live giving you the latest news at seven o'clock on the morning of 21 August 2017 read by Richard Simple.

"It is reported that the crew of the Royal Navy's submarine *HMS Excalibur* has just returned home to a heroic welcome from their families and from certain US Military staff at the submarine's home base on the River Clyde.

"Shortly after half past five this morning, the British submarine surfaced after being at sea for seven months. Its epic voyage…"

The news report then listed the series of strange events and assignments the British submarine had been engaged upon, while under its operational code name Blindfold.

The newscaster continued, "The Royal Navy stand ready today to receive the many cherished honours the crew were awarded for acts of gallantry and bravery. The medals were earned while undertaking duties demanded by the shroud of departments in charge of the military operation. These awards have been given to persons spanning from ordinary seaman to officers, and men serving in the Royal Navy's operations at their headquarters and special forces departments, plus others attached to the Royal Navy's intelligence Headquarters at Northwood.

"The British Government confirms it will, in due course, release and hand back to the Russian authorities a total of thirty survivors and seventeen bodies the British submarine brought back from its exploits. Unfortunately, one of the survivors has subsequently died from his injuries, while *HMS Excalibur* was on the final leg of its homeward journey.

"The Prime Minister has sent a message of congratulations on behalf of the Government to the submarine's crew and Commander. The message acknowledged that a huge debt of thanks and gratitude was owed and that the crew of the submarine acclaimed a well-deserved honour. It was advised that the Prime Minster gave a special commendation to all concerned in finally bringing the Russian tyrant to heel.

"The Royal Family has sent a special message of thanks and congratulations on behalf of the British people."

When the crew disembarked there were warm welcomes from waiting families and friends, tears of happiness and joy, the shaking of hands and hugs of welcome from parents and loved ones. Cries of, "Thank God. Thank heavens your safe," could be heard."

As the morning progressed the sun shone high in the sky. Its warm, mid-summer rays shone brightly which allowed the sea to yield a beautiful colour of blue and shimmering gold. It was a beautiful clear day; not a cloud was visible to dampen or turn the joyous scene into the dull colour of battleship grey.

Two ships passed *HMS Excalibur* and gave a full turnout of their crews. Each hailed a victory cry of three cheers and gave a tumultuous welcome home. Slowly the frigates glided gracefully past. Their flags signalled 'Leaving Port'; both were departing on a routine voyage.

Away from the pageantry of the special arrival the Royal Navy was soon back to normality in its daily role in seeking out any hidden enemy alien or foe. Admiral Marchant stood watching as the ships passed by. As he did he turned to Commander Thompson and remarked, "Well, Derek, I suppose when all this exciting stuff has died down it will be business as usual."

On further investigation and searching of records that had spanned a period of eighteen years, a plan had been deployed by certain adventurous terrorist renegades who had planted fully trained 'sleeper' persons from the al-Qaida organisation within the military and political powers of Russia and the Commonwealth of Independent States, and other countries in the world. These sleepers operated quietly and unnoticed until directed otherwise.

It was these persons whose evil wish was to seek dictatorial supremacy so that eventually they could yield sufficient strength to control the whole world by tyranny. Such evil was directed to discredit the peaceful policies sought by the West after the fall of communist powers, and after the exit of Boris Yeltsin. Also, failure of the destiny of the man whose honourable name had been given to the ill-fated and doomed Russian submarine, and it being applied by the Captain who was found out to have had Russian parents but was born in Ta'if in Saudi Arabia, and had grown up there and in the Yemen before returning with his parents to Russia for his education. From here the story was to begin to build.

THE END

Printed by BoD˚in Norderstedt, Germany